PRAISE FOR

T0013029

"A fast-paced, sometimes brutal thriller reminiscent of Dan Brown's *The Da Vinci Code*."

—*Booklist* (starred review)

"A hair-raising thrill ride."

—*Library Journal* (starred review)

"The fascinating historical information combined with a storyline ripped from the headlines will hook conspiracy theorists and action addicts alike."

—*Kirkus Reviews*

"Fans of *The Da Vinci Code* are going to love this book . . . One of my favorite reads of 2016."

—*Crimespree Magazine*

"This suspenseful tale has something for absolutely everyone to enjoy."

—*Suspense Magazine*

PRAISE FOR *MERCY'S CHASE*

"An immersive voice, an intriguing story, a wonderful character—highly recommended!"

—Lee Child, #1 *New York Times* bestselling author

"Both a sweeping adventure and race-against-time thriller, *Mercy's Chase* is fascinating, fierce, and brimming with heart—just like its heroine, Salem Wiley."

—Meg Gardiner, author of *Into the Black Nowhere*

"Action-packed, great writing taut with suspense, an appealing main character to root for—who could ask for anything more?"

—Buried Under Books

PRAISE FOR *THE TAKEN ONES*

"Setting the standard for top-notch thrillers, *The Taken Ones* is smart, compelling, and filled with utterly real characters. Lourey brings her formidable storytelling talent to the game and, on top of that, wows us with a deft stylistic touch. This is a one-sitting read!"

—Jeffery Deaver, author of *The Bone Collector* and
The Watchmaker's Hand

"*The Taken Ones* has Jess Lourey's trademark of suspense all the way. A damaged and brave heroine, an equally damaged evildoer, and missing girls from long ago all combine to keep the reader rushing through to the explosive ending."

—Charlaine Harris, *New York Times* bestselling author

"Lourey is at the top of her game with *The Taken Ones*. A master of building tension while maintaining a riveting pace, Lourey is a hell of a writer on all fronts, but her greatest talent may be her characters. Evangeline Reed, an agent with the Minnesota Bureau of Criminal Apprehension, is a woman with a devastating past and the haunting ability to know the darkest crimes happening around her. She is also exactly the kind of character I would happily follow through a dozen books or more. In awe of her bravery, I also identified with her pain and wanted desperately to protect her. Along with an incredible cast of support characters, *The Taken Ones* will break your heart wide open and stay with you long after you've turned the final page. This is a 2023 must read."

—Danielle Girard, *USA Today* and Amazon #1 bestselling author of
Up Close

PRAISE FOR *THE QUARRY GIRLS*

Winner of the 2023 Anthony Award for Best Paperback Original

Winner of the 2023 Minnesota Book Award for Genre Fiction

"Few authors can blend the genuine fear generated by a sordid tale of true crime with evocative, three-dimensional characters and mesmerizing prose like Jess Lourey. Her fictional stories feel rooted in a world we all know but also fear. *The Quarry Girls* is a story of secrets gone to seed, and Lourey gives readers her best novel yet—which is quite the accomplishment. Calling it: *The Quarry Girls* will be one of the best books of the year."

—Alex Segura, acclaimed author of *Secret Identity, Star Wars Poe Dameron: Free Fall,* and *Miami Midnight*

"Jess Lourey once more taps deep into her Midwest roots and childhood fears with *The Quarry Girls,* an absorbing, true crime–informed thriller narrated in the compelling voice of young drummer Heather Cash as she and her bandmates navigate the treacherous and confusing ground between girlhood and womanhood one simmering and deadly summer. Lourey conveys the edgy, hungry restlessness of teen girls with a touch of Megan Abbott while steadily intensifying the claustrophobic atmosphere of a small 1977 Minnesota town where darkness snakes below the surface."

—Loreth Anne White, *Washington Post* and Amazon Charts bestselling author of *The Patient's Secret*

"Jess Lourey is a master of the coming-of-age thriller, and *The Quarry Girls* may be her best yet—as dark, twisty, and full of secrets as the tunnels that lurk beneath Pantown's deceptively idyllic streets."
—Chris Holm, Anthony Award–winning author of *The Killing Kind*

PRAISE FOR *BLOODLINE*

Winner of the 2022 Anthony Award for Best Paperback Original

Winner of the 2022 ITW Thriller Award for Best Paperback Original

Short-listed for the 2021 Goodreads Choice Awards

"Fans of *Rosemary's Baby* will relish this."
—*Publishers Weekly*

"Based on a true story, this is a sinister, suspenseful thriller full of creeping horror."
—*Kirkus Reviews*

"Lourey ratchets up the fear in a novel that verges on horror."
—*Library Journal*

"In *Bloodline*, Jess Lourey blends elements of mystery, suspense, and horror to stunning effect."
—*BOLO Books*

"Inspired by a true story, it's a creepy page-turner that has me eager to read more of Ms. Lourey's works, especially if they're all as incisive as this thought-provoking novel."

—Criminal Element

"*Bloodline* by Jess Lourey is a psychological thriller that grabbed me from the beginning and didn't let go."

—*Mystery & Suspense Magazine*

"*Bloodline* blends page-turning storytelling with clever homages to such horror classics as *Rosemary's Baby*, *The Stepford Wives*, and *Harvest Home*."

—*Toronto Star*

"*Bloodline* is a terrific, creepy thriller, and Jess Lourey clearly knows how to get under your skin."

—Bookreporter

"[A] tightly coiled domestic thriller that slowly but persuasively builds the suspense."

—*South Florida Sun Sentinel*

"I should know better than to pick up a new Jess Lourey book thinking I'll just peek at the first few pages and then get back to the book I was reading. Six hours later, it's three in the morning and I'm racing through the last few chapters, unable to sleep until I know how it all ends. Set in an idyllic small town rooted in family history and horrific secrets, *Bloodline* is *Pleasantville* meets *Rosemary's Baby*. A deeply unsettling, darkly unnerving, and utterly compelling novel, this book chilled me to the core, and I loved every bit of it."

—Jennifer Hillier, author of *Little Secrets* and the award-winning *Jar of Hearts*

"Jess Lourey writes small-town Minnesota like Stephen King writes small-town Maine. *Bloodline* is a tremendous book with a heart and a hacksaw . . . and I loved every second of it."
—Rachel Howzell Hall, author of the critically acclaimed novels
And Now She's Gone and *They All Fall Down*

PRAISE FOR *UNSPEAKABLE THINGS*

Winner of the 2021 Anthony Award for Best Paperback Original

Short-listed for the 2021 Edgar Awards and 2020 Goodreads Choice Awards

"The suspense never wavers in this page-turner."
—*Publishers Weekly*

"The atmospheric suspense novel is haunting because it's narrated from the point of view of a thirteen-year-old, an age that should be more innocent but often isn't. Even more chilling, it's based on real-life incidents. Lourey may be known for comic capers (*March of Crimes*), but this tense novel combines the best of a coming-of-age story with suspense and an unforgettable young narrator."
—*Library Journal* (starred review)

"Part suspense, part coming-of-age, Jess Lourey's *Unspeakable Things* is a story of creeping dread, about childhood when you know the monster under your bed is real. A novel that clings to you long after the last page."
—Lori Rader-Day, Edgar Award–nominated author of
Under a Dark Sky

"A noose of a novel that tightens by inches. The squirming tension comes from every direction—including the ones that are supposed to be safe. I felt complicit as I read, as if at any moment I stopped I would be abandoning Cassie, alone, in the dark, straining to listen and fearing to hear."

—Marcus Sakey, bestselling author of *Brilliance*

"*Unspeakable Things* is an absolutely riveting novel about the poisonous secrets buried deep in towns and families. Jess Lourey has created a story that will chill you to the bone and a main character who will break your heart wide open."

—Lou Berney, Edgar Award–winning author of *November Road*

"Inspired by a true story, *Unspeakable Things* crackles with authenticity, humanity, and humor. The novel reminded me of *To Kill a Mockingbird* and *The Marsh King's Daughter*. Highly recommended."

—Mark Sullivan, bestselling author of *Beneath a Scarlet Sky*

"Jess Lourey does a masterful job building tension and dread, but her greatest asset in *Unspeakable Things* is Cassie—an arresting narrator you identify with, root for, and desperately want to protect. This is a book that will stick with you long after you've torn through it."

—Rob Hart, author of *The Warehouse*

"With *Unspeakable Things*, Jess Lourey has managed the near-impossible, crafting a mystery as harrowing as it is tender, as gut-wrenching as it is lyrical. There is real darkness here, a creeping, inescapable dread that more than once had me looking over my own shoulder. But at its heart beats the irrepressible—and irresistible—spirit of its . . . heroine, a young woman so bright and vital and brave she kept even the fiercest monsters at bay. This is a book that will stay with me for a long time."

—Elizabeth Little, *Los Angeles Times* bestselling author of *Dear Daughter* and *Pretty as a Picture*

PRAISE FOR *THE CATALAIN BOOK OF SECRETS*

"Life-affirming, thought-provoking, heartwarming, it's one of those books which—if you happen to read it exactly when you need to—will heal your wounds as you turn the pages."

—Catriona McPherson, Agatha, Anthony, Macavity, and Bruce Alexander Award–winning author

"Prolific mystery writer Lourey tells of a matriarchal clan of witches joining forces against age-old evil . . . The novel is tightly plotted, and Lourey shines when depicting relationships—romantic ones as well as tangled links between Catalains . . . Lourey emphasizes the ties that bind in spite of secrets and resentment."

—*Kirkus Reviews*

"Lourey expertly concocts a Gothic fusion of long-held secrets, melancholy, and resolve . . . Exquisitely written in naturally flowing, expressive language, the book delves into the special relationships between sisters, and mothers and daughters."

—*Publishers Weekly*

PRAISE FOR *MAY DAY*

"Jess Lourey writes about a small-town assistant librarian, but this is no genteel traditional mystery. Mira James likes guys in a big way, likes booze, and isn't afraid of motorcycles. She flees a dead-end job and a dead-end boyfriend in Minneapolis and ends up in Battle Lake, a little town with plenty of dirty secrets. The first-person narrative in *May Day* is fresh, the characters quirky. Minnesota has many fine crime writers, and Jess Lourey has just entered their ranks!"

—Ellen Hart, award-winning author of the Jane Lawless and Sophie Greenway series

"This trade paperback packed a punch . . . I loved it from the get-go!"

—*Tulsa World*

"What a romp this is! I found myself laughing out loud."

—*Crimespree Magazine*

"Mira digs up a closetful of dirty secrets, including sex parties, cross-dressing, and blackmail, on her way to exposing the killer. Lourey's debut has a likable heroine and surfeit of sass."

—*Kirkus Reviews*

PRAISE FOR *REWRITE YOUR LIFE: DISCOVER YOUR TRUTH THROUGH THE HEALING POWER OF FICTION*

"Interweaving practical advice with stories and insights garnered in her own writing journey, Jessica Lourey offers a step-by-step guide for writers struggling to create fiction from their life experiences. But this book isn't just about writing. It's also about the power of stories to transform those who write them. I know of no other guide that delivers on its promise with such honesty, simplicity, and beauty."

—William Kent Krueger, *New York Times* bestselling author of the Cork O'Connor series and *Ordinary Grace*

MERCY'S CHASE

OTHER TITLES BY JESS LOUREY

SALEM'S CIPHER THRILLERS

Mercy's Chase

Salem's Cipher

STEINBECK AND REED THRILLERS

The Reaping

The Taken Ones

THRILLERS

The Quarry Girls

Litani

Bloodline

Unspeakable Things

GOTHIC SUSPENSE

The Catalain Book of Secrets

Seven Daughters

CHILDREN'S BOOKS

Leave My Book Alone! Starring Claudette, a Dragon with Control Issues

YOUNG ADULT

A Whisper of Poison

MURDER BY MONTH MYSTERIES

May Day

June Bug

Knee High by the Fourth of July

August Moon

September Mourn

October Fest

November Hunt

December Dread

January Thaw

February Fever

March of Crimes

April Fools

NONFICTION

Rewrite Your Life: Discover Your Truth Through the Healing Power of Fiction

MERCY'S CHASE

JESS LOUREY

THOMAS & MERCER

Text copyright © 2018, 2019, 2024 by Jess Lourey

Published by Thomas & Mercer, Seattle

www.apub.com

Amazon, the Amazon logo, and Thomas & Mercer are trademarks of Amazon.com, Inc., or its affiliates.

ISBN-13: 9781662519208 (paperback)
ISBN-13: 9781662519215 (digital)

Cover design by Caroline Teagle Johnson
Cover image: © Mehul Patel / Arcangel; © matejmo / Getty Images

Printed in the United States of America

For Zoë, as smart as she is fierce, as funny as she is kind

TUESDAY

September 19

CHAPTER 1

Blessington, Ireland

"She was a witch, a'course."

Salem's head snapped up so fast that loose curls tumbled over her eyes. "Excuse me?"

Pivoting her neck like that exploded the pain, shooting hot needles down her arm and toward the cell phone she'd been peeking at. Bel's encouraging words—*Pretend like you know what you're doing! Everyone else is faking it, too*—had soothed her as she'd fought the cottony panic of impostor syndrome. That comfort was now shoved aside, the unpleasant thump of Muirinn Molony's words echoing off the rustic cottage walls.

"A witch. My grandmother." Mrs. Molony, several times a grandmother herself, smiled, revealing tiny twisted teeth.

A kettle bubbled behind her. Its steam perfumed the air with cinnamon and sage.

Salem guessed the woman didn't receive many visitors on this lonely County Wicklow road. In fact, she'd assumed that's why Mrs. Molony had phoned the UN's threat line, her tip forwarded to cryptanalysts at the FBI. *Forced Bedside Interrogations* is what Agent Len Curson, Salem's partner for the day, labeled these visits. The thankless errands had spread like a virus since the UN had advertised its line, which was dedicated to taking nonimmediate threats related to the upcoming International

Climate Change Summit. An environmental treaty was on the table, one requiring G20 countries to radically divest from fossil fuels.

The accord, if signed, would disrupt the global economy like a dropkick to an anthill.

The threat line had been overrun with calls.

"Many women were considered witches back then," Mrs. Molony continued, her smile still in place. "At least that's what they were called by those who didn't understand the country ways. Really, my mamó was a midwife, not that it would've mattered, would it? Nurse, healer, cook. They were all labeled as witches. You sure I can't offer you a spot of tea?"

The woman had spoken this as one long word, her accent thick. Salem was still trying to catch up. "Your grandmother was a witch?"

Mrs. Molony exhaled a gentle disgust. *Och.* She stood, her head nearly brushing the low ceiling. "It'll be easier to show you, won't it? Here's a bit for you before we tramp outdoors." She offered Salem, not Agent Curson, a plum-size sachet of herbs. It was string-tied in a scrap of blue cloth dotted with red flowers. "Protection against evil."

Salem glanced at her partner as she tucked the aromatic bundle in her parka pocket. Judging by his sour expression, he was more certain than ever that they were on a snipe hunt. He brushed imaginary dust off his ironed jeans and followed the woman out of her cottage. Salem took up the rear, allowing her initial shock at the mention of witches to pass. Mrs. Molony had been referring to country superstition, not a dark conspiracy.

Salem followed them both outdoors, inhaling deeply of the scent of wet campfire. Chickens burred and clucked at her feet, scratching at the rain-softened earth. The weather had changed three times since she'd left the Dublin Airport. Most recently, a coy sun was elbowing out the drizzle, its fairy light dancing with shadows at the edge of her vision. The play of bright and dark suggested movement where there was none, causing her to stare too long into the misted thickets and dripping brambles that defined Mrs. Molony's yard. Beyond the hedgerow grew a vivid field of red poppies that mirrored the tiny blooms on the fabric of the sachet she had been given. The flowers were framed by a sea of emerald green Salem had yet to grow accustomed to, the lush, high hills of Ireland appearing liquid and timeless.

Agent Curson had driven the forty-seven miles to Mrs. Molony's cottage. When he'd entered the directions into the GPS, Salem had studied the sky rather than swallowing an Ativan. She found she didn't need her medicine, not here. Something about Ireland tugged at her gut in the most peculiar way, comforting her by bringing her home to a place she'd never been. As unsettling as the sensation was, it was better than anxiety, and she was grateful for the reprieve. She'd thought she had her agoraphobia under control when she agreed to join the FBI, but then she'd been assigned to London, and suddenly Minneapolis was forever away and the world too large.

The agent recruiting her had been insistent. *Your country needs you. Your cryptanalysis will save lives.*

Reluctantly, she'd joined the top-secret Black Chamber.

The covert branch had been dreamed up in 1919, when the US State Department and the army proposed a peacetime cryptanalysis department. The organization initially disguised itself as a commercial coding company and set up stakes in New York City. The front office produced toll-saving telegram abbreviations for businesses while the back office cracked the diplomatic communications of the world's most powerful nations.

Secretary of State Henry Stimson had shut it down in 1929, famously declaring that "gentlemen do not read each other's mail." Gina Hayes, the first female president of the United States of America, felt no such compunction. Her first unofficial act after taking office in January had been to revive the Black Chamber as a clandestine arm of the FBI.

Not counting the recruited code breakers, fewer than five people knew.

The Black Chamber 2.0 was licensed to operate across international boundaries in service of Americans. They were to be the United States' conduit to Five Eyes—the intelligence alliance among the

US, the United Kingdom, New Zealand, Australia, and Canada that allowed the countries to spy on one another's citizens, sharing relevant SIGINT: impending terrorist attacks, assassination plans, destabilizing movements.

Len Curson and Salem Wiley were the first Black Chamber 2.0 analysts hired; another ten had followed. The middle-aged Curson was the only one who came to the table with field experience. The other eleven analysts had been speed-trained at Quantico. The battles that decided the fates of nations were now waged in cyberspace, physical soldiers replaced with computer warriors.

Nonetheless, the new hires needed to know how to defend themselves on the corporeal plane. During her sixteen weeks at Quantico, Salem had learned the proper use and maintenance of firearms, close-space defensive tactics, survival skills, and intelligence gathering. She'd been by turns terrified and exhilarated during the training.

Her first, agoraphobia-stoking assignment upon graduation? Work with Five Eyes agents in London to intercept and decode every threat arriving in advance of the climate change summit. The conference was drawing leaders from all over the world, including President Gina Hayes, the new German chancellor, leaders of NGOs and progressive organizations, professors and researchers, and internationally famous artists and activists.

Not that Salem would see any of them.

Since she'd been stationed in London, she'd been chained to a cubicle, tasked with sifting through piles of dead-end codes and paper tiger threats while simultaneously charged with developing a quantum-based SIGINT intercept program. After a full day of coding and cracking, if she had the energy, she'd trudge to the on-site gym to lift weights before tromping upstairs to the gray temp barracks and a private room not much bigger or brighter than her cubicle. Then she'd wake up and start all over again.

She loved the work.

She *hated* being so far from home.

She'd also developed an antagonistic relationship with her computer chair. It was an old model designed to wheeze up or down and that was it. No matter how she messed with it, the angle was wrong. Her elbows either hung too low or were stretched too high, and the armrests irritated her after twelve hours in the chair.

Hence the Gordian knot swelling in her neck.

When Agent Curson, a twenty-five-year veteran of the FBI and a trained linguist, had requested Salem on this field job, she'd been almost relieved to escape that iron maiden of a computer chair, even though it meant flying in a four-seater across the sea to Dublin, a journey that would have been unthinkable this time last year.

Agent Curson had imparted that a Mrs. Muirinn Molony had phoned the threat line. She'd claimed she'd received an airtight tip from a relative that President Gina Hayes would be assassinated at the upcoming environmental summit. She insisted she needed to speak to agents in person, to show them the danger. That lives were at stake.

The one qualification she demanded? These agents must be able to crack codes.

Agent Curson had devoted the hour-long drive from the airport to Mrs. Molony's Blessington cottage to complaining about what a monumental shitcan time-waster this visit was sure to be, his grumbling interspersed with travel suggestions should Salem ever return to the area, including a recommendation that she visit St. Brigid's Cathedral just up the road.

Salem had granted him half her attention. The rest of her was marveling at Ireland's atmosphere, a steely gray sky studded with jagged, wet clouds, the heavens seemingly close enough to whisper a secret. She'd been in Europe less than a month, her first journey off the continental United States. What if there were more places in the world that felt as *right* as Ireland?

The squawk of a chicken snapped Salem back into the moment.

Mrs. Molony was tightening her apron as she led them behind her house. "The coded message is just ahead." She raised her voice to be heard over a rustle of rain-scented wind rattling the branches. "It's after I uncovered it that I had the dream about the shooting of your president. Straight from the mouth of my dead mamó."

Agent Curson tossed a glance over his shoulder.

Told you so, it said. *Snipe hunt.*

Salem stepped past her partner as they crested a small rise, determined to treat the lonely woman with respect. So what if Mrs. Molony had a fanciful imagination? She'd gotten them out of their cubicles and into this green countryside under a sky that felt like an embrace. "You weren't actually informed of a threat, Mrs. Molony? You dreamed it?"

"Aye, at first." She had a humping walk, as if one leg were shorter than the other. She limped through the hedgerow and over a line of stones. "Then the visions came. I see them eyes open or closed now, I do. I wouldn't have wasted your time otherways. Right around this bend we go, to my mamó's grave."

They stepped toward a clearing surrounded by knobby, gnarled trees that cast skeleton shadows over the earth. Salem smelled it before she saw it: fresh-dug dirt, loamy and alive in the middle of the glade. Near the fresh hole, a weathered headstone perched atop five feet of sunken earth.

Salem shuddered. One grave old, one grave new. Except the new hole was round and not yet filled in. The final resting place for an ailing pet?

Mrs. Molony nodded. "Here's where I was talking. The well I was to dig. That's how I uncovered the urgent message that brought you here."

Salem's instant relief—the freshly dug pit wasn't a grave—made way for curiosity. "You dug a well by your grandmother's grave?"

The woman shrugged. "That's where the water is."

Salem didn't meet Agent Curson's glance. Instead she smiled encouragingly at Mrs. Molony and began planning the story she'd relay to Bel. Bel, who'd threatened to drug Salem and tattoo *loser* on her forehead if she didn't take the Black Chamber job, who'd joked that it was easier to land dates in a wheelchair because all the women she met wanted to mother her, whom Salem could not imagine life without.

Salem was smiling when the bird swooped at her. "Gah!"

She swung wildly at the air, ignoring Agent Curson's startled bark of laughter. The magpie flapped and screeched before landing in the nearest tree.

Salem straightened her jacket and glanced around, heart thudding with surprise and embarrassment. Mrs. Molony was staring at her, her rheumy eyes suddenly clear, her gaze sharp and deep.

Salem's stomach clenched in response.

A ripple passed across Mrs. Molony's lined face. She pointed a bent finger at Salem and then the bird. "Tip your hat at the magpie, or you're destined for a life of bad luck."

Lady, you don't know the half of it.

But Salem made a saluting motion with an imaginary hat.

Agent Curson coughed.

Mrs. Molony's smile returned just as a cloud scudded over the sun. She indicated the pocket Salem had tucked the sachet into. "That's all right, then. You'll want to wear those protection herbs at your belt. That's what the string is about. And now, here's what you come for."

She stepped to the hole and indicated that Agent Curson and Salem should do the same. "When I first laid eyes on the symbol, it put the heart crossways in me. Thought it was a wee set of graves right next to me mamó's."

Agent Curson reached the hole first. He grew bedrock still.

Salem stepped beside him, drawing the sachet out of her pocket as she moved. She followed his gaze, her breath turning to dust.

CHAPTER 2

Blessington, Ireland

There, in a divot of dirt as thick and fresh as arterial blood, someone had first dug and then scraped away an area the size of a manhole cover. In the center of the cleared spot, a diorama jutted like teeth from the ground.

It was an almost perfect replica of Stonehenge.

The difference? Mrs. Molony's featured an extra stone.

And if archaeologists could see what Salem was looking at now, they'd have no question what Stonehenge was built for.

But that wasn't why Salem's heart was pounding at the cage of her chest.

No, what had her suddenly feeling like a hunted animal were the five tiny letters carved on that added piece, their edges dull yet still legible: *mercy.*

The same plea found on the locket worn by Bel's mother the night she was murdered.

Salem grabbed Agent Curson's arm for support. Her tongue thick, she pointed a shaking finger toward the ancient code and turned to him.

Can't you see it? Something that all modern archaeologists have missed, the truth that their training has taught them to overlook? It's a feminine explanation for Stonehenge!

Her blood bubbled with the awareness.

But she couldn't speak, not with Agent Curson sneering at her like she was a silly girl.

Not with Mrs. Molony cutting her with those sharp-again eyes.

So she closed her mouth and released Curson's arm. She shoved her knee-jerk Stonehenge hypothesis down deep, where she stored all her stupid ideas. It was her mother's fault the crazy thought had even entered her mind. It was Vida who viewed the world as a conspiracy against women, not Salem. It was Vida who belonged to the Underground, a centuries-old organization created to protect women from the men of the Hermitage. Salem's mother had wanted to induct her into the Underground, to teach her its history and purpose, had in fact secretly molded her to become the Underground's code breaker.

Salem had zero interest.

She intended to live a life in plain sight, an existence where she knew the expectations. She would crack codes, but she would work for an aboveboard agency. Conspiracies, ancient organizations, and hidden trails that led to even more clandestine histories had driven her anxiety to an unbearable level and cost Bel her ability to walk. Salem planned to remain in the orderly world of mathematics and computers, truth and logic, a place where the rules were clear and incontrovertible.

Nothing would drop her back into the shadowy world her mother had exposed her to.

Nothing.

CHAPTER 3

Rome

Former FBI agent Clancy Johnson sat across the table from the informant, surrounded by the hot-blooded clamor of Rome. He'd been on the move since he'd bungled the assassination of then Senator Gina Hayes last November. He was tired of running. That made it okay that they'd tracked him down.

"It's got to happen in London," Clancy said. "During the climate change summit."

The informant's brow furrowed. His face was so potato-bland that Clancy suspected the man could blend in anywhere. Definitely an asset in this line of work. "The president's security detail will be even tighter at such a high-profile event," he said, his voice as unremarkable as his face.

"Yes and no." Clancy patted his rumpled shirt and tugged out a pack of Camel Straights. He'd quit six years earlier but had recently decided that, as a dead man walking, he deserved to smoke. "More security, less focus," he continued. "It'll be chaos at the summit. Protestors. Media. Hayes has the world on fire. Everyone will be watching her. Plus, we have someone the president trusts on our side."

"Who?"

Clancy grabbed the sleeve of a passing waiter. "Light?"

The waiter scowled but flicked a matchbook out of his pocket. The good thing about Rome was that everyone smoked. That, and the pepper cheese pasta served in every corner bistro. Clancy could bathe in the stuff, it was that good. He inhaled deeply on the soothing fingers of smoke, letting them stroke his lungs. "Before I give up that information, I'm going to need verification you're with the Hermitage."

Across the table, the man's potato face started twitching. Clancy at first thought the informant was going to laugh. When that didn't happen, he decided the guy was hiking the north side of a seizure. That'd be a damn shame because it would mean he'd need to dress up and sell this plan to someone else. Before Clancy could muster a reasonable response, the man's twitches rode deeper, and a sound like wishbones snapping popped off his face.

Clancy wondered if he was on some bizarre hidden-camera show.

Or maybe he was asleep, the past year a single dream, his wife of forty years lying next to him in bed, his reputation intact?

Turned out to be neither of the above.

With a jerk, the man's face completed its metamorphosis. Suddenly, he was so beautiful it hurt to look at him.

If Clancy'd had any food in his body, he'd have shit himself.

The man spoke, his eyes watering from pain, his face an angel's. "In Europe, we don't call ourselves the Hermitage. Here, we're the Order."

WEDNESDAY

September 20

CHAPTER 4

The Campus, London

By the time Salem returned to London, she'd reclaimed the safety of rational thought. There was no global plot to suppress a feminine explanation for Stonehenge. There was only a lonely lady who'd created a kitschy model and used it to garner attention, exactly as Agent Curson had argued on the drive back. Once he'd dryly observed that *mercy* was neither Irish nor Proto-Indo-European, the language of the UK at the time of Stonehenge's construction, she'd had to agree with his take on the whole day.

She'd typed the report as soon as she'd returned.

A waste of time, it essentially said.

Her first FBI field experience, and it was a bust.

Clearly, she belonged behind a desk. She'd been a no-name master's candidate two years earlier when global security agencies had begun wooing her. They were all interested in the quantum computer theory she'd developed while writing her thesis. If translated into a functioning program, her theory would revolutionize cybersecurity. Whichever nation developed the program first would possess the equivalent of a nuclear bomb in a butter knife war.

She'd turned all the agencies down.

She'd planned on staying in the safety and comfort of her Minneapolis home as she developed GAEA (*Gee-uh,* as she called her), the program she'd sketched in her thesis. But forces beyond her control had shoved her out of her comfortable routine. In that new state of mind, she'd accepted the FBI's offer to join. That they'd promised she could continue her work on GAEA was a deciding factor.

They hadn't exactly delivered on that promise, though.

She'd been allotted little development time at the Campus, the nickname for the Marylebone building where Black Chamber analysts lived and worked while in London. The Campus was a 1960s block of an apartment building currently registered as an American diplomatic base. That claim wasn't too far off the reality: the analysts housed inside did interact with foreign representatives, work on behalf of the United States' citizens, and write a lot of reports.

The key difference?

At the Black Chamber, the "diplomats" never left their chairs. They toiled in an enormous room, what had been the communal gathering space back when the building housed apartments. There were no walls between their workstations. The openness was designed to encourage collaboration among the dozen analysts employed at the Campus.

They started each day with a typed task list. No one knew better than cryptanalysts how easily most computer programs could be hacked. If FBI agents needed to keep something secret, they used a typewriter and hand-delivered it. The task lists were shredded and then burned at the end of the day.

Not that they normally contained high secrets.

Based on their proficiency in a specific foreign language, each analyst at the Campus was assigned servers to track and clean. Cleaning involved running their assigned server's data through ECHELON, their code-breaking software, and manually decrypting any code that ECHELON couldn't crack or had red-flagged. On particularly long days, Salem saw the analysts as factory workers sorting through nuts and bolts, looking for defects in the assembly line of information.

Thanks to her mom, Salem spoke Persian, which meant that her job was to decrypt all Persian messages originating in European servers. She had to finish her assigned code cleaning before she was allowed to work on GAEA. Her quantum program would exploit the fact that all existing computers could process in only one direction, meaning they could only be made faster or stronger. Once it became a reality, Salem's theory would allow designated computers to also process sideways, backward, and into themselves without breaking a sweat. That meant that a line of code could be encrypted and decrypted on multiple levels.

In short, GAEA would make ECHELON look like a cereal box decoder ring. She would protect the United States, starting with shoring up private records, voting systems, government data, weapons algorithms, and individual citizen privacy. There was not a code the quantum computing program couldn't crack or a code breaker she couldn't repel.

However, the FBI, for all its strengths, was still a bureaucracy, one that assigned value based on measurable outcomes rather than more speculative activities, like theory testing. With Salem cleaning code and now working in the field, that left only five hours a week for GAEA. Salem's boss, Assistant Director Robert Bench, hadn't been convinced by her multiple pleas to be assigned more development time.

She'd resorted to sacrificing sleep to work on GAEA.

Tonight was no exception. She'd finished the Blessington field report around midnight, grabbed her laptop, and padded to the study hall, a retrofitted storage room that housed a couch, three swaybacked recliners, mismatched tables, and a television. It was one of a handful of afterthought rooms tucked around the Campus.

Salem figured she'd be less likely to fall asleep if she couldn't see her bed.

She set her steaming mug of peppermint tea on the table and dropped onto the sofa. If she balanced her laptop on crossed legs, her neck hardly hurt at all. It didn't take long for her to fall into the rhythm and security of programming, playing numbers like notes, writing a quantum symphony one line at a time.

The clock ticked away the minutes and then hours. She was exhausted. The couch was so comfortable, and the work was mesmerizing, lulling her into a dozy trance. She didn't hear the door open behind her.

"London treating you well?"

Lucan Stone's low rumble startled Salem out of her seat. She yelped as she flew to her feet, nearly toppling her laptop.

"What are you doing here?"

He chuckled. Had she ever seen him laugh before? She did not know the FBI agent well. He'd saved her and Bel's lives almost a year ago, but it felt further in her past, occupying that murky dreamscape when Salem and Bel had been on the run, chased by the Hermitage and the law, racing to save their own mothers. She hadn't known back then if she could trust Agent Stone.

She still didn't.

He crossed his arms languidly as she collected herself. He wore a well-cut suit, hair shaved close, his skin so dark it reflected purple in the dim light. He exuded calm power. "The president is coming to town for the summit. I'm on her advance team."

Salem sat back down on the couch, only partially facing him.

Agent Stone made her nervous.

Nearly everything but computers made her nervous.

"Oh," Salem said. Something didn't line up, but she wasn't sure what. "I see."

"What are you working on now?"

Salem glanced at her laptop. This was the first conversation between her and Stone that could be considered personal. She still couldn't believe he was here, at the Campus. Non-crypto FBI weren't supposed to know the Black Chamber existed, and Stone wasn't a code breaker. He was a straight-up G-Man. She didn't think he had clearance to hear about GAEA, so she lied.

"A new social media filter that tags unsourced news. That way you know if you're getting your information from a legit source or some Eastern bloc computer rat."

Stone leaned over for a look. "Still protecting the world, even during your downtime?"

She tried to close her laptop so he couldn't see, but he smelled so good. Freshly showered. His breath reached her neck, the slight caress of air like a finger trailing from her ear to her shoulder blade. He was heat and smooth darkness, safety and danger and so close. A thrill burned along Salem's skin.

She told herself to be calm.

They were professionals.

Colleagues, apparently.

"Saving time, not the world." Salem's voice cracked. "People are too busy to check all the news they read."

She risked a glance at him, swiveling her head until their eyes locked. Amazingly, her neck no longer hurt. But she shouldn't have turned toward him. He was too much, his lips a magnet. She set her computer on the table, unwilling to fight the pull.

She exhaled softly as she leaned toward him. Her pulse throbbed at her wrists.

Their lips met, his soft and then more passionate. This had been a long time coming.

She grabbed the front of his shirt and helped him over the back of the couch and onto her. The weight and hardness of him were electric. His edges melted into her curves. She wanted to touch every inch of him, her skin naked to his.

She ground her hips upward. Her sexual courage embarrassed her, but her body was insistent.

He drew back, pushing her curls out of her face. When he saw his desire enthusiastically reflected in her, he kissed her deeply, tipping his weight so he could touch her, lingering on her neck before brushing over her right nipple, causing a shiver the length of her. His hand moved slowly and deliberately across her hip before sliding between her legs.

The pleasure was building inside her, a spark that flickered and then caught, growing, consuming her with heat. She moaned, swung out her arm, and knocked her computer off the table.

Crash.

She blinked, disoriented, woken by the sound of her laptop clattering to the ground. She was in the study hall, alone. The calm repetition of programming had put her to sleep as she'd been typing. The crash of her computer had been real, everything else a dream. The delicious heat and weight of Lucan Stone were gone, but the echoes of her orgasm remained. She blushed in the quiet of the room. It had been a while since she'd had a clutch dream; she hoped she hadn't been so . . . expressive during the previous ones. What if someone had been walking by?

Agent Stone.

She sighed. It'd been months since she'd thought of him. Last she'd heard, he was on another of President Hayes's secret projects, much like the Black Chamber. He likely lived and worked in DC. Bel would know, if Salem dared mention his name. She sat up, stretched, and asked her phone the time.

"Five forty-five a.m. Would you like to hear the weather?"

Nope. She would be strapped to her computer today and for the foreseeable future, unless another field job came her way. She doubted Agent Curson would request her help if it did. She'd behaved like the greenhorn she was, with a dash of hysteria thrown in for good measure.

She rolled her eyes at herself before standing to make her way to her room, grateful that everyone else seemed to be asleep as she walked down the hall. Her X-rated dream was surely playing over her head on a movie screen, visible to anyone she met.

She slipped inside her room with a plan. She didn't need to be at her work computer until eight, and her dream had made clear she had some juice to work off. She changed into sweats. At Quantico, she'd discovered muscles she didn't know she had, plus an affinity for weight lifting. She wanted to keep both. The designers of the Campus had knocked out walls and removed kitchens and bathrooms to make dormitory-style bedrooms for the analysts, keeping the original apartment building's pool, steam room, and weight room surrounded by an elevated track.

She leaned over for her running shoes and knocked the blue-flowered sachet off the bedside table. It smelled of sage. *Mrs. Molony.* A familiar, hot rush of shame flooded her cheeks. Should she have said something about her Stonehenge hunch after all?

She picked the sachet off the floor and was inhaling deeply of its spice when her phone rang. She glanced over.

Bel's image winked at her from the brightly lit phone. Salem's guts jerked.

It was midnight in Minneapolis. This would not be good news.

CHAPTER 5

The Campus, London

"Everything is okay, don't worry."

Isabel Odegaard's smiling face filled Salem's screen before the room behind Bel shifted. She was in the kitchen of Salem's childhood home, filling a glass with water from the refrigerator dispenser. She'd pimped out her wheelchair so it held a phone, a laptop, and a table for taking notes, all hands-free. Until last year, her life had been built around her physical prowess. Bel had been a Chicago police officer, best shot in her class, a self-defense instructor.

The assassination attempt had changed that.

The first bullet had passed overhead, missing its target. The second had paralyzed Bel from the waist down.

Both shots had been meant for Gina Hayes. Bel had used her body as a shield. Publicly, she was hailed as a hero. Privately, she struggled with excruciating physical therapy and even more painful depression as she traded power and police work for something different. Throughout, she'd made it clear that Salem should not feel sorry for her, and better not stay in Minneapolis to care for her. To this day, Salem wasn't sure if she'd ultimately joined the Black Chamber to protect Bel from worrying she'd *not* joined because of her.

"Yes," Bel said, answering Salem's question before she had a chance to ask it, "it *is* midnight here. But that means it's six a.m. there. I wanted to catch you before you went to work. It seems like all we do anymore is text. I wanted a real conversation."

"Mercy is okay? Mom?"

Bel swiveled the phone so it faced the refrigerator and a crayon drawing of two broccoli-shaped trees with a rainbow joining them. Two people held hands underneath, one tall, one short, both with dramatically five-toed feet and five-fingered hands.

"They're great. Mercy said this is a picture of you and her under a lucky rainbow."

Salem's heart melted. She and Mercy Mayfair had developed an unbreakable bond. When they'd first met, the child had been as skittish as a wildcat, fierce-eyed and bony, trusting only her brother, Ernest. During the cross-country journey to save Bel's and Salem's mothers, Salem had tutored Mercy, bought her coloring books, and made sure she ate her vegetables. Gradually, the alley-cat girl had warmed to Salem. It had been nearly as hard to leave the child behind as it had to abandon Bel.

Salem retrieved a mental image of the mini-Stonehenge with *mercy* written on the extra stone, and her chest tightened. *Coincidence, surely. One is a name, the other a plea.*

"Mercy seems happy?" Salem snapped open her laptop as she spoke and attached her phone to it via a simple USB connection. She propped up the phone so she could type while she talked. Bel had given her permission to test GAEA as needed during their conversations. One of its planned features captured background images in video calls, triggering an alert if they were of note: stolen items with visible serial codes, drug paraphernalia, illegal weaponry. She wanted to test how GAEA would translate the drawings taped to the refrigerator.

Bel reholstered her own phone, a grin lighting up her beautiful face. She'd decided not to regrow her strawberry-blonde hair after Salem had chopped it on the run. The pixie cut suited her delicate features, eyes the sweet blue of a cloud-free sky, creamy skin, elegant nose, full lips. "Mercy is better than happy. That kid is a goddamned genius. You know how she picked up the math you taught her when we were on the run? She's the same with physical training."

Salem's face pinched before she could smooth it.

Bel chuckled. "Good thing you're not a poker player. You'd be flat broke inside of an hour. Yeah, in answer to the question your face asked, I train her. Krav Maga, plus evasive moves. The top of my body works just fine."

Salem leaned toward her phone, eyes wide. "I didn't doubt you, Bellie. I worry about *her*. She's only seven. Do you really need to teach her to be afraid of the world?"

"Not afraid of it. Able to survive it. And I want her to *know* she's getting trained."

They sat in the silence, together. Bel spoke truth.

It wasn't only Salem who'd been tricked into working for the Underground. She and Bel had both been secretly groomed by their parents, Salem for code breaking and computers and Bel for strength and spycraft. They had excelled in their fields. When their parents' worst nightmare materialized and the Hermitage hunted Bel and Salem in the hopes of destroying the Underground, they'd had to call on all their training to survive, to save Gina Hayes, and to crush the Hermitage.

The training had stuck. The betrayal as well.

The sticky pain of being lied to by their parents, of being groomed for a life they had no say in, reared its ugly head. Salem needed to silence it. Two possible topics of conversation came to mind, neither of which she particularly wanted to bring up: Stonehenge and Lucan Stone.

"I saw something in Ireland yesterday," she blurted. "I went out there with another agent, Len Curson? I thought we were called out on a fool's errand. There's all sorts of them with the summit coming. The caller was a sweet old woman. Said she had something to show us."

Bel's face lit up with interest.

"You wouldn't believe it, Bel." Salem's voice went high, sounding fake even to her own ears. Her rational side was warring with her intuition, trying to muzzle it from voicing its ridiculous theory. "The woman had uncovered a little replica of Stonehenge in her backyard, right next to her grandmother's grave. The word *mercy* was carved on one of the stones."

Bel saw Salem's distress. She didn't waste time on tangential questions. "Was it a code?"

Salem squished her lips together. "It was—"

But the words didn't come. *Hey, I don't know what* mercy *has to do with anything, but if you see the placement of the stone it was written on, guess what? Things fall into place, and you see that Stonehenge is a profoundly stationary version of something you and I carry in our purses every day.* It sounded stupid in her head and would certainly crush her under its silly weight if she uttered it aloud.

Bel inhaled loudly. "You solved the mystery of Stonehenge, didn't you?"

If they were together, in person, Salem could maybe confess what she thought Stonehenge really was, and they'd laugh about it. She couldn't bring herself to do it over the phone, though. She shoved an easy smile on her face and waggled her eyebrows. "For sure. And for my next trick, I plan to identify the Zodiac Killer."

Bel studied her, squinting. Salem held her breath. This could go either way.

After a long three seconds, Bel went with the laugh. "That's my girl." She drank the water she'd drawn from the refrigerator. When she set down the empty glass, she wiped her mouth with her arm. "In honor of our unbreakable friendship bond, I should tell you that your mom has a surprise for you."

Salem tensed. "What?"

"If I tell you, it's not a surprise." Bel winked and pivoted. "Hey, don't suppose you've found any sexy British women for me to date? I need someone who takes no shit."

The conversation continued for another ten minutes. Bel updated Salem on the freelance work she'd been doing. Salem shared as much as she could about her work at the Campus, which wasn't much at all. After a promise to talk again soon, they hung up.

It was 6:30 a.m.

That left enough time to work out.

Salem finished lacing her shoes and snapped the elastic band that held her room key around her wrist. She bound her wild morning hair in a topknot and stepped into the hallway. The dormitories were housed on the west end of the building, the conference rooms and offices of the brass in the middle, and the code breakers' computer lab was tucked at the east end. The workout area was below it all, in the basement. She could reach the gym from either end or the center of the Campus, but the middle stairs were better lit. She trotted toward those.

She was playing with the blue plastic band at her wrist when she heard a murmuring from one of the conference rooms. Cleaning staff? No one else would be in this early. She didn't have a chance to reverse her course before the conference room door opened.

Assistant Director Robert Bench stepped into the hallway. Other than a brief orientation when she was first assigned to the Campus, she had encountered her supervisor only when she'd tried to convince him to assign her more GAEA time. In those brief run-ins, he'd come across as a gruff man with a twitchy muscle in his cheek that made her think he was always chewing on a bit of leftover meat. His face was jowled, his hair more gray than black.

He appeared neither pleased nor surprised to run into her at this hour.

"Agent Wiley. Just the girl I wanted to see."

Salem stopped, flustered. "Yes, sir?"

He got right to it. "President Hayes is arriving tomorrow to attend the summit. She has specifically requested you on her cybersecurity detail. She wants you to deploy GAEA."

Salem flinched. That made no sense. The FBI hadn't given her the time to develop the program, yet she was being asked to use it? For a moment, she wondered whether this was a continuation of her earlier dream. With the president coming to London, Lucan Stone might also be near. "It's not ready."

"That's what I told Hayes. She said you'll employ other means as well. But she was very specific that it is you she wants running code interference for her while she's here, and that she wants you to test the new program in her presence."

Salem nodded.

"One more thing." He tipped his head toward the open door of the conference room he'd exited. "You have a new partner."

CHAPTER 6

Moscow

"What would you like to drink, sir?"

US Speaker of the House Vit Linder crossed his arms. "I don't drink."

The Russian butler kept his expression serene. "Tea, perhaps?"

"I'll take a Diet Pepsi."

It was Vit's second trip to Russia, and his first meeting with the Order. His staff had cleared the visit with the State Department, his spokesperson had lined up a press conference to spin the visit in the best possible light, and off they'd gone. The first and second days had been boring—shaking hands, feigning interest in the minutiae of Russian politics.

Today, the minister of economic development had invited him to a private engagement. His security detail had been allowed to sweep the mansion's third floor for threats, and then they'd been forced to stay in the foyer, leaving Vit to this meeting, where he'd been invited to the most exclusive club on the planet.

It was a coveted offer.

He leaned back in the executive chair. It was a rich brown he'd never seen in his fifty-eight years. When he'd asked the butler about it, the man had informed him that the leather was prerevolutionary reindeer, discovered by divers on a sunken Danish brigantine. The chair was one of thirteen rimming the dark violet African blackwood table. Vit didn't know what any of that meant except *cha-ching*.

Probably the abstract paintings mounted on all four walls were priceless originals, too, and the liquor he sniffed in the air fifty-year-old Yamazaki. Vit didn't drink because it had been his father's downfall, but real estate tycoon George Linder had referred to the $140,000 whisky in reverent tones often enough that it had stuck. George only spoke to his son when he was drunk, and during a particularly agitated bender, he'd mentioned the Order.

"They run the world," George had said, pouring his fourth scotch.

Despite his father's apparent desire to connect with him, Vit remembered feeling guarded. Sometimes his father would tell him some real corkers and then make fun of Vit when he believed him. "They're rich?"

George had laughed and then drunk both fingers in a single swallow. "They're not rich. They are *beyond* money. Do you understand?"

White spittle gathered at the corner of his mouth. "They start wars and end them. They control the media, the internet, food production, and now, even the weather."

Vit had perfected an expression he'd employ when he wanted to look like he understood something. He slid it on then. His father didn't notice, saying no more on the subject no matter how many times Vit asked.

Intrigued, Vit had called in the private detective he used when he wanted to know what his sisters really thought of him or when he planned to ask out a famous actress and needed to make sure she'd say yes. The PI sniffed around, uncovering just enough to confirm that everything George had said about the Order was true and then some.

Then the PI had disappeared.

Vit hadn't thought much more about it in the intervening two decades. Until last week, when the invitation had arrived from Moscow. It was routed through his office, addressed to the Speaker of the House. He was to fly over and discuss trade sanctions, a trip that was beneath him and that he would have declined if not for one specific line: *We understand you prefer the Four Seasons and have the presidential suite reserved in the hopes that you and your staff will join us to discuss . . .*

The reference was discreet. Maybe the author, the Russian minister of economic development, didn't know about the "incident" at the Four Seasons the last and only time Vit had traveled to Moscow. That had been before he'd considered a career in politics.

Then again, maybe the minister did know about it. Maybe he even had video evidence.

In either case, Vit considered it expedient to accept the invitation. And here he was, seated at a table with two of the world's most powerful men: Cassius Barnaby, one half of the Barnaby brothers and co-owner of Barnaby Industries, a multibillion-dollar multinational corporation based in Missouri, and Mikhail Lutsenko, a Russian steel tycoon whose command of the Russian mafia was the country's most poorly kept secret. They'd invited Vit because they wanted him to replace Carl Barnaby, Cassius's brother, who was currently serving twenty-five to life for the kidnapping of Vida Wiley and the theft of millions of dollars of gold, jewels, and artifacts discovered by Wiley's daughter when she cracked the Beale Cipher.

"You understand what's at stake?" Lutsenko asked Vit after the butler had returned with his diet soda. Lutsenko's martini glass was sweating directly into the magnificent blackwood. "We have twelve on the board. We need an odd number."

"I understand," Vit said. He was comfortable at a high-stakes table.

"I don't think you do, son," Cassius Barnaby said, leaning forward. He reminded Vit of his own father in age and manner. In other words, he was a condescending prick. "We fart and an economy collapses."

Vit Linder smirked, hiding the surge of rage he felt at Barnaby talking down to him. Vit was the son of a wealthy man, but it wasn't his father's millions that had secured his own empire, though they had provided a hefty start. Neither was it his father's connections that had gotten him elected to the third-highest office in the land, though they hadn't hurt. That left charisma, brains, and looks—except Vit's personality was a shallow pool; he'd barely graduated college, even with a team of tutors; and his physical attractiveness had peaked at twenty-three and wasn't anything to write home about even then.

So what *had* launched Vit Linder to the top?

Canniness, he called it.

In laymen's terms? Nobody read a room better.

Specifically, no one in business or politics could glance at a person and immediately sniff out exactly what would piss them off. He kept everyone around him off-balance, like a martial artist, and his power had never failed him.

Not that he needed to call on it to get Cassius Barnaby's number. The man was back on his heels. He was trying to keep his face smooth, and he mostly succeeded, but his eyes kept flicking to Lutsenko. Vit didn't need a tutor to see that Lutsenko was at the top of the ladder and Barnaby barely hanging on to the bottom rung, likely because of the bad publicity he and his brother had brought to the Hermitage, the American branch of the Order.

Always plant your foot on the neck of the bottom man, his dad had taught him. *It makes you stand taller.*

Vit addressed Cassius Barnaby directly. "That may have been true before your brother was arrested with his hands in the Beale Vault. Tell me about the Order's power now."

Vit leaned back, a deceptively relaxed gesture. He kept his eyes locked with Barnaby's while registering Lutsenko's body language. He was satisfied to see the Russian imperceptibly relax. Lutsenko had not been sure about Vit.

Now he was.

"This isn't a pissing contest," Barnaby said. The sweat that had formed on his upper lip put the lie to his words. "The regulations that come with the climate accord are going to cost us dearly. Is it a coincidence that we are losing assets while female-led enterprises gain them?"

Lutsenko laughed. It was a dry sound. "It was luck that they decrypted the Beale train," he said, using their archaic term for connected ciphers.

"You'd gamble everything on that?" Cassius Barnaby asked. "On *luck*? Because we've overcome regulations in the past. The accord will sting, but if the Underground uncovers the remaining trains before us, we are done. Women will realize how many resources they have at their disposal, how many they've always had. Our money? Power? Gone. What's at the end of those trains will make what Wiley uncovered in the Beale Vault look like a waitress stealing tips."

"Enough," Lutsenko said. Vit got the impression the man didn't put as much stock in the rising power of women as Barnaby did. He was also a vain man, straightening his hair and stroking his mustache, an observation Vit filed away for later. "We have our own men searching for the trains."

"Bring Salem Wiley and Mercy Mayfair in," Barnaby argued. "Bring them in as insurance."

"We've made a deal with the Grimalkin."

Barnaby flinched at the name. Vit sat up with interest.

"We let Wiley remain a free agent so we can learn from her," Lutsenko continued. "We know where the child is. We can call them both in for an interview when needed. No earlier."

Vit sat back, disappointed. If he wasn't making deals, he wasn't interested, and there was no money to be had in this talk of a woman and a child. "I'll let you gentlemen handle that. My focus is on the United States. If I join the board, I get what I want?"

Barnaby's mood shifted for only a flash, distaste replaced by something that looked like humor. Vit didn't like that at all, the feeling that he was being laughed at. He made a note to make Cassius Barnaby pay, sooner rather than later. He would make the man squirm in shame.

In the meanwhile, the Order needed an odd number on the board. Their covenant demanded it, and they wanted someone they thought they could manipulate—that much was clear. Vit would pretend to give them what they wanted because only they could facilitate his greatest desire.

Revenge.

Vit would join the Order.

He'd use his position to have President Gina Hayes and Vice President Richard Cambridge assassinated. Next in line for the presidency of the United States of America?

Speaker of the House Vit Linder.

Who's stupid now, George?

❖

Vit's head was thrown back in laughter when the secretary walked in. Vit was not an exuberant man. An occasional chuckle or snicker. Barnaby and Lutsenko wanted him to be a buffoon, though, and so he'd expose his neck. It's not like anyone here was taking pictures. Besides, it was funny, their plan for keeping the American poor at each other's throats.

The secretary stopped behind Lutsenko's chair. "Sir."

"*Da?*"

The secretary held himself like he had a glass stomach. Vit didn't care one whit for male secretaries. It wasn't right.

"We have an intercept," the man said, staring forward.

Vit recorded how Barnaby and Lutsenko each demonstrated interest. Barnaby scowled. The Russian grew more rigid.

"Speak, then," Barnaby said impatiently.

"Ms. Wiley spoke of Stonehenge." The secretary's hands were clenched. "It seems she is interested in its code."

Barnaby barked, "See!"

"What exactly was said?" Lutsenko asked, signaling for Barnaby's silence.

The secretary glanced at the paper in his hand. It fluttered with an almost imperceptible tremor. "It was a phone call with Ms. Odegaard. Ms. Wiley: 'You wouldn't believe it, Bel. The woman had uncovered a little replica of Stonehenge in her backyard, right next to her grand-mother's grave. The word *mercy* was carved on one of the stones.' Ms. Odegaard: 'Was it a code?' Ms. Wiley: 'It was.' Ms. Odegaard: 'You solved the mystery of Stonehenge, didn't you?' Ms. Wiley: 'For sure. And for my next trick, I plan to crack the Zodiac Killer's code.'"

Lutsenko laughed. "That is a joke."

Barnaby's lips drew tight. "You don't know that."

Vit took charge. "What was their tone?"

The secretary consulted his sheet again. "There was laughter after the final line. None before."

Barnaby spoke through clenched teeth. "She solved the Beale Cipher. This is not an idle threat."

Vit's blood began bubbling nicely. It looked like he would get to cast his first tiebreaking vote. That would leave an impression. He kept score as the men continued arguing across the table.

"We bring in only the girl. Solving Stonehenge is nothing without the child in hand."

"We bring them both in. The Grimalkin can locate the end of the Stonehenge train."

"That hasn't worked before. Why would that change?"

Vit saw his opening and pounced. "If your Grimalkin is as good as you say, ask for verification when she's solved Stonehenge. She won't know she's being tailed. You have nothing to lose, everything to gain. You can bring in the child and use her like a gas pedal to speed up . . . what'd you say her name was? Salem Wiley? Speed up her search for the train."

He was just reordering their own words and parroting them back to them, but he'd counted, and they were the only words both Barnaby and Lutsenko would buy. "It's the one plan with the most exits. You need Wiley brought in? You can do that later."

Barnaby's eyes sparked, but he was beginning to nod.

"You're in favor?" Lutsenko asked.

"With one modification," Barnaby said, his tone icy. "We acquire the child now, as Mr. Linder has proposed. We let Salem Wiley continue to freelance, but *only* until she cracks Stonehenge. After that, she is retired once and for all. If her talents are that strong, she is too dangerous to continue as a free agent."

"Agreed," Lutsenko said.

Just like that, Vit's patience reached its limits. There was no money on the table, nothing that benefited him, only smoke and conspiracy and talk of *girls*. "I'll leave you fellows to the boots-on-the-ground planning of that one. Because I have the inside information, I'll oversee the . . . retiring of the president and vice president."

"The president only," Barnaby said, once again reminding Vit of his father, "or it's too much unrest."

Vit's testicle spasmed. They'd mentioned that idea earlier, but he hadn't thought they'd been firm about it. He had overplayed his hand. "Of course. The president only."

That would not work. Richard Cambridge would ascend to the office and appoint a new vice president. Vit Linder would remain only the Speaker of the House.

Lutsenko steepled his fingers, reclaiming control of the meeting. "We'll connect you with Clancy Johnson. He's being brought in to retire the president."

Vit's eyes shot up before he could hide his reaction. "Johnson's still alive?"

Rumor was the FBI had shot their own and dumped his body after the traitor bungled his assassination attempt.

"Very much," Lutsenko confirmed.

"But he failed last time he tried to kill Hayes," Vit whined.

Barnaby's and Lutsenko's faces shifted. They had discussed this before.

"More incentive to get it right this time," Barnaby finally said. He took clear pleasure in denying Vit his worry. "You'll make it look like a Middle Easterner did it, of course."

Vit nodded like a petulant child. The whining had not been an act.

Fortunately, being denied his due was Vit's greatest motivator. It took him only a second to arrive at a work-around, which he wisely kept to himself. Johnson had messed up an assassination once. Nobody would point fingers at Vit if it happened again and Johnson "accidentally" fumbled another, killing two instead of one.

The shortest route to looking good is surrounding yourself with fuckups was another of Vit's father's sayings.

Barnaby relaxed pompously, Vit thought, exactly as planned. "Jason will acquire the child," Barnaby said. "And if we are letting Salem Wiley freelance while she solves the Stonehenge train, I want Jason assigned to mentor her along with the Grimalkin. If we lose her, we lose everything."

"The Grimalkin won't like that." Barnaby's face made clear he didn't care.

"It's settled, then," Vit said. They needed to move to another subject before the plan changed again. "I get Johnson. Your Jason 'acquires' the girl. The Grimalkin and Jason work together on Salem Wiley, retiring her when she cracks the Stonehenge code."

The absurdity of his sentences was almost lost on Vit. *Almost.* He'd smile about it later, but for now, he was too near the pot of gold. "And by this time Saturday, President Gina Hayes is fired."

Barnaby and Lutsenko nodded.

Vit took a swig of the best diet soda he'd ever tasted.

CHAPTER 7

The Campus, London

"Not your cup of tea, eh?"

Salem snapped her mouth shut. It was ridiculous, but she'd expected Agent Lucan Stone to stride out of the conference room. This man was his physical opposite—bony where Lucan was muscled, the uniquely translucent white skin of a Brit to Lucan's smooth darkness. She guessed he was in his early forties, crinkled hazel eyes beneath a mop of brown hair more suitable to the lead singer of a boy band than an FBI agent.

Her disappointment must have been emblazoned on her face.

He held out his hand. "Charles Arthur Thackeray, but please call me Charlie."

She took it. Her own palm was sweaty and shaking. What did it mean that she being was assigned a new partner the day after her only fieldwork with Agent Curson?

"Salem Wiley."

"Charlie is British intelligence." Assistant Director Bench was peeking at his watch. He wore a business suit, as did Charlie.

Salem grew keenly aware of her sweats and messy topknot. "The British know we're here?" It was a stupid question.

Charlie's smile crinkled the corners of his eyes. "MI5, in any case. It's a pleasure to finally meet you. You're a bit of a legend in our department. We've crowned you queen of cryptanalysis. I look forward to working with the best."

Salem frowned. This was happening too fast. She already didn't have enough time for GAEA, and here she was getting a directive to work with the president this coming weekend as well as a partner from another agency. "What is our assignment?"

Bench gave her his full attention. "Same as it's always been. Intercept threats, develop GAEA, and now, check in with the president's team while she's here. Charlie has full security clearance. He'll fill you in on the details. I have a meeting to get to."

That was his goodbye. Salem watched him walk away, resentment burrowing into her chest. She didn't know her new partner. He wasn't even American. He was another distraction from what she was good at, what she had been hired for: developing computer programs that would protect her country. "Agent Thackeray—"

"Charlie. And believe me, I understand." His chuckle was rueful. "I was a week's work shy of cracking the ISIL Shard Code when I got pulled to work with you on fuck all."

Her hand flew to her mouth. "I'm that transparent?"

He politely refrained from answering. "Part of the job, these assignments. It's a wonder we get anything done." He tipped his head toward her sneakers. "On your way to lift some weights?"

She followed his gaze. "Yeah. I mean yes. Then I'd planned to be at my computer at eight. Should I change that?"

"Let's walk and talk. The gym is this way?"

Salem nodded. The familiar hallway felt too narrow now that she had to share it with a stranger. If Bel were here, everything would be okay. Her fingers twitched, and she began the soothing motion of touching her thumb to each of her fingertips, starting with her pinkie and working toward her pointer finger. She didn't want to work out anymore. She wanted to sit in front her computer and organize the information into clean pillows of code that followed her command.

Charlie walked a little bit to the front and as far to the side of her as the hallway would allow. It meant she could watch him without openly staring, which soothed her somewhat.

"Can't believe you cracked the Beale Cipher." His voice was soft and shaded with something. Envy? "How did that feel?"

"It wasn't me," Salem said truthfully. "It was someone else."

"Maybe someone else saw it first, but they were using your theories." He turned to give her a soft smile. "Is what we're told about GAEA true? You've almost pinned down the variables?"

She rubbed the back of her neck. The crick had returned. "Almost. Do you need my data?"

They'd reached the gym. It smelled like sweat and unwashed socks. An analyst was bench-pressing on the opposite side of the room, his grunts interspersed with the clang of the metal weights. Someone was jogging the overhead track that hugged all four walls. The space was too big. Everyone here was a stranger, including Charlie.

Especially Charlie.

She could feel his eyes on her, and she mentally retraced the steps to her Ativan bottle. She didn't want a partner, not unless it was Bel. She should quit. She should go home to Minneapolis. She could work on GAEA just as well there, probably better. There would be no interruptions. She wouldn't have access to the real-life code threats, but she could imagine them. She could prototype off that.

"No data," he said, but his voice came from far away. "We're to work together solely on cleaning and sorting SIGINT while your heads of state are in town to avoid an international incident on UK soil, yeah?"

Salem heard his words but couldn't process them. All her attention was now on the track. Who was running up there? There was something eerie about him. The length he was currently jogging meant he wasn't facing her, but his longish hair and lean build looked familiar.

Her blood drained.

She realized who he reminded her of. Jason.

The freaky face-changing assassin. The man who'd tortured Vida and brutally murdered Grace, Bel's mom and Vida's best friend. The monster who'd hunted her and Bel like rabbits, terrorizing them.

He'd tracked her down in London.

But it couldn't be.

Her presence here, the Campus—they were top secret.

Salem's heart was pounding in her ears. Could she run to her Ativan without making Charlie uncomfortable? It couldn't be Jason. Could it? She'd know one way or another in three seconds, when he reached the corner and ran this direction, revealing his face. Or he'd exit through the door before he hit the corner. She never should have gone to Ireland. It had thrown everything off.

"Salem?" Charlie's voice was soft. She'd forgotten he was standing next to her. Her neck jerked, and she looked at him, the pain pulling her back into the present. He appeared worried.

"Sorry. Did you say something?"

He coughed. Clearly, he'd said her name more than once. Her cheeks burned.

"Not a thing." He tipped his head toward her sneakers. "I'll leave you to your workout. We'll talk later?"

He walked away without saying another word. Salem wanted to crawl into herself. Two coworkers were laughing over by the drinking fountain. The man who'd been using the jogging track had in fact left through the door rather than running into her sight line. He was probably a new analyst, or an office worker from the front of the agency.

She felt foolish, just as she had in Ireland yesterday. She couldn't get so deep into her own head, be so thrown off by haunting reminders. Fighting the urge to run back to her dormitory and hide, she walked toward the weights. Physical exertion had pulled her back from the edge of a panic attack before. Maybe it would work now.

She tried working her usual circuit, but her neck hurt too bad. Leg curls, it would twinge. Bench press was agony. She probably needed a masseuse, or a chiropractor. She'd have to settle on the steam room.

She glanced at her phone as she wiped down her equipment. Fifteen minutes for a quick steam and then a shower and off to meet Charlie. She headed to the women's changing room and located her locker. She swirled the dial on her combination lock. In a crypto cave like the Campus, a dial lock offered about as much protection as duct tape, but old habits died hard.

Locker open, she traded her workout clothes for a swimsuit, slid her feet into flip-flops, and padded toward the steam room. She hoped the heat would relax her muscles and ease the knot in her neck. When she opened the door, the steam rolled out of the dark room. She squinted. She thought it was empty, but the steam was too thick to be sure.

She felt along the wall until she reached the far corner.

She dropped onto the wooden bench and slid her feet out of her sandals.

Beads of sweat immediately formed on her forehead and began trickling down. She tipped her head back, rubbing her own shoulders. The steam slickened her skin. She located the knot immediately. It was a hard nugget the size of a peach stone between the base of her skull and her right shoulder. She pressed her pointer finger into the center of it, pushing with all her might even though the pain made her tongue taste like alum.

The knot released the slightest bit. She sighed deeply.

A counter-noise emerged from the opposite side of the room. Salem's every muscle tensed for flight. Her hands dropped to fighting position, the knot forgotten. She blinked, trying to clear the air, but the steam was as thick as paste.

"Hello?"

No sound. Was a person sitting on the other bench? Only ten feet separated one seat from the other, but with the thick air, it might as well have been a wall between them. She stood, her knot having grown its own knots.

"Is there someone there?" She waved her hand. The motion provided a tantalizing inch of visual clarity. Someone was definitely sitting across from her. "Charlie?"

No answer.

Her flesh turned icy beneath her sweating skin. The discordance curdled her stomach. She backed toward the door. "Len?"

The person shifted.

A savage part of her wanted to jump at the stranger, slap his face, demand to know why he wasn't answering. She took another step backward. The heel of her flip-flop caught in the wooden flooring slats, and she tumbled backward, catching herself before she hit the floor. She felt vulnerable as she flailed. He could have a knife. Or a gun.

The person most certainly was a male.

It wasn't his silhouette that finally gave him away. That was shifting like a genie's behind the steam. It was his smell, a sour musk magnified by the steam.

Jason.

She wanted to yell and fight.

Instead, she charged the door, grabbing blindly for the handle, feeling his hands racing toward her neck as she struggled to escape.

CHAPTER 8

The Campus, London

The panic attack swallowed her whole.

She ran all the way along the basement level to the dormitory end of the Campus wearing only her swimsuit. Her ragged breath pounded like footsteps in her ears. She was too terrified to glance behind her, too shaken to care that she was half-naked. Her hands vibrated as she tried to shove her room key into the slot, but she finally managed, slamming the door behind her, falling against it, gulping for air.

Salem slid to the floor, fighting nausea.

The panic eventually receded, replaced by the scrape of rock bottom.

No villain had been lurking in the steam room. Jason, the face-changing assassin, was not after her, never really had been, in fact. He'd hunted her mother and Bel's mother, and Gina Hayes. He wanted the Underground leaders; Salem and Bel had gotten in his way but had never been primary targets. He was from a different time and place. She'd imagined him in the steam room with her like a child in bed fabricates a sharp-toothed bogeyman in the closet.

She'd acted like a weirdo.

Again.

She'd been able to skate on the surface of this new job for nearly a month, to tell herself she might be good at it, but her nerves had finally caught up. It had been a mistake to come to Europe by herself. The world was too big. She belonged in Minneapolis with Bel, and Mercy, and even her mother. She knew she was in bad shape when spending time with her mother was appealing.

Salem realized she was freezing. God, she hoped no one had seen her mad dash in her swimsuit. She replayed her frenzied flight in her head, trying to remember if she'd passed any gawping faces. It was no use. The run was a blur. She showered in her room, changed, returned to the locker room to retrieve her phone, and made up her mind to quit.

Bel would hate her for her weakness, but she had no choice.

"Ready to go?"

She spun. Charlie stood outside the locker room, an expectant smile on his face.

Salem opened her mouth and closed it, opened it again. "Where?"

"Parliament. The president arrives today."

Salem squared her shoulders. "I can't."

"Oh." His expression shifted to concern. "Are you unwell?"

"I . . ." She'd intended to lie. Instead a concrete stream of truth poured out. "I'm a shitty analyst. I'm scared all the time. I don't even like to go outside. I only pretend to be interested in fieldwork, swallowing just enough Ativan to get through the day. This isn't me. I want to be at home, staring at a computer screen, working on GAEA and—"

"—knowing what time breakfast, lunch, and dinner will be, eating the same thing for each meal so you can feel safe in your routine?"

That wasn't what she'd intended to say, but it was close enough. "Something like that."

"Me too." He flashed a sad grin and pointed at the ceiling. "Same with everyone working in your lab, my guess. It's the curse of our kind. We are not people of action and espionage, but our talents land us here and so we learn the rest, reluctantly. I spent the first five years of my MI5 career feeling like a fraud."

Salem realized her shoulders were gathered up around her ears. She relaxed them. "How'd you cope?"

"Drank too much, probably." He chuckled. "If you want to drop out of this assignment, no one would fault you. I'll even go with you to talk to Bench. And in fact, it's a ridiculous shame they don't have you on GAEA all the time. It'd be better for your country, you leaving the FBI to devote your full attention to quantum computing."

Relief hit Salem so hard that tears flooded her eyes. "Thank you."

He pursed his lips. She sensed he didn't want to say the next part. "Yeah, but if you want my opinion? Wait until after the president leaves. Things aren't looking good for her."

The small respite dried up. "What do you know?"

"Not much more than everyone else." He glanced over his shoulder, suggesting the opposite. "A female president is a tempting target is all, yeah?"

"Yeah," Salem said, the world weighing heavy on her.

❖

"The driving really isn't that bad."

Charlie disproved his words by running a red light, nearly hitting a boxy black cab, and practically shaving the whiskers off a startled pedestrian. The sky was gunmetal gray, brushing the top of the car. It could rain but probably wouldn't, Charlie had informed her when they'd left the Campus. He'd brought an umbrella for her in any case. "You get used to it snap quick."

Salem gripped the interior door handle, a gurgling sound escaping her lips. She'd so far only ridden a bus or the Tube in London. This was her first car ride. The streets seemed impossibly narrow, the buildings squeezed together as tightly as teeth threatening to topple on their vulnerable car. Salem found herself nauseous if she concentrated on the road—driving on the opposite side had been fine in a bus but was puke-worthy in a car—so she studied the architecture, focusing on the Georgian terraces and Victorian mansions, few buildings taller than five stories or more modern than the late eighteenth century.

She realized she was dressed far more casually than the people on the streets, the women wearing fashionable overcoats and heels, the men in hats and smart trench coats. People in Minneapolis never dressed that nice for anything short of a wedding or a funeral. Salem had worn comfortable slacks, a warm cardigan over a white peasant blouse, and thick socks with her boots. She wouldn't have minded a pair of mittens even though it was technically still summer for a few more days. The damp of London was making her bones soggy.

On Charlie's advice, she'd amended her plan to quit the FBI. She would stay on the job while the president was in London—through the twenty-fourth. After, she would apologize to the FBI for the time and money that had been wasted training her. She would offer to continue the GAEA project as a private contractor, and then she would return home.

Bel, Mercy, rules, structure.

Familiar weather, food, bed, and house.

Safety.

They approached a second red light and Charlie slammed on the brakes, screeching to a stop with only a microscopic space separating his front bumper from another vehicle's rear. He drummed the steering wheel as he waited for the light to change. "Have you visited Parliament before?"

"No." She tried breathing exercises to calm herself. *Inhale through the mouth to the count of four, hold breath to the count of seven, exhale through the nose to the count of eight.* When her pulse slowed, she concentrated on her surroundings. The Campus was housed in the cheap corner of Marylebone. They'd passed through the tony section and were now on to the retail. The buildings were still squat and ornate, each one an identical, scolding gray, but their bottom floors were well lit and devoted to Nike, Topshop, and Tezenis among others, their pedestrians more diverse.

"It's quite something," Charlie promised.

The president was visiting Parliament purely for the optics. The accord would be signed there on the twenty-third, three days from now, and Gina Hayes wanted photos of her there as a tourist to humanize her in advance of the grand event. Salem and Charlie were to meet with her today if there was time, stand around with their hands in their pockets if there wasn't.

The second option was the more likely scenario.

For the duration of this assignment, Salem had been allotted a ball and chain, or B&C, the shorthand name for the FBI's supposedly indestructible field computers. She was to be prepared to do her job wherever she was needed. Charlie was a good crypto, her SAC had promised in the too-short briefing she'd received when she picked up the computer, but that's not the only reason he'd been assigned to her. He was an excellent shot, and he knew the city. Not a bad person to have on her team for the next week, though he was no Bel.

The light changed.

Charlie bumped forward, handling his vehicle like a bucking horse. While driving on the opposite side of the road was disorienting, he'd be a terrifying driver in any country. She chalked it up to one more reason she shouldn't be here.

They passed a King's College sign trumpeting a Rosalind Franklin exhibit. Several plays were advertised on the side of double-decker buses. They were passing Russell Square when Charlie informed her they'd need to travel farther east than he'd like due to extra security for the presidential visit and road construction. "It's a bit of a circle, but you'll get to see the Tower of London, at least the outside. You haven't been there, either?"

Salem shook her head.

"The Gherkin!" She pointed at the black-and-silver, pickle-shaped skyscraper, its exterior constructed entirely of diamond-shaped windows. She'd seen photos of it online.

Charlie chuckled. "True enough. And up ahead is the Tower, though you won't see much more than a gray stone wall. Tower Bridge up there is a bit more impressive. We'll turn here and follow the Thames back to Parliament so we can enter the secure zone."

Salem craned her neck, pressing on the knot to keep the pain in check. From this angle, she could see the ornate suspension bridge spanning the Thames. She knew that some people confused Tower Bridge with London Bridge, a much plainer structure just up the river. Tower Bridge seemed straight out of Cinderella, the blue and white of its cables and the glass-bottomed tourist walkway teetering several stories above the actual bridge, giving the structure an aristocratic feel. The thought of being up that high jellied her spleen.

Honking snapped her attention back to the ground level. A sloe-eyed woman with thick black hair was staring at her from the edge of the sidewalk before disappearing into the pedestrian crowd. The woman's glance had been fierce, personal, but she was a stranger.

"Traffic is terrible, eh?"

Salem shook off an unsettled feeling and glanced at the clogged road through the windshield. "I have a Google Maps hack I can run."

Charlie smiled and slapped the steering wheel. "Of course you do! I'd be delighted, love."

Her cheeks warmed. She snapped open the B&C and navigated to a blackout page she'd created. It connected two information sources—Google Maps and law enforcement routes—and ran them through a statistical analysis of past traffic patterns to estimate the best course for this time of day. The results popped up in ten seconds.

"You're already on the fastest route." She hunched her shoulders, expecting him to be disappointed.

He grinned at her, tapping his forehead with a knuckle. "Reassuring that the ol' noggin can be as reliable as a computer."

He pointed toward a snarl of traffic ahead. "So, you haven't yet visited Parliament or the Tower of London. You traveled to Ireland, but only for a pop to Blessington and back to the airport. Please tell me you've left the Campus other than that."

She didn't know if it was the shame she felt at being exposed for the homebody she was—other than the Tube and then bus ride from Heathrow and the single trip to Ireland, she *hadn't* left the Campus—or the fact that the mention of Blessington called to mind Mrs. Molony's model, but the lie blurted out before she could stop it. "I've seen Stonehenge," she said, cheeks tightening. She wanted to pull the words back in, but there they were, hanging in the air like big fat dummies.

He cut his eyes at her. "Aye, that's a magical place." His voice turned authoritative. "Not built by Druids, as many people believe."

"I've never been there," she corrected. She wanted to hit herself. "I don't know why I said that."

He tossed her a concerned look and then smiled. "I'm a fan of the old stones. You must have sensed that." He continued his speech, one he'd clearly delivered before. "The site was a gathering place starting over ten thousand years ago, but the stones themselves weren't brought in until much later. Did you know that? They're fit together like huge Lego blocks. Nobody knows who brought them, or how. Each stone weighs about twenty-five tons, yeah? The bluestones, some of them, came from two hundred forty kilometers away."

"Hmm," she said. She flipped open the B&C. She should have been working on GAEA the whole time rather than trying to socialize. *Talk to computers, not people. Talk to computers, not people.* The laptop screen lit up immediately. She clicked on GAEA's nascent visual decoder, checking for glitches that her conversation with Bel would have exposed. The report waiting for her showed GAEA had recognized Mercy's crayon drawing for the kid's doodle it was, but the program was hung up on decoding what appeared to be a splash of spaghetti sauce on the refrigerator.

Charlie continued without pause. "Archaeologists and anthropologists think Stonehenge may have been a burial ground. There are certainly a lot of graves, human and animal. Many of the human skeletons are women, and quite wealthy ones, they say. What do you think of that?"

"Wow," Salem said, but only halfheartedly. She'd discovered the line of code that needed tweaking.

"The Druids came two thousand years after the prime of Stonehenge. By then, the bluestones were already in place."

She couldn't get away with another mumble. She had to do more for her end of the conversation. "You sure know a lot about stones."

His mood darkened immediately, his energy change so drastic that it jerked her out of her programming.

"Parliament ahead," he said curtly. What had she said?

They veered past Big Ben, then turned again after Charlie flashed his credentials to a guard. "And there's your woman." President Gina Hayes stood behind a phalanx of guards in Parliament Square Garden. The president was smiling and shaking hands. Her assistant, Matthew Clemens, held a black umbrella over her even though the sky was being civil.

Charlie steered sharply to the right as a guard ushered them into an underground parking ramp. It wasn't until they were in the dark cool of the garage that Salem processed the rest of what she'd just witnessed.

Lucan Stone had been standing near Hayes. He'd had his back to Salem, but she'd recognized the outline of his sleek head and broad shoulders. But that's not why her heart was echo-thumping.

Little Mercy Mayfair had been standing next to Stone. And near her, Salem's mother.

Vida Wiley was in London.

CHAPTER 9

Parliament, London

Vida Wiley, world-famous history professor and controversial women's rights activist, had been born in Iran. Her family moved to Iowa when she was ten, and she retained a lilt from her home country and from being shielded from the outside world by her parents. She still spoke fluent Persian and had taught Salem to do the same.

She'd met Daniel, Salem's father, when he recruited her and Bel's mom for the Underground. Both women had been high school seniors at the time.

Daniel Wiley, Irish born and Iowa bred, became Vida's world from the day she met him.

After his death, their house grayed. Salem had been twelve years old.

Frozen dinners replaced home-cooked meals. Vida worked and slept, nothing else, never smiled unless Gracie was around. She treated Salem like an inconvenience. When Salem won the eighth-grade science fair blue ribbon for a weather-predicting computer program she'd back-rigged to break into any word processing program, Vida had been working late. Same with band concerts, parent-teacher conferences. Her mom had always been competent, distant, but after Daniel's death, Salem grew up without her.

Betrayal and her mother were braided together like strands of DNA, and the sting of that emotion hit Salem slapshock every time she laid eyes on Vida. Right now, the burn of duplicity was polluted with a sense of disorientation. What was Vida doing in London? And why was Mercy with her?

The answer came to Salem as a guard escorted them from the parking garage to Parliament's Robing Room, where they were to meet the president. Bel had all but given it away in this morning's phone call: *In honor of our unbreakable friendship bond, I should tell you that your mom has a surprise for you.*

Seeing her mom out of context knocked loose a memory Salem had long buried. Bel was eleven, Salem eight. They'd agreed to meet at the playground halfway between their childhood homes, just as they'd done countless times before. It was late October, the Minneapolis air crisp and apple-scented.

They planned to practice the penny drop off the monkey bars. It was the middle-school rage, even more popular than striped Benetton rugby shirts and strap-off-the-shoulder overalls. A penny drop was simple: Hook your legs over the bar. Swing, upside down, until you build enough momentum to pull your feet around and under you.

Bel nailed it on her first try.

"Booyah! It's your turn." She grinned at Salem, so sure of her friend's abilities, always. The autumn light shaded her eyes so dark blue they edged toward violet. If Bel thought she could do it, Salem had to at least try, even though the physics didn't match up in her mind. She grabbed the cool metal of the monkey bar and hoisted her legs over. Her jeans squeaked and the rip in one knee opened a little more. She stretched her hands, reaching toward the sand two feet beyond. Leaves skittered across the ground.

She forced her upper body forward and then back. Forward and then back. By the third swing, she'd gained enough thrust to put her shoulders even with her knees. The fourth time would do it. She'd be high enough.

"Now!" Bel yelled.

Salem flung her feet over the bar. She concentrated on pulling her head toward the clouds and pushing her feet toward the ground. She was parallel to the earth when she allowed herself to consider how unlikely it would be that she—dumpy, awkward Salem—could pull off this move. Her body froze and she dropped to her stomach, the gritty earth forcing her breath out of her.

Unable to draw air, she wheezed.

Bel flipped her over, wiping sand off Salem's chin. "Are you okay?" Salem tried to nod.

"Oh!" Bel pointed at Salem's knee. "You scraped it. Let's go to my house. We've got Band-Aids."

"No." Salem forced herself to sit up. She didn't want Bel to feel bad for her. "I'm fine. I think I'm just going to head home."

Bel squinted but didn't challenge her.

Salem scanned the playground. A group of kids from their school rode the swings, but they didn't seem to have witnessed Salem's belly flop. Her knee screamed when she stood. She forced a weak smile for Bel.

Bel wasn't buying it. "Call me when you get home?"

Salem nodded. She walked as normally as she could, waiting to limp until a glance over her shoulder confirmed Bel was out of sight. She allowed a single tear to roll down her cheek. Sand clung to her fall jacket, shedding as she walked. By the time she reached her house, she had almost worked up to a full-on cry. It was a Saturday, her mom and dad home. Her dad would take care of her. He'd wash out the scrape, apply salve and a bandage, and make her feel good about trying a penny drop even though it had been scary.

She'd probably find him out in his workshop. He was nearly to the varnishing stage with a table he'd been working on since the order arrived three weeks ago. It contained seven secret compartments, the most he'd ever incorporated into such a simple structure.

She planned on hobbling through the house to find him, but she heard voices when she stepped inside the front door. Maybe he'd come in for lunch? Salem cocked her head. The sounds were coming from her parents' bedroom.

Curious.

They both had work to do; they'd been clear about that when she asked them to join her at the park. She shambled toward the noise.

Her mom's giggle separated from the hum of conversation. That was even more odd. While Daniel made her belly laugh occasionally, Salem had only heard her mom giggle when Gracie was around. But surely Bel's mom wasn't in the bedroom with Vida?

Salem's hand was reaching toward the doorknob when her dad's voice cut through the giggle. "Honey, Salem could be home any minute."

A sensation pressed against Salem's throat. "Who cares?" Vida said. "We're adults."

The pressure squeezed. Salem tried to swallow past it but couldn't. She backed up from the door. She knew what they were doing now. It was gross, but they had a right. It was her mom's words that had struck her down.

Who cares?

Not Vida.

Never Vida.

Salem tiptoed to the bathroom, dug the dirt out of her knee with a warm washrag, and padded to her room to read. The book was *Abraham Sinkov's Elementary Cryptanalysis: A Mathematical Approach*. Her father had bought it for her.

She snapped back into the present. Her mother wasn't in London as a surprise for Salem, as Bel had said. For all her honesty and awareness, Bel wasn't able to see Vida and Salem's relationship as it was. Instead, she saw what she wanted to see, and what she needed more than anything was for Salem and her mom to have a connection that had been lost to Bel forever.

Vida was in London to see the president, likely. Or for the summit. Or maybe as a tourist. But she certainly was not here for Salem.

If Salem had needed any confirmation, it was written on Vida's face when the guard led Salem and Charlie into the Robing Room, a lush, gilded cavern set aside for state occasions and for the queen to prepare in prior to the State Opening, a highly formal ceremony that marked the beginning of the annual Parliament session.

The guard explained all this as he led her and Charlie into the room. The queen's ladies-in-waiting would help her to don the imperial robes and crown before beginning her ceremonial walk through Parliament. The room housed a wooden miniature of the Houses of Parliament in its center, and next to that, a temporary table had been set up.

The walls featured five frescoes, all painted by William Dyce. They featured images from a medieval version of the King Arthur legend to depict the chivalric virtues of generosity, religion, mercy, hospitality, and courtesy. Dyce had been commissioned to produce two more paintings for the room—fidelity and courage—but died in 1864, before they'd been finished.

When Salem and Charlie were ushered inside the Robing Room, Vida, Mercy, and Agent Stone were standing near the wooden miniature. While Vida's mouth twisted like she smelled something bad as soon as she laid eyes on Salem, Mercy's face lit up. The child's cheeks were plump and the color of rose petals, her hair glossy, two huge buck teeth coming in where her front baby teeth had been. She'd grown at least an inch in the last month and—except for the rag doll she clutched, the one Salem had bought for her—was now unrecognizable from the greasy street urchin she'd been a year ago. The realization hurt Salem's heart. She was missing out on Mercy's life.

Mercy wasted no time on reflection, instead squealing when she laid eyes on Salem. She ran to her and leaped into her arms, talking the whole time. "Auntie Sale! I got to take a plane and they brought food and I got my ears pierced and everyone talks so cool here and . . ."

The child wiggled like a puppy in Salem's embrace, chasing out all the self-doubt Vida's appearance inspired. Tears flowed as Salem squeezed warm, perfect, loving Mercy Mayfair. She'd wasted her whole life hoping to share this unconditional love with her mother. She would instead shower it all on Mercy.

A prickle at her hairline told her that she was being stared at. She glanced behind her, her heart *ba-thumping* as her eyes connected with Lucan Stone's. He was as beautiful as she remembered and exactly as unreadable. Her glance dropped but not before she caught Charlie winking at her, almost as if he knew how uncomfortable this situation was.

"I feel like you all know each other," Charlie said, amiably. "Introductions all around. I'll start with me." He placed his hand over his heart. "Charlie Thackeray, at your service."

"No need for introductions," Vida said archly, stepping forward. Charlie stepped back. Vida addressed only Salem. "Mercy wanted to see you, and the president approved. I'm here as an adviser on her team. We have a full day of activities planned."

Mercy dropped out of Salem's arms, leaving a cold spot. She skipped over to Vida and took her hand. Vida smiled at the child with a warmth that she had previously reserved for Daniel and Gracie. Salem hated the way it twisted in her gut.

"Can we have dinner tonight?" Salem asked.

"No." Vida's mouth pursed. She was a handsome woman, her salt-and-pepper hair piled on her head in a neat bun, her face free of makeup except for red lipstick, her eyes bright. "We have obligations this evening as well."

Salem's heart began beating in her cheeks. Charlie and Lucan were witnessing how little she mattered. It might be punishment. Her mother had been disappointed when Salem hadn't wanted to continue as a code-breaking puppet for the Underground. Or it might simply be that Vida did not much care for Salem.

Charlie stepped forward again, his hand out, his body language making clear he would not be dismissed this time. "Agent Thackeray. I'm your daughter's partner. A real pleasure to meet you."

Vida shook the hand reluctantly, studying the man. Her eyes flicked to Lucan Stone, and something passed between them. Salem was surprised and then embarrassed by a surge of jealousy. Lucan Stone was nobody to her. It wouldn't do her any good to act like a ten-year-old who hadn't been invited to the party.

"But I want to play with Salem!" Mercy dropped Vida's hand and reached for Salem's.

Vida smiled, years falling off her face. "If we have time, dear. Come now. Don't you want to see some of the most famous paintings in the world?"

Mercy glanced from Salem to Vida. "If you promise I can play with Salem later."

Vida sighed. "I promise. Tomorrow, if Salem is free."

Salem glanced toward Charlie. He lifted one shoulder slightly. They didn't know their schedule. It depended what they were assigned at today's meeting.

Salem crouched. "We'll make it work, Mercy. No way am I going to let you be in London and not spend time with you."

Mercy smiled, satisfied, and walked off with Vida.

"It was nice to see you both," Salem mumbled at their backs. She felt lonelier than she had since she'd arrived in London.

"We have this room for the next hour," Agent Stone said, his voice a deep rumble as he indicated the table in the center of the room. "I can brief you both."

"Not much for introducing yourself in America?" Charlie said, his smile wilting around the edges. "Name is Agent Thackeray. Agent Wiley and I are working together while you blokes are in house."

"Agent Stone." His hand could have wrapped twice around Charlie's, and Salem thought she saw Charlie wince at the grip. It was a good distraction as Salem swung from the shock of seeing her mother to the heat of last night's clutch dream. Had it been only last night? Recalling everything Dreamland Stone had done to her, and she to him, made her feel naked in front of real-life Stone. She needed to gain some semblance of control over the situation.

She picked up the B&C she'd set on the ground to catch Mercy. "Are you going to need us to work here on-site, Agent Stone?"

He glanced at her, a hint of a smile in his expression. "It is up to your SAC to assign you location. My understanding is that you'll be updating the president on GAEA and then work from wherever makes the most sense to you."

He walked to the table and sat down. A brusque nod at the uniformed guards got them to step outside and close the door behind them. Salem walked toward the chair opposite Lucan—too far away, really—and took a seat. That left Charlie the option of either sitting next to Salem, next to Lucan, or halfway in between as if they were a family of three fighting at the dinner table.

He chose a spot next to Salem.

The move was not lost on Stone, whose eyebrows lowered. "Congratulations on entering the force," he said to Salem. "I was happy to hear of it."

Salem had the feeling that Stone was making fun of her but couldn't figure out how. She didn't understand most social interaction that couldn't be programmed into a computer. It warmed her that Charlie had chosen to sit next to her, though. It felt like loyalty, like he'd had a choice between sides and chosen her. Such a contrast to her own mother.

"Thank you," she blurted, focusing on Stone. "It's been a wild ride."

Stone nodded. His expression made clear that he recognized the understatement, his smile now obvious because it revealed dimples. "The president has plans for you."

CHAPTER 10

Westminster Pier, London

Jason enjoyed London.

First, the rich blend of sizes, skin colors, and languages made it easy to disappear into a crowd. He seldom had to completely alter his face. A pair of sunglasses plus a light tweak that created a hook in his nose were all it took, hardly any pain at all.

Second, and more importantly, London was the home of the Viktor Wynd Museum of Curiosities, Fine Art, and Natural History.

He visited the museum whenever he was in the city, paying his ten pounds for a cup of tea and access to the dusty aisles crowded with shrunken heads, pickled fetuses, and archaic books. The cacophony of oddities soothed him, somehow. It was the only place in the world he felt completely at home. He supposed it reminded him of his childhood in New Orleans. He'd lived for a time above a cluttered French Quarter store, in a home where his mother at turns tortured and ignored him.

It was more than nostalgia that attracted him to the Viktor Wynd Museum, though.

The museum was a place where the rules were upside down. Here, the deformed and demented were brought into the light. They were celebrated.

He liked to think of his skull ending up at the museum once he died. That would be a thing.

He'd discovered the ability to change his facial features at age six, after his mother had squeezed her hand into a fist and punched his face. He could call up the *pop-squish* noise of his nose exploding at will, all these years later. The blast of pain so sharp it momentarily blinded him. The satisfied expression on his mother's face.

He could no longer remember why she'd hit him, but he knew he'd been unable to breathe. Hot blood had gushed. His destroyed nasal passages sent the liquid the wrong way. His mother watched him struggle, sipping and sucking on the cigarette that she hadn't even set down to punch him.

He'd instinctively put his hand to the hamburger of his nose and pulled it away from his face. The pain was excruciating, but it meant he could breathe. He chewed air like a starving person and bolted to the bathroom, locking the door behind him.

He stared in the mirror, his eyes already bruised from the blow. His nose was altered—broken, certainly, but also a whole new appendage. It amazed him how quickly a new nose changed his appearance. He stayed in the bathroom that entire day. When the bleeding stopped, he worked the cartilage like a muscle, flexing bits, suspending them in place, twitching others. It hurt a hundred times worse than any punch, the pain driving him to scream out, but it was worth it when he discovered that he could morph and hold the shape of his nose as readily as other people could raise an eyebrow or crack their knuckles.

As time passed, with repetition and a growing tolerance to pain, he'd learned to modify the shape of the skin around his eyes and mouth and raise or lower his cheekbones as well. At the time, he figured it was some rare double-jointedness. When he was old enough, he researched it. As near as he could tell, he had sentient Sharpey's fibers, the microscopic fingers of collagen that connected bone to muscle to skin.

If he'd been born one hundred years earlier, he'd have been killed or put in a freak show.

Instead, the ability to adjust his appearance at will had led him to this job. With wigs, colored contacts, a variety of clothing, and his fingerprints shaved off, he was impossible to trace.

He carried the Mare Street Museum's peacefulness with him as he rode the Tube toward Parliament. He had a job to do before he met with the Grimalkin.

Reluctance tugged at his shoulders like a too-tight coat. He preferred to work alone but understood he had to reestablish himself after the Alcatraz fiasco. It had cost him his beloved mentor, Carl Barnaby, who was now in jail. After a workplace error on such a grand scale, Jason recognized he was lucky the Order had allowed him to continue living.

He would prove himself worthy of this second chance, even if it meant working with a partner.

Besides, the Grimalkin was mythical, a genius code breaker and assassin equally skilled with a gun, poison, or a knife. The Grimalkin was purported to be the manager who'd fired Peruvian activist María Elena Moyano, Russian human rights activist and journalist Anna Politkovskaya, and the most famous firing, Benazir Bhutto, the first and hopefully last female prime minister of Pakistan.

Attributing these deeds to the Grimalkin could be baseless lip-flapping meant to bolster a reputation. The world of assassins was not above that, though Jason had never resorted to telling lies about himself.

And truly, he didn't care which famous women the Grimalkin had let go. Jason was only interested in the famed assassin's knife skills, which were superhuman, if true. One story went that the Grimalkin had been dining with a man who was eating a steak. The Grimalkin had stood, sliced the man's throat, and sat back down so silently, so whip-quickly, that the man didn't know his neck had been cut until he tried to swallow his meat.

Jason knew such a thing was possible, technically. He'd slit enough throats himself. Knowing it was conceivable didn't mean that it had happened, though. He would have to ask the Grimalkin. He might have the opportunity to improve his own knife work.

As he detrained, Jason patted the sheathed blades inside his suit-coat pocket the way another man would check for his wallet. The Westminster stop was crowded with tourists and locals alike, green wristbands and scarves identifying those in town for the accord. He fought the urge to push back against the flow, instead melting into it, thinning his lips and extending his forehead as he strode to Westminster Pier, face down.

He didn't glance toward the Eye, the enormous Ferris wheel. He hugged the Thames, flicking his glance toward the benches.

People ate popcorn. They laughed. A bearded man wearing a soaring British flag hat shoved Stonehenge tour pamphlets toward people, who shook their heads and walked on. The conversations were a loud hum of American English, British English, French, and Arabic.

Fifteen feet ahead and to the right, a young man with Middle Eastern features studied his phone. He appeared pensive, as if he'd meant to meet someone who hadn't shown up. He glanced to his right and to his left, massaging his neck.

Jason neared. He smiled, brilliantly. The man, certainly no older than twenty-one or twenty-two, couldn't help but beam back, his eyes confused, apologetic.

I'm sorry, I don't remember you, they said.

Jason nodded. He held out his hand. The man mirrored the gesture. People slid by on each side, chattering. Jason raised his other hand, the handshake morphing into an embrace. The man was too polite to correct Jason's familiarity.

What happened next took seven seconds.

Jason's right hand circled the youth's neck, slitting his throat from behind. The young man struggled slightly, and Jason laid him on the bench, as gentle as a lover. He unclasped the bomb belt he wore under his trench coat and threaded it around the man, his features going slack for a moment from concentration. He unfolded a newspaper and laid it across the young man's face. If someone walked by, they'd think Jason was checking on an itinerant who'd maybe had too much to drink, and they would avert their eyes, not wanting to get involved.

The belt clicked and the timer set, Jason stood, smoothing his face. He strode toward the nearest steps, a sign telling him he could choose to walk toward Parliament or Westminster Abbey once he attained street level.

There was not a lick of blood on him.

He reached the street before the screaming started.

CHAPTER 11

The Eye, London

Clancy entertained no doubt that the London Eye was a fancy bit of bullshit. He'd waited in line for forty-five minutes for his chance to board the 443-foot-tall Ferris wheel. He had to admit that whoever'd invested in its creation back in 1999 had been a genius. Rolling in the money now. For about thirty bucks, you got a molasses-slow trip around a circle.

Not a treat for anybody except snipers.

For snipers, it was ideal.

You couldn't shoot from up here. The pods that turtled you around were glass enclosed. You could get the lay of the land, however, and you wouldn't look one bit suspicious if you slapped a pair of binoculars to your face and peered first at Tower Bridge and second at Parliament, measuring the angles and sight lines, catching a glimpse of the president of the United States.

The first time Clancy'd been tasked to kill Gina Hayes, back at Alcatraz the day before the election, he'd been the third line of defense. By all rights he never should have had to step up to the plate, but Jason had fumbled, and then Geppetto dropped the ball, and that left Clancy, who would have succeeded if not for Isabel Odegaard.

As far as Clancy was concerned, the former Chicago cop had paid a fair price for ruining his shot. Wheelchair girl must have been an excellent police officer. You couldn't teach courage like that. You were either born a warrior or you weren't.

The problem with the Alcatraz plan was that it had been too complicated. This time wouldn't be. Simple point and shoot on September 23, using the Order's specially manufactured sniper rifle and their private room above Tower Bridge as his home base.

The Order had sniper towers ferreted around all major cities. Locate the top of the highest building, guess that the Order owned a few rooms up there and had access to upmarket rifles that could shoot twice as straight and three times as far as military issue, and you'd be right. No better angle in London than Tower Bridge—he'd already checked that out, and riding on the Eye was just to get a second perspective.

He wouldn't mess up the hit this time.

He took no pride in that thought. Gina Hayes and her vice president weren't as bad as the news would have a person believe. They never were—he'd learned that and plenty more in his three decades at the FBI. This assassination was not personal. Hayes was a woman and she threatened the Order. That was all.

He'd kill her and the vice president, and then he'd disappear forever. That was the deal.

He imagined what his life would be after the assassination. The details sometimes changed, but he knew one thing: it was time to hit up one of those unnamed Caribbean islands and become the eccentric old guy who lived in a straw shack out on a secluded beach and only tramped to the one-store town to pick up rum, eggs, milk, and bread every other week.

He'd fish all day, read some good spy novels before bed. Hell, maybe he'd write his own book. He'd certainly seen enough in his life to fill fifty novels. Yeah, that sat right; that vision of him clacking away on a typewriter, Hemingway-esque, a half-empty bottle of rum and a full ashtray within reach.

Maybe he'd even get a cat.

"You've been standing there the whole ride."

Clancy dropped his binoculars and swiveled his head slowly—
everything moved slowly on this tourist trap—toward the unmistakably
American voice. The man was half Clancy's age, round and soft in the
middle, and quivering with the need to usurp Clancy's unobstructed
view of London. Clancy fought the urge to punch the guy. People in
Rome had been rude, almost as an art form, but it was never personal.
Americans, on the other hand, insisted on shaming a person. Clancy
hadn't missed that when he'd fled the country.

He made a note to put this guy in the book he was gonna write.
"Count on that not changing," Clancy grumbled, smacking the binoculars back to his face. He would never get back on this ride if he could
help it, which meant tracking all possible angles and escapes on this
single trip.

He scanned the countryside. They were at the apex of the ride, and
if he wasn't mistaken, he could spot Windsor Castle twenty-five miles
to the west. Impressive. He focused back on Parliament. The weather
for the next week was supposed to be cloudy and cool. In other words,
London. There was a bit of luck in that no wind was forecast. If that
held, he'd have the clearest of shots.

The president was now being herded inside Parliament.

He wondered if she was meeting with Lucan Stone, who Clancy
had spied entering the building just a few minutes earlier.

Lucan and Clancy had been partners before the Alcatraz goat rope
of an assassination attempt. Stone had exploded through the FBI ranks,
but he didn't have that hotshot air most wunderkinds did, and Clancy
had worked with more than his share of young guns. Stone was quiet,
and he did his job. Clancy Johnson had liked him better than fine as
a partner, but it had always been a mystery whose side he was on. Was
he a NOC—a nonofficial covered officer, the agency's most clandestine
operative—or was he simply running a one-off assignment?

Didn't really matter anymore.

It was interesting that the FBI was so openly active in London,
though. They were primarily domestic. If they needed to second-layer

the Secret Service in Europe, that ought to be CIA territory. Clancy made a note to ask his connection at Five Eyes what he knew. It'd give him something to do with his free head time now that he'd decided exactly what his retirement would entail.

"Some people would share their space," the American whined, under his breath, but not really. "If they had the best seat in the pod, I mean. If they could see stuff that no one else could."

Passive-aggressive was another trait Americans excelled at. Clancy considered giving the man a piece of his mind but thought better. Someone who wasn't embarrassed to be ignorant wasn't going to listen to Clancy. He *did* toss the guy a second glance to make sure his face hadn't changed, though—a recent habit since his meeting with Jason in Rome.

A shudder tickled his neck. He didn't know if the man was even human. It was a waste of talent, the Order treating him like a gofer.

Thinking of Jason recalled Salem Wiley, who'd driven up to Parliament just as Clancy's Eye pod had cleared the building's roofline. She must be cracking codes for the FBI now, though her companion had looked more MI5.

Clancy smiled. That kid. Too bad she was on the Order's radar.

He'd heard the Grimalkin was assigned her—or if the rumors were true, had demanded her. The smile turned into a grimace. That meant she wasn't long for this world. He hoped for her sake that the Grimalkin was as efficient as the lore suggested.

None of this—Lucan Stone being on-site, Salem Wiley being in town—changed his instructions. Vit Linder had been specific: Clancy was to assassinate the president and the vice president. Normally they did not travel together, but there would be a single, very public photograph taken on the twenty-third featuring President Gina Hayes and Vice President Richard Cambridge on the front lawn of Parliament just moments after the signing of the accord. The event was being staged purely for optics, a risky but photogenic illustration of the United States' commitment to a new, globally responsible environmental policy.

Both of them cut down at that moment would send a clear message.

Vit Linder had been shifty, unctuous on the phone. Clancy knew the type. Rich dad and a staggeringly dumbfuck certainty that he'd earned it all himself. The good news was that Clancy didn't particularly care what sort of man Linder was, or even that his voice had slid sideways when he'd mentioned the double assassination. The guy was uncomfortable with some part of it, but Linder was what men like Clancy called a soft hand. Probably didn't want blood on them.

No, all that mattered to Clancy were these nine words, whispered by Linder toward the end of their conversation: *Once they're dead, you'll be free of the Order.*

The details were straightforward. The president would exit Parliament at the same time the vice president was driven there. They would meet for a highly orchestrated handshake, at which time Clancy would shoot them both from the Order's Tower Bridge penthouse. He would then be driven to the airport.

Linder had said a Muslim group would be framed for the killings. That told Clancy that this assassination was being marketed for Americans. "A Muslim group." That's all the Rust Belters and Bible Thumpers would need to know. He'd be toes-deep in the sand before the American intelligence community discovered it wasn't Muslims.

If they ever did.

He felt a twinge in his gut as the pod started its descent. He realized he cared about his country, at least for a second. The president and vice president both dying would plunge the United States, and maybe the world, into chaos.

The twinge passed.

He thought about fishing and writing that book, a golden sun turning him brown as a nut, his rum at his side. He swung his binoculars to the east and glanced at his watch. He would be staring through the spyglasses in full view of multiple witnesses when the bomb went off.

Exactly as planned.

CHAPTER 12

Parliament, London

The largest door of the Robing Room opened and Gina Hayes stepped inside, accompanied by her ubiquitous assistant, Matthew; two Secret Service agents; and a steady stream of staffers coming in and out with questions and updates.

Salem, Charlie, and Stone all stood when they saw the president. "Salem!" Matthew said, waving, indicating she should leave the table and join the president.

Salem smiled. She remembered Matthew as having a gift for putting everyone at ease and remembering names. Salem had met him only once, at President Hayes's inauguration last January.

"Hi, Matthew, Madam President."

Gina Hayes was a formidable woman, solidly built, her eyes steel gray. She was as efficient as she was smart. "Update me on GAEA."

Salem tipped back on her heels. She should have anticipated the question, but her mind was as blank as a sheet. Charlie appeared at her elbow to rescue her. "Agent Thackeray of MI5, Madam President. I'm Ms. Wiley's partner. GAEA has amazing potential, but I'm afraid Ms. Wiley hasn't been given enough dedicated time for it. With all due respect, it should be her full-time job."

Salem flushed with gratitude. President Hayes reminded her of her own mother, cold and authoritarian. The similarity made it difficult to keep her wits in her presence. And Vida Wiley and Hayes shared more than a demeanor. They were both connected to the Underground at depths Salem hoped never to know.

The president arched an eyebrow at Charlie. Instead of responding to his defense, she strode toward the nearest painting, Matthew, Salem, and Charlie following. "I'm a fan of William Dyce's."

The painting depicted a man on a white horse returning to King Arthur's court, the king stretching a sword toward him in welcome. The painting was titled *Hospitality*, and the plaque below it read "The Admission of Sir Tristram to the Fellowship of the Round Table."

Hayes tipped her head toward the words. "Dyce was a Scotsman, did you know? My grandmother emigrated from Scotland."

"That explains how well she held her whisky," Matthew said, not glancing up from his ever-present iPad.

The president's chuckle was surprisingly warm. "Possibly." Her eyes grew faraway. "'The best laid schemes o' mice and men, gang aft agley, and leave us nought but grief and pain, for promised joy!'"

"Robert Burns," Charlie said, admiration apparent on his face.

"Yes," President Hayes said, turning her attention to Salem. "Luckily, Salem, we are neither mice nor men. What do *you* think would be the best use of your time with the FBI?"

The question caught Salem off guard. *Quitting it.* "I'm not sure—"

"Don't be modest," Charlie interrupted. "You're brilliant. Once you've built her, GAEA will revolutionize computers."

The president and Matthew exchanged a look. Hayes moved on to the next painting, this one featuring a man kneeling before a queen and her ladies. It was named *Mercy* and was half the size of Dyce's hospitality painting. Its plaque read "Sir Gawaine swearing to be merciful and never be against Ladies."

"This one has always looked to me more like justice than mercy," Hayes said, hands behind her back as she studied the art, "but of course there can be no justice without mercy."

A loud bang interrupted their meeting.

It sounded to Salem like a very large door being slammed, but Lucan Stone, Charlie, and both Secret Service agents were in motion before the sound faded. All four of them shielded the president with their bodies and escorted her out.

The door to the hallway opened. It was chaos outside. "Bomb!" someone yelled.

Salem's knees gave way, and she reached for the wall below the painting. She was suddenly alone in the Robing Room. A bomb had just gone off somewhere close enough to hear. Where were Mercy and Vida?

Heart thumping, she rang her mom, frantic to make sure she and Mercy were all right. When there was no answer, she called Bel. "I'm in Parliament. I was talking to the president when a bomb went off somewhere."

Bel had never allowed lag time in her reactions. "Is anyone hurt?"

"Not that I know of."

"Vida and Mercy?"

"I don't know where they are. Mom isn't answering her phone." Saying that out loud made Salem nauseous.

Bel hung up without question. She called back two minutes and forty-five seconds later. "They're fine. They're on their way to their hotel. The news hasn't gotten wind of anything yet. Start researching."

Salem didn't know she'd been holding her breath until the aching in her chest signaled her. She sucked in a mouthful of air, staring at the B&C. Of course. "Thank you," she said, but Bel had already hung up, likely to follow up on her end.

Salem set down her phone and clicked on GAEA, talking to the program in soothing tones. "I need SIGINT on what's happening, honey."

She typed on the industrial laptop's keyboard, her fingers flying like a concert pianist's. GAEA may be a baby, but she was a gifted child. She could manage the terrorist networks, at least when looking for something as loud as a bomb. Within five minutes, GAEA had established a terrifying fact: the marquee terrorist groups were as surprised by the bomb as the president and her team had been, so caught off guard that they didn't even bother to code their communications.

GAEA wasn't needed; a simple language translator would do.

Salem commanded ECHELON to run in the background before tapping GAEA to scour the major news networks.

Thirty-seven minutes later, she had it.

A man believed to be Saudi Arabian and in his early twenties had set off the bomb while sitting on a bench near Westminster Pier, only about a thousand feet from where she now sat. The act was being treated as a suicide bombing, his ties still buried, two tourists killed and eleven injured in the attack.

The rest of the afternoon and the night ticked away. Charlie checked on her sometimes, reporting on the lack of action outside. Salem stayed at the B&C in the Robing Room, running and tweaking GAEA, listening for any SIGINT tying the attack to a specific group. She was the best in her field, she recognized that without ego, and she couldn't find anything. Three groups had publicly claimed the bombing, but their backdoor communication put the lie to that.

Something was way off.

A bombing in London with so many heads of state gathering would be a jewel in the crown of any known terrorist organization. The internet was alight with talk of it, but no one in the surface web or dark web knew who had done it.

❖

"Hey."

Salem glanced up. Charlie was standing there, looking as though he'd been there for a while. "Sorry. Hey."

"Have you left your computer today?"

She glanced at her phone. She'd been sitting in the same spot for seven hours. "No."

He wrinkled his nose. "That's what I thought. Everyone else is off—everyone who works for the president, that is."

"Agent Stone?"

Charlie nodded, his eyes hooded. "And one of his fellow field agents. We're all going out for a pint. Care to join us?"

Salem blinked, still not oriented to reality after spending the afternoon in a rabbit hole. "Did they identify the group for the bombing?"

Charlie shrugged. "No. And even if they had, it doesn't change standard operating procedure. Security is tight. Scotland Yard is on the case. The summit moves forward as planned. And tired men need a drink."

He ran his hand through his hair and slapped on a smile. "Women as well. You're joining us?"

CHAPTER 13

Mayflower Pub, London

London's Mayflower pub had stood on a cobbled street, tucked into the edge of the River Thames, for more than four hundred years. It had been erected on the original mooring spot of the *Mayflower* ship before its trip to what would become Cape Cod. The pub was dark wood and heavy stone, scarlet walls and crosshatched windows, the sour smell of four centuries' worth of beer spillage complementing the hearty fryer smell of London's best fish and chips. Stepping inside the cozy interior was a stroll back in time, the brightly lit cell screens and modern clothes of the patrons jarring.

The FBI agents' grim faces, however, perfectly matched the interior.

Salem sipped her second pint. She hadn't eaten since breakfast. She'd never cared for beer, but she also had never had a Guinness straight out of a keg. It was creamy, chocolaty, more dessert than beverage. She'd been listening to the agents talk, Charlie slipping easily into the group.

"ISIL, you'd think," he was saying. "But they'd have claimed it by now, right, Salem?"

Salem knew he was being nice, pulling her into the conversation. As the beer began to line her veins, she realized she didn't mind. "Any group would have," she said. "Unless this is only a warm-up leading to something else."

Lucan Stone sat across from her, his expression inscrutable. Nina, one of his agents, sat to his left. If Salem wasn't mistaken, Nina and Stone had a thing going, or were at least very comfortable with one another. She fought the lick of jealousy, leaning toward Charlie. He threw his arm over her shoulder companionably.

"If Salem hasn't discovered a claimer, no one has," he said. "This girl's the best in the business."

Nina leaned forward, her elbows on the table. She was a redhead with a sharp nose. "Word on the street is that GAEA is at least a year out from being workable. Padding expectations?"

She had said it conspiratorially rather than meanly, but her physical nearness to Stone set Salem on edge. "If I was, I wouldn't come clean in a bar." Salem pulled on her beer. She really should order some food. Or slide her hand into Stone's under the table. The more she drank, the more difficult it became to separate a good decision from a bad.

Nina wouldn't let it go. "My Quantico cyberterrorism professor couldn't stop talking about you," she said. "There must be more than you're saying. If you can build a quantum-based code-breaking software before anyone else, doesn't that mean that the United States wins the cyberwar? We'd be light-years ahead of all the other nations."

Salem shook her head. "Quantum computing is like an engine or, more accurately, a whole new roadway. GAEA will be a vehicle on that road, that's all."

Charlie sat forward. "You're being modest." He looked at Nina. "Once Salem has GAEA working, it'll be a constant fishing line trolling the internet, updating itself real-time as the bad guys create new code."

Salem frowned. "Not until I figure out the missing algorithms."

Stone flashed her a look. He seemed angry, his drink untouched and his shoulders stiff. The bombing had him tense, surely.

Nina held up her drink for a toast. "Cheers to bureaucracy standing in the way of progress. The FBI is the same all over, eh?" She glanced at Stone for agreement, but he was staring at Salem.

It sent a thrill like a kiss down Salem's neck. She was terrible at reading people, she accepted that, but there was something in his eyes. She clinked her beer with Nina's drink, a smile on her face.

Charlie touched his glass to theirs. "It sounds like the FBI is the same as MI5 as well." He downed his own pint. "They want to make enthusiastic bureaucrats out of all of us."

Salem found herself unexpectedly filled with the desire to talk. "Some days I think we might be heading in the wrong direction with GAEA," she said, swallowing the last of her beer and holding it up for a refill. "The latest hidden is *not* hidden. Messages written on paper, delivered by couriers, burned or swallowed once they've been received. I'd like to see all agents taught old-school cryptanalysis for security's sake."

"I agree!" Nina said. She was going to add more when a scuffle broke out to her left, followed by an ape of a man flying onto their table, scattering their drinks. All four agents jumped to their feet. Stone took a step toward Salem, but he didn't intervene when the man stood, dripping beer, and turned toward her, glaring at Salem's open-mouthed gape.

"What're you staring at?" The man was at least six and a half feet tall but hunched over, his knuckles all but dragging on the ground.

Salem closed her mouth, opened it, and closed it again. A dark-eyed woman stood behind the giant, hair pulled up in a dark ponytail, her stance lean and confident. She appeared to be judging Salem, curious about her next move. She also looked familiar. Salem found both points equally distracting. Was the sloe-eyed woman with the guy who'd toppled their table?

"She's just having a pint, mate." Charlie inserted himself between the man and Salem, his hands palms out. "You should cool down."

He glanced at the table, glasses knocked over, beer dribbling off the edge. "And you owe all of us a beer."

The man swung at Charlie. Charlie blocked the first hit, but the second caught him square in the jaw, sending him to the ground.

Salem stepped in, her body acting before her brain could talk her out of it. She grabbed the man's wrist, turning into the arc of his swing so her back was to his chest. She kept the momentum of his punch going, leaning forward and thrusting her butt backward to throw him off balance. He didn't have time to right himself. He fell over her bent back and toward Charlie, who rolled out of the way in the nick of time.

The assailant hit the ground.

Salem blinked so loudly she was sure everyone in the pub could hear it. It was a move she'd practiced a hundred times in Krav Maga training with Bel, and fifty more at Quantico, but she couldn't believe it had actually worked in real life. Her first bar fight, and *she'd won*. She hooted and pumped a fist into the air before she could stop herself.

Out of the corner of her eye, she saw Stone smile. She guessed that's why he'd stepped aside. He'd banked on her being able to take care of herself. That confidence felt good. She looked for the dark-eyed woman, but she'd disappeared.

Another guy stepped forward and helped up his friend. "Sorry. He's had too much to drink."

"Get him out earlier next time," Charlie said, standing with Nina's help.

They nodded and scurried out.

Charlie turned on her, an angry, cherry-red welt growing on his chin but a grin lighting up his face. "Not poor in a pinch, are you?"

He wasn't a bad-looking guy, Salem realized. Small, pasty, but when he smiled like that, he appeared younger. "It must have been all my training kicking in. Muscle memory." She laughed too loud. Adrenaline.

"Our shots have arrived!" Nina said, motioning to the waitress, who was ferrying the drinks they'd ordered before the kerfuffle. She handed Charlie and Salem a shot glass each while she and Stone righted the table and another waitress swept up the broken glass.

The minty liquor burned Salem's throat, warming her belly. She was reaching for another glass when her stomach pitched and the room shifted. If she didn't get fresh air, she would be sick. "I need to go."

Agent Stone nodded, his jaw set. Had he appeared that angry all night long? "I'll see you to a cab."

Salem glanced at Charlie, who was watching her, expressionless, his own second shot paused halfway to his mouth.

"I'm fine," she said. A burp was pushing up her throat.

"I'll see you out," Agent Stone repeated.

Salem commanded her legs to walk toward the door. The adrenaline backlash combined with the shot made her feel like she was walking on the moon, though she did not stumble. She hoped she wasn't lifting her feet too high. Once outside, the cool drizzle cleared her head, marginally. She gulped deeply of the London air, its mist curling into her stomach and settling it. When she felt like herself again, she turned. Agent Stone was watching her with his ageless eyes.

"I think the bomb was a distraction," she said. She had no intel to back it up, and she didn't want to believe in hunches, but the thought had been nagging at her. She'd planned to sit on it until she had data, but being outside, alone with Stone, made it feel like an idea worth sharing.

He cocked his head. Salem thought he was auditing for listeners, practicing discretion, being a spy, doing everything she should be doing. "How so?"

"Because no group has credibly claimed responsibility for it. The only logical explanation is that it's a setup for something bigger."

"Connected to the president or the accord?"

"I'm not sure." The bomb was set off near enough to the president, but it had virtually no chance of harming her. It was the first strike. Salem didn't know what the second would be or who it would be targeting.

"We need hard intel. Use GAEA."

It was a command, and she discovered she liked it when Stone issued orders. He was strong and confident. His spicy cologne, clear eyes, and full lips all seemed to be whispering to her, reminding her of the erotic dream, filling her with something like courage. If she reached out and laid her hand on his chiseled cheek, would bright sparks fly from her fingertips? Would he wrap his arms around her, holding her tightly, safely, keeping the confusing world at bay? She suddenly, urgently, needed to know.

She leaned toward him, anticipating the hardness of his body, staring up and into his eyes. "I think it's time for me to trust someone," she said softly, offering her heart and mouth.

He moved quickly, putting distance between his body and hers before she even had time to register mortification. His face was shadowed by the entryway overhang. "I think you've had too much to drink."

Her mouth formed an O. She'd read the situation 100 percent wrong. Stone did not want her. He'd simply walked her out so she wouldn't embarrass the Bureau anymore.

"Of course. Sorry. No cab. Some exercise will do me good." She strode off into the night.

Lucan Stone watched her go.

And Charlie Thackeray watched him watching her.

THURSDAY

September 21

CHAPTER 14

Russia Dock Woodland, London

A steady drizzle fell.

The air smelled like the color gray, like rock dust and damp and cold, like rejection.

Salem walked, her shoulders clenched up around her ears, hands shoved deep in her pockets, shivering. The Campus was four kilometers from the pub; Charlie had assured her of it on the ride over. She could walk four kilometers.

It was a chance to walk off the shame.

Ooh boy.

What was she, a horny teenager? Who lunges at a colleague outside a bar? Especially when he had something going on with Nina. The farther she walked from the Mayflower, the clearer that became. Little looks they'd tossed each other. How Stone had been mad when Salem had monopolized the conversation. She may not be good at reading people, but she wasn't blind.

Well, there was one more reason to leave the FBI.

Quitting would mean living with her mother, and her mother's disappointment that Salem hadn't taken up the mantle, but Salem could survive that if it meant being safe at home with Bel and Mercy.

Mercy.

The mercy stone.

The mystery of it scraped at the edges of her attention like an annoying child.

She ignored it.

Her wet hair clung to her cheeks. She wished she had a cap to yank snug over her cherry ears, and mittens to tug onto her cold-swollen fingers. Could she see her breath? She stopped, swiveling to study her surroundings, a nudge of worry worming its way into her chest. She'd been walking for almost an hour. Her surroundings should look familiar by now as she neared the Campus. The streets had started out well lit, crowded, but the farther from the river she walked, the sparser humanity became. She was the only person on her current street, the fronts of the businesses all leaden and wet, her world painted black and white by the night rain.

She mentally retraced her steps.

Dammit.

She'd covered at least two miles, but she hadn't crossed the Thames, which was what she would need to do to reach the Campus. She must be walking the exact wrong direction. Her eyes burned, but she wouldn't let the tears fall. She wouldn't be warm anytime soon, and there was no use crying over it. She had no choice but to walk back the way she'd come.

She'd left the B&C in Charlie's car, but the reassuring weight of her phone pushed against her chest. She was tempted to pull it out and call a cab, but a woman staring at her phone in an isolated street in the middle of the night was a target. She'd get somewhere more populated, and then she'd call.

London was one of the world's largest cities, she reassured herself. There were people around, even at two in the morning, even if she couldn't see them. It couldn't be more than forty-five minutes that she'd been out here, far less than that since she'd seen people. In fact, hadn't she passed a quiet neighborhood bar several blocks back? She could tuck in, use her phone to call a cab, and be in her toasty bed inside of an hour.

Shoulders set, she started back down the street.

A dark alley was ahead and to her right. She hadn't noticed it the first time she'd passed, but now that she realized she was lost, the whole world seemed a danger. The sliver of darkness, ink against charcoal, was narrow, maybe four feet across. Surely no one was hiding in there. Still, she stepped in the middle of the street to put distance between herself and the unknown.

She stumbled on the uneven terrain.

She was nearly abreast of the alley when she heard the whimper creep out of it.

Her skin rippled down her spine. She wanted to keep walking—no, she wanted to *run*—but what if someone was hurt?

"Hello?"

No answer.

"Is anybody in there?"

Still nothing. The whimper had stopped. She must have imagined it. Her hands felt powerless in her pockets, so she tugged them out despite the cold.

"Help."

The baby hairs on her neck stood up. There was no mistaking the plea. It was soft, a breath formed around a word, and it had come from the alley.

She stepped toward it, reaching for her phone.

"Hold up, love."

An average-size man stepped out from the alley and into the dim ambient light of the London night. He walked toward the center of the street, not glancing her direction. He wore his collar up, his trench coat open at the waist to reveal hands deep in his pants pockets. He approached close enough that she could smell his drugstore cologne, sweet and chemical-based. His slow pace and refusal to look her way were darkly soothing, hypnotizing, in the way it must be to encounter an apex predator. *This will be over soon,* his movements whispered.

When he stood dead center in the street, ten feet in front of her, a second man, this one a giant, loped out of the alley. She recognized him immediately as the ape who'd slammed into their table at the Mayflower, the one Salem had brought to his knees with her little Krav Maga move. He had more curiosity or less intelligence than the first man because he stared straight at her.

Now it was she who was whimpering.

A third man emerged from the shadows immediately behind the second, this one lean and dry-looking, his furtive movements reminding Salem of a lizard darting out from beneath a rock. He couldn't decide who to look at, his eyes scurrying between the leader, the ape, and Salem. A dirty little smile flickered across his mouth.

A scream jerked up from Salem's brain stem. Her prefrontal lobe immediately knocked it down, but not before it turned into a grunt that leaked out her mouth. Yelling would not help her now. She looked around for escape, for help, and saw neither. She would need to get herself out of here, and that didn't seem possible. Her front jacket pocket held her single room key on its plastic band. Threaded through her fingers, it would be the weakest of weapons.

She still clutched her phone. She was trembling too much to type, but she could yell a command for her cell to call 999, London's version of 911, and hope the order got out and was answered before the men were on her.

The leader still hadn't glanced her way, the ape couldn't stop staring at her, and the third man kept playing eyeball ping-pong.

Salem heard the clacking of castanets. With a start, she realized it was her teeth chattering. Or her bones. This fear was one that every girl, every woman had experienced—a metallic, powerless certainty that she was about to have something fundamental ripped from her. The helpless terror tasted like warm silver poured down her throat, slicing through her blood with the high-pitched wail of a funeral keen, finally settling in her bones, hard and inevitable.

She found herself growing impossibly tired. This was not a fight she could win.

The leader finally spoke, his eyes still pinned to the ground, hands deep in his pockets. His accent was surprisingly smooth, aristocratic. "Out late?"

The ape chuckled. "I think she is. You shouldn't have touched me, lassie. Hurts a man to be shamed like that, yeah?"

The leaden torpor she felt was the wrong response, but she just wanted to sleep. A soft whooshing sound, almost like water, cut through the chilly air, growing steadily louder. She thought only she could hear it, but when the light changed at the far end of the street, she realized it was a car approaching. The three men stiffened. Salem felt hope for the first time since the men had appeared. If the vehicle drove this direction, she would run toward it, no matter how those men tried to stop her. She would yell at her phone as she ran.

Her pulse soared with hope. The light grew brighter.

The car was driving this way. Headlights played across the trees.

The sound of its engine, its tires crunching, grew louder. Salem imagined she could even hear the radio inside that toasty, safe car. Was it playing Bob Dylan?

The leader didn't look toward the car. He studied his shoes.

It's going to save me! Salem wanted to yell. She clenched her leg muscles, preparing to run. The front of the vehicle came into view. It was a dark, four-door sedan with only the driver. Those were the only details she could make out because it sped by, not even slowing for the intersection.

No!

All three men stared at Salem now, openly leering, as if the nearness of escape had been a twist they'd planned.

Salem's bones turned soft. She knew she had strength in her arms, steel in her thighs, that she had to fight, always fight, but it would be no use, not with three against one.

"Who gets her first?" the third man asked.

"Can't leave any evidence," the leader said.

"All right, that," the ape said. "We'll wear our rain jackets, yeah?" He held out his hand toward Salem, rubbing his thumb against his pointer and middle finger. "Here, pussy, here here, little pussy. Come to Daddy."

The third man laughed, the sound high and creepy.

Salem's right leg slid back to fighting position without consulting her brain. *Muscle memory.* The movement recalled more of her Quantico training. *The parts that hurt in you hurt in them, no matter how big they are: eyes, base of throat, genitals.* That memory triggered an image of Bel showing her how to punch someone in the throat with her right hand and scoop their eyeballs out with her left, using the weight of one swinging arm as ballast for the other. *Stay solid in your center and gouge the fuck out of them.*

A heat low in her belly began to burn off the silver fear. She would lose this fight, but they would not walk away in the same shape they'd arrived. The heat was solidifying into a war cry that was pushing its way up her throat. She opened her mouth to release it when a projectile whizzed past her ear, halting the yell on her tongue.

The missile carved a tunnel through the air, tracking directly to the crotch of the third man, the one with the restless eyes of a lizard. It plunged into his groin with a juicy *whisk*, its hilt protruding, vibrating in the air like a curious antenna. The man fell to his knees groaning and then tumbled onto his side, his hands pawing at the knife like a fishing frog trying to work a hook out of its throat.

A woman stepped forward into Salem's line of sight. Her thick black hair was piled on top of her head, clasped in a ponytail. She was strongly built, curvy on the bottom and lean above, just like Salem.

Salem recognized her as the same woman she'd locked eyes with in the bar. The shock of the situation jarred loose a memory of why she had looked familiar back at the Mayflower: she had also crossed the street in front of Charlie's car earlier today.

The dark-eyed woman had been following Salem. And, apparently, was now rescuing her.

She held two more knives in her left hand.

She flicked one of them into her right hand and released it in a move so liquidly efficient, so coolly automatic, that it looked like a heartbeat. The blade hit the leader dead center in his stomach, angling down. His suave exterior fell away in the face of deep distress, his mysterious eyes gone wide and terrified. Gurgles escaped his mouth as he dropped.

The female knife slinger stepped toward the second man, the ape from the bar, the one who moments earlier had been taunting Salem. His face had gone slack with fear.

She held up the third knife, her voice velvet. "I appreciate the invitation, *Daddy*. You might not like what comes of it, though. See, this pussy has teeth."

CHAPTER 15

Russia Dock Woodland, London

She strode toward the third man with the confidence of an Amazon. Her knife rested in the palm of her hand, its sinister blade pointed toward the ground.

"Please," the third man said. He dropped to his knees between his partners, who were writhing in pain. He held up both hands like a supplicant.

The woman stopped and cocked her hip. She held the knife up like a finger testing the wind. She waggled it.

Salem remembered how to breathe. She sucked in air with such force that she pulled up half the street.

The woman turned with a jaunty smile. "Don't worry, sweets. I'm not gonna hurt this one."

She made a shooing motion in the man's direction, like he was a raccoon she'd discovered in her garbage. "Off with you."

He dragged himself to his feet, sparing a last glance to his pals. They were alive and in deep pain. He turned and ran toward the alley, disappearing into the darkness.

The woman spun on her heel. Salem fought the urge to raise her hands defensively.

"Who are you?" Salem asked.

The woman studied her, unblinking. "Name's Alafair." The knife disappeared under her coat and behind her back. She held out a hand, her voice melodic. "Pleased to meet you."

Salem shook it, pointing toward the alley with her free hand. "You let him go."

Alafair shrugged. "It's best. He can get help, and all three can spread the word like the plague dogs they are. Infect the pack with a healthy fear of women."

Salem's neck creaked as she turned toward the two squirming men on the ground. Men who'd meant to rape and possibly kill her. Her stomach heaved. She caught the bile before it left her mouth.

They brought this on themselves.

"I need to call the police," Salem said, directing her focus toward her phone.

Alafair stepped forward, her face dominated by huge brown eyes. "Wrong. We need to get out of here, Salem Wiley."

Salem had been dialing. She froze midgesture.

"Don't look so fearful. You're famous. In my world, in any event. You had to see me following you the last few days?"

Salem tried to disguise her surprise. She'd made the woman only today. "Why are you tailing me?"

"It's better I show you. Come on, then."

"I shouldn't go somewhere with a stranger." Salem recognized how silly her words sounded too late.

"You've got a tracker on your phone." It was not a question. "Turn it on."

It was on, always, but while Alafair removed her knives from the men, cleaning them with a handkerchief from her leather jacket, Salem took a photo of her location and wrote a brief email on a timer: Bel, this is weird, but I'm in London with a woman who says her name is Alafair.

She looked up at Alafair, who had casually shoved down the shifty-eyed man as he tried to get to his feet, using her boot to hold him in place. "Can I take a photo of you?"

93

Alafair shrugged. "Knock yourself out."

> I've attached a picture of her. If I disappear tonight,
> look for her.

She set the message to send in two hours. "If I don't follow up on that in an hour," Salem lied, "they'll look for me."

"We better hurry then." Alafair turned and began jogging back the way Salem had come, blending into the night as if she'd been born to it.

CHAPTER 16

Russia Dock Woodland, London

"This area used to be a pier," Alafair said, pointing at the sign that read RUSSIA DOCK WOODLAND. "It mostly took in shipments of cheap wood. The jetty was infilled in the seventies and turned into a park. The Thames is a half mile on each side of us." She pointed due west. "The Mayflower pub is a twenty-minute walk that way—unless you wander like you did—and the Campus a two-hour walk past that, if you're feeling foolish."

Salem's pulse twitched. Unless the woman was FBI, she shouldn't know about the Campus. "Who do you work for?"

By way of answer, Alafair tipped her head toward the thick woods that defined the city park. Salem had to squint to make out anything other than the trees. The tent was the same shadowy black as the tree line, a camouflage so successful that Salem's ears had identified it before her eyes. It emanated a clicking sound, reminding Salem of Chinatown mah-jongg under the cover of dark, a soft clacking as ivory tiles were shuffled and stacked. A step closer and she felt the heat, smelled the ionized electricity.

Salem realized what the dark tent contained before Alafair drew back the curtain.

People typing on at least a dozen computers.

No one glanced up when Alafair and Salem stepped inside. Salem counted fourteen people sitting at Frankensteins—desktop processors cobbled together from various parts and models. They wore street clothes. The heat of the server magnified their smell in this small space, sour sweat and unwashed hair.

"We've been following your career," Alafair said. She indicated the workers. "We all have."

This was the first time this evening that Salem had a chance to examine Alafair in the light. She guessed the woman was a decade older than her, maybe midthirties. She had the coloring of the Roma, a dispersed group originating in northern India.

Everyone in the tent had the same coloring. "Are you MI5?" Salem asked.

Alafair threw back her head and laughed. The sound was deep and raspy, rolling up from her belly. "You hear that, brother? She wants to know if we're MI5."

The man nearest the tent opening nodded, a smirk at his mouth, but he didn't look up from his screen. He shared Alafair's black, glossy hair and sharp features.

"We're independent," Alafair clarified. "Cryptanalytic freelancers. We work as needed, move as necessary."

Salem nodded, the idea thrilling her. The fourteen computers dominated the center of the tent. The perimeter contained stacked bedrolls. What looked like a food station stood near the flap, a stack of water bottles, dry goods, and a hot plate.

A crackle at her neck told her Alafair was watching her. "We have everything we need to live in here," Alafair confirmed. "Outside the tent, behind it and out of sight, we park our trailer. We can have this whole operation shut down and packed up in under twenty-two minutes. It's quite a sight."

Salem bet it was. She'd seen a similar operation in Chinatown. It wasn't just the sounds that had reminded her of San Francisco; it was the energy. "Are you part of the Underground?"

Alafair arched an eyebrow. "We are part of *an* underground."

Salem didn't know if she was deliberately avoiding answering the question. She decided not to pursue it. She unzipped her coat, the heat of the enclosed space making her lightheaded.

"Stop there." The woman pointed at Salem's belt, her voice incredulous. "They've got to you."

Salem glanced down at the flowered sachet Mrs. Molony had given her. For the third time that day, she found herself thinking about the Stonehenge replica and its mercy stone. "I got this from . . . from a friend in Ireland. It was a gift."

Alafair pinned Salem in place with her eyes and scoured her up and down, as if looking for more sachets. "The 'friend' who gave it to you. She didn't say what it meant?"

"She said it was for protection."

The mirth bubbled in Alafair's eyes, but she did not throw her head back this time. "I'll say it is."

A wave of exhaustion washed over Salem. Today had been one of the longest days of her life. She was hungry, stumbling around in that dry-mouthed, headachy land between drinking and hungover, and emotionally spent. "What is it you want from me?"

She assumed they were after her research. Or maybe they wanted her to update their ancient computers. She wasn't good at hardware, but she'd help if she could, as long as it didn't interfere with her work at the FBI or break any laws.

Alafair placed her hands on her hips, intelligent, striking, and deadly. She reminded Salem of a superhero. "We want you to help us track down Rosalind Franklin's code."

Salem's forehead crumpled. She and Charlie had driven by a King's College banner with Franklin's name on it earlier today, at about the same location she'd first spotted Alafair. Salem had only the most distant awareness of who Franklin was. "The X-ray scientist?"

"Yes. She's best known for Photo 51. You've heard of it?"

"I'm afraid not."

"It's the diffraction X-ray that first revealed the basic structure of DNA. Franklin parlayed what she learned from that image into groundbreaking stem cell research. I suppose you're not familiar with that, either?"

Salem shook her head.

Alafair's brother glanced their direction. His expression was sad. Salem saw he was closer to her age than Alafair's, his face beautiful in its symmetry. While he shared Alafair's skin and hair coloring, his eyes were the startling ice blue of a husky.

"Not surprising," Alafair said. "Most of the research has been lost. Some say it never happened, others claim it was stolen. We have reason to believe that neither is true. Rosalind Franklin completed the research and then she hid it herself, leaving a code trail to find it."

Salem's brain was spinning. She came at this from every direction and decided there was one question that needed asking above all others. "Let's say all that is true—why do you want to find the research?"

The man who Alafair had called her brother separated from his computer and rolled toward Salem. Her eyes widened as she saw what his workspace had hidden. His wheelchair was not as nice as Bel's, but it served the same purpose.

"If we find it, he can walk again."

CHAPTER 17

Queens Inn, London

The hotel room smelled of pear ginger shampoo and carpet cleaner. It could have been any of a hundred suites Jason had stolen into, silent as a revenant, watching his target sleep. His routine had always been the same once he entered the room.

Slip inside. Stand with his back to the door. Scan the perimeter. Once sounds have separated—cars outside, the breath of sleep inside—pad toward the bed. Study target. Choose a location to plunge the blade. He usually preferred the soft hollow of the neck, the indent where the heart beat like velvet butterfly wings.

Stabbing it choked blood and speech.

Other times, the Order requested the knife go directly into the heart.

Jason didn't ask questions.

In any scenario, his final act before selecting the insertion point was to unsheathe his knife. He carried the set in the inside left pocket of his suit coat, cradled in galuchat leather, an ensemble of metal and glass blades, each of them mounted on a bone handle and sharp enough to slice between cells.

His daggers were his only extravagance.

This night called for a different plan, however, and it was throwing him off. He wasn't here to kill. He was here to kidnap.

He observed the child sleep, her hair a mess of snarls suggesting she had gone to bed with it wet. It wasn't the first time he'd watched her slumber. She'd been a different child then, wild and more bone than muscle, curved in Salem's arms. Bel had slept in the bed next to them, all three crammed into a cheap roadside motel, on the run. Thinking of Bel inflamed the familiar heat of sexual arousal. He'd sliced a lock off her strawberry hair that night.

He no longer possessed the hair. Anger at the memory snuffed his growing erection. The past would stay where it belonged.

This moment was all there ever was.

Vida Wiley snored in the bed opposite Mercy. Both were gripped in the muscular arms of jet lag, sleeping deeply. His gaze lingered on Vida, something like fondness easing his chest. The woman was a survivor. A fighter like him. He'd sliced her, broken her bones, whispered terrible words in her ear, and she'd never bent. Her seeping, swollen wounds had been allowed to fester, and still, she'd kept her head. The echoes of his work were visible in the twitches and moans that bothered her sleep, but he'd watched her walk into the hotel earlier in the evening, her head high, her eyes fierce.

He allowed himself a moment to consider what his life would be like if he'd been reared by this woman. His own mother had been beautiful and wicked, dedicating her life to ascending from her swamp roots to the gilded arms of the New Orleans aristocracy. He had been an unwelcome hitch in her plans. Subsequently, she alternated between using him as a best friend or a whipping post, depending on her mood, and she looked the other way when her boyfriends used him as well.

He'd never met his father. The sentient Sharpey's fibers had likely been inherited from the man, though, as Jason's mother had never evidenced the gift. Maybe his father had possessed even more talents? Jason would never know. His mother was his only family, at least until Carl Barnaby had recruited him for the Order, training him in psychology, physical combat, spycraft, and marketing.

And now Barnaby was gone.

He guessed his mother was, too. For the last several years, he'd kept her tied to a chair and hooked up to an IV, a box of kitty litter poised below the chair's special opening. He'd had to leave her when he was recently assigned overseas. He'd propped a photo of him as a child, before he knew how to change his face, next to a glass of water, both just out of reach of her bound hands. She might make it until his return. She might not.

Relationships with mothers were complicated.

For this moment, he would imagine Vida Wiley as his own mother. No one would know. He stared at her, tasting the shape of the word on his lips: *mother*. It felt right. Foundational. He would neither wake her nor hurt her. It would be easy to remove the child without a struggle.

He glided toward Mercy, leaned over her. She radiated the drowsy warmth of sleep.

His right hand covered her mouth at the exact moment the edge of his left hand snapped her Stomach 9 pressure point, near where most people were taught to check their pulse. The pressure to her carotid sinus's baroreceptor would render her unconscious for two to three minutes, a generous amount of time.

He laid the note on her pillow:

Solve the Stonehenge Train for the girl.

You have until midnight 24 September.

He hoisted her up so her head rested on his shoulder, much like he imagined a loving parent held their child. She was light. He moved backward toward the door, eyes on Vida. His tonight-mother moaned but did not wake. He stepped into the brightly lit hallway and strode toward the elevator at the north end.

He pushed the "L" button.

The up arrow lit up, the elevator humming toward him.

Its doors opened. A loud man and women were hanging off each other inside. They stumbled out.

Jason glared at them. *My little girl is sleeping.*

The female widened her eyes and nodded while the male giggled and hurried her along.

He continued the ruse as he walked out of the lobby.

The kidnapping would have gone just as well without the Grimalkin, he thought sourly, opening the passenger-side door and strapping Mercy in. Their meeting had turned out to be a tremendous annoyance. Jason had come to talk business, to relay the Order's plan, but the Grimalkin had been unfocused, almost childlike, intent on planning ways to play with Salem like a goddamned cat rather than follow her according to protocol. There was no talk of knife work or anything of interest to Jason.

After the unsatisfactory meeting, Jason had done his own recon on Salem, following her to the Mayflower pub, watching her through the window. So uncomfortable, so out of her element. He verified—not that he needed to—that assigning the Grimalkin to work alongside him was overkill, no pun intended. Jason could do all this on his own. He could stay close to Salem, record her results the moment she solved a section of the train, and kill her when she cracked the mystery of Stonehenge.

The Grimalkin on board only mucked it up. Jason didn't even know what role he was to play after he kidnapped the girl. He had to wait for instructions from his partner, who wasn't a rule follower, who cared nothing for structure.

The only pleasure he had experienced during the meeting was the surprise at learning who the Grimalkin was. A smile twitched at the memory. It was clear why both the Order and the Grimalkin kept the assassin's identity hidden.

Such a delicious secret.

CHAPTER 18

The Campus, London

The craggy sunlight scraped across London's rooftops. The rain had stopped an hour earlier, morphing into a hoary frost. Salem was sure she'd never be warm again. She'd been raised in Minnesota, the land of four seasons—almost winter, winter, still winter, and road construction—but that had been an honest cold. *Snow. Ice.* A serious cold that scrubbed the air, razing it of germs and pests, wiping the earth clean, rebooting it for spring.

London cold was sneaky. Damp-that-crept-into-your-bones sneaky. It weakened Salem, where Minnesota cold fortified her. She shivered as she walked toward the Campus, but her mind ran hot. It had shifted into whiteboard mode, scribbling hypotheses, running algorithms, noting random facts that arose. Rosalind Franklin. Stem cell research. Freelance Romani computer nerds on the hunt for a paralysis cure.

A snippet of 702's "Where My Girls At" popped from Salem's pocket.

"Shit!"

A man in a rain parka glanced her way, scowling. The streets were starting wake up, people hustling to work, businesses opening.

"Sorry," she said, scrambling for her cell. The song was Bel's text tone, a joke from their favorite song of 1999. She'd emailed her friend a dire warning two hours earlier and never followed up on it.

She thumbed the button on her cell and the screen lit up, revealing Bel's text.

You switching teams?

Relief washed over Salem. Bel had taken the email as a joke, thank god, focusing on the photo of Alafair, the suggestion that Salem was spending the night with a woman. Salem's fingers flew over the keyboard.

Naw, still benched by the home team. What are you doing up so late?

Research. Didn't even check email until just now. Who was the hottie?

Her name is Alafair. Met her last night.

Is she single?

Salem couldn't fight the smile. I'll ask.

And she would, if she ever saw Alafair again. Salem had agreed to help her; of course she had. If there was a way to give Bel her legs back, Salem would move heaven and earth to find it. Alafair would send her all the Rosalind Franklin research over a secure channel. As soon as Salem finished out this week in the FBI, she would devote every waking minute to poring over it, sending updates over the same channel.

Before letting her go, Alafair had filled Salem in on the minimal data they'd so far uncovered. It amounted to only three suggestions that Rosalind Franklin had discovered a way to regenerate spinal tissue and nerves: a newspaper clipping dated 24 February 1958, referring to "an exciting development from Birkbeck College, something our paraplegic soldiers and polio victims will be interested in"; a note from a friend warning Franklin that she was becoming too famous; and a page purported to be from Franklin's diary where she wrote, *I must hide the cure seven levels deep or the men will take this, too, from me.*

Salem had checked on her phone to confirm that Franklin had been working at Birkbeck College in 1958, but that was a thin connection, especially since cursory research suggested Franklin's DNA and RNA work was isolated to the tobacco mosaic virus while at Birkbeck. Alafair had seen the doubt in Salem's eyes, had convinced her there was more, that Franklin's lab assistant confirmed that she'd perfected human cell regeneration and had made a medical discovery that would alter the world: she could make the paralyzed walk.

That lab assistant was Alafair's grandfather. He'd passed down the story.

He swore that Franklin had been murdered for the discovery, her death by ovarian cancer a public ruse. The grandfather, upon learning of her passing, had returned to the lab for Franklin's notes. They had vanished. He believed Franklin had hidden them.

The story was ludicrous built on top of ridiculous, but the sad thing was Salem had heard even weirder. This, at least, was a cause she could fight for: Bel.

She started to type I'm coming home Sunday but stopped herself. Miss you, she typed instead. She would tell Bel in person, all of it.

Miss you too, Bits. Olive juice.

Salem smiled. The last part was code for "I love you."

The Campus was just ahead. Salem could not wait to get to her room and strip off her damp clothes. She might even pop an Ativan and return to the steam room to leach the cold out of her bones. The door felt lighter than usual as Salem opened it, the warmth of the foyer welcoming. She avoided eye contact with the security guard, emptying her pockets into a tub before stepping through the metal detector, waiting on the other side as he recorded her entrance into the computer docket.

After this week was over and she left the FBI, she definitely would not miss the institutional feel of this building, more nursing home than office suites, no images on the walls, not even the pale globbiness of dentist office art.

Her tub came through on the conveyer belt. She reached for it.

Vida Wiley flew into the lobby just as Salem was fishing her phone out of the tub. Assistant Director Robert Bench followed Vida. His face was grim, gray hair askew as if he'd been woken.

Vida's expression was violent, twisted with pain and accusation. It was the same face Salem had woken up to on the beach the day her father had died. They had not yet discovered his body, but the police had arrived. Water search and rescue was out on the lake. Salem was being treated by EMTs. She was coming to, still mercifully unaware that her father had drowned.

Gracie's car had pulled up. Salem didn't know then that the authorities had called Vida, and that Gracie had driven her to the lake. She only knew that she was sitting on the bumper of an ambulance, and that everyone surrounding her was a stranger, and no one was telling her anything.

Salem had looked over at Gracie's car, overwhelmed with relief when her mother fell out. Vida lurched toward Salem, her face the gruesome color and shape of a broken heart. She held her hands toward Salem not in comfort but in accusation.

"What have you done?"

The same words then as now.

Vida lunged at Salem, stopping only when Assistant Director Bench restrained her. Her hair was loose, her pajamas out of place in the harsh light of the Campus. She held Mercy's rag doll in her hand. It would have been a relief to see her crying. Her face was dry, though, her eyes hollowed pits in her face, her mouth condemning.

"What have you done?" she repeated.

Salem backed up, stumbling against the hard plastic of the metal detector. She knew she wasn't twelve anymore. She realized her brain was her strongest weapon, that it could compute at incredible speeds. She understood there were resources available to her now that she hadn't possessed back then.

But for the life of her, she couldn't recall what they were.

She wanted to look at Bench for a clue as to what the situation was, how she should react, but she couldn't pull her gaze away from her mother. Vida was Salem's only parent, and she *hated* Salem. That truth was tattooed across Vida's face, the brittle veneer of courtesy fallen away. All the raw emotion her mother really felt for her—the betrayal, the fear, oh god, the envy—was laid bare.

Salem couldn't track the situation. What *had* she done? Alafair had assaulted two men, but that felt more like a cartoon attack than a reality. Alafair had assured her they were not the type who would go to the police. Salem planned to quit the FBI, but no one knew that, not even Bel.

What had the power to so upset Vida?

Her eyes were drawn to the rag doll, a blank smile stitched on its face, its yellow-yarn braids askew. The sharp-clawed awareness of what was missing from this picture hit her so fast and hard that she could not duck. She stood her ground even though the realization felt like a body blow. "Mercy?"

She swayed. Hands reached out to her, but they weren't her mother's. She would have recognized Vida's touch, had been craving it for the past fifteen years. No, her mother was not embracing her, but her words were burying her.

"They kidnapped her. Do you understand? They have her now. That innocent child is with the men who did this to me." Vida pushed her hair back, showing the ear with the missing lobe, one of many scars she carried.

Salem shook her head, pushed against the hands trying to pull her toward a chair. It wasn't the security guard, or Bench. Charlie? "I don't understand."

Vida drew close to Salem, so close their noses nearly touched. Her voice hissed, her morning breath sour. "We've all been so careful. Every one of us. You're the only one who refused to listen. The only one who isn't taking this seriously, who refuses to learn about the Underground. Because of you, they took the girl." Vida pulled on her hair. "What did you say? What were you stupid enough to utter on an unsecured line?"

Vida threw down a ball of paper she'd been squeezing in her fist. She stood, stepping back from Salem, hate illuminating her eyes. Salem reached for the paper with shaking hands. Smoothed it out.

Solve the Stonehenge Train for the girl.

You have until midnight 24 September.

Salem moaned because she knew in that moment, she saw it all. There was only one person she spoke with socially, one woman in the whole world who she didn't use an unsecured line with because they only talked about middle school and dating, and if it started to get real, Salem would change the subject.

Bel.

"You wouldn't believe it, Bel. The woman had uncovered a little replica of Stonehenge in her backyard, right next to her grandmother's grave. The word mercy *was carved on one of the stones."*

"Was it a code?"

"It was—"

"You solved the mystery of Stonehenge, didn't you?"

"For sure. And for my next trick . . ."

It had been innocent. A joke. But somehow those words had caused Mercy's kidnapping. There had been power in them. Conspiracy.

Those words were pulling Salem back into the witch hunt web. The child. The stone. The Underground.

"What *is* Mercy?"

"She's the last." Vida sounded hollow, hoarse. "She's the code that sets us free."

"Why didn't you tell me they wanted her?" Salem didn't recognize her own voice.

Vida squeezed her stomach as if trying to hold herself in. "Because you wouldn't listen."

CHAPTER 19

Drive to Stonehenge

The English countryside sped past, blotches of greens and browns, hillocks and grazing cattle. The air smelled of freshly cut grass and diesel. It had taken them nearly half an hour to reach the western outskirts of London, even using Salem's map hack. Charlie said it'd be another hour or more until they reached Stonehenge.

Salem rode in the passenger's seat, grief cloaking her. Charlie allowed her silent space.

The president's directive had been clear: get Mercy back. Salem would have searched for the girl even if the president hadn't ordered it, but she was grateful for the official assignment. It meant she had a partner and access to FBI resources.

Vida had provided precious little detail. She'd confirmed there was a Stonehenge train just as there had been a Beale train, and they were two of many. The Underground had been formed to create the trains, their goal to safeguard women's intellectual and financial wealth from the Order, who would either claim or destroy it. Each train was a series of ever-deeper codes that eventually led to a single location that housed land deeds, scientific achievements, formulas, maps, jewels, and gold— the treasure of women throughout the ages.

But the keepers of the trains were hunted and killed, and what they knew died with them. Through the millennia, the Underground had lost the solutions to many of their own trains and, in some cases, the awareness that there was a train at all. Between that and time destroying many of the hiding spots, no one knew for sure what was left. It had fallen into the mists of legend. But the Order searched, and the Underground scoured, racing against each other, one to maintain the power, the other to restore the balance.

Salem hadn't cared. She did now.

Vida had revealed that Mercy Mayfair's lineage was the key to cracking the code that would tumble the patriarchy once and for all. It had nothing to do with her blood, which had been drawn and studied by the Underground's scientists. It was not anything Mercy could recall, no passcode murmured to her by her mother, who'd had it whispered to her by her own mother, and so on down the line through the tunnel of history. The truth was that the Underground had no idea *how* Mercy fit in, only that as the last living Mayfair, she was the key.

The Order knew the same.

They'd previously thought it more prudent to monitor the child than take her. Vida suspected that they wanted the Underground to do their heavy lifting, to show them how Mercy unlocked it all. But then there was Stonehenge, one of the first and biggest of all the code trains, uncrackable for thousands of years, and Salem sniffing around Stonehenge, connecting Mercy to it, must have tipped the scales. They'd clearly decided it was too much of a risk to leave the girl at large. They'd kidnapped her, gambling with four days—how long they'd given Salem to solve the train—to discover what was at the end of the fabled train.

Salem assumed they'd be watching her the whole time.

Charlie always carried an overnight bag in the boot of his car. Salem was given twenty minutes to pack. She brought Mercy's doll as well as her Ativan, popping two along with three aspirin and a bucket of water before they left for Stonehenge. With presidential approval, Assistant Director Bench had allowed them four days to retrieve the child.

Salem got to work immediately, ignoring Charlie's erratic driving. The B&C was tethered to her cell phone for Wi-Fi access. She typed furiously on the laptop, uninterested for the moment in Stonehenge. Her dad had always told her that to solve a puzzle, you had to locate the beginning.

Salem needed to find out who Mercy really was. If she could uncover what the Order wanted from the child, she might be able to bargain that information to save her. Screw the Stonehenge train, the Underground, the Order, and anything that didn't involve her, Bel, and Mercy living a safe and boring life back in Minneapolis.

She began with a search on the Mayfair name. The first hit showed her that Mayfair was a district in London. The second pulled up information on a two-week fair held in London from 1686 to 1764.

She filed both facts away, digging deeper for the name's genealogy. The lack of information frustrated her. Mayfairs had immigrated to the United States since the earliest of records, but only a handful, and all from Ireland. They settled in New York or San Francisco, mostly, some making it inland to Illinois in the late 1800s. When she tried to trace the root of the name back to Europe, though, she dead-ended time and again. No coat of arms. No mottoes or family crests. No famous explorers or governors or even cobblers with the name.

She tried her own name, backward knocking at the problem. Her screen flooded with information. Wiley, alternative spelling.

Wylie, a surname of Northern Ireland and Scottish origin. The name was first used by the Strathclyde-Britons in the late 1590s. An Irish woman, Ann Wiley, was the first Wiley to arrive in America, landing in Maryland in 1674. Salem could have read all day if she wanted to learn more about her own surname. When she returned to Mayfair, though, nada.

Maybe she could nail down more facts about the actual Mercy Mayfair.

Ernest, Mercy's older brother, had told Salem and Bel that Mercy had been born in Georgia and that their mother had died in childbirth. Ernest, who couldn't have been more than thirteen at the time, had stolen his sister rather than have them both turned over to the county.

He may have lied about that, but Salem didn't think so, and ultimately, it didn't matter. She didn't have anything else to go on.

Fourteen keystrokes were all it took to call up the Georgia state birth records. She'd need GAEA to break through their firewall. The program may be young, but this was code breaking at its most basic.

That left Salem's own ethics as the remaining boundary. She was rulebound—every mathematician was—and without a warrant, what she was about to do was illegal. Her SAC could get her one, but that could take days. She realized she was grinding her teeth, an old habit from after her dad's death. She really had no choice but to slice through the firewall. Research, that's what she'd call it. No way to perfect GAEA if she wasn't tested.

Salem turned GAEA on. It took all of four minutes for her baby to punch gleefully through the firewall. She plugged the name Mayfair into the DOS screen that appeared, offering a five-year window starting ten years earlier as the parameter dates because she didn't know exactly what year Mercy was born.

Zero results.

She groaned in frustration.

Charlie kept his eyes on the road. "Search not going well?"

Salem hadn't told him she wasn't researching the Stonehenge train, but she figured he'd catch on. He'd been moments behind her when she'd walked into the foyer, had been the one to help her off the floor, had heard everything. "Mercy's last name is Mayfair, but I can't find any history of her birth or even the origin of the name. It's like someone went into the system and erased even basic Wikipedia data."

Charlie tapped the steering wheel. "It's possible."

Salem's head jerked back. "You think someone would go through the trouble of removing *a last name* from the internet?"

He shrugged. "I've seen weirder. I bet you have, too."

It was true. "What kind of work did you say were you doing at MI5 before you got yoked to me? Cryptographer or cryptanalyst?" The first was a code maker, the second a code breaker. While most computer analysts were good at both, they usually specialized in one area or the other.

"I worked where they put me. Are you familiar with the Coogan case?"

Salem shook her head.

"It was big in the UK three years ago. Serial killer was chopping up girls in South London. Fancied himself a bit of a coding genius. Like your Zodiac Killer. Left a clue at every scene. Got seven girls before we caught him."

His words hollowed out a spot in Salem's stomach. "How did you crack his code?"

"I was just part of the team. And the truth is that Coogan got lazy. He repeated an earlier cipher pattern in his last note. The repetition allowed us to crack it."

"I'm glad you were able to stop him," she murmured.

A comfortable silence settled between them, unspooling itself. "Hey," he finally said. His quiet tone drew her full attention. "We can talk about your mother."

She stiffened.

"Or not. At your own pace. That was a bit of a bad job she laid on you back there, is all."

Salem's vision narrowed. "She had reason to be upset."

Charlie looked like he wanted to say something, his brain warring with his mouth. He pinched his lips together and glanced out his window before looking back at the road. "Yeah. Maybe."

Salem stared out her own window. She desperately wanted to call Bel, to tell her that the Hermitage had been only a tentacle of the octopus they'd fought, to ask for her help in fighting the larger monster. But she couldn't think of a way to tell her that her indiscretion had gotten Mercy kidnapped. She couldn't bear the reprobation in her best friend's voice.

She shifted in her seat. "How far are we from Stonehenge?"

"Another half an hour, maybe. I can't drive any faster," Charlie said, not unkindly. When she didn't respond, he fiddled with the radio buttons. He landed on a station playing jangly folk tunes. He sped up to the bumper of the car in front of him and then slowed down when the westbound M4 motorway passing lane filled up.

Charlie seemed to want to keep the conversation going. He nudged her. "Nina and Lucan slept together last night after we had drinks. Bet on it."

Salem didn't have the stomach for a response. In a normal time, that news would have twisted her rib cage, but it was only hours earlier that Stone had rejected her in no uncertain terms. Even if he had wanted her, she didn't have the mental space for him now. It took all her concentration to keep her brain from eating itself, caught in a loop imagining poor Mercy, afraid, begging for Salem, not understanding why no one came.

"Sorry. Was there something between you and Stone?"

Salem snapped into the conversation. "No. I don't care about him, only Mercy. You heard my mom. It's my fault that she was taken. If anything happens to her, I'm done."

Charlie drew a breath deep enough lift his chest. "I know she's your ma, but that doesn't mean she's right. In fact, on this front, she seems straight wrong."

Salem didn't want to think about it because then she'd cry.

Charlie must have sensed her distress on the subject. He pointed toward her computer screen, taking his eyes off the road for far too long. "Maybe it's time to consider Stonehenge. Your mother seems to think there's a mountain of a conspiracy there, and if your president is setting us on this merry chase, I'm inclined to agree. There's got to be something to it that every archaeologist has overlooked."

Or misunderstood. Salem angled her rotating screen so the sun didn't flash off it. *Because now that you mention it, when I was in Ireland, I saw Stonehenge in a new light, and I wonder if . . .*

But she didn't want to tell him about her graveside hypothesis. Or did she? She had to trust someone.

But maybe not just yet.

She began a wide-net search on Stonehenge, skimming the information. "Nothing much here," she said. "Stonehenge's basic history that the stones we recognize now have been around for five thousand years, and that no one really knows what the structure was built for. Pretty much what you told me earlier."

He tapped the side of his nose. "I'm a bit of a history buff. But what's that I hear in your voice?"

His attentiveness warmed her and made up her mind. She would share her theory. "The day before we met, I went to Ireland."

"Sure. With Agent Curson. Dead end, the report said."

Salem realized she hadn't seen Agent Curson since. "It was. At least as far as what we were called out for. There was no threat to the president that we could discern. The woman had uncovered a tiny replica of Stonehenge."

"What, made of stone?"

"Yeah, but it had an extra stone in it."

The radio crackled, and Charlie changed the station. "There used to be quite a few more stones, you know, more than what we see now. The original had around eighty, and postholes indicate there was more to it, maybe even a timber structure built atop. Have you heard of the Aubrey Holes?"

Salem didn't want to make him feel bad for pivoting the subject from her big reveal. He didn't know she'd been about to share something with him that she hadn't even told Bel. "No. What are those?"

She clicked the phrase into her search bar as he spoke.

"Chalk pits surrounding Stonehenge. There's fifty-six of them in all. John Aubrey discovered them in the 1600s, but they believe they predate the construction of Stonehenge as we know it, from around 3100 BC. Can't tell if they contained wood posts or stone. Plus, there's the Heel Stone, outside what we recognize as Stonehenge. It marks the midsummer sunrise. There's the Slaughter Stone, the Altar Stone. Who can say if the stone you saw was even an extra? Maybe it was just an earlier construction."

"Maybe." Salem verified everything he had just said. She'd commented earlier that he seemed to know a lot about Stonehenge, and it had bothered him. She kept that observation to herself this time. She searched for a sketch of Stonehenge in its prime to run against what she'd seen at Mrs. Molony's.

He indicated her screen again. "You know I love computers, but it's not good to type while sitting in a moving vehicle. Unsettles the stomach. Besides, it's lonely out here in the real world, and we need a plan going in. You're the only one who's solved one of these code trains. Tell me what we're looking for at Stonehenge."

Salem clicked her screen shut. "I don't know." He waited.

She sighed. "I know I have to save Mercy. That's it." She couldn't hold the tears back.

He made tsking noises. "Why, if you can crack the Beale train, then Stonehenge will be a piece of cake. Count on it!" He patted her shoulder awkwardly. "Hey, you'll cheer right up when I tell you the best part."

"What's that?"

"I got us inside Stonehenge! They'll clear it for our arrival. We have fifteen minutes to solve an apparent code that's evaded centuries of attempts." He chuckled. "Not a thing to worry about there."

It wouldn't be enough time. Panic stroked Salem's throat. She grasped on to an earlier thought to distract herself. "Do you know what happened to Agent Curson?"

Charlie shrugged. "I assume he's back at the Campus." He gripped the steering wheel and pointed to the right. "Here we are. Look at those gorgeous rocks."

Salem followed the path of his finger.

Her jaw dropped. She was looking at history's most famous mystery.

CHAPTER 20

Stonehenge

If the sun had been able to crash through the clouds, it would have appeared directly overhead. Salem was unaware of its position, or its feeble heat, or the chilly breeze whispering at her neck, or even the handful of visitors talking in a clot, blocking the path leading away from the private parking lot they'd been ushered into.

All she cared about was connecting to that beautiful stone structure again.

A hill hid Stonehenge at the moment, but the initial glimpse had stolen her breath away. Photographs of the monoliths were a pale shadow of their majesty, even from the road. It was epic, stunning, awesome.

Stonehenge had awoken something true in her blood, almost a song, not quite a story.

She tightened her parka's belt, yanked the shoulder strap of the B&C on one arm and her purse on the other, and pushed through the crowd.

"Salem! Wait up."

She didn't turn. He could hurry up. She needed to examine the rocks. Her feet crunched on gravel. Her eyes ate the fields billowing to her right and left, chewed on the poppies that dotted them. She inhaled deeply, smelling cow and country, prairie and field. She'd felt this grounded, this comfortable in her skin, only once before, and that had been in San Francisco's Chinatown. The bustle and aroma there had made her feel both anonymous and part of something bigger.

The land around Stonehenge was different. Stonehenge made her feel *powerful*.

She crested the hill separating the private lot from the beginning of the interpretive trail and, beyond that, Stonehenge. Her shoulders relaxed when it was again in sight. The field of scarlet poppies ringing it was even more glorious at this height. They reminded Salem of the flowers surrounding Muirinn Molony's house and decorating the sachet she'd been given. It hung off her jean's belt loop. She patted it through her coat, speed walking toward the structure.

"Quite the eyeful, yeah?" Charlie caught up with her, out of breath. He was hunched against the wind. He nodded toward the stones and the security guards who were opening the rope gate for them. "They're expecting us."

The thrill of entering the ancient circle heightened Salem's senses. "We have free rein?"

"Almost." He held out a hand to indicate Salem should enter the rope circle first. "The only rule is that we can't touch the stones."

Salem scowled. If there was a code hidden in one of the rocks, as there had been inside Emily Dickinson's grandmother's gravestone, which had led them to Beale's buried treasure in Virginia, she would need to lay hands on it.

She'd cross that bridge when she came to it.

Salem stood just outside the stones, suddenly hesitant. Once she entered, she sensed she would not be the same. "Does it matter which stones we enter through?" she asked a guard.

He shrugged and pointed at a well-traveled path separating the base of the nearest trilithon. It looked like a doorway through time.

She nodded.

She stepped through the megalithic arch. She held her breath and closed her eyes.

Time and space interacted differently inside the stones, trailing against her skin like a broken cobweb. She knew when she was inside the circle because it was warmer. The temperature change was dramatic. Probably just the stones blocking the chilly wind.

The caw of a bird startled her, and her eyes flew open. A blue-eyed raven had settled on the Altar Stone, a greenish-purple rock the size of a sedan that rested inside the circle of Stonehenge. Another movement caught the edge of her vision, but when she turned, she saw only the stones. It must have been a trick of the light.

"Quite something, isn't it?"

Salem was almost surprised Charlie had been able to step through. It seemed too precious in here, too magical. But of course it was just her head playing tricks on her. Twenty-six tourists were allowed in here twice every day, once at dawn and once at dusk. They were called special access tours and were the reason there were paths in and out of the stones.

"Yes," she breathed.

He held up his watch. "Clock's ticking."

She turned to take it all in. There was no clear beginning spot.

Her dad's voice found her, suffused her with warmth. *Start with what you know.*

Once you'd inventoried the familiar, you could find what didn't belong.

Well, rocks were familiar. Salem counted ninety-three of them making up this incarnation of Stonehenge, a mix of broken lumps and freestanding rocks.

That told her nothing.

Next, she evaluated shape. The original structure was a circle of stones around a horseshoe shape. Salem was currently standing inside what remained of the formation. Beyond the stones lay a circle of embankment and, even farther, burial mounds. The Heel Stone lay approximately 250 feet northeast, a lumpy, fifteen-foot-tall rock shaped like an eel poking its head out of the ground.

Her research had verified what Charlie told her on the drive, which was that on the summer solstice, if she stood in the center of Stonehenge, she'd see the sun rise directly over the Heel Stone. The winter solstice sun set opposite that.

Charlie strode to the Altar Stone behind her. He knelt beside it. "They don't think anyone was sacrificed here. Just a fanciful name."

Salem turned and nodded. She had number and shape. Now she needed surfaces. All the stones were pockmarked, gray and green, three tons each, and as large below the earth as above. The rocks were ancient and timeless, witness to five thousand years of humanity: feasts and festivals, rituals and rites. These stones would not give up their secret lightly. She felt that, and below that certainty the friction of discomfort itched at her brain stem.

She recognized it: she needed to find a pattern. She needed to soothe herself. She stepped toward the nearest stone, her hand raised.

"Stop that!" The guard stared at her fiercely. "You can't touch the stones."

Salem dropped her hand but felt no shame. Normally, getting in trouble would drown her in embarrassment, but she was a different woman inside the stones. Or maybe her perspective had shifted now that she was responsible for Mercy getting kidnapped.

"Nothing like the fear of finger oils destroying a five-thousand-year-old rock, eh?" Charlie said under his breath.

Salem's lip twitched. She wasn't alone in here, and that felt good, but knowing how closely they were being watched made their impossible task even more difficult. She would have to crack this using only her mind. She didn't know if the code train had been put in place by the Neolithic builders or if it had been placed here later, camouflaged for hundreds of years. It could be a disguised drawer, a cipher carved into the stone, something buried below the soil, or any of another thousand possibilities.

She turned on her heel, studying the stones as if they were old-fashioned slides and she in the center of the projector. It only took half a turn before she spotted it.

CHAPTER 21

Stonehenge

She dashed toward the stone, her blood thick in her veins. A sliver of sun had broken through the clouds and glinted off the rock face. The stone was covered in lichen, like the others, but the sun had also caught metal.

"What is it?" Charlie called, rushing to her side. She pointed.

He squinted. "Yeah, it's Stone 52. That's a nail."

"What?"

"Sure. Someone pounded it there, no one knows when. Lookit this." He led her around to the south side of the stone. I WREN was carved into it. "Archaeologists believe Christopher Wren carved this in here."

"The seventeenth-century architect?"

"Among other pastimes. He may have been a freemason. Someone pounded a hole above the name." He pointed toward it, overhead. "But don't bother looking inside because that's been examined more than a whore's orifice."

Salem recoiled.

He ran his fingers through his thick hair, chagrined. "Excuse my French. I spend too much time with men, I think. Truly sorry. It won't happen again. But if it might be helpful, there's more graffiti over here. Let me show you."

They had stepped outside the circle to examine the outer edges of Stone 52. He brought her back inside to examine more markings. Now that he was pointing it out, she could see the graffiti everywhere. A dagger carved in one rock. Victorian names and dates in another. In some places, merely the suggestion of a name. She suddenly had so much visual information that the lichen and natural pebbling on the stone were starting to take on a pattern.

"How can we possibly find anything here?"

Charlie nodded sympathetically. "It might be helpful to consider what the original builders were after, if the code was hidden way back then. They were a preagricultural society. Feeding themselves would have taken up most of their day, if not their life. What force would've compelled them to forgo survival to create this monolith?"

Salem found herself nodding.

He continued. "And how did they call others here? The Neoliths were only beginning to create pottery, for Pete's sake. They had no method of communication, yet forensic study of the bones buried here prove that some came from as far away as Egypt, returning home and then visiting Stonehenge again, multiple times. What gathered them? Who organized them to build once they arrived?"

"Human instinct?" Salem whispered.

"What did you say?"

The blue-eyed raven cawed, pulling her gaze upward. She cleared her throat. "Maybe an ancient human instinct now bred out of us drew them here, the same drive that causes salmon to swim upstream and birds to fly south in the winter."

A strain of music yanked her attention toward the guard. Except he was no longer standing there. No one was in earshot. Salem must have imagined it.

Charlie's expression was doubtful, but it lit into a smile. "Maybe. In any case, this is the most interesting code-breaking mission I've ever been on."

He held his hands out and twirled like a dancer. The wind outside the henge had ruffled his hair, and he hadn't bothered to straighten it after entering the interior. "Cracking the meaning of Stonehenge! Who would have thought?"

Salem had no urge to join his excitement. Poor Mercy was terrified somewhere. Time was short. She yanked her camera out of her pocket. She would take photos now and study them later. If she discovered something, if GAEA's image-reading program sniffed out something Salem's eyes had missed, they could return to the rocks.

Charlie returned to the Altar Stone while Salem snapped photos. "This rock's nickname came from Inigo Jones, who was sent here by James I to suss out what Stonehenge actually was."

"Another seventeenth-century architect," Salem murmured.

He pointed in the direction of the Heel Stone without moving his eyes. "Some researchers believe the Heel Stone was named that after the Anglo-Saxon word for conceal: *helan*."

Salem squinted toward the Heel Stone, wondering again how he knew so much about Stonehenge. "You think there's a code in there?"

"I don't know." Charlie looked at her, measuring her. "My dad was a stonemason. He taught me everything I know about this place."

She hadn't been expecting that. It brought a smile to her face. "Mine was a carpenter."

"I know."

Her face must have reflected her annoyance at him knowing that detail about her when she knew nothing about him because he stood, hands palms forward. "It's not my fault you're famous among us computer nerds."

She noticed his dimples for the first time. "Is your dad still alive?"

He shook his head.

"Mine neither." In that moment, she made up her mind; he had shared something personal with her, and she would return the favor. She said it all in one breath before she lost the courage. "When I saw that replica Stonehenge in Ireland, it wasn't just that it had an extra rock, one that isn't standing here now. It wasn't even that the extra rock had the word 'mercy' carved on it."

Charlie's eyebrows shot up.

"It's what that extra rock made me see." She dropped the B&C to the ground and opened her purse, riffling around until she found what she looked for. She yanked the plastic clamshell out and held it toward him, snapping open the top.

"It made me see that Stonehenge is arranged just like a packet of birth control pills. Well, the ones that come in the clamshell, anyhow. Do you see it? The circle of pills on the outside are the birth control. The ones on the inside are placebos, for your . . . period."

She didn't dare look at him. She let her hair fall over her eyes. "Once I saw that Stonehenge is shaped like a packet of birth control pills, it made me think there must be a feminine explanation for this site, that it's related to a woman's cycle, somehow."

There. She'd said it all, every stupid word. Had he heard?

His silence became too much. She pulled up her eyes. His face was shifting.

CHAPTER 22

Stonehenge

Charlie couldn't contain his laughter, but he had the good grace to turn away from her until it was under control. Once he calmed himself, he faced her again. "I'm sorry. I know the best ideas come from brainstorming. It's just that you caught me off guard with that." He indicated the clamshell she still held. "My mom used the same brand."

Salem snapped it closed and shoved it in her purse. The tips of her ears grew hot. She swiveled and walked toward the nearest opening. She didn't really have a destination other than *away*.

"Salem, I'm sorry! Don't be like that. I shouldn't have laughed."

She was mad at herself for saying her stupid theory out loud. And now a guard was walking toward them. Their time was up. She had wasted their precious access talking. Glancing around, she sighed. It wouldn't have mattered if they'd had all the time in the world. She didn't have any idea what she was looking for. At least she'd gotten photos.

"No luck?" The guard, a different one, a woman in her early sixties, asked as Salem exited through the same trilithon she'd entered.

"No, but thank you for letting us in."

The gray of the sky darkened. A possible storm.

Charlie was still trying to catch up with Salem.

"If you're motoring back to London, you'll want to leave soon, avoid congestion hour over lunch," the guard said. "I take the train back to Piccadilly, near my house, but I saw you have a car."

"Thanks," Salem said. Charlie reached her side. They walked toward the private parking lot, heads lowered in misery.

The guard called after them. "You might want to pop in the visitor center if you haven't yet. You can't see it from here, but it's only a short tram ride. You'll find some pottery, jewelry, animal bones, the like, all from this site."

"Thank you," Salem said over her shoulder.

Charlie walked alongside her, keeping his distance. "You mean it, yeah? It's a good idea. We'll check out the center. I haven't been since they built the new one."

The need to save Mercy outweighed Salem's shame by a long shot. She nodded curtly, then realized it served no one for her to ignore him. "If they have a museum, or information on the structure, we might be able to find where they could hide a code in a way we couldn't see standing inside of it."

"That's right, now!" Charlie was visibly pleased. "I'm sorry again for that bit back there. It was dumb. Why couldn't women have had input into Stonehenge? Preagricultural societies had less gender stratification, and a woman's cycle would certainly have appeared mystical to a people without an understanding of anatomy. Maybe you are right about what the henge was built to represent. What do I know?"

"Sounds like we'll have a better idea once we get inside," Salem said.

"Certainly." A new wave of Stonehenge arcana spilled from his mouth, stories of the explorers who'd discovered the stone, the men who'd come to measure it. The more he talked, the more Salem moved from her shame and toward a hunch. There *was* something inherently feminine about the site. Having Charlie laugh at the possibility had strengthened her belief in it.

They boarded the tram that would deliver them to the visitor center, Charlie still talking. She studied the monument as they pulled away.

The feminine wasn't obvious, but it was whispered in the way the stones rode the land and seemed to interact with the curves of the hill and the stain of the poppies. She felt it somewhere low in her hips, but her brain wouldn't let her *see* it. It was programmed for data, facts, and codes.

"Here's the plan," Salem said, interrupting Charlie. She kept her voice pitched low even though their fellow passengers appeared deep in conversation. "With the Beale train, the codes were hidden by women throughout history. We're going to look for the same thing here, for any evidence of women being connected to Stonehenge, and we're going to follow it no matter how stupid it seems."

"Salem." Charlie stopped her by squeezing her shoulder. "I don't think the feminine is stupid. I—" He glanced around, studying their fellow passengers. He must have seen something he didn't like because he dropped his arm and shifted the conversation.

"You tell me what to do," he finished. "I swear I'll do it, no questions asked. Let's find your girl."

CHAPTER 23

Stonehenge Visitor Center

They waded through a cluster of thatch-roofed Neolithic houses, each of them designed to replicate the homes the Stonehenge workers would have occupied. They were single-room dwellings with chalk walls, the interior rimmed with wood and woven furniture, a firepit in the center.

Real-life children ran in and out of the replica village, giggling, chasing each other toward an enormous stone tilted on its side. Its placard declared it the size and weight of one of the original sarsen stones. It had a rope embedded on one end.

No one could move it.

A towheaded girl was hopping beside the stone, a raggedy bunny doll clutched in one hand. She reminded Salem of Mercy, which brought a wave of grief that felt like a gut punch.

Salem forced her attention away, striding past the stone and through the sleek metal poles of the visitor center. The structure was steel and glass, but cleverly constructed to blend seamlessly into the English countryside. The gift shop to her right had a line snaking out the door. The museum to the left required tickets, but Charlie flashed identification to the guard, and they were immediately ushered inside.

The museum's interior was dark and crowded. Salem kept to the periphery, her eyes scanning the bones and blades under glass, the landscape murals behind them, the interpretive signs all around. An informative lecture played on a background loop.

She'd known since she was young that she saw the world differently than most kids. Where her classmates would charge the playground at recess and fight over the swing set, Salem would study the ground, searching for patterns. It had soothed her even back then.

The jungle gym was a tetrahedron.

In winter, she could spend hours studying the sixfold symmetry of snowflakes.

In summer, she'd search out the Fibonacci petals of a black-eyed Susan and drift into its endless possibilities. Or she'd duck into a shady spot and search out ferns, counting the fractal pattern, thrilled if it was pinnate beyond four.

When her mother introduced her to patterns in code—starting with simple substitution ciphers and working toward more complex sequences—Salem realized she'd finally found her world, the place where she wasn't an odd duck and where everything could be broken down into mathematically precise logic.

She'd been excited to discover how many women had been pivotal in the development of computers. Jean Jennings Bartik was one of six women who created programs for ENIAC, the first electronic general computer, in the 1940s. A decade later, Grace Hopper led the creation of COBOL, the original widely used computer programming language. Computer science had been built on the work of women, who in the early years entered through the field of mathematics.

But it wasn't just that it was a field that accepted women. With computers, Salem felt like she was home.

Bel had always made her feel loved—beautiful Bel, who was as kind as she was popular—but computers introduced Salem to a world where she could *fly*.

Her pattern-finding gift grew rusty, lazy even, once she hit her teens. Her talent became almost exclusively focused on computers. That changed when she was forced to crack the Beale Cipher.

She needed to call on that latent skill again.

Charlie disappeared and then returned to her side, guiding her toward another room. "I asked a docent. The recreation of the henge through all its iterations is back here. Maybe we'll see something in there?"

Salem nodded. "When was the last time you were on-site?"

"Maybe five years ago. It's grand, isn't it?"

Salem nodded, studying the artifacts in the room as they made their way to the next. The stone implements used by the workers on-site thousands of years ago didn't seem helpful. The plaque sharing the Stonehenge worker diet—pig, whose charred foot bones suggested they were cooked over an open flame, sloe and blackberries, hazelnuts and honey—was worthless. Same with the pottery shards, the stone axe heads, and the recreation of Neolithic man, which reminded Salem of a young and confused Charlton Heston.

She dismissed each of these bits of information as irrelevant, but the truth was, Salem could be staring right at a clue and have no idea. Her heart sank with the realization. She couldn't do this without Bel.

She probably couldn't do it even *with* Bel.

"Hey." Charlie was at her side, looking concerned. "You okay?"

Salem's voice was high-pitched. Her Ativan was wearing off. "I'm worried I can't do this. Not alone."

A woman standing next to Salem tossed a worried glance her way. She must have spoken louder than she'd thought.

Charlie smiled, transforming his features, softening him. Salem realized that her guess back at the Mayflower had been spot on; he was not even ten years older than her. "But you're *not* alone. I'm here with you. This failure lands squarely on both our shoulders, should it come to that. Same with a success, you know. We share what we find."

Salem drew a ragged breath. He was right. It didn't matter what she thought she was or was not capable of. Besides, she had more Ativan in the car. "Is this the model the docent told you about?"

They were standing in front of a reproduction of the original Stonehenge, all ninety-six stones in the definitive circle, erected around 3000 BC. They stared down at it. Unlike the actual stones outside, these lacked the graffiti and the pitting. Salem was disappointed to confirm that Charlie had been right—the full model contained the stone that she'd seen in Muirinn Molony's tiny Stonehenge, only in this version, nothing was carved on it.

It was merely Stone 28.

The word carved in Mrs. Molony's version had made the stone seem more prominent, causing the trick of the eyes that made Salem see a way to mark a woman's cycle where the rest of the world saw a stone circle.

Charlie spoke firmly. "We can do this. We're looking for a simple code. What was the timeline of the Beale Cipher, the 1800s? Probably that would be the latest the code was placed here, more likely earlier, but in any case, pre-computer as we know it. Something basic, maybe akin to a Morse code, or along the lines of a Playfair Cipher? Or if it was put here by the Neolithics—and I can't see how that would be—it would . . ."

But Salem wasn't listening. She wasn't even breathing.

His word—*pre-computer*—had shaken loose what she should have noticed all along.

She saw it, clear as a clarion, and her mind was exploding with the realization.

She wasn't looking for a code *in* something. Stonehenge itself was the code.

❖

Jason watched her dispassionately.

She'd cracked it. He could see it in her eyes. He knew no one else had been able to, guessed the Grimalkin would be livid that Wiley had done it so quickly. That planted a small smile on his face, one that didn't mar the bland mien he'd cultivated, his appearance rendered even less remarkable by a pair of round-rimmed glasses and a baseball cap.

She turned to Agent Charlie Thackeray, hands shaking as she pointed at the replica of Stonehenge. Thackeray hooted, lifted her up in the air, then set her back down before turning on his heel toward one of the guards, likely to acquire a private room so they could verify whatever Wiley had discovered. The genius cryptanalyst turned back to the replica, visibly trembling with her discovery. Her fingers twitched at the zipper of her portable computer.

Jason wondered briefly what it would be like to possess a mind like hers.

He returned his attention to the pig teeth he'd been pretending to study, his heartbeat drumming pleasantly. The plaque said that deterioration suggested the pigs had been fed honey until they were harvested at nine months old for an apparent feast. He imagined they were delicious.

He slid his cell phone out of his pocket, his thumb dialing as he brought it his ear. "She's got it."

There was an intake of breath, small and sharp, followed by a moment of silence. Finally: "Call the Grimalkin."

Jason's second call was a hair longer. The Grimalkin spoke first. "You're calling because she's broken the first wall of the Stonehenge train."

"Yes."

Jason thought he heard wheezing close to the phone, the hum of a crowd behind. He realized it was the Grimalkin laughing.

"She's going to Blessington next, count on it, to finish what the old witch started for her there." The Grimalkin sounded happy, which disappointed Jason. The assassin must have already cracked this part of the code.

The Grimalkin continued. "I'll see you at the Dublin Airport. I can't wait to see her face right before I kill her."

Jason hung up.

The Grimalkin knew Jason would follow his orders. There was nothing more to say.

CHAPTER 24

Stonehenge

Binary, a deceptively simple word, originated in the fifteenth century. It meant *dual*, or *a pair*. A light switch is a binary system because it consists of two options: on or off.

A question that can be answered true or false is binary. Black and white are binary colors.

But when most people think of *binary*, none of that comes to mind. What we think of are computers, which run the most complex of data using a binary system of ones and zeros.

In 1679, Gottfried Leibniz invented what modern humans know as the binary system. Leibniz was looking for a way to organize verbal logic into mathematics. It turned out that ones and zeros were the bridge. His breakthrough was popularly credited to his Christian search to represent the concept of *creatio ex nihilo*: out of nothing, creation.

Less well known was his true inspiration: the *I Ching*.

The *I Ching* was a Chinese divination text dating to 1000 BC. The manuscript contained collected wisdom examining the ultimate binary choice—chaos or order—and created a method for seeking guidance on the most complex and philosophical of questions. Consulting the *I Ching* was so effective that it was used throughout history to answer questions of state, warfare, money, and love.

The first step of the method was to frame a focused question. Next, the seeker threw a bundle of yarrow sticks into the air and read how they landed. They could fall as either a broken line or an unbroken line, thereby, at their most basic reading, becoming the oldest known use of binary data.

At least, that's what historians had believed.

What Salem was looking at would shred that theory. Stonehenge had been built at least 1,500 years earlier than that. Her mouth was dry, her senses heightened.

Stonehenge was a binary code.

The circles, and there were two—the outer and the inner—were the zeros.

The stones were the ones.

The ASCII, or American Standard Code for Information Interchange, had assigned binary numbers to the letters of the alphabet. Lowercase *a* was 1100001, for example. The builders of Stonehenge wouldn't have used the same categorization, would not have even spoken English, a language that didn't emerge in its earliest form until at least 550 CE. They would have their own language and code keys, but once Salem saw it, it was impossible to deny the binary nature of Stonehenge.

Charlie had seen it as soon as she'd pointed it out.

Neolithic humans had sent them a message in the most ancient of codes.

He'd whooped, then run off to secure them this private room, some administrator's cloistered office with a desktop computer he could use while Salem field-tested GAEA for the second time that day. "I need you to find all the various iterations of the monument," Salem said, unaware she was taking the lead. Her fingers were a blur of typing. "Include all possible variables: the Heel Stone, the wooden posts that could have been here, counting the trilithons as a single stone as well as three, everything."

"I'll send them to you when I get them." Charlie was already firing up the desktop, circumventing the administrator's password as easily as if it were a tissue-paper wall. His cheeks were flushed. The excitement in the room was ionized.

"No!" Salem said, pausing. "Put it on this jump drive. We don't have time to encrypt it, and I don't want it accessible in the ether."

"Of course. How foolish of me."

Salem nodded and dug back into her work. She'd been disappointed to not have the time to expand on her quantum computing breakthrough, now more than ever. Every computer system running used the same binary system as the first computer invented. Quantum computing, once a reality, would be based in qubits, which were the ones and zeros of the binary system on steroids. They operated as a one or a zero, but through the quantum physics principles of entanglement and superposition, those ones and zeros could swap their identity. They could also do more than be on or off. They could be up, down, in, out.

If Salem had access to quantum hardware, she could quickly create a sophisticated algorithm that could access any document ever uploaded that contained the word *Stonehenge*, collate all visual and written records of the stones throughout the millennia, and look for any patterns that would break the binary keytext of Stonehenge.

It would take less than a second with a fully realized quantum computer. Salem could only guess at how long the B&C would take.

Charlie ran the jump drive to her. "They're all here."

"Good work! That was quick." She plugged it into her USB port, feeding Charlie's data to baby GAEA.

They peered at the screen, not unlike how ancient people must have stared at their campfires.

The administrator's wall clock ticked audibly. How did she get any work done with such a loud noise?

"Is GAEA up for the task?" Charlie asked.

A rose bloomed on Salem's screen by way of answer, hitching her chest. She really would have to come up with a better image. "That means she's ready."

Charlie glanced at his wristwatch. "Thirty-four seconds. Pretty goddamned impressive."

"We'll see." Salem bit her lip. She tapped the "Enter" button. "I asked her to run your Stonehenge data against any she found on the internet—sorry, she's fast—and collate it into all possible binary constructions and then translate that into the languages most likely spoken by the Neolithic people, and then translate any recognizable words from that into English. She may come up with several possibilities."

A single word appeared on the screen, centered, 12-point Arial typeface.

Second

Charlie and Salem tipped their heads to the left, identical quizzical expressions on their faces.

Charlie spoke first. "Well, fuck me."

Salem glanced over at him. "Yeah," she said. "There must be more."

She keyed in some commands. This result took half the time but was identical.

Second

"What's that mean?" Charlie asked. "Second?"

Panic was brushing the edge of Salem's view. She would not give in to it. "I don't know. But I know someone who might."

CHAPTER 25

Stonehenge

"GAEA confirmed that the language of Stonehenge was Proto-Indo-European, which is what Agent Curson told me," Salem said.

They'd packed up their evidence and hoofed it to the car, buzzed from their discovery.

"Makes sense." Charlie opened the trunk for her.

She tossed the B&C inside and opened the passenger door. "Blessington's a long shot."

He slammed the trunk closed and offered her a lopsided smile. "It's all we've got. Besides, it's a nice day to fly to Ireland."

Salem nodded, but something was bothering her. A faint but persistent prickling at the base of her neck, her instincts telling her to do something that seemed unnecessary. "Hey, I have to run back to the bathroom. Is there time?"

He'd already slid into the driver's seat. He nodded, completely involved with his phone. She assumed he was calling in favors to book a flight.

She did need to use the bathroom, but that wasn't why she ran back. She dashed into the gift shop and grabbed the first envelope and greeting card she saw, featuring a photo of the sun setting across Stonehenge. The line took forever, packed with sticky children and exhausted travelers. She wrote her name and the Campus as the return address as she inched forward, sneaking furtive glances toward the parking lot. She'd been gone too long. Charlie would worry.

Finally, she was at the front. She threw down her cash and walked away, not waiting for the change. She slid the jump drive inside the envelope, the one she'd made as backup while GAEA ran the Stonehenge numbers. She was licking the envelope when she remembered she didn't have any stamps. Her eyes and cheeks grew hot. She couldn't wait in line again. There wasn't time.

She budged to the front, feeling like the worst human being ever. She looked away from the scowls. "I'm sorry," she said to the cashier. "I just bought this card but forgot stamps."

"Sorry, love," the woman said. "We don't sell postage."

Salem's body grew heavy. It wasn't that she didn't trust Charlie. A scientist always backed up her research, that was all. She didn't know what *second* meant, but she knew it was too big to die with her should something happen to her and Charlie. But who could she trust? Even if she had postage, she couldn't send this to her mom, or the president, and it was too risky to send it overseas to Bel.

"Hey, you're still here! Any better luck?"

Salem squeaked, she was so startled. She turned to the security guard who'd recommended they check out the visitor center.

"Not really," Salem said, feeling bad about the lie. The woman's face was so lovely and open. So much so that it gave Salem an idea. "You said you're taking the train back to London?"

"Yep! All the way to Piccadilly Station."

Salem dug in her purse and yanked out a twenty-pound note. "I have a favor to ask. Can you drop this off at Parliament for me?" She scribbled a name on the front. "They'll know who to get it to."

The woman smiled at her, puzzled. "Stamps wouldn't cost you as much."

"They don't sell them here."

"Ah." The woman didn't take the bill but did take the envelope. "I was going to eat near Parliament tonight anyways."

Salem knew the woman was being kind. She'd seen only one restaurant near Parliament, and it catered to tourists. "Thank you," she said, gratitude etched on her face.

"It's not a thing. I hope you find what you're looking for." The guard pointed over Salem's shoulder. "Oh, and here's your chap coming back."

Salem swiveled just in time to witness Charlie walking toward the glass wall of the gift shop. Her chest tightened. She'd need to tell another lie. She thanked the guard one more time and charged out to him.

They left immediately.

They were ten minutes from Stonehenge when Salem realized she still had to go to the bathroom.

CHAPTER 26

Dublin Airport

Clancy pretended to read the spy novel, which was what he had legitimately been doing moments earlier. The book was pure crap. It made an agent's life seem glamorous when in fact it was mostly being on stakeout, pissing into a jar, holding your shit until it went wherever a shit went when you did not take it, and if you were super unlucky, fucking up an assassination bad enough that you had to spend the rest of your life in exile.

But maybe it wasn't bad luck. Maybe it was a self-destructive streak.

There was no other explanation for why he was sitting in the Dublin Airport when Vit Linder had been clear that Clancy was to stay in London until the assassination was complete, and that the killings must happen on the twenty-third, right before Hayes signed the accord. Striking her down then would send a warning about what would happen to those who opposed industry. It would terrorize the leaders and send a righteous message to the masses already bored with the topic of climate change and who wanted cheap gas and inexpensive clothes without the guilt. The timing of the assassinations was meant for them. A war won in the mind was much cheaper than one fought on land.

The timing was important to the Order, and it was why they wanted him to stay in London, close to the action, poised to pivot if necessary. If they knew he was in Dublin, they'd have him finished off, no question.

But here was a truth he couldn't dodge any longer: they were going to kill him no matter what. He'd hung on to that Caribbean escape fantasy for as long as he could, longer than he should have. It tasted so good. But under the imaginary sombrero, he was a sensible man. Once he'd taken out the president and vice president, there was not a single reason to let him live and ten good ones to off him.

So, he figured, might as well sate his curiosity.

Specifically, he wanted to know what Salem Wiley was up to.

That kid.

When he'd first tailed her in the Minneapolis Institute of Art, he'd pegged her as either the kind to break and shatter on impact, a grenade taking down those near her, or one of those rare birds who had steel hidden below the feathers. Damn if he hadn't discovered she was composed of pure metal, brain and body, although the way she carried herself made it difficult to see.

She must know by now that the Order had kidnapped Mercy Mayfair, a move that Clancy did not truck with. It shouldn't have mattered because it wasn't his fight, but still.

The curiosity.

It wasn't so much Clancy's fault. Linder was the one who'd dropped Wiley's name in his single phone call with Clancy. He'd done it "by accident," trying to gauge what reaction it would evoke from Clancy, that much had been clear.

The Grimalkin has been assigned to Salem Wiley . . . oh! Wrong file.

The guy was a Jerry Lewis pratfall of a human being. Clancy had known that before Linder's phone call. The man had a reputation and a nickname in the intelligence community. In fact, it'd been all Clancy could do to bite back those three words when the Speaker of the House introduced himself: *You mean One-Ball?*

Clancy had read Linder's file, as he assumed most FBI and CIA agents at the upper levels had. Anybody who was a leader, or rich, or famous had a similar collection of intelligence gathered on them. What made Linder's file stand out, at least in watercooler discussions, was the video of Linder in his room at the Moscow Four Seasons twelve years earlier.

Linder's recorded behavior fell more on the Newt Gingrich than the Fatty Arbuckle side of the sexual impropriety scale. In fact, it would not have stood out if not for his diaper fetish. Watch a video of a man born with one testicle begging to get his nappy changed by a Russian thug he'd paid to call daddy, and it stuck with you.

Nothing illegal, but damn memorable just the same.

It was safe to assume that the Russians possessed a similar tape. The Kremlin collected kompromat like fish breathed water. When Linder, to everyone's surprise, was elected to the House, and then, slap Clancy's ass and call him granny, became the Speaker of the House, that tape was trotted out again. At least by the FBI. Clancy had last watched it maybe four years ago, recently enough for it to immediately come to mind when Linder called him on the Order's dedicated phone.

Tell me you love me, Daddy!

Clancy wondered if the video could be leaked online. He'd been wondering about a lot of things since talking to Linder, because despite his apparent buffoonery, Linder's ploy had worked, in a way. He'd gotten into Clancy's head. Besides Wiley, Clancy couldn't stop thinking about the Grimalkin, who, if half the legends were true, made Satan look like a middle-aged cruise director. And once Clancy had Wiley on his mind, he'd wanted to see her. And not like he'd seen her walking into Parliament from his perch in that ridiculous Ferris wheel.

No, he wanted to know what she was *up to.*

Wherever that kid went, it was sure to be interesting.

He'd gone to her mom's hotel—talk about another piece of work, that woman—and scoped it. That's how he'd seen Jason leave with the girl. Turned his stomach. Next, Clancy motored over to the Campus, where he spotted Wiley leave with the MI5 guy, looking like she'd been forced to eat her own stomach with a knife and a spoon. Clancy had tailed their car until it was clear they were going to Stonehenge.

He'd turned off to avoid detection. No telling how good the MI5 agent was, not this early in the tail. An hour later he located their empty car in the private lot, picked the lock, and dropped in a bug.

Next stop? The airport for some shut-eye. It was a guess, but a smart one because it put him ahead of them if they were leaving the country and near them if they were returning to London. When his bug caught them discussing that they were going to Blessington, he chartered a puddle jumper to the Dublin Airport, and voilà, here he was.

They'd landed twelve minutes ago, walked in front of him six minutes after that.

He'd let them go.

It was a hunch, and one that played out.

Ho-leee shit. He hadn't planned for this. Lucan Stone was striding across the Dublin Airport. No way could he have flown in the same plane as Salem and the Brit. He appeared to have been waiting for them, which was interesting. They hadn't called their destination in to the London Bureau, at least not after they'd returned to the car.

Clancy guessed Lucan would only go as far as the airport's front doors. A Black man blended in rural Ireland like coal in snow. Shame, that. Unfair for a gifted agent to be hobbled by something he couldn't change, but that was life.

Stone walked out of sight, a few women turning to watch him go. He was a handsome man, no doubt. Probably a double agent, too, but Clancy wasn't in a position to judge.

He'd been about to return to his book when Jason separated from the magazine rack across the way. Clancy recognized the man's eyes even though the shape of his face had changed. He'd lost sleep thinking about those eyes. Worse than being so close to him was the fact that Jason made Clancy immediately. His gaze connected with Clancy's, flashing neither hope or threat, only icy recognition.

Clancy peed himself a little bit.

He'd told himself since Rome that he'd commit hara-kiri if it ever got to the point that he needed adult diapers, but decided on the spot that he would not count Jason-based incidents.

His ears buzzed as a happy thought occurred to him. If, as Linder had said, the Grimalkin was on Wiley, and both Jason and Wiley had just passed through this airport, then the Grimalkin must be working with Jason.

The Grimalkin was here.

Hot damn, Clancy might be the first agent to positively ID the legendary assassin. He squinted into the crowds; preternaturally relaxed Irish in their pointy-toed shoes blended with harried, moonfaced tourists and suited business travelers. He needed to pick out someone not quite right, a person whose gaze lingered too long, a man who appeared to be following Jason.

He kept it up for nearly ten minutes. For nine minutes and fifty seconds of that, he knew it was a fool's errand. Someone of the Grimalkin's caliber would not be made so easily.

Clancy put his book back up to his face. Bullshit spy novel.

CHAPTER 27

The Road to Blessington, Ireland

They'd navigated the hectic area around the Dublin Airport and were entering the more scenic countryside. Salem's skin felt tight, her heartbeat light and fast in a way the Ativan hadn't been able to soothe, but the near gray of the clouds comforted her like a blanket. There was relief in returning to Ireland's close skies, its smell of wet woodsmoke, the fairyland green of the hills unfurling toward her like a welcome mat.

She flipped the B&C open, tethering it as she'd done on the journey to Stonehenge.

Charlie was wiggling in his seat. "The historical implications of this discovery are staggering. How will this affect the field of cryptography? Archaeology? Anthropology?"

He'd started to talk about Stonehenge a dozen times on the plane ride, stopping himself as he realized they could be overheard. He'd swallowed each question before fully offering it to Salem, let them gurgle in his belly as they walked through the airport, coughing to keep from burping them as they filled out the car rental paperwork.

They spewed forth once they slipped inside the Lilliputian Nissan Versa.

"Who'll believe Bronze Age builders created a binary code that withstood the ravages of time?"

Salem was only half listening. Questions drove research, but she had plenty of her own. She needed answers. The Wi-Fi signal came through immediately. All four bars. Salem pulled up a search engine, fighting against the contagion of Charlie's childlike enthusiasm. For all her fears for Mercy, she felt a thrill growing. Solving a puzzle had always done that for her. "You and me, for starters, and that's all I'm worried about right now."

He bent his head toward her screen. "What're you after?"

Such a good question. When she blinked, the whole of the internet unfurled itself against the back of her eyelids: loops and swirls, locked doors, long hallways, data that could reach to the moon and back a thousand times over, answers to questions she'd never even thought to ask, mysteries created and solved in black holes that collapsed on themselves. "Anything. Everything. There must be more to this than what we're seeing. There is no way Stonehenge is nothing more than the world's largest, sturdiest Post-it note, you know?"

Charlie laughed. It was the first time she'd heard it. The sound was sweet, a little high and breathy, like a mouse caught off guard. "She jokes! I wasn't sure if you had a sense of humor." He collected himself. "In all seriousness, your point is excellent. We can't get too married to the first clue we've found."

"Exactly." Salem pushed her hair behind her ears. "We need to find out if Stonehenge served dual purposes and, if so, what they were. Regardless of that, we need to dig until we know exactly who created the binary-based message, and who its intended audience was."

"Spend your time researching the people who built it and who came to it, because I've got all the stonework information you'll need on Stonehenge up here." Charlie tapped his skull and then pointed to the dash-mounted GPS. "Satnav says we have forty-five minutes to your Mrs. Molony's house. Do your worst."

He didn't need to tell her twice. Like Mozart at a piano, she dived in, tapping out search terms, backing off when they offered the gentle pushback of a bottomless dead end, following up ruthlessly when the points of information began to connect, to hum with the unique frequency of pattern, a Fibonacci-esque orchestra of meaning and purpose that appeared as coincidence to the untrained eye.

A twinge of doubt stained the thrill of pursuit: Had her mother not necessarily molded her to be the Underground's code breaker, but rather observed and nurtured a natural talent? That thought triggered a memory. In it, Salem was twelve.

A self-defense instructor had been invited to their home. It was the second time such a thing had happened. The first time, it had been a judo instructor brought into the Wiley household to train both Bel and Salem. It was strange how normal such a thing had felt, but then, Grace and Vida were always doing stuff like that for their girls: dance classes, first-aid training, dragging Bel and Salem to community ed knot tying or immersion Spanish workshops at the local high school after hours.

Salem wouldn't even have questioned the close-quarters self-defense instructor coming into their home for a private lesson except for Bel's absence.

"Bel would love this," Salem had said. "She'd think it was supercool."

Vida and Daniel had exchanged a look. They could pass so much to each other without using words. Salem understood that's how it worked when you married someone. You learned to read their mind. Salem could do that with Bel. She knew how good it felt.

Vida must have won the eye-wrestle because she spoke. "Bel doesn't need this class. She's too advanced."

Salem felt her face crumble into her turtleneck sweater. Of course Bel didn't need another self-defense class. She was beautiful and strong and smart and perfect, and Salem was holding her back. Their parents had had the girls take fewer and fewer classes together. Even with the judo instructor, Bel had ended up teaching him something by the end of the session. She was a physical genius. Salem was a computer nerd, not good for much if the electricity went out.

Daniel must have seen her expression. "Honey, we all have our strengths. Bel is good at sports, strength, and speed. Your gift is in your noggin." He'd tapped his head.

"Then why do I need this class?" The instructor was supposed to arrive any moment. How gross would it be to wrestle with a stranger in your living room with your parents watching? Grody gross.

Vida had scowled. "Because you're a girl." She said *girl* like it was a dirty word. That was confusing. Vida was famous for her support of women's rights, and didn't all women start as girls? Daniel reached for Vida, but she pulled away. A gray shadow had fallen over her face. Salem had seen it there before, mostly when her mom had that third glass of wine, or on the rare times when Daniel had to travel without her and she had to sleep alone.

"You know what, Salem?" Vida continued, that gray shadow pinching her mouth. "Even if you get all the training in the world, you still might not be able to stop them. They might steal your most precious center, take it without a second thought, as if it wasn't even yours to begin with."

"Vida!"

Salem had never heard her father use that tone. It was clear they were talking about something else, and it was terrifying. Salem began to cry.

"That'll get you nowhere," Vida had said, even as Daniel led her away. "It's better you learn that in this world, girls don't get to play."

The instructor had shown up, and Salem had worked so hard to do everything right. Her mom didn't come out for supper that night. Daniel said he was tired and went to bed early. When Salem leaned her ear against the painted wood of their bedroom door, she heard her mother crying softly, and Daniel whispering soothing words.

Salem wiped away the memory and the blotch of uncertainty it brought with it—what had happened to make her mom like she was?—as best she could. It didn't matter if she'd always had an inclination toward mathematics and logic; it gave her mother no right to conceal her connection to the Underground. She should have told Salem about it.

GAEA offered a rosebud, her signal that she'd collected data that could be something or nothing. When Salem clicked on it, she was surprised to see it was an earlier line that she'd cast, the one looking into the bombing outside Parliament.

Across the World Wide Web, GAEA had found only two servers sourcing any reliable data connected to the bomb, and maybe not even that. One server was housed in Moscow, the other in London, and they'd shared a message that contained the exact day and time of the bombing embedded in what appeared to be an innocuous business email. It was likely only coincidence, but Salem sicced GAEA on both servers just the same, creating an algorithm that would scour those two servers for anything else that might shed a light on who was behind the bombing.

Then she refocused on her Stonehenge search. As a computer scientist, she had automatically laid her hunches to the side. Fears and feelings could not be allowed to steer her work. If there was no evidence to indicate Stonehenge was grounded in the feminine, it would be a waste of time to research based on the subjective sense that women and Stonehenge were inextricably linked, even if she'd been unable to shake that feeling since being introduced to Mrs. Molony's unearthed replica.

Did the fact that Vida saw everything bad that happened—political, local, global, environmental, getting cut off in traffic—as a conspiracy against women affect Salem's decision to put aside her hunch? Didn't matter. Science was science.

After cross-referencing multiple sites, Salem established that the English Heritage site contained the most comprehensive Stonehenge research. The data they presented posited that the Heel Stone may have been the earliest component of Stonehenge, followed by a circular ditch. Inside the ditch were the Aubrey Holes. As Charlie had said, the Aubrey Holes had held timber and possibly stone, an earlier but similar version of Stonehenge that was lost to the ages. Cremated remains were deposited in the Aubrey Holes, one per hole, enough remains to qualify Stonehenge as the largest known Neolithic cemetery in the British Isles.

Five hundred years after the digging of the ditch and the creation of the timber-based monument and graveyard, the enormous sarsens and smaller bluestones that still stood today were brought in. They were erected in a vaguely similar pattern, the sarsen stones following the circle pattern of the Aubrey Holes but also erected in a horseshoe shape in the center. The bluestones were placed between the sarsens. As she read this research, Salem fought the urge to glance at Charlie, who was vibrating in his seat. It felt like a small betrayal to look up this information rather than simply ask him. After all, he'd been the one who first told her about the holes.

Still, science.

She had to be sure for herself.

Three hundred years after the sarsens and bluestones were brought in, the bluestones were rearranged to form an oval and a road was built between the structure and the River Avon. That formation had produced the code they'd cracked today. Around the same time, barrows—burial mounds for the respected and wealthy—began appearing immediately next to Stonehenge or on hills within view of Stonehenge, indicating that Stonehenge had been considered either a holy place or an homage to the powerful. Also, celebrations drawing as many as four thousand people began, the festivals occurring at midsummer and midwinter every year.

Salem felt the warm and familiar tingle that sparked when she located the beginning of a thread she was trying to unravel. Stonehenge had been a gathering place for the Neolithic leaders. They had ordered its creation through whatever means available, and they gathered twice annually on constellation-based dates.

Who were these exalted leaders? Knowing that would help Salem to understand who had orchestrated the code and, potentially, their reasons for using it. The loudest hits on Stonehenge and Stonehenge-adjacent burials came back from a hundred years or so after the construction period of Stonehenge as they now knew it. These discoveries included the burial mound of the "Amesbury Archer" along with other males interred with pottery, amber, gold, and flint, which would have represented great wealth at the time. More interesting were the oxygen isotope analyses proving that the powerful people buried at Stonehenge had traveled from all over what was today known as Europe as well as western Asia and northern Africa, again, as Charlie had said.

Salem programmed GAEA to gather all research related to Stonehenge, stack it all on top of each other, collate and dismiss any repetitive information, and create a separate document of the outliers. A minute after she ran it, Salem found herself looking at something unusual, something unsettling. "Oh my god."

"What?"

Salem jumped in her seat. She'd forgotten Charlie and the rest of the world were here. She was looking at whispers—a bone fragment discovered here or there, articles peppered around the internet rather than one cohesive document—but they all said the same thing: the bodies cremated or buried at Stonehenge immediately before, during, and after the construction of the monument that had produced *second* were women.

"Stonehenge research from 2300 BC, which is when the version of the monument that we saw in the visitor center was created." Salem instinctually turned the laptop screen toward him, even though he couldn't study it while he drove. "Did you know that mostly women were buried there at that time?"

He smiled, a quiet, soft gesture. "What do you think it means?"

"Something inconceivable," she said.

"Yet your hypothesis is . . . ?" he gently prodded.

There was only one explanation.

"That four thousand years ago, women held the power."

CHAPTER 28

Blessington, Ireland

Salem tugged a hair tie from her wrist and wrapped it around her tumultuous curls, an unconscious gesture that appeared whenever she was wrestling with two puzzle pieces that needed to fit together but were resisting. "But that makes no sense. Archaeologists would be all over this if it were true."

Charlie's lack of response caused her to pause her research. He was clenching his jaw so tight that his skin had gone white around his ears.

"What is it?" Salem asked.

"Are you familiar with the Birka, Sweden, Viking grave? Bj 581?"

Salem shook her head. "No."

"Find it." His voice was low, intense.

She obliged. The article she found had been published two short weeks earlier.

"I'll save you the trouble," he said. "History tells us that warriors and leaders were always men. Stories of powerful women have been whispered or sung, tales of Valkyrie and Amazons, but they were always dismissed as mythology. This bias has shaped everything we know about the past, has influenced what archaeologists choose to see or not even look for."

Salem couldn't help but think of her Stonehenge hunch.

Charlie continued. "So, when a grave is discovered and searched, and it's found to house the tools of war or, even more telling, evidence of leadership, the unquestioned assumption is that the skeleton is male. Bj 581 was no exception. Inside the grave, archaeologists found the remains of one human, two horses, swords, armor-piercing arrows, an axe, a battle knife, two shields, and strategy pieces used to plan combat. Obviously, they'd stumbled upon the chamber-grave of a powerful— and so, *male*—tenth-century Viking general."

He wrinkled his nose. "Except they were wrong. A few years ago, a female osteologist was studying the bones for unrelated reasons when she noticed their feminine characteristics. An osteological test proved they were female."

He signaled an upcoming turn, his words heavy in the car. "Think about that. How many other beliefs about the roles of men and women do we have completely wrong?"

Salem was researching as he spoke, corroborating his words within seconds of their leaving his mouth. "How do you know so much about this?"

Charlie's expression hooded. "I have a fascination with women's history." He glanced at her as if he wanted to say more, but then stared back at the road. Night was falling. The traffic had been thick leaving Dublin, but as they neared Blessington, they saw more horses than cars on the road. The world was slowing down the deeper into Ireland's hidden places they drove.

Salem let it go. He'd tell her more when and if he was ready, as he'd done when he revealed that his father had been a stonemason. "Will we get into trouble for flying to Ireland without permission?"

"I have some clout," Charlie said, his mouth set in a grim line. "I am cashing it all in to buy us two days to follow a lead. Told your man Bench that it was related to the president's safety on top of the girl's, in case he was up for arguing."

Salem had filled Charlie in on Muirinn Molony and her belief that the Stonehenge replica was tied to an assassination plan. "Do you think it is?"

"Who knows what to think anymore?"

Just then their attention was drawn to the console between them, where Salem's phone had been resting, the B&C sucking Wi-Fi off it like a tick. It was suddenly lit up.

"You're getting a call," Charlie said unnecessarily.

Bel's face lit up the screen, her photo smiling, untroubled, worlds away from the emotions she was certainly feeling as she called Salem from across the ocean. Salem's stomach lurched. Bel had to be calling about Mercy.

"Is that Isabel Odegaard?"

Salem's pulse flared, suspicions about Charlie surfacing before she remembered the reluctant fame that she and Bel had acquired. Their faces had been plastered all over the news after Bel had thwarted the assassination attempt on Gina Hayes.

"Yeah," Salem said, hitting the button to send the call to voice mail. "I'll get back to her later."

But she wouldn't.

She couldn't bear speaking to Bel until Mercy was safe, even though this wasn't the first time Bel had called or texted. In fact, she'd been reaching out so frequently that Salem had created a folder to route Bel's incoming texts to so she didn't have to read them, to risk seeing Bel's anger and disappointment and pain.

Salem stared out her window at the farms zipping past. Evening had laid its blanket on the ground. The air washing in through the vents smelled different, crisper, the wet of the woodsmoke grown musky, spiked with the cold promise of rain.

"Her house is right up here."

Charlie pulled onto the small patch of gravel in front of Mrs. Molony's cottage, parallel to the stone fence separating her house from the road. Déjà vu tugged at Salem. She'd been here only two days earlier, but it felt like another lifetime.

The house appeared exactly as it had before, cozy in a hobbity way. Salem climbed out of the car and stretched and then hopped out of the way. The dirt parking strip was so narrow that Charlie had to crawl out her door.

"Cute place."

"Yep." Salem studied the house. Something cold twisted in her gut. She sniffed the air. Manure and night. Traffic coasted far off, and nearer, a chicken *bawked*, probably in search of a safe spot to roost.

"What is it?" Charlie asked.

Salem pointed at the chimney. "No smoke coming out. And no lights inside."

"Maybe she's run to town," Charlie said, but he removed his gun from its holster.

"Maybe." A frown line formed between Salem's eyebrows. Mrs. Molony hadn't struck her as the type who left her house after dark.

She took the lead, walking through the fence's gate and up to the house. She knocked on the heavy wooden door. The noise was sharp.

Rap rap rap.

No answer.

Charlie raised his eyebrows.

Salem shrugged, stepping off the front stoop to peek inside a window.

What she saw inside turned her blood to chalk. Mrs. Molony's orderly home was in complete disarray. The two dining room chairs were toppled. Clothes were strewn everywhere. A cast iron pot was bubbling at the stove, gas flames flickering below it as if Mrs. Molony had been attacked while cooking dinner.

Charlie glanced over her shoulder and saw the same scene. He pounded on the door. "Mrs. Molony, this is Charlie Thackeray. I'm here with Agent Salem Wiley, who you met two days ago. We are going to come in."

He didn't wait for an answer. Gun in his right hand, he reached for the doorknob with his left. It was unlocked. He pushed the door open. "Mrs. Molony, I'm stepping inside now."

Salem followed him into the house, her chest heavy with dread. The small, well-insulated cottage was claustrophobically hot inside, the air redolent with bubbling stew and fresh-baked soda bread. Charlie flicked on the light and cleared the combination kitchen, dining, and living room while Salem walked over to the stove, scouring the shadowy corners for evidence of blood or body.

She reached the cast iron pot and removed the lid. "It hasn't been cooking long enough to burn." She turned off the burner, placing her hand over the mound of brown bread. Still warm.

"I'm going to check the bedroom and the bathroom. You stay here."

Charlie stepped through one of two open doors, likely the bedroom. Salem was staring into the unlit pantry off the kitchen. She thought she was looking at a huge flour sack, but then as her eyes adjusted, she realized it had arms and legs.

And eyes.

Mrs. Molony stepped into the light. "Knew you'd be back. You're a dead ringer for your pa, you know."

CHAPTER 29

Blessington, Ireland

"An off day of housecleaning shouldn't be so severely judged." Mrs. Molony sniffed, filling Charlie's ceramic bowl with a second serving of savory beef stew.

Salem was full but still tempted to ask for another helping. She didn't know when she'd have another chance to eat anything so delicious. Mrs. Molony had sworn the recipe couldn't be easier. Cut up generous chunks of carrots, onions, and celery, heat them up with some oil for a handful of minutes, dredge the beef in flour and salt, and then toss it in the pan with the mirepoix, sautéing until the beef was cooked through. Then in go the potatoes, a bottle of Guinness, a few scoops of tomato paste, and beef stock to fill the pot. Salt as needed.

"Oh, but you have to grow the vegetables yourself and eat it on Irish soil," she'd cackled, when Salem insisted that such a simple recipe couldn't have produced this thick, rich stew, perfect for a chilly Irish night.

Salem had tried not to moan when she took her first bite of buttered bread. "What is this butter?"

"Irish," Charlie answered for Mrs. Molony, holding up his own slice. "Cheers. No one does it better."

Mrs. Molony stopped at the table where her guests were eating, her arms weighted with the clothes she'd picked off the furniture. She claimed they'd been drying about the house, not flung, that the chairs had tipped under the weight of the wet pants on them and she hadn't bothered to lift them up. "Nice words from a Scotsman."

Charlie's face lit up in delighted surprise. "Not many catch that. Me mum's from the Highlands, traveled to southern England as a teenager. Sometimes her burr sneaks in."

"All right, then."

"But the butter," Salem asked, still amazed. "I've never tasted anything like it. It's sweet and salty, creamy. Is this what all Irish butter tastes like?"

"Any worth eating." Mrs. Molony had sat them both down and fed them, refusing to answer questions until they were done eating, insisting it was rude to talk business over dinner. She started a fire in the hearth, calling it a blessing against the coming night, and then picked up while they ate, offering fresh slices of the warm bread.

"Can I help you clean?" Salem asked, deciding against the second bowl of stew.

"You're finished with the meal?"

Salem stared longingly at the pot of butter and half loaf of bread. Curiosity won over gluttony. "Yes, I am. Thank you for a delicious meal. You knew my father?"

"Join me by the fire for some tea. Your lad can join us when he's done with his soup."

Charlie's head was bent over his bowl. It'd take him a few more minutes at least. Salem tried to clear her spot at the table, but Mrs. Molony scolded her.

"Take this, instead," Mrs. Molony said, offering her a steaming mug of smoky tea, waiting to speak until Salem had taken the chair opposite her. "That's all right now."

Mrs. Molony nodded and blew on her own mug of tea. "I wouldn't say that I *knew* Daniel Wiley. Met him only once. He came by to see my stones."

"The ones you showed Salem?" Charlie asked without giving up his spoon.

"Hush with you. You don't talk with your mouth full. There's time for questions when you're done eating." She returned her attention to Salem. "It was the stones I showed you."

Salem realized she liked Mrs. Molony a lot. She did things her own way.

"Your father wasn't the first to come by to see them. He was in the area to see family, that's what he said, and asked about my wee Stonehenge with its mercy stone."

Salem took a sip from her tea and burned her top lip. "You told Agent Curson and I that you'd just recently uncovered your Stonehenge replica."

"'Tis true, in a manner. Your father, before he left, said I should bury the stones and not speak of them until I received the phone call. It came last week. The women I spoke with said it was time to dig the rocks back up and give a call in to the number. Ask for a code breaker, tell them the president's life was at stake. So it's true that I had recently uncovered them." She winked at Salem.

Charlie tipped his bowl to pour the last of it into his mouth and showed it to Mrs. Molony. "Can I come to the fire now, Grandmother?"

Mrs. Molony smiled, revealing her tiny twisted teeth. "Bring your smart mouth with you."

Charlie brought his chair and took the mug of tea Mrs. Molony offered. "Can you back the story up for us, say? All the way to the time you first discovered the stones until today."

"Aye." Mrs. Molony tilted a little forward and then a little back, setting her chair to rocking. "I found the stones just as I told your girl here. I was digging a well next to the grave of my mamó, except it first happened twenty years ago. I brought a neighbor over to show him what I'd discovered. Paddy Walsh was his name, and he's long dead. Paddy told someone, who told someone else, and pretty soon I had visitors, mostly women."

The fire crackle-popped. Salem jumped.

Mrs. Molony laughed. "Paddy saying hi is all. He was a lovely man."

Salem squared her shoulders and waved at the fire. "Pleased to meet you, Paddy."

Mrs. Molony's eyes instantly narrowed. "That's a kindness," she told Salem. "And I'll return it to you with this: Do you know the three signs that someone's a witch?"

Salem went still. "No. What are they?"

Mrs. Molony stopped rocking. "One, she's a woman. Two, she's got a long life. And third? She was born with three nipples."

Salem's eyes widened.

Mrs. Molony let that go on for only a second before she burst out cackling. "That was a joke, lass. Same with me saying the fire sparking was Paddy greeting us. You shouldn't take everything so serious."

Mrs. Molony wiped the mirth from her eyes and started rocking again as she returned to her story. "As I was saying, all the women who visited here were grim as well. Told me the wee Stonehenge were actually a message, that there were ones like it hidden all over the Isles."

"Exactly like yours?" Salem asked, sore at the edges from being the butt of a joke.

"More or less. It wasn't until your father showed that I got more of the story. It works that my mamó was part of the Underground. You know a bit about that?"

Salem nodded, her blood gone still. She moved only her eyes, measuring Charlie for his reaction. Vida had referred to the Order and the Underground when she'd accused Salem in the foyer, but Charlie and Salem had not yet spoken of it.

"I know about it," Charlie finally said.

"Of course you do," Mrs. Molony responded. She didn't elaborate. "And not only was my mamó a member, she was a leader in these parts. It was those leaders who had the wee Stonehenges brought to them. Daniel

Wiley said the others scattered around the Isles are identical to the one my mamó had buried near her."

"It's like a gravestone?"

"More like copies of a key," Mrs. Molony said, jolting Salem. "You probably do the same for all your important locks? One key you keep, the other you give to your friend so you're never locked out of your home."

Salem called up a mental image of Mrs. Molony's Stonehenge. It was identical to the modern layout of Stonehenge, not the original stone shape that they'd gotten the word *second* off. "Is the whole thing the key, or only the word *mercy*?"

Mrs. Molony slapped her knee and chortled. "Your father was right about you! Said you wouldn't waste a second on fluff once you showed up. *Mercy* is the code. But that's tied to Stonehenge, you see. Come with me and I'll show you something."

Both Salem and Charlie stood. Mrs. Molony gestured for Charlie to remain in his seat. "Not you. I need you to keep an eye on the fire. We'll be right back."

Charlie sat without an argument.

Salem felt apprehensive as she followed Mrs. Molony out the front door. The night had gone black, not a single light beyond the cottage, the crescent moon, and the sparkle of stars. For a wild moment Salem imagined that if she could fly to them, they'd taste like Irish butter. She shivered.

"You should really dress for the weather," Mrs. Molony said.

"Do you know what the forecast is for tomorrow?" Salem asked.

"It could be as warm as it can be." Mrs. Molony stopped to grab Salem's hand, hers rough and gnarled. "Don't want you to stumble. We need to walk out back."

Salem didn't question her, still startled by the intimacy of holding hands, reeling from the thought that her father had been here before. "You said my dad was only here for a bit?"

Mrs. Molony stopped in her tracks and cocked her head at Salem. The shifts and shadows of the moon made her look like a raven. "Not long a'tall. He gave me a message for you, though. Said there were forces at work, ones that would break you against ones looking out for you."

Mrs. Molony started walking again, still holding Salem's hand, her humping stride making it difficult to find a rhythm.

"That's all?"

Mrs. Molony laughed. "He said you were impatient—that's the truth. And no, that's not all. Here we are then."

Disappointed, Salem discovered that they were back at the grave. Mrs. Molony had covered the Stonehenge, the fresh-moved dirt catching the starlight differently than the compact ground. Salem had imagined Mrs. Molony might have an actual note from her father for her, not just some more graveside fancy.

"Do you smell it?"

"Excuse me?" Salem asked, her eyes darting toward the grave.

"The roses. Lean over to these and smell them."

Salem inhaled. The smell came to her so strongly that she was amazed she hadn't caught it earlier. She stepped forward and leaned toward the shoulder-high tangle of wild roses. The spicy night air perfectly complemented their sweet perfume. "That's lovely."

"That's thirty-five million years old," Mrs. Molony said firmly.

"What?"

"Roses have been on this planet for thirty-five million years." She indicated the field beyond her stone wall, an inky rolling darkness covering it. "You can't see it, but the same is true of the poppies out there, the mustard, the thrift, thistle and clover, the flowering chamomile. They seem delicate, yet they last, yeah?"

"I suppose." Salem wasn't sure where she was going with it.

Mrs. Molony squeezed Salem's hand. "Same with women. Men build towers and walls. Women plant flowers. You see which stands the test of time."

Salem felt like she was speaking a foreign language. "I don't know what you mean."

Mrs. Molony tapped the sachet at Salem's waist. "Look for the help that's out there, and remember the water, the flowers, and the power of women. That's what your father wanted me to tell you when you came. He even left me a picture, so I'd recognize you when you showed up, if you'd like to see it." She drew a 3 x 5 photograph out of her apron pocket and handed it to Salem.

Salem studied it underneath the sparkling stars, her face puffy with emotion: it was a photo of her and her father. Vida had snapped it the first day of summer break before seventh grade. Her father had taken her and Vida to Sebastian Joe's ice cream parlor near Bde Maka Ska to celebrate. Salem had ordered cinnamon ice cream in a waffle cone. Daniel had ordered Pavarotti in a cup because he claimed a spoon was necessary to ensure each bite contained equal parts banana, caramel, vanilla ice cream, and chocolate chips. Salem couldn't remember what Vida had ordered, only that she had brought the camera.

Salem and Daniel had made deliberate ice cream circles around their lips and were grinning into the camera, heads together, Daniel's arm slung over Salem's shoulder.

Salem was surprised at the pain she felt looking at the photo. She still missed him so much, yet oddly she felt surprisingly close to him in that moment.

Charlie's voice coming from the front of the house broke the spell. "Everything all right back there?"

Salem glanced up at Mrs. Molony, who was watching her with those glittering crow eyes. "It will be, right, love?"

Salem offered the photograph back to Mrs. Molony, who waved it away. "I don't need it any longer, not now that you've come."

Salem's shoulders lifted with the force of her inhale. She realized she was exhausted. She hadn't slept last night, had been on the run since she'd learned Mercy had been kidnapped.

Mercy.

"There you are!" Charlie said, coming around the corner. "Did she tell you what the *mercy* on all the little Stonehenge keys mean?"

Mrs. Molony finally dropped Salem's hand. "I'm afraid that's beyond my talents."

"Then you won't know what it means to refer to Stonehenge as *second*," Charlie said, his tone deceptively lighthearted.

Mrs. Molony made a *pffft* sound. "Well now, that's easy for anyone's not a cabbage. Your Stonehenge is the second rock circle on the Isles. The first is found in Scotland. The Standing Stones of Stenness, they're called. The first true stone henge."

CHAPTER 30

The Road to Dublin

"I should have known."

Charlie had been mumbling since they'd pulled out of Muirinn Molony's. Salem had only been partially listening. Research into the Standing Stones of Stenness was calling to her. Her head was tipped so far forward that she was at risk of falling into her computer screen.

"Should have known what?"

"About other rock formations. I knew the British Isles is poxed with them, but I'd assumed Stonehenge was the first. My da would be ashamed. Tried to teach me everything he knew about working with rock. I lapped it up. Took in everything he said about Stonehenge, too, and thought myself smart. Too smart to see what I didn't know."

Certainty is a prison. Be soft to the truth.

Daniel Wiley had said that to her often, when she was frustrated during one of his games to release a hidden drawer on some magnificent piece of furniture and argued with him that there was no way that she hadn't uncovered all the secret springs.

"Learn your lesson and keep on moving," Salem said. It was another motto of her father's, though it had sounded less harsh when he said it.

"I suppose that's all there is to it." He slowed down for a corner. "Tell me what else I don't know. What are these other Scottish stone circles, and please don't tell me they're found in the Highlands near my mother's people. That'd be too much ignorance to wear for one day."

Salem inputted the final variables into the line of code she fed to baby GAEA. It hadn't taken long to create a research program that would cover the Standing Stones of Stenness. She'd only had to swap out keywords from the Stonehenge search, as both algorithms would serve the same function—sweep the web for historical data, collate duplicate information, create an outliers document.

Once she had the Stenness search running, she checked GAEA's net for more information on the London and Moscow servers that had pinged the day and time of the Parliament bomb going off. GAEA hadn't dug up anything else bomb-related in the past communication from or between the servers, so she'd paused herself until issued a new command. Salem fine-tuned that algorithm to wake up should any-thing suspicious originate in either server and added potential terms to look for, coded or open: "Parliament," "environmental summit," "Gina Hayes."

Next, she checked what GAEA had caught on Stonehenge and was disappointed to see nothing there. Yet GAEA hadn't automatically paused this search as she'd done with the bombing algorithm when it had dead-ended. There couldn't be many cyber-stones left unturned, yet GAEA churned. It must be a bug in her code. Salem would look at it later. For now, she'd let GAEA do as she'd been told—collate research on the Standing Stones of Stenness in the background while Salem researched old-school in the foreground.

Salem read her screen out loud. "They're in Orkney. Is that the Highlands?"

"Yes, damn it all to hell." Charlie chuckled ruefully. "But it's off the farthest northern tip, so I'll hardly count it. Plus, I've never visited. Tell me what else I don't know."

"The stones date to around 3100 BC, so still the Neolithic period, but at least a few hundred years before Stonehenge was constructed. Stenness only ever had twelve stones in its circle, plus a nearby

Barnhouse Stone and Watch Stone. Only four of those original twelve remain standing, and they're spindly, like tall gray baby teeth, and spaced far apart." She tilted her screen so he could see it.

"'Spindly' is right. What's their height?"

"Twenty feet, more or less, so taller than they look."

He returned his attention to the road. "Bit of a disappointment, those. I don't feel so bad for never hearing about them. Is there anything circling it?"

Salem kept reading. "Yup. There's a ditch, six and a half feet wide and thirteen feet deep, chiseled into the bedrock. Bones were discovered in the ditch, but I haven't found yet if they were animal or human, or a mix. There's considerably less research on this monument than Stonehenge."

"That means less money for it, which means less security and easier for us to search. I'm confused. If these Standing Stones are what Stonehenge was meant to send us toward, why hide it? Why not just directly send the seeker to Stenness?"

"For the same reason you hide anything," Salem said, thinking again of Daniel Wiley, and the day he'd driven that lesson home.

Her father was hand-sanding a walnut monk's bench. She remembered the sun poking through the shop window's dusty glass, and sawdust the color of heartsblood dancing in its beam. Salem had trailed her finger through the specks, upsetting their fairy dance. She was on summer break, between second and third grade.

"You know why people hide things, don't you, Salem?"

She'd helped her dad pick out the wood for this bench, held and handed him tools while he measured, cut, drilled, and Dremeled, watched in awe as he carved the lions' heads that would decorate each end of the two armrests.

"So other people don't find them?" she'd guessed.

He'd reached for the varnish. She remembered wanting him to open it more than anything in the whole sweet world. He'd always made her leave at this point in a project, said little girls with developing brains mustn't be in close quarters with varnish. She imagined it smelled like butterscotch.

"That's right." He smiled, encouraging. He wore the cut-off jean shorts and faded, paper-thin Led Zeppelin Icarus T-shirt he always wore at that stage in the project, that time of year. "And why don't they want other people to find them?"

Salem pushed a sticky curl from her face. "Because they don't have enough to share?"

He studied her and set down the can. "You know what, I think you're old enough to stay for the final step."

She couldn't believe it. "You're going to let me watch the varnish?"

He chuckled. "If you like, but I have something that comes right before the varnish that I think you'll enjoy even better. It's the final test of the furniture."

He reached into the mouth of a carved lion's head and tugged its wooden tongue. Next, he turned the head forty-five degrees and slid the top of the armrest toward the center. Underneath lay a long, narrow hidden drawer. He repeated the action with the other lion's head.

Salem was speechless.

"I added the compartments while you were sleeping. I do that with every piece of furniture I make."

He flipped the varnish lid and stirred the viscous liquid underneath. She wrinkled her nose against the acrid odor. It didn't smell like butterscotch at all. He painted quietly, carefully, until he was done and the monk's bench gleamed as if it had been carved of liquid gold.

"Remember the question I asked you earlier?" He scraped the excess varnish off the stir stick using the lip of the can. "There's only one reason a person ever hides something."

She blinked, waiting.

He clicked the lid back into place. It made a hollow snap, like a metal bone breaking.

"Fear. That's it."

Salem wondered if her dad and Charlie's dad would have gotten along, if maybe they'd even been in the Underground together. She studied his silhouette as he drove, found herself feeling reassured by his jawline and the way he tugged at his ear when he was feeling frustrated.

"This is the same way it was with the Beale train," Salem said. "The treasure was buried several codes deep, each serving as a gatekeeper for the next."

Charlie nodded. "I know. I read the report. I *memorized* it. Some of the most famous women in American history hid that treasure so well that only a master code breaker could find it. Can I poke the elephant in the room?"

Salem felt a furrow plowed between her eyebrows. "What?"

"You're certain that's what we're dealing with now? A situation like the Beale train?"

Salem scowled. "We know that Mercy Mayfair was kidnapped by people who believe there's a series of codes connected to Stonehenge that lead to some unknown treasure. They want us to find it, and they'll return her." She didn't want to acknowledge that the Order was behind it, though. She was breathing shallowly. The Order had killed Grace Odegaard without a second thought, carved slabs of flesh out of Vida Wiley. What would they be doing to tiny, frightened Mercy Mayfair?

"You told Mrs. Molony you were familiar with the Underground," she continued.

"Aye."

"Then you must believe that the Order exists, that there's a shadowy cabal of men who run the world's economies, decide wars, create laws, and devote their lives to keeping women from personal or political power."

He didn't answer her right away. The corrosive poison of hysteria began to bubble at Salem's sanity. "Say it," she said. "Say you believe in this crazy conspiracy bullshit."

Charlie sighed. "Here's what I believe. There are no conspiracies, only people born with more money and power than the rest of us, facing the same choice the rest of us are up against every day: Do I do the right thing, or do I do the easy thing? And when you are a man, and the whole world is set up to make you believe that your comfort is the right thing, always, that choice becomes muddier. You don't even have to be that smart to be on top. You start out with money, with the chutes already greased for you. You're shown the rule book that the rest of us can only guess at. Best yet? You own the media, so you get to tell the story. It's not a conspiracy. It's how society has been run since time immemorial. Hell, it's how elementary school playgrounds are run. So yeah. I believe that the Order exists."

"And the Underground?"

He shot her a quick, troubled glance. He was less forthcoming on this point. "It's real. I've met members."

Salem had, too. It had cost her dearly. It was time to admit to the obvious. "And you think the Order has Mercy."

"I know it." His voice was husky. "I need you to be certain, too. Else we might miss what matters."

Salem dug in her purse for an Ativan pill and swallowed it dry. "I just want to solve the train and get Mercy back. That's all."

I'm coming for you, baby girl. Don't give up. Please don't give up.

A rose bloomed across Salem's screen, GAEA using a version of the computer program that had won Salem the eighth-grade science fair to break in and tell Salem she'd found something. "Hold up."

"What is it?"

"GAEA uncovered a Stonehenge outlier. Or at least she thinks she did." Salem's pulse picked up. GAEA didn't have a bug; she'd kept working because she knew there was something more out there. Salem clicked on the rose. A document appeared. Salem whistled low. "She gathered another page of outlier information."

"Impressive. Anything we can use?"

Salem scanned the data, disappointment forming a heavy ball in her gut. "Not at first glance. It looks like wacky theories about Stonehenge. Aliens building the site, Stonehenge having great acoustics because it was really an ancient concert hall, Stonehenge being the gateway to the lost city of Atlantis, another postulating that Nephilim built Stonehenge."

He chuckled. "I've heard that one. The Nephilim were supposedly a race of giants, now extinct. An image from the 1100s depicts them constructing Stonehenge with Merlin's help." He pointed his thumb at himself. "A bit too far-fetched for this one. Anything else?"

"Here's one that says Hypatia designed Stonehenge."

"Hypatia? The mathematician?"

"I imagine so, but the dates don't line up. She was born between 360 and 350 BC, thousands of years after Stonehenge was built." Like any self-respecting math geek, Salem had fangirled over Hypatia during high school. At a time when few women had been taught math, let alone allowed to teach it, Hypatia had risen to the head of Alexandria's Neoplatonic School, where she taught astronomy and philosophy and was admired for her intellect and dignity. A pagan, Hypatia was stripped and murdered by a mob of Christians worried that her correct calculation of the vernal equinox would undermine the Church's authority, which had scheduled Easter based on Ptolemy's incorrect computations of the date.

"Whoever forwarded this theory must have conflated her astronomical research with Stonehenge's alignment to the winter solstice's sunrise and sunset." Salem kept scanning the page. "There's also a theory here suggesting that Stonehenge was a place of healing, like an ancient Lourdes. Apparently, a lot of the bones discovered in the area show evidence of injury and illness. That's about all that's here. GAEA provided links to the sources of these outliers. We can follow up on them later, but I don't see anything urgent."

"Agreed." He slowed down so a sheep could finish crossing the road. "Tell me again how it is you don't go green reading on a computer as we careen and carom on these narrow Irish roads?"

"Never get carsick," Salem said, already tweaking the original Stonehenge search so that it was now looking for mention of mercy-stone replicas like Mrs. Molony's. She checked the Stenness net and the bomb net and found them both still empty. She shifted in her seat, scaring up the smell of sage from the protection sachet tied at her waist. The smell made her think of Alafair. They had another half hour until they reached the Dublin Airport. With GAEA running all her research for her, she decided to do some digging on Alafair and Rosalind Franklin's DNA research.

Salem had little to go on with Alafair's group except that they were freelance hackers. She entered as many identifiers as she could think of, without much hope. If they were any good, they'd use concrete firewalls. After several frustrating minutes, all she'd uncovered was an organization called the Indigo, a group of freelancers and code breakers that would work for anyone if the price was right.

They'd been tied to some high-profile, high-skill hacks, including crashing all the Google servers for a day. The little information she found on them indicated that they were a well-resourced but clandestine group that demanded—and received—a very high price for their work. If Alafair was a member of the Indigo, she would be fabulously wealthy. The tent she and her brother traveled in made that unlikely.

Oh well, good practice for GAEA. Salem programmed her progeny to follow Alafair's trail and moved on to Rosalind Franklin. This research was much more discoverable, but Salem couldn't locate anything specific to DNA research and paralysis recovery. She set up GAEA to devote space to collating and removing redundancies. That meant Salem's baby was running five research and code-breaking algorithms simultaneously, and so far, all was well. A good sign.

"Look at this." Charlie was signaling and slowing down. "A hitchhiker."

Salem squinted into the darkness, startled. "I don't see anyone."

"Passed him a few meters ago."

Salem's heart thudded unpleasantly at her throat as Charlie pulled onto the shoulder. "We shouldn't pick up a hitchhiker."

Charlie shrugged. "That's what we do in the UK."

Salem snapped her computer screen shut. The thought of a stranger sitting behind her, out of her line of sight, crawled like bugs across her flesh. "I'm moving to the back seat."

Charlie's head hinged back on his neck. "That'd be rude."

"That's what we do in the US." She felt bad, but staying in front would be worse. She unhooked her seat belt, gripped the B&C and her phone close to her chest, and slipped out the front door and into the back without glancing around. She locked both rear doors, snapped her buckle, and waited.

Charlie's expression in the rearview mirror appeared amused. "You could have left the door ajar for him."

The hitchhiker managed just fine. The front passenger door swung open. "On your way to Dublin?"

"Yes, sir," Charlie replied. "The airport. We can drop you off anywhere between here and there but don't have time for anything more specific."

"That'll do." The man stuck his head in and swiveled to stare at Salem. His hair was long, gray, and stringy, hanging forward. The lack of wrinkles around his mouth was at odds with his hair color. The shadows might have erased the lines. It'd be easier to place his age if his eyes weren't covered by large sunglasses, the comprehensive kind that followed eye surgery. "Kind of you to make room for me."

Salem wished she could melt into the seat. As a child, she'd had elaborate fantasies of being able to surround herself with a panic room at will. Whether provoked by social anxiety or straight-up fear, her power would allow her to drop down into the floor through a secret chute that led directly to a padded room with a computer, books, and enough food and water to last until the threat passed, whether a minute or ten years. The chute's entrance would close behind her and become part of the panic room's impenetrable walls.

"You're welcome." Salem silently applauded herself for not remaining in the front seat just so she didn't appear rude. Bel would be proud of her for looking out for her own comfort.

The man slid in and snapped his own seat belt into place. "Not a bad evening for a walk, though I always prefer a ride."

"That's right," Charlie said. The two of them settled into small talk, volleying it back and forth as if they'd known each other their whole lives. Salem had witnessed that instant camaraderie among UK natives. She didn't know if it was because they were politer or more gregarious or shared a longer history as a country.

The B&C was warm on her lap. She flipped it open. GAEA already had a hit. The frisson of discovery sparked along Salem's veins. If this was what it felt like to go fishing, she could understand the thrill. She'd assumed GAEA was delivering the initial report on Franklin. When the report turned out to be an email sent from the office of the United States Speaker of the House, it took Salem a moment to reorient.

Of course. GAEA wasn't running five search-and-collate programs—Stonehenge, Stenness, the bombing, Alafair's group, and Rosalind Franklin. She was running six. Salem had forgotten her priority, the reason she was working in London: detect viable assassination threats against the president.

Salem read the email, her shoulders tight with shame. She was relieved to discover that this wasn't a legitimate threat, just an official email containing hot words:

> We understand that you advise against Representative Vit Linder attending the International Climate Change Summit as your department will already be taxed providing security for the president and vice president. Representative Linder had been excited to attend and is disappointed in your recommendation, to say the least, but understands that protecting President Hayes and Vice President Cambridge must always be given precedence. As Representative Linder's country is his priority, he will remain in the United States and not attend the summit.

Salem understood why GAEA had plucked the email out of the massive sea of words flowing across cyberspace. Besides containing nearly every hot word, it had been sent from the office of a government official to the Secret Service. While it featured all the key ingredients, they weren't in the right order. The Speaker of the House's email was obviously not a threat.

Salem could use this misstep to tighten GAEA's net.

She'd already peeled back a layer of code to pinpoint the source of the misread when a tingle at the base of her neck told her that she was missing something important. She reread the email. *Nothing to see here, folks.* She wished Charlie and the hitchhiker would quit talking so loudly. It made it difficult to concentrate.

She read the email one more time. Still nothing.

She'd already sent the Stonehenge data to Agent Stone via the thumb drive she'd handed the female guard at the visitor center. He may or may not receive it, but there was no reason to keep pretending she didn't trust him. He'd kept his word during her and Bel's cross-country race nearly a year ago. More than that, Lucan Stone had saved her and Bel's lives and then risked his career for them, all in a short five minutes.

At the time, they were wanted fugitives, set up for the planned assassination of Gina Hayes. Stone tracked them to the front of Dolores Mission in San Francisco, but so had the Hermitage, the American branch of the Order. Stone had inconvenienced the contract killers who had Bel and Salem in their grip, causing them to leave their prey for a more expedient time, but not before the more terrifying of the two men had dislocated Bel's shoulder.

Stone could have arrested them at that point, but instead he'd let them go. She didn't know who he was working for, if it was more than the FBI, but for those thirty-six hours, he'd been a man of his word. Good or bad, he also kept his secrets. He had no romantic interest in her, and sure, that stung, but he was a good agent. She had to rely on someone other than Charlie, who was in as much danger as her, maybe more. With Bel out of the picture, it would be Lucan Stone.

Mind made up, she ran a deceptively simple encryption on the email from Linder's office and, as an afterthought, did the same on the Moscow to London email GAEA had flagged. Salem had developed the encryption program at the Campus. She'd also created a sequencer to crack it. As of yesterday, at least, the code was still airtight to anyone outside the FBI.

Once the email was encrypted, she forwarded it via her computer to Agent Stone's cell. The B&C whirred and buzzed, cleaning and compressing the text so it could move efficiently through the ether.

Sent.

She sat back, surprised at the relief she felt at sharing the data with Stone, at the thought of it arriving on his phone in mere seconds.

Ding ding.

Her relief was short-lived.

The sound had originated in the front passenger seat. The hitchhiker had just received a text.

CHAPTER 31

Kensington Palace Gardens

London Offices of the Order

They didn't make you Speaker of the United States House of Representatives if you were a fool. That should go without saying, but it didn't. Not in Vit Linder's experience, in any case. Between the opposition party, members of his own party, and the damn press, defending himself had become a full-time job. He told himself he was used to it. He'd been born an underdog, the third-favorite of the three children born to George Linder and his wife, Mrs. George Linder.

Vit had had to beg and scrabble for every loan his father had given him, and even when he transformed those beans into fame and fortune, George had still preferred his sisters over Vit, threatening to leave all his money to his grandchildren, of which Vit had contributed none.

Vit told himself he didn't need the money, and he supposed it was true. He'd built his own empire. And when his father had said offhandedly that the only real power in the United States fell in the hands of politicians, Vit ran successfully for the House seat of the First Congressional District of New York. He'd been nominated to the Speaker position his third term.

His father had lived to see his only son elected fifty-fourth Speaker of the House. His congratulations? "That's all well and good, but you're still not the president."

George Linder had suffered a fatal heart attack one month later, a full decade after his wife had passed. True to his word, he'd left the entirety of his wealth to his grandchildren. The only way Vit could get even was to become president of the United States of America.

He was third in line. That would all change in two days.

He thought having his people send the email to the Secret Service was a nice touch. Sometimes reporters liked to dig, and his constituents seemed to believe emails were extra-meaty evidence. He played the future interview in his head as he left the Order's London offices.

Reporter: How tragic that the president and vice president have been killed. Thank god you weren't there, too.

Vit Linder, wearing a suitably sad/capable face that he'd have to schedule time to practice: I almost was. The environmental summit leaders had requested my attendance. Almost like they wanted all three of us there, though I don't want to suggest there was a conspiracy against the United States. No, I would have been there if not for the Secret Service's monetary concerns. I didn't want to further weigh down our already bloated budget. Trimming the DC fat will be one of my first priorities as president.

Reporter: Wait, *you* were supposed to be at the summit?

Vit Linder: You bet. I even communicated with the Secret Service about it. Jeannie, can you round up that email? I'm sure we have a copy somewhere.

Even if a single reporter never saw the email, it was a beautiful smoke screen for the requisite investigation into his involvement in the assassination, a record establishing that it was no less than the Secret Service who presented him his alibi.

While Vit would not attend the summit, he couldn't help popping into London on his return trip from Moscow. There'd be so many reporters there. He wouldn't have time to hire a model to wear on his arm, but he could stop by the Order's London offices. He wanted photos out there of him entering one of the priciest pieces of real estate in London, next to Buckingham and Kensington Palaces. The creamy white mansion was registered as the private residence of a Saudi. Simply being seen entering it would drive up the price of his stock.

Besides, he wanted to see the girl.

The ancient conspiracy shit still hadn't gotten hold of him, but he had natural curiosity. She was just a kid, yet the world's wealthiest men believed she could take them down. What did a girl that powerful look like?

Pretty much like any other blonde seven-year-old, it turned out, except this one was scared as hell. They had her locked up in a basement room behind two-way glass with theater seating on the viewing side of it. Linder wondered who else they'd had locked up in there before. He made a note to ask about getting on the list to watch. He bet there'd been some really interesting women in that room.

The kid didn't do much, just alternated between shivering in a ball in the corner and launching herself at the glass, spitting and hissing like a feral cat, too slight to make any impact. Vit thought they should at least get her some street clothes. Those fuzzy bunny pajamas she wore made a guy feel bad staring at her.

He stayed as long as he thought necessary so he didn't look like a coward, nodding brusquely at the other men watching before he took the elevator back to the main floor. He'd hoped to meet the Grimalkin while he was here, but he'd been informed that the assassin was on the road, tailing Salem Wiley. He'd tried to force Clancy Johnson to tell him something, anything, about the Grimalkin, but Clancy had been too dumb to know what Vit was fishing for. Vit wanted to be friends with the Grimalkin. He thought someone so respected by the Order would be worth having on his side.

But nope, the Grimalkin was out following Wiley as she solved the secret of Stonehenge. Talk about another load of bunk. If they couldn't go public once it was solved and there was no serious money in it, who cared?

The Order, that's who.

Vit knew the twelve of them thought he was a buffoon. That worked swell for him. Kept everyone off balance. He'd surprise them with how well he managed the double assassination and stoked the fires of division in the United States. He'd deliver for them, deliver his whole country, and then they'd respect him.

Once he was president, the whole world would bow at his feet.

It was nice how smoothly the Order's interests dovetailed with his own—other than them having a Muslim and an African on the board, which he'd discovered on his way out of the Moscow meeting. Vit assumed that was for show. He had no problem personally with Blacks, in fact had found them quite useful when it came to upsetting the voters who made up his base, but he didn't think they belonged at the table of power any more than women did. It wasn't a global conspiracy. It was the order of things.

Vit paused as he reached the mansion's front door. *I wonder if that's where they got their name? The Order. Huh.* Made sense.

Together, Vit Linder and the Order would return the world to the way it had always been, with men ruling and women cooking and cleaning and getting fucked. Once he was president of the United States of America, maybe he'd volunteer his time to restructure the Order, modernize them, get the coloreds out. He'd been told the group was originally founded by St. Peter. Certainly there were now better ways to do business. Time for an update.

He was smiling as he stepped outside the mansion, but he quickly swapped out the expression when he saw that the reporters he'd had tipped off were out there. He looked goofy when he smiled—that's one thing his dad had been right about. He adopted a gruff mien instead, one that clearly conveyed his displeasure at being caught leaving an important business meeting.

It was difficult to keep the serious face. He was so happy.

FRIDAY

September 22

CHAPTER 32

Journey to Orkney Islands, Scotland

The hitchhiker's text had come from his wife, its timing coinciding with Salem's message to Lucan a fluke. The text had prompted the hitchhiker to make a call, speaking in Irish, his voice rising in what sounded like an argument, but may have been only an animated conversation. He'd ridden all the way to the car rental return with Charlie and Salem, caught the same shuttle as them to the airport, then parted ways at the airport bus stop.

Agent Lucan Stone had not responded to the encrypted text. Salem and Charlie had to run to catch their plane to Edinburgh.

They made their flight, just, and slid into their seats. At the Edinburgh airport, they had a two-hour wait for a private puddle jumper that would take them to Kirkwall, the main airport in the Orkneys, an archipelago of seventy islands off the north coast of Scotland. They'd wolfed down sandwiches, then found a quiet spot to catch some sleep, their heads bobbing against each other. It was the middle of the night when they finally boarded the four-seater. Salem was too exhausted to be scared by the plane's size. She fished around her bag for a sweatshirt to turn into a pillow and came out with Mercy's rag doll.

She held the doll to her face, inhaling the sweet scent of Mercy's shampoo. The force of the tears surprised her. The child hadn't asked for any of this. Like Salem, she'd been forced into a dangerous world, her path decided for her, her life always at risk. But Salem had been allowed a fairly normal childhood, at least until her father's death. Mercy had never known stability, and now was being held by the most violent men Salem had ever encountered. A wail grew inside her when she imagined what they were doing to the little girl right at this moment. They had to hurry. They had to save Mercy.

She fell asleep with the tears still on her cheeks, holding the doll as if it were her own child. She was jarred awake when the plane's wheels grabbed the Kirkwall tarmac. She stretched. Her eyes and mouth were gritty, her hair and clothes disheveled. Surely the last two days had lasted longer than forty-eight hours. The world had taken on a surreal, foggy quality, the light oddly violet, her thoughts liquid.

The pilot didn't leave his seat as they deplaned. "Your guide will be here soon. Lad's roommate needed to wake him."

"Thanks, mate," Charlie said. "I owe you one."

"That's right," the pilot said. "Except I'll be home in bed in another two hours, and I don't think that's true for you, so let's call it even."

Salem grabbed her duffel and the B&C. Charlie had only his overnight bag. They trudged toward the small airport. Its single public structure was a cross between a pole barn and a naval training building, made all the smaller by the vastness of the sky.

"Have you ever been to Kirkwall?" Salem asked. She was trying to blink the gunk out of her eyes, but she couldn't. The weird eternal twilight effect lingered. Maybe someone had left the light on in the Orkneys? She began to laugh at her internal joke but stopped when she realized she was delirious.

"Never." Charlie held the terminal door for her. He glanced over the flat terrain as she entered. "This is my first simmer dim, as well."

Salem stopped and stared in the direction he was looking. She didn't see anything except flat green fields under the lavender-tinted sky. "What?"

"This time of year, this far north, the sun only sets for a few hours. It's called simmer dim. We're on the far end of it—the phenomenon peaks midsummer—but the change in light and color is enough to unsettle you."

Salem blinked. The sandpaper of her eyelids scraped against her cornea, but at least she now knew why everything appeared surreal. "Might make it easier to find what we're looking for."

His gaze landed on her, deep and intense, like he'd discovered something new about her. It was the same way Lucan Stone had looked at her in her dream, before he began kissing her. "I like your optimism. Thank you."

Salem didn't know why she blushed. "Do you know the guide who's meeting us?"

"Not a bit." Charlie smiled, breaking the mood. "We might as well get comfortable."

The inside of the airport was much more welcoming than the exterior, featuring rows of comfortable chairs, televisions turned to twenty-four-hour news, and a restaurant that wouldn't open for two more hours.

"I'm going to use the loo," Charlie said. "Shall we take these chairs?"

They looked as good as any. Salem dropped into one, keeping her eye on their bags while Charlie went, and then grabbing her toiletries and taking her turn. The bathroom was simple and clean. She washed her face in the sink and wiped it clean with scratchy paper towels. Digging around in her pouch, she found her toothpaste and toothbrush. She felt a million times better after scrubbing her teeth.

When she returned to her seat, Charlie had purchased a couple bags of what he called crisps along with two colas from a vending machine. "Fine Scottish dining." He smiled his lopsided smile.

She took the food gratefully. "I've never had salt and vinegar potato chips."

"Well then, my darling, you have not yet lived."

She dug into her bag. The crisps were so tangy they puckered her lips. The icy-cold cola provided a perfect contrast. They munched in companionable silence. They were the only people in the airport besides a janitor and a security guard, who were talking over a garbage can on the far side of the terminal, and near them, a man sleeping on a bench.

Still, when a thought occurred to her, Salem pitched her voice low. "The plan at Stenness is the same as Stonehenge, right? We look for a code on or around the stones."

"Sounds about right." Charlie crunched thoughtfully. "I've never been here."

Salem nodded. "You mentioned that."

"No, I mean Scotland."

Salem looked at him, surprised. "But your mom was from here?"

"Born and raised, until she moved south. Quite a woman, her. Name was Elizabeth."

"She's not alive?"

Charlie's eyes dropped. "She passed when I was eight."

Salem softened toward him. "I'm so sorry."

"I was lucky to know her at all." His smile took on a boyish quality. "You would have loved her. Everyone did. She was a bit of a rebel spirit. Raised on a horse farm, left for England to join the British Army when World War II began. She was in London for the bombings, you know. They'd blitz every night, but my mother refused to leave because she was a nurse and she was needed."

"She sounds like a brave woman."

"You don't know the half of it. One night her hospital was bombed. The army forced the evacuation, but she stayed behind to pull bodies from the rubble. She was a wee woman, could reach places the soldiers could not."

"She survived the war?"

"She did. After, she found a scrap of land in southern England and began raising her own horses. She met my father then. They never married. She had me much, much later in life. I expect I was an accident, though she never made me feel it. I had the best tutors and free rein of the countryside."

Salem sighed as she stared into her now-empty chip bag, the silver foil reflecting muddy shadows back at her. "Sounds like a wonderful childhood."

The smile dropped off his face. "It was up until her death."

"I'm so sorry." He'd revealed that his father was also dead, which made him an orphan. She took a leap. "Your mother was in the Underground?"

He crossed his arms. "Yes. She and her friends would meet in our parlor. This was before the internet, of course. I thought it was a bunch of country women meeting for tea, but sometimes I'd eavesdrop. They'd talk of codes and plans to buy land and free their sisters across the world. I was quite taken with it. Likely explains why I joined British intelligence straight out of college."

Salem grew quiet. Since it seemed she couldn't escape the reach of the Underground, maybe the answer was to not fight it but coexist with it, as Charlie appeared to.

"Can I talk to you about something?"

She smiled. "If it's whether we should buy more crisps, the answer is yes."

The lopsided smile returned. "I can get us more. But no, I wanted to ask you about Agent Stone."

Salem stiffened.

"I'm sorry to bring it up," he said, "but I'm afraid I hurt your feelings earlier when I spoke about Agent Stone and Nina. It was unprofessional, and I apologize."

"You didn't—" Salem stopped herself. She wasn't going to lie to Charlie. "I had a little crush on Agent Stone, but there's nothing between us."

"You aren't dating?"

"Nope." Salem planted her smile back on her lips. "I'm as single as a dollar."

Charlie's eyes cut away. "I'll get us the crisps. You watch for the guide?"

"Sure. What's he look like?"

Charlie stared at the sleeping man on the other side of the terminal and then out at the lonely tarmac. "Awake."

CHAPTER 33

Orkney Islands, Scotland

The Standing Stones of Stenness

The northwest Orkney Islands had the same melancholy, make-do smell of a doused campfire as Ireland, but the air was brinier, leaving salt kisses on Salem's lips as she walked from the terminal to the guide's car. The cola Charlie had bought her had sharpened her senses but also made her jittery.

Their guide, a mop-haired Patagonia type named Bode, was unbothered by the late—or early, depending which way you were coming in—hour. He was an American who reminded Salem sweetly, sadly, of Mercy's brother, Ernest.

"I've been here eight months," he said as he pulled out of the airport parking lot. "I'm on a grant to study Orkney's geography as part of my master's degree, so I won't be able to help too much with the history of the Stones. I'm the best you can get at this hour, I guess."

His laugh was good-natured, relaxed, but his fingers twitched with excitement. "What's the FBI after at Stenness, anyhow?"

"Nothing too exciting, I'm afraid," Charlie offered from the back seat. "You've heard of the climate change summit coming to London this weekend?"

"Dude, the whole world has."

Charlie laughed. "I suppose. Well, some ecoterrorism groups think it's not going far enough. They've threatened to vandalize UK monuments this weekend unless the accord is rewritten to offer more environmental protections. We've been assigned the thankless job of checking out Stenness to make sure they haven't disturbed it and aren't planning to."

Salem was surprised at how smoothly the lie rolled off his tongue. She supposed she shouldn't be. If she stayed FBI, she'd grow skilled at lying, too.

Bode scratched his beard. "There's worse gigs. Have you visited Stenness before?"

"No," Salem said.

"I hope you're not expecting Stonehenge. You'll be let down."

"We were just there," Charlie said. "First stop."

"How long of a drive is it?" Salem was considering checking in with GAEA to see if she'd uncovered any new information.

"Twenty minutes."

Not long enough.

"What can you tell us about the area?" Charlie asked.

Salem appreciated the question, considering the necessary skills Charlie was bringing to this investigation. He'd mentioned having years of experience as a field agent, which meant he knew how to conduct an investigation. Where Salem went directly to her computer for research, Charlie talked to people.

"It's an archaeologist's dream," Bode answered. "Everything here is built of stone, so it lasts. It's not bad for geographers, at least with my specialty. I'm part of a geophysical survey team studying all the drowned paleo-landscapes in the Orkneys, with a specific focus on the Loch of Stenness, which is just west of the Stones. We only have a basic idea of what's been covered by rising water."

He pointed out the windshield, where the landscape was still bathed in the unsettling violet of the simmer dim. "See what looks like lakes out there? In the Neolithic period, most of this was swampland.

Our project is developing methods for studying the submerged shores of the UK."

"Do you think there are more standing stones underwater?" Salem asked.

"Possibly, but it's unlikely they'd still be standing against the ocean currents." He slowed down for a turn. "Don't quote me on this, but I heard one of the archaeologists say the Neolithic people got the idea for the Stenness circle when they started to move rocks so they could farm the land. That's how all the stone fences dividing property began, and building a stone circle, sorta an outdoor community church, grew from there. People made pilgrimages to the Stenness Stones twice a year, just like at Stonehenge, bringing offerings and food for a festival."

Salem was looking at a patchwork quilt of white stone fences bisecting the green earth as he spoke. "Where do you go to college?"

"University of Colorado, Boulder. I was lucky to land this cherry gig." He reached behind him to grab something stuffed in the rear pocket of Salem's seat. "I brought rain slickers for you both. The weather changes on a dime out here."

"Thanks," Salem said, unbuckling to pull hers on. Charlie did the same.

Bode looked at her appraisingly. "Do you have a hair tie, too? The Orkney wind can give you locs in under a minute, I swear."

Salem held up her hand, and the slicker fell away, revealing an elastic at her wrist. "Always. You learn early with curly hair."

He smiled and pointed at the bun on top of his head. "With long hair, too."

Charlie's head appeared between them, his hand pointing beyond the center of the windshield. "Is that *it*?"

Salem looked where he was indicating. Across the green flats, atop a small rise, stood a row of fence posts. As they neared, some of the posts separated from the rest, growing and then morphing into the sparse rocks of Stenness.

"Yeah," Bode said. "I warned you. The good news is that it's open twenty-four hours a day, not that I suppose that matters to FBI agents. Hey," he said, directing a question at Charlie, "if you work for the FBI, why do you have an accent?"

"I'm a transplant," Charlie said, a grin lighting up his face.

"All right, man." Bode offered his hand, palm up, so Charlie could slap it. He pulled into the empty lot and turned off the car. "The parking lot is a bit of a hike from the monument, so prepare yourselves."

Salem pushed on her door. At first, she thought it was stuck, but then she realized the wind was holding it closed. She shoved harder, and it whipped open as the direction of the gust changed. The briny squall tried to rip her hair out of its tie, but she'd bound it tightly.

She squinched her watering eyes, trying to make sense of a dark patch of water near the stones. She didn't remember a lagoon that close to the structure. Two blinks brought the area into focus. It was a field of flowers bent against the ground. The violet light kept her from identifying their color, but their existence recalled Mrs. Molony's words.

Look for the help that's out there, and remember the water, the flowers, and the power of women.

With a silent apology to Mrs. Molony, Salem acknowledged that that advice was a load of bunk. She was a mathematician and a cryptanalyst, a scientist to her core, not a woo-woo palm reader. She would search for questions and answers she could see and hold, codes she could solve. That was the only way to save Mercy.

"Is everything okay?" Bode asked, raising his voice to be heard above the wind.

Salem jumped. She hadn't realized she was that tense or he that close. "Yeah. Thanks. Just getting my bearings."

"I know what you mean. Scotland feels like a door into a different world, especially up here in the Orkneys. It took me weeks to acclimate."

Salem nodded. Charlie appeared at her side, the hood of his wind slicker tied tight around the oval of his bright white face. He reminded

Salem of a little boy whose mother had let him outside to play in a storm. "Onward!"

Bode handed them each a flashlight. "The light of the simmer dim is deceiving, too. You'll think you see more than you can and miss what's right in front of your face. Trust me."

Salem found that she did.

They trudged toward the stones, leaning into the gale. When Salem raised her eyes to check their progress, the wind wicked away their moisture and she'd have to glance down and blink rapidly. It wasn't until Bode yelled that they'd made it that she realized she was standing right next to one of the stones.

It was twice her height at least, but slim, shaped more like an ancient tabletop on its end than a timeless stone monolith. It couldn't be more than a foot thick, sharply angled at the top. She stretched out her hand to touch it and then paused. That had gotten her into trouble at Stonehenge.

"It's okay," Bode said. "They've suffered worse."

He pointed toward the middle, where a flat slab of stone lay on the ground next to two thick standing stones. All three appeared to be twice the weight and half the height of the four perimeter stones. "See those? They used to be set up like a table with the flat stone you see on the ground over the top of the others. It was called the Altar Stone, though it wasn't erected the same time as the rest of the circle. Some drunks toppled it September 1972. We're probably close to the anniversary of that event."

"I'll check those out, and you take the perimeter stones," Charlie called over the wind. He didn't wait for Salem's response, striding toward the center stones.

In the preternatural violet light, he reminded Salem of a supplicant approaching the altar. She closed her eyes, hearing the lapping of water against rock from the nearby ness, the shout of the wind across rolling plains, and nothing else. She had no idea the sound of a medieval night, but it surely must have been similar.

She opened her eyes. Charlie was almost to the fallen altar stones. Had he always been so slender? She wouldn't be surprised if the wind whipped him away like a dandelion seed. When he knelt in front of the stones, Salem felt a lurch like her soul had shifted. The disorientation was complete, the same unsettling sense she'd been overtaken by inside Stonehenge. She felt like she was slipping back in time, falling outside herself.

Charlie's triumphant shout snapped her attention back to the here and now. "Here! I found something."

She jogged toward Charlie, the earth spongy underfoot. The wind fought her, pushing back like a magnetic field. She latched on to the circle of his flashlight, the wind rustling in her ears.

She was short of breath when she reached him. She bent toward him. "What is it?"

Charlie shook his head, his expression sheepish. "Sorry, I thought it was some sort of inscription, but it's just some grass lying against this stone. I'll keep looking." He ducked his head between the standing stones.

Salem swallowed her disappointment. She walked once around the altar stones and spotted nothing to help him with. Bode had remained standing patiently next to the first stone she'd touched, arms crossed over his chest. She ran back to him, licking her lips and tasting salt.

She clicked on her flashlight, appreciating his quiet as she began a grid pattern across the face of the stone, slowing for every inch, peering at anything that might be an imperfection hiding something more. She did the same to the narrow sides, and the back. She was not tall enough to view the top, even when she backed up and shined the flashlight toward it.

"You folks are real thorough in looking for any vandalism," Bode said.

Salem thought she heard suspicion in his voice underneath a layer of genuine curiosity. "That's not exactly why we're here," she said.

"I figured." He grinned. "Anything I can help with?"

Salem considered his question. She could be ladylike, or she could do everything in her power to help Mercy. Put that way, the choice was clear. "This is weird, but do you think you could hoist me on your shoulders? I want to get a better look at the top of the stone."

He shrugged. "Sure. I used to give my little sister shoulder rides all the time."

"I probably weigh more than your little sister," Salem said.

He tucked his mouth up to the side. "You look strong. Like you'd be good at snowboarding."

He knelt next to the rock, bracing himself with it. Salem climbed onto his shoulders, tempted to use the stone to take some of her mass. She did not think the Neolithic builders or the current archaeologists would approve. She trusted Bode with her full weight.

"Can you see the top?" he hollered up at her.

She ran the flashlight over the nubby, shadowed surface. "Somewhat. Can you back up a touch?"

He did. The top of the stone appeared as unbroken as every other side of it, at least from this angle. She wouldn't be able to investigate any closer without a ladder.

"Good work, both of you!" Charlie yelled from the center of the monument.

Salem flashed him a thumbs-up. "Nothing to see up here," she called down to Bode.

He returned her to the ground as smoothly as possible. She hopped off. "Thank you. Are you okay doing that with the other stones?"

He was. The remaining three perimeter rocks received the same treatment. They were pitted, covered in lichen, rough with age and the elements, but they contained no hidden messages or drawers that Salem could detect. Her gut grew heavy. It had been a long shot to think that they would find something at the Standing Stones of Stenness.

She stared at the landscape. What the hell was she doing in Scotland? Mercy was in London, she knew it, and here she was cobbling together the thinnest of possible leads, building an imaginary world where she could control her fear by solving puzzles.

Charlie joined her and Bode, looking as dejected as she felt. "You didn't find anything, either?"

She couldn't respond. Her brain had retreated into the darkness, the place where she was a failure, where she didn't get anything right, where her stupidity had gotten Mercy kidnapped, where even her own mother saw her as an inconvenience. Once the dark got a hold of her, it dug its sharp claws into her gray matter, sending her images of Mercy being tortured, crying for Salem, for her brother, for anyone to save her.

A warm hand gripped her shoulder. "Don't cry."

It was Bode, his brow furrowed in worry. "I'm not sure what you're looking for," he continued, "but just because you didn't find it here doesn't mean you won't find it somewhere else. The trick is not giving up. Lemme show you."

He took off toward the sea of flowers. Now that the sun had shifted below the horizon, offering a more honest light, Salem could see that they were a field of red poppies.

Bode plucked one and ran back, offering it when he reached her. "These flowers aren't native and shouldn't even survive, as saline as the soil is. And look at them!" The wind tore at the petals, but they held firm to their center.

Salem took the poppy. It would do nothing to help her, nothing to save Mercy. Her tears broke loose of their growing mass and slid down her cheeks, the greedy wind lapping at them.

Bode was undaunted. His hands free, he spread them large. "These flowers grow all over the place around here. There are so many of them, they gave the archaeologists the nickname for the Flower Stone over at the Ness of Brodgar."

Salem inhaled audibly.

Flowers, water, the power of women.

Computers and science had failed her. She had nothing to lose. "The Flower Stone? Is it near?"

Bode pointed northwest, where the sea was consuming a strip of land only as wide as the road on top of it. "You can see it from here. That house on the other side of the road? The Ness of Brodgar dig is directly behind it. Not even a quarter of a mile away, though with the tide coming in, it won't be passable for much longer."

Salem took off running toward the disappearing road.

CHAPTER 34

Orkney Islands, Scotland

Ness of Brodgar

Ness of Brodgar's earliest structures were erected in 3300 BC. Built of carved and painted stone, they were too finely wrought to be a domestic settlement. In 2003, the then-underground complex was accidentally discovered when a farmer plowed up a slab of it. Archaeologists began digging. To date, eight main buildings had been uncovered, surrounded by a wall five meters wide and estimated to be a hundred meters long, though much remained to be dug up.

On top of the uniquely decorative stonework, archaeologists had uncovered spatulas, spoons, pottery, and hundreds of animal bones. The accepted theory was that Ness of Brodgar had been a religious complex.

Bode yelled all this to Salem as she ran across the land bridge, the wind provoking the waves. Fresh water on one side and seawater on the other licked and sucked at her, drowning her socks and shoes. She did not slow down, or she would succumb to the fear.

It helped that she could see Bode and hear Charlie charging behind her.

"It's in the shed, over there!"

Salem's breath dragged at her lungs, but she pushed through. Leaning against the shed, she took stock of the massive dig site. What she could see consisted of stone-lined holes in the ground, most the size of three-room houses, some covered in tarp.

Bode unlatched the shed's door and gestured for Salem and Charlie to enter ahead of him. Salem happily agreed. She'd been standing in the wind for so long that it took her a moment to knock its conch-shell echo out of her ears.

Bode stepped in and flicked on a light. An anemic yellow illuminated the room. The shed was no larger than ten feet by ten feet. Labeled bins ringed the walls. It smelled of dirt floor and the sea. A large, tarp-covered object dominated the center.

Bode removed the covering to reveal the Flower Stone.

"It was discovered in 2013, covering an empty crypt. They haven't figured out whose museum it'll end up in yet, so it lives here for now. It's the largest complete Neolithic piece of art yet discovered." He pointed at the designs, turning on his flashlight to better illuminate them. "The back of it is carved with the same pattern as the front. That identical design has been found here on smaller slabs, etched into some of the walls and buildings, but none of them look as much like a flower as these. At least that's what they tell me. I don't see it, unless maybe they're thinking tulips?"

Charlie stepped forward, cocking his head. "I don't see a flower, either. It's more of a repeated chevron pattern." He stepped aside. "What do you think, Salem?"

She counted thirteen triangles on the face of it. Some were rough isosceles triangles, shaped like a V with a wide top. Others were double triangles, more diamond shaped with an inner chamber replicating the outer shape. All of them were covered in cross-hatching.

It was plain to her as the hair on her head what the patterns represented.

Yonic, Vida would call them. The sacred feminine.

If Bel were here, she'd say the stone looked like a map to Cooter City, Iowa.

"This pattern is replicated all around this area?" Bode nodded, studying the stone.

Charlie knew her well enough at this point. "What is it, Salem? What do you see?"

Lotsa vaginas, Charlie. You?

He'd laughed at her at Stonehenge when she'd shared her theory about the clamshell of birth control pills. It had not been mean-spirited, but neither had it been supportive. Being mocked for this observation would bury her.

Both Bodie and Charlie were now staring at her. If they didn't see what was so obvious, how could she possibly utter it loud? She couldn't, that's how.

A fierce gust of wind slammed the door closed. Its breath scared up the spicy odor of the sachet at her belt. She was overcome by a punch of grief as she envisioned Mercy somewhere dark, alone.

Remember the water, the flowers, and the power of women.

It wasn't just a hunch, she told herself. It was a code—a different kind than she'd ever seen before, but a cipher nonetheless. She had nothing else to go on, nothing to lose by looking for what this rock meant to point her toward.

Still, her knees trembled, and her cheeks burned. She dropped her eyes and sucked in a shaky breath. "Bode, is there anything around here, anything near water, that reminds you of . . . a woman's genitals?" She cringed at his bark of laughter, squeezed her eyes shut. Her shoulders slid up toward her ears, trying to shield her ears from the ridicule.

"Oh, I'm so sorry!" He stepped toward her but stopped short of touching her. "I thought you were making fun of me."

Shock made her stare at him straight on. "Making fun of *you?*"

"You really don't know?" His eyes were wide. "Man, have I got something to show you."

CHAPTER 35

Orkney Islands, Scotland

Arcaibh Inn, Kirkwall

Bode would drive them to the Gloup as soon as the storm passed. The collapsed sea cave was a half an hour journey south and then east of Kirkwall, perched on the farthest east edge of the Orkney Mainland. Depending who you asked, it had been named after either the sucking sound it made when you stood atop it or *gluppa*, the Old Norse word for *chasm*.

But when Bode showed Salem a photo of it, she understood where locals had come up with its nickname: the *fud*, which roughly translated to "where the sun don't shine."

Truly, it was impossible to look at the image and not feel like you were upskirting Mother Nature. Carved into the earth and separated from the sea by a narrow land bridge, the sea cave was modestly sized, approximately 130 feet long and 80 feet deep. Bode said it was a popular spelunking spot because it had been used as a garbage dump a hundred years earlier and so, depending on the whims of the sea, you could make the odd discovery down there. Nothing great, but still exciting, like a mossy wagon wheel or a horse femur.

"There's even a rumor of a pirate's booty in the cave, though I've never unearthed anything more precious than sea glass. Even without finding treasure, it's a beautiful place, though. Peaceful."

"We'd have to climb into it?" Salem asked doubtfully.

"Depends what this storm leaves behind." Bode clicked off his phone and shoved it into his car's console. He'd pulled over to research their options. "If the wind keeps this direction, we'll be able to steer a small boat in from the sea. If the wind switches, which it does a lot around here, we'd have to climb down."

"*You* will have to climb down," Charlie said to Salem. "You're the only one who knows what to look for."

Salem frowned. A hunch she'd been batting around moved to the forefront, but she didn't want to embarrass Charlie in front of Bode.

Bode mistook Salem's pause for fear at climbing, an inevitable emotion she hadn't had time to arrive at yet. "It's not difficult at all," he said. "With those strong arms, I bet you'll be great at it. Women are the best climbers, everyone knows that. Lower center of gravity, plus they have practice relying on brains over brawn. Thinking all you need is strength gets a lot of new climbers in trouble."

"Thanks," Salem said, "but I still hope we can take the boat."

Bode smiled and pulled in front of a small Kirkwall inn. He'd promised the owner wouldn't mind the hour at all. "I'll get us there one way or another. You two grab some shut-eye, and I'll meet you back here at eight a.m. This place offers a rad breakfast. Best in Kirkwall."

Salem exited the car and grabbed her bag and the B&C. Her eyes were sticky and sludge-coated. She felt twitchy, like her bones had been replaced with electric power cords, but she knew Bode was right. She and Charlie needed sleep.

Charlie held open the door to the inn. He looked like she felt. "I'll book the room."

She nodded, dropping into the only seat in the lobby while Charlie strode to the front counter and pushed the buzzer. She clicked on her phone, drawn to the folder she'd created for Bel's incoming texts. It was pulsing, stamped with a blue "72."

Salem's ribs tightened over her heart. She would save Mercy and Bel surely would forgive her. *Then* they'd talk. But what if Bel had information on Mercy? It'd be irresponsible to ignore her because she couldn't handle Bel's justifiable anger. A happier thought pushed that aside: What if Mercy had already been saved and Bel was trying to give her the good news?

Salem opened the folder before she could talk herself out of it. She started with the most recent text.

I CAN'T BELIEVE WHAT VIDA SAID!! EXPLAIN TO ME WHAT IS SERIOUSLY WRONG WITH YOU!?!

The message landed like a punch to her gut. She closed it and exited the folder, but the damage was done. She couldn't blink without seeing Bel's accusations on the inside of her eyelids. Salem's carelessness had resulted in Mercy's kidnapping, and without a doubt, Bel knew that awful truth.

The pain of Bel's words still hot in her belly, Salem needed to acknowledge two hard truths. First, she was dealing with the Order. They'd kidnapped Mercy because something important loomed at the end of the Stonehenge train, something that would damage the cause of women. Well, she didn't care if there was a damn Bible at the end claiming Jesus Christ was a woman. She would hand it over to Mercy's kidnappers for them to destroy if it meant they'd return the girl.

And that brought her to the second realization. Once Salem cracked the ultimate code, they'd have no need for her, or for Mercy. They were certainly following her and Charlie, ready to snatch the information the moment they got their hands on it. If she was truly going to save Mercy, she needed to be vigilant, and she needed to be smarter than them.

She also needed to have an uncomfortable conversation with Charlie. She'd been paying only peripheral attention to his dealings with the grumpy Scotsman behind the counter, who'd obviously been woken up to check them in. The men were arguing. The Scot apparently won.

Charlie slid some money across the counter in exchange for a key. The innkeeper watched Charlie walk back toward her, his hands flat and firm on the counter, his mouth set.

"They only have one room available. I had to tell him we were husband and wife to get it, but he refused me a cot. Said if we're married, we can share the same bed. No worries, though. There'll be a comfy chair in there. Besides, one of us should stay awake to keep watch anyhow. It's no good to let down your guard on a case like this." Salem could not have agreed more, not to mention the fact that she was so tired she would have slept in a baby sling strapped to the crabby Scot's chest if it meant she could close her heavy eyes.

"Works for me."

She followed Charlie to a first-floor room. Its interior was clean and plain: a double bed, nightstand on each side, armoire in the corner next to the bathroom door, and a rocking chair near the television. Charlie whisked the curtains open to reveal a glorious view of a brick wall.

"Perfect," he said. "The bed is all yours."

She should shower. It would feel like heaven to rinse off the tacky salt the sea air had painted on her skin and to scrub days' worth of grit and grease out of her hair, but once that bed was in sight, she toppled onto it like a felled tree hitting the forest floor.

Charlie chuckled. "Way to put your shoulders into it. I'll be right here if you need me."

She was more asleep than awake when she heard the *humph* of his rear hitting the chair cushion, followed by the mouse-quiet, rhythmic squeak of the chair rocking. Their uncomfortable conversation would have to wait.

"Wake me up halfway through so I can take over the watch?" she said. Or at least she thought she did. She may have only grunted.

The tickle of dust and the lavender odor of laundry soap scratched at her nose. The right side of her face was tingling. She swiped the back of her hand across her mouth. It came away wet. She'd been sleeping so hard that she'd drooled.

Her right eye was buried deep in the comforter and she was not yet ready to move, so she opened her left eye. It felt swollen. Daylight, true daylight, was peeking around the curtain.

She blinked.

She was in Kirkwall, Scotland, sprawled on a bed at the Arcaibh Inn. Charlie must not have woken her as he'd said he would. No sounds emanated from the room. He must have left the rocking chair, and that cessation of noise had woken her. She heard nothing, not even movement outside their door. Surely the hotel had other guests.

Thirsty for sleep, her body tried to drag her back down, but some internal alarm was too loud. *Something* had woken her.

Her heart thick-thudded as her brain finally shook her body awake.

She'd slept for too long. There was danger in this room.

Adrenaline shot through her veins and she leaped off the bed. Blood rushed to her head, and the room shifted. She tried to turn toward the rocking chair, but the swift movement erupted an agony in her neck so searing that she dropped to the floor.

She could see the rocking chair from this position. It was empty. The bathroom was also vacant.

She had to turn her whole upper body to peer at the corner nearest the curtains, a shadowy spot brushed with grays and blacks.

That's when she saw him. A stranger.

Watching her.

CHAPTER 36

Orkney Islands, Scotland

Kirkwall

Jason sat in a rental car across the street from the Arcaibh Inn.

He was fuming.

He'd done plenty of stakeouts before. *Plenty.* That's not what was bothering him. He'd also been trained to modulate his emotions. Not just on the surface, but to erase them completely through meditation and distraction. This was a standard stakeout. The only twist was that the building was set up in such a way that someone could sneak out the back without setting off an alarm. Jason had secured the back door with a shovel and parked out front.

Problem solved.

Yet he found himself frozen with a rage so cold that he imagined he would shatter like ice if he moved too quickly.

The issue was that the Grimalkin had known Salem Wiley would end up at the Gloup—just like he'd known she would travel to Blessington—before Salem Wiley herself knew. Jason didn't like that. It wasn't that he needed to know all the ins and outs. In fact, he preferred to avoid the politics and the debates and be told only the desired end goal. Rather, the problem was that the Grimalkin was *playing*.

The Grimalkin was toying with Jason, leading him forward inch by inch rather than telling him where to go, and he was downright *clowning* with Salem. The Grimalkin had ordered Jason to keep watch on this hotel, to follow Salem if she should unexpectedly leave her room.

The Grimalkin wanted to hide a present for her. It was unprofessional. Dangerous.

"A present?"

The Grimalkin had giggled. Nodded. Like they were kindergarteners rather than assassins for the most powerful organization in the world.

Jason had scowled. "Is the Gloup the end of the Stonehenge train? Is she about to solve its mystery?"

The Grimalkin answered the question with a command. "Let me watch you do it."

They'd both been sitting in the rental car at that point, parked near the hotel, as conspicuous as aliens in this small town under this unnatural sky. Jason's eyes narrowed. He knew what the Grimalkin was asking. Jason gripped the steering wheel. His hands seemed to be trembling, but that could not be. Steadiness was his calling card.

"I will not," Jason said. A childish retort reached his tongue but did not make it past his lips: *And you can't make me.* What was the Grimalkin doing to him?

"You will. Change the shape of your face. I want to see it."

"No," Jason said. The tremble had reached his voice. His knives weighed heavily against his chest. How fast could he draw them? Fast enough to kill the legendary Grimalkin?

"Yes." Like a playground taunt.

The unfamiliar, uncontrolled rage caught Jason off guard. It was so powerful that it popped his Scottish nose out of joint. The shape he'd taken care to create flattened as if it had just been smashed by an invisible fist.

"Marvelous!" The Grimalkin had clapped. Jason had stewed in fury. "That's all for now, but I'll need to see more later. An entire face change." The Grimalkin stepped out of the car. "But first, I must run this errand. It's important to leave gifts for women so they know that you see them and appreciate them. Watch the hotel. I don't think she'll leave, but if she does, track her."

Jason followed the Grimalkin's command for thirty minutes. Then his almost religious dedication to the Order took over. The Grimalkin was costing them something important, Jason knew that, and he needed to inform them, even if it violated the chain of command.

He decided to phone the remaining Barnaby brother.

Cassius's brother, Carl, had hired Jason, mentored him, become almost a father to him. All Jason's directives had come from Carl. He'd felt a weakening of his personal discipline since Carl was jailed. Maybe Carl's brother could stabilize the imbalance Jason was experiencing?

The inside of the car was hovering near fifty degrees. Jason lifted the collar of his coat to keep his body heat close. He dialed the phone.

Barnaby picked up on the fourth ring, his voice thick with sleep. "What is it?"

Jason stuffed down the unpleasant sense that he was tattling. "I have a report to deliver," he said, falling back into the corporate-speak he'd perfected with Carl Barnaby. "About the business prospect."

The silence made Jason feel good, like Cassius Barnaby was weighing his words. That sensation dissolved when Barnaby came back on the line. "And?"

"I can offer a recommendation at this point. She's good at her job and has the exact skills we're looking for." Jason gripped the phone. "Unfortunately, my colleague is not using our time wisely. It's hurting our acquisition. I'd like permission to complete this project on my own."

Barnaby's second silence lingered longer. A light flicked on in the bakery up the street. The town was waking, though Jason didn't imagine these people ever slept deeply, not with the haunted light. He'd never tried Scottish baked goods. There must be a specialty for this region. There always was some—

"You called me at home in the middle of the night to complain about your assignment?" Cassius Barnaby popped off each word like a bullet.

Blood drained from Jason's face. With it slipped his control. He could feel his flesh melting. He'd spent so many years stretching and morphing it that it pooled near his chin without constant concentration. "I'm sorry."

"Goddamned right you're sorry. Don't call me again until that job is done. No, don't even call me then. I only want to hear from the Grimalkin." Barnaby hung up.

Jason held the warm phone, feeling more unsettled than he had in his entire tenure with the Order. There were protocols to be observed, the most basic of which was not to name names.

Barnaby had spoken a name.

A name most guaranteed to alert security agencies.

Jason pulled himself back together. He needed to destroy the phone. He and the Grimalkin needed to leave the Orkneys as soon as possible.

Always, the Order had known best.

But they were shaken. Cassius Barnaby dropping protocol evidenced that.

And that shook Jason.

CHAPTER 37

Orkney Islands, Scotland

Arcaibh Inn, Kirkwall

Salem lunged toward the stranger in the corner, needles of fear piercing her chest. If she'd had time to fully wake, she'd have talked herself out of it. This was pure instinct. The sudden movement reawakened the pain in her neck, throwing her off balance. She grabbed the shades to steady herself. The curtains came down, washing the room in clean yellow light.

The corner was empty.

Charlie made a snuffling sound as he sat up. He'd been lying on the floor next to the bed. "What is it? Time to get up?"

Salem spun to look around the room, desperate to search every corner at once. "I thought I saw someone."

Charlie stared at the window. Without the curtain, it offered an unobstructed view of the alley and the brick wall. "That'll happen."

He stood and stretched, rubbing his face. "It's the mission. We're tired. A little girl's life hangs in the balance, and we don't even know if we're on the right track. It's a surefire recipe for seeing ghosts."

Salem gulped in air, telling herself to calm down.

Charlie picked the curtain off the floor and jimmied the rod back into the hooks. He'd doffed his jacket and was wearing only a black

T-shirt. His arm muscles flexed as he fixed what Salem had broken, his movements confident and reassuring. "We need to look out for each other."

Salem nodded. She stepped forward, meaning to straighten the flower-patterned curtains, but when she raised her hands above her shoulders, the pain squeezed out an involuntary yelp.

"What's this? You've been favoring your left arm this whole trip, you know."

Salem rubbed at her neck. "I thought it went away, but I must have slept funny. It started with my office chair," she finished lamely.

"Government issue, I'll bet. Might as well have us perch on a block of wood while we work." He indicated she should sit on the edge of the bed. "Let me have a look. Can't make it any worse."

Salem hesitated.

"I've been told I give good massages," Charlie said. He held up his hands.

Salem perched gingerly on the corner edge of the mattress, her back to the window.

Charlie rubbed his hands together until the friction created warmth. He laid his toasty palms on the exact source of her pain. Salem moaned.

"Sweet Mary," Charlie said, kneading gently. "You've a knot here the size of a caravan. That'll take some time to dissolve. Hot and cold compresses on and off, some good massages, and rest are what you need. I can't offer any of that." He squeezed each side of her neck, testing. "What I can do is put your neck back in alignment to at least take some pressure off. Are you all right with that?"

Salem wasn't sure, but her options were limited. "Yes."

"Good," he said. "Because I can be very helpful." He jerked her head without warning, denying her time to tense up and fight the adjustment.

The pop was loud and satisfying.

"Oh my god," she said. Her head felt ten pounds lighter. She swiveled her head to the left and to the right. There was an achy twinge where the knot was, but full range of movement had returned. "You're a wizard."

Charlie's smile dipped. "I may be good with necks, but I'm bollocks when it comes to keeping watch. I'm so sorry that I fell asleep."

"I should have set an alarm. We were both so tired." She knew now was the time to have the conversation they'd been putting off. She squared her shoulders. "Charlie, can I ask you something personal?"

"Is it about my snoring? I've been told it's quite the horror show." He rubbed his cheeks. "Or that I'm long overdue for a shave?"

His boyish face was so open, almost innocent. In this small clean room, an honest sunlight pouring through the window, they were just two scared people. Salem weighed her words. She didn't want to hurt his feelings, but she had to know.

"That case you told me about earlier? The Coogan case? You said that you were part of a team that cracked the serial killer's code. What was your role?"

Charlie's nostrils flared. The energy in the room shifted. "Ask what you mean to ask," he said quietly.

Salem didn't want to continue. At Stonehenge, at the Standing Stones of Stenness, examining the Flower Stone, Charlie had been invaluable in terms of getting them where they needed to be, acquiring access, paving their way, and even in his knowledge of stonework, but he did not understand code. Not computer, and not ancient. She'd wanted to make excuses for him, to cover his deciphering ineptitude, but there was too much at stake. "Are you really a cryptanalyst?"

A movie's worth of emotions played across the screen of Charlie's face. He clenched his jaw. "I am not."

Salem's breath caught.

He looked her dead in the eye. "I *was* on the Coogan case. I was the arresting agent, not the code breaker. I've taken some cryptography workshops, the standard MI5 training, but I know about as much about cryptanalysis as you know about guns. And that's exactly why I was assigned to you."

"What?"

He ran his fingers through his hair. "I'm your standard in-the-pocket spy. Your president, Gina Hayes, pulled some strings to have me assigned as your partner. They brought me in as your overqualified London bodyguard, I thought at first. We were supposed to remain in the city, and I was to protect you while you worked on GAEA." He cleared his throat. "You weren't supposed to know. Then your girl was kidnapped, and here we are."

Salem scanned all that information. "I don't answer to Hayes. How could she have anyone assigned to me?"

Charlie shrugged. "You're the president of the United States, you get to do what you want."

Salem stayed quiet.

"For what it's worth, I'm sorry I had to lie to you. It's part of the job, but now that we've grown close, it no longer felt right."

Salem tasted his words. Swallowed them. They didn't go down easy, but it wasn't the worst she'd ever digested. While she could use another code breaker with her now, she had to admit that his actual talents had proven useful. It chafed to be lied to, but if the choice was between hanging on to a sense of betrayal and going all in to save Mercy, it was no choice at all.

He watched her.

"Mom was a spy, you know," Salem started.

"It's true, and in the spirit of total transparency, it's important you know where my loyalties lay. My mother was a nurse, but she also worked for the Special Operations Executive, the British espionage organization at the time. She was one of several women who were successful spies. I know it's difficult for some to step outside the torpor of opinion. 'Men do this, women do that, and never the twain shall meet.' But that's not how I was raised. I know women can do *anything*." He stepped forward, a yearning in his eyes. "That's why I felt so terrible when I'd laughed at your Stonehenge theory. I was just out of my element, and it was a shit thing to do."

Salem's chest was suffused with warmth. It was freeing to have the air cleared, but there was something more than that. They'd forged a connection in the last three days. She'd had some internal pushback, but she found herself trusting him. Even more, she discovered she wanted to kiss him. He was so close, his lopsided grin so inviting.

And there was a bed right there.

He must have been on the same wavelength because he leaned forward, his smile replaced with a softness to his mouth. It would be so easy to meet him in the middle, to work off the incredible stress of the past seventy-two hours, to feel *good*, even if it was only for a pocket of time.

She yanked herself back abruptly. An image of Agent Stone had bloomed in her mind, followed by a picture of Mercy, shivering in the corner of a cell somewhere. Salem would not be so selfish as to steal time from the mission.

Charlie was watching her, confused.

"I'm sorry," she said, though she wasn't sure exactly what she was apologizing for. Maybe, like Stone, Charlie had neither expected nor would be receptive to a kiss, forget a roll in the hay. Salem had certainly read that situation wrong before, and recently.

"Here is what," she said. "Now that you're being truthful about your talents as well as your original mission, we need all our cards on the table. Tell me everything else you know about what's going on."

He did not hesitate. "Your mother was right, I'm afraid, and you've known it the entire time. The Order has Mercy Mayfair. The Underground wants to save her because she's the code breaker for some ultimate secret that will destroy the Order once and for all. I suspect that your mother keeps the child close because of what she represents rather than her love for her."

That struck close to Salem's heart.

Charlie continued. "Your president is a member of the Underground, as I'm sure you know, which is why she signed off on you tracking down the girl."

She'd already known, or at least guessed, all that. "That's it?"

"No." Charlie rubbed the back of his neck. "We've been followed since Stonehenge."

Salem's stomach plummeted as her worst fear was confirmed. "How do you know?"

"Little tells. Been in the business long enough. Someone watching us longer than they should. A car turning off at the right time. A man at the Dublin Airport pretending to read a spy novel."

"The Order?"

"Would make sense. That's all I know for sure, though my gut tells me that you're onto something. Otherwise, they wouldn't be following us. They'd be ahead, waiting for where we should be."

"You think they've already solved some of the train?"

"That's my hunch, and it lines up with SIGINT I've seen. MI5, like most intelligence organizations, watches the Order. There's not much we can do because they mostly stay on the right side of the law, and when they can't, they rewrite it, but that doesn't mean we don't keep track of what they're up to. Our current director has quite a hard-on for the Order, excuse my French. Apparently, the Stonehenge train is one the Order has been trying to crack for a while, and our best analysts believe they've broken at least two or three of the levels. Their analysis is that there are five or six levels in total before the payoff. Must be quite a nugget at the end."

Salem grimaced. "I hate every bit of this." Her stomach chose that moment to growl so violently that she was sure the room next door could hear it.

Charlie smiled. "Right then. Enough philosophizing. Sounds like mealtime." He glanced at his wristwatch. "We have half an hour until Bode picks us up. Should be plenty. If you've never had a proper Scottish breakfast, you're in for a real treat."

✦

Salem was grateful that any sexual tension that may or may not have momentarily flared between her and Charlie went unacknowledged.

They easily fell back into a routine, taking turns in the bathroom before making their way to a wooden table in the corner of the inn's cozy dining room. There were no breakfast choices other than "Scottish breakfast," and so the massive plates of food were slid in front of them within minutes of sitting down.

"A Scottish breakfast to start your day right," the innkeeper said, his mood considerably improved since they'd checked in.

"What is all this?" Salem asked.

Charlie pointed at her plate with his fork, talking around a mouthful of food. "Black pudding, white pudding, fried haggis, sausage, tomatoes, mushrooms, eggs, toast, and jam, plus cream for the black tea, and I suspect that's a basket of scones he's bringing our way right now."

Salem started with the black pudding, which reminded her of grainy sausage. The white pudding was just as good, salty and satisfying, particularly when swiped through the bright yellow egg yolk. She'd never tasted a slice of roasted fresh tomato with breakfast, but she found its sweetness perfectly balanced the spicy pop of the sausage and made an excellent complement to a toast-and-egg sandwich.

The sublime food was enhanced by the fact that she was starving. The last hot meal she'd eaten was Mrs. Molony's delicious stew and homemade bread. Salem ate so fast that she sometimes forgot to chew. She was slurping her last bit of tea when Bode joined them.

He smiled at their nearly empty plates. "Aren't Scottish breakfasts the best?"

"I'm so sorry," Salem said, glancing down at the carnage. "We didn't save you anything."

"No worries. I ate back at my room. I'm sharing a house with a bunch of other interns." He pointed toward the front of the restaurant, where his car was parked. "I've got good news and I've got bad. The good news is that the storm has passed, which means it's safe to explore the Gloup. The bad news is that the water is too high to take the boat in. We're going to have to climb. And by that, I mean *you're* going to have to climb." He smiled encouragingly at Salem.

Salem glanced at Charlie, who seemed to be trying to look supportive as well, except the lines around his mouth suggested he was worried. "There's no other way?" he asked Bode.

"Not unless you want to wait until this afternoon. Then the tide will be out and driving a boat in will be easy peasy."

Salem wanted that option so badly. She began rubbing her fingernails with her thumb to soothe herself. A little girl at the front of the restaurant laughed just then, a carefree calliope of sound. Salem and Charlie both looked at her, and then at each other. Charlie's eyes appeared as haunted as Salem's felt. Wherever Mercy was, she was certainly not laughing.

"We don't have time," Salem said. "We have to go now."

"All right," Bode said. "Then let's hit the road."

Charlie threw some money on the table and followed Bode out. Salem took up the rear. A prickle along her hairline told her she had left something on the table. She glanced back. Empty plates, cups, and napkins were all she saw. But the innkeeper was staring at her, she sensed it. She looked his direction. He winked, the gesture friendly, then resumed his conversation with a middle-aged man who reminded Salem, somehow, of a gray-haired cat.

The cat-man smiled warmly at her as if he knew her.

CHAPTER 38

Orkney Islands, Scotland

The Gloup

The drive was blessedly short and the wind tranquil beneath the cold lemon sun. When they pulled into the Gloup parking lot, Salem saw that between the early hour and the departing storm, the area was empty except for a flock of orange-footed puffins guarding the cliffs.

It was the smallest serving of luck, but Salem welcomed it.

Bode had given her a spelunking crash course on the drive over. "Stay close to the rock and look for handholds. We'll keep you secure up top so you can focus on finding what you're looking for."

He offered her more climbing minutiae, which she had to trust her ears to store because her lizard brain was writhing at the thought of being dangled over the sea. She felt like a virgin sacrifice as they strode up the path toward the sea cave's opening, its yawning mouth protected by only the smallest of fences.

"What will you use as a counterweight?" Charlie asked.

"There's two anchors on the other side of that nearest fence post." Bode pointed toward them. "We cover them with grass when we're done so no one trips on it, though you're not supposed to cross the fence."

Charlie seemed almost more nervous than Salem, the flesh of his face a split-pea green.

"Are you feeling okay?" Salem asked.

Charlie tossed a glance toward the cliff, where the puffins were strutting and squawking like small, colorful penguins. "Not a fan of heights."

Salem nodded. "Me neither."

She was afraid of the sea, too, but as the only true code breaker here, she was the one who had to climb down. Bode threaded and tested the harness and ropes while Salem and Charlie huddled near each other, not talking, just drawing on the nearness of another human for comfort.

Bode's setup was alarmingly quick.

"Good to go! I've roped both anchors, so we've got a backup if you need me to drop down, which you won't. Legs go right in here." He indicated holes in the harness and strapped it around her waist once she'd stepped through. She felt like she was watching him suit her up from a great distance, his tugs and cinches reaching her through a novocaine-like haze.

"This bandolier holds your flashlight, your phone, an emergency medical kit, and this empty pocket is for whatever you put in it." He held up a flashlight trailing a safety cord. "Do not pull this out of your bandolier until you've slipped on the strap. If you drop it by accident and it falls all the way down, we have to pull you back up and give you another one. That takes time it doesn't sound like you have."

Salem nodded.

"Hey," he said. "It's okay to be scared. It doesn't mean you're doing anything wrong."

She attempted a smile, but her lips were frozen.

He snapped a carabiner over her harness, tugged leather gloves onto her, and showed her how to hold the rope above and below the contact point to let herself descend in controlled bursts.

When he trusted that she had the basics, he patted her arm. "The lip is the hardest part of the entire climb. It juts out before curving back in, which makes it hard to reach the face for purchase. Once you're past that, this is going to be safe. I promise. You decide how fast and how slow you go, and when you yell, I pull you back up."

"Can I back up toward the ledge?" She thought it might be easier if she couldn't see where she was going.

"Yeah, for sure. Keep your eyes on me. I'll guide you." Bode planted a confident smile on his face. "That's good. Little steps are the best. You're about ten feet from the edge. I want you to start leaning back, give the rope a test. That's it. See? It'll hold you. I won't let you go."

Charlie stood behind Bode, looking for all the world like he was trying to keep his breakfast down. Salem found herself flashing him an encouraging smile. That's when she noticed the patch of yellow flowers to her left, not visible from the trail. She took it as a positive sign.

"I'm ready to go over!"

Bode's grin lit up his face. "That's the way! Take one leap back, feet straight out in front of you. Trust gravity and your rope."

Salem closed her eyes.

Below, the sucking *gloop gloop* sound of the sea squeezing through the cave walls was oddly soothing.

She pushed off from the solid earth, one hand instinctively rising to shield her face as she inevitably slammed right back into the rock lip.

But she didn't.

Instead she dropped, just as Bode had promised. She hung there, twirling slowly.

She opened one eye and then the other. She'd descended at least fifteen feet, smoothly. The light trickled down from above, and less so from the openings on the east and west, but the sea and shadows refracted it, giving the cool cave walls an underwater feel.

"I did it!" she yelled, overcome by something like euphoria. She whooped.

"Yeah!" Bode shouted back. "Start swinging yourself side to side so you can see more of the walls. Remember to always look for something to grab on to."

Salem nodded. Her palms were sweaty and her heartbeat rapid, but she was discovering strength she hadn't known she possessed. Part of her still felt vulnerable, like a giant worm dangling on a hook over the roiling sea, but a deeper, stronger part of her realized for the first time that she could do this. She began swaying to the left and the right, gaining momentum exactly as she'd done on those Linden Hills playground swings with Bel.

Left and right, left and right.

She guided her hand to the flashlight as she pumped, careful to slip the safety strap around her wrist before releasing the flashlight from its Velcroed perch. She clicked it on, its surgical brightness jarring inside the brackish cave.

While the wall to the east traveled out to sea and the wall to the west cleaved deep into the earth, the cave itself was an isolated pocket. If an Underground cryptographer hid something here, she'd have to have done it in the cave's 3,300-square-foot area. The swath of each wall to be inspected was the size of a large house's floor plan.

Searching for a code here amounted to reading a giant stone book written in an unfamiliar language. Salem was on the lookout for anything out of the ordinary, any man- or woman-made structure or sign. She expected the code to be rudimentary, as Stonehenge and the Flower Rock had been, so basic as to easily blend in with the scratches and dips of these ancient walls.

She must be meticulous.

Her brain ran a grid pattern of the north wall, the one she was presently facing. She located markers to her left and to her right and swung toward them, playing the flashlight across the moist surface. The swinging motion required her to scan the area, and to wait until momentum brought her back if she saw anything out of the ordinary. *Down there, you are your own force, your own counterweight,* Bode had instructed her. It felt good to work in this protected space, to use the strength in her body coupled with the power of her mind. It left no room for her characteristic worry.

She was also comforted by the thought of Bode and Charlie looking out for her above.

Once she'd made a complete scan of the top portion of the north wall, she changed the direction of her momentum, pushing off the wall once she was close enough.

She dropped five feet and repeated the lattice pattern at the new level.

The rhythm soothed her, each pass requiring six or seven minutes, and then she'd switch direction, approach the wall, bend her knees, push off, and drop another five feet. The smell of the sea was different nearer the shoreline. Salty, elemental. The rocks gave off an eternal chill, but the physical exertion kept her warm.

A small rivulet cut its way down the rock on the next pass. She directed her weight to return her to the spot. The rock changed color at the water source, became froggy and warm-looking, but when she tapped the spot with her toe, there was no give. Still, she reached for a promontory near the waterfall, grabbed on, and held herself with one hand while shining her flashlight into the hole with the other. She was looking for anything out of the ordinary—a shelf, a recess, maybe a huge *X*.

Nothing.

But the murmur of the sea comforted her. She'd previously had an antagonistic relationship with water. A lake had stolen her father. The ocean hid threats. It could rear up and grow angry at the drop of a hat.

This sea felt more maternal. Protective. Familiar almost.

She began her pattern anew, starting at the far west point of the line that had brought her to the rivulet's mouth in case she'd overlooked anything when she'd first caught sight of the anomaly.

Flex legs, straighten them, push off, then left and right, left and right.

She saw it instantly. She didn't even need to make another drop. A flash of white.

Guano? There must be bats down here.

She swung past the spot, searching for a handhold.

She located one four feet to the left of the bright blotch. Perched on a small ledge, her toes curled with exertion, fingers bent into a claw to keep her attached to the wall, she flashed her light at the aberration.

There was definitely something abnormal there. An indent, she couldn't tell how deep, and inside, the splash of brightness against the dark.

"I think I found something!" she yelled up.

There was no response. A fissure winked at her two feet closer to the indent. She stretched toward it. It was deep enough to dig her hand into. She grunted with the strain but brought herself near enough to look inside the hole.

The opening was the size of a carry-on bag.

While her hand was shoved deep in the fissure, though, she couldn't aim the flashlight into the recess. Her position was precarious. The sea was as far below her as the opening was above. Stress twisted her belly. There was no way to stabilize herself and peer inside the hole at the same time. She could swing past it, but that wouldn't allow enough time to examine. A trickle of sweat escaped her hairline and stung her eye. The panic began to rise, but there wasn't time or space for it. She took a deep breath and remembered Bode's instruction.

There's always a place to grab on to. Trust the rock.

She swiped her forehead with her forearm. Her attention drawn upward, she spotted a handhold directly above, just within reach. Grabbing it would take her farther away from the recess, but it would put her within reach of another handhold off to the right, and another after that. In five moves, she'd be staring directly into the hole, her feet lodged in a shelf below the recess.

Her movements were constrained but certain. She needed to hug the wall and trust all her senses. The cool moss welcomed her touch, its softness leading her toward the sharp edges of the handhold. Inch by inch, she felt along the wall, plunging her fingers and toes into every opening she felt, testing her weight before releasing the previous support.

The air changed when she finally reached the recess, sweat running down her back from the pressure of restrained exertion. The flashlight still hung from her right wrist.

She swung it into her hand and snapped it on.

She blinked. The recess's ledge was two feet across, and it looked to be forever deep. When her eyes adjusted, she spotted the white against the back of the ledge that had first caught her eye. It was only a few feet in but too deep to reach from her current spot.

She would have to crawl inside.

"I'm checking out a hole dead center on the north wall!" she yelled, not expecting a response this time. Sound must travel differently from down here.

She was inside the hole up to her waist when she noticed the change in smell. It was sharp and sour, the odor of fish rotting in the sun. Her heart slid sideways. She didn't want to find anything dead.

She sucked in a deep breath. She'd power through it. Pulling a knee onto the ledge, she pushed herself forward. And was rewarded with a face full of rotting seaweed.

It didn't slow her down. She brought the other leg up and in, brushing aside the seaweed with the flashlight. She shoved her body all the way to the rear of the mini-cave, almost on top of the flash of white that had called her back here.

It was a pile of shells. She touched them to be sure, and they crumbled in her fingers.

Disappointment wanted to join her in the small space, but she didn't allow it. She'd only explored a quarter of the Gloup. There was work to do. She shimmied out backward, waiting until her feet were over the ledge and tucked inside her toeholds before she pushed herself off the wall.

She expected to swing to the left because she'd pushed off with her right foot. So confident was she in the rope holding her that she hung in the air for a split second, defying gravity like a cartoon figure, before hurtling toward the jagged rocks below, the end of the rope following close behind.

She didn't even have time to scream.

She smacked a sharp ledge at an awkward angle. Her world went black.

CHAPTER 39

Orkney Islands, Scotland

The Gloup

She woke to wet puppy kisses lapping at her face.

When she tried to push the dog away, she realized she couldn't move. A lurch of panic ripped her completely back to consciousness.

She lay on her stomach. It was the sea, not a dog, trying to wake her.

The solid smack of a ledge had caught her. The rock was unforgiving, but if she'd missed it, she would have drowned. She did not know how long she'd blacked out.

The sharp tang of metal flooded her mouth.

Blood.

She tried to sit up again, but with no more luck. Fear rolled in like storm clouds. She was a child again, paralyzed by a nightmare, unable to even call for her father.

But wait.

Her fingers wiggled under her belly. She'd landed on them, pinned them under herself. Leaning to the left, she freed one arm. The same happened when she tipped her weight to the right. Both elbows felt tight, skinned, but they worked. She pushed her upper body off the ground and rolled over onto her butt.

She moved both feet, causing a blinding sear of pain in her left leg.

Her pants were ripped, a dark liquid staining the edges of the tear.

Her flashlight had disappeared. The strap must have torn off in the fall.

Thoughts buzzed like bees. She swatted at them. Likely, she was concussed. The rope was still looped through her harness, except rather than running taut to the surface, it hung limp down to the sea. She drew it toward her, making a loop with each section. Fourteen loops later, she held the other end.

It had been sliced cleanly. "Bode? Charlie?"

She'd whispered their names, knowing it was pointless. If they hadn't heard her before, they wouldn't hear her now. She rubbed her hand over a goose egg the size of a peach at her temple. How long had she been out? The water appeared the same height as it had been before she'd fallen, but that could be a trick of the angle she'd looked at it from. Was it possible her blackout had lasted only seconds?

She stood, gently putting weight on her wounded leg. The pain burned, but she could stand. Thank god for the first-aid kit Bode had packed in her bandolier.

And her phone!

She unzipped the pocket and tugged it out. No signal. Not surprising given that she was deep inside the earth, but at least the clock worked—she was relieved to see she'd been unconscious for no more than a few minutes—and she could use its flashlight function. Propping her cell on a rock, she removed the first-aid kit and located gauze squares and a roll of medical tape.

She pulled aside the torn cloth of her pants, revealing a deep three-inch gash. It made her feel woozy looking at it, so she tamped the bandages over the top of the cut. The white turned red instantly. She wrapped the tape around her pants leg as many times as she could, hoping to slow down the blood flow.

"Charlie!" she yelled, strength returning as she took control of her body. "Bode!"

No answer.

She glanced out to sea, a slice of sky and brightness two hundred feet beyond the cave. Bode had warned her of open water currents. Even if she could swim through the cold water of the cave, she'd have to hug the sheer cliffs of the Orkney shore for another half mile before she could climb ashore.

The only way out was up.

The wall opposite her appeared massive, the circle of light at the top a world away. She tried to recall every bit of Bode's rock climbing advice. She'd listened with half an ear, never intending to need it, sure that she'd have a rope and would be doing more swinging than climbing. Bode had instructed her to establish a solid foothold before moving an arm, hug the wall like a lover, and always plan a step out. It was good life advice. She was sure he'd told her more, but she couldn't recall it.

Salem couldn't hold her phone and climb at the same time. She turned off its flashlight function and tucked it away. She must rely on the dim light and her instincts to find the hand and toeholds.

She tackled the wall, refusing to think of what awaited her on top.

Once she compartmentalized her leg pain, climbing the first few feet was methodical. *Foot in crevice, reach for handhold. Foot in new crevice, reach for new handhold. Periodically glance down and then up to get bearings.* It was slow, agonizing work. Despite the cold temperature, sweat poured down her spine and into the waistband of her pants.

Twenty feet above the ledge that saved her life, the bruises and bumps that had gotten in line behind the sharp pain of the slash in her leg began to scream for attention. Her back was on fire. She suspected that the hot slipperiness in her shoe was accumulating blood. She looked up, estimating by the angle of the sun that she'd been climbing for half an hour.

At this rate, she had another hour to go.

The next handhold was an inch beyond her grasp. Her shoulders were quivering with the effort. She'd need to place her foot higher to reach it. She pushed off from the wall, gently, so she could look down at her feet in search of a new spot.

Her eyes snagged on a shape, something unusual carved into the rock. She squinted. It was a V, at thigh level, cross-hatching carved inside it.

The identical design as found on the Flower Rock. Her heart pumped a jolt of energy to her extremities. "I found something!" she yelled.

The wall was damp under her hand, jagged. Straining, she felt for the shape of the V, tracing it with her fingertip. She needed to move down so it was at eye level. It hurt, mentally and physically, to give up ground. She slipped the first time she tried to lower herself, barely catching her weight. With grit and determination, her foot found a new toehold and she eased herself two feet lower.

She found herself face to face with thirteen Vs.

They were weathered, but they were there, carved into the stone. Because there was no way to hold her phone and cling to the wall, she would have to explore the Vs with her hands, searching for an irregularity or a trip switch. Starting with the etching farthest from her, she ran her finger along its interior. Each of its legs was four inches tall and as smooth as soapstone.

She felt inside the cross-hatching.

No irregularities there, either.

She repeated the search with the next two Vs, which were connected at their wide ends to form a diamond. Same with the fourth and the fifth Vs. The exploration was oddly soothing, like rubbing a giant worry stone. Her dad had given her one when she was five and scared of the monsters under bed, telling her to rub her thumb across the surface of it, so smooth that it felt wet.

Remembering her dad gave her courage.

She reached for the sixth V, this one a complete triangle.

All three of its arms were smooth. She touched the whorls inside.

The first and second were sleek.

The third was not.

Its center hid a marble-size indent. She pushed it.

The bottom half of the V popped out of the wall like a drive-up bank drawer. The rock that had concealed it clattered to the ledge below.

Her angle prevented her from seeing inside the metal trough. Salem forced herself to be patient, inching slowly to the left, closer to the drawer, attaching herself to the wall with two solid footholds and a handhold. She was rewarded. Her new position allowed her to peek in the drawer.

It held a jewel-encrusted box the size of a harmonica. On top of that lay a sheet of white paper folded in half. Salem reached for it.

It was thicker than printer stock, the texture and weight of kindergarten construction paper.

She dipped her thumb into the fold so she could look inside.

The light was shadowy, intermittent, but bright enough that Salem could see what was drawn on the paper. She began trembling so violently that she feared she would not be able to cling to the wall. A wail began to build deep in her belly, threatening to explode up her throat. The paper featured a crayon drawing of two people holding hands, one a curly-haired brunette woman, one a yellow-haired little girl, both with dramatically five-toed feet and five-fingered hands. Round blue tears fell on the child's cheeks. HELP was scratched underneath her in uneven block letters.

Salem struggled to breathe. Mercy had drawn this picture, Salem would have known that even if Bel hadn't shown her a similar drawing on the Minneapolis fridge. The message was clear: *Time is running out.* She fought to calm herself. The Order had been one step ahead of her and Charlie the entire way. They'd known this code was down here, and that she'd find it. Why were they playing with her?

Breathe in through your mouth to the count of four. Hold to the count of seven. Breathe out to the count of eight. You can still save Mercy. They still want something from you, or you'd be dead. Don't give in to fear. Don't give up.

When she had her breathing under control, she slid the drawing into the back pocket of her jeans. She then reached for the metal box in the drawer, grasping it, the cold gems sharp against her palm. She unzipped a bandolier pocket with the same fingers that held the box, slipped it inside, and zipped it closed.

She jammed the metal drawer shut. A spelunker with lights would be able to discern the imperfection in the wall, but they'd have to be looking for it.

Eyes back on the surface, she started her climb to the top.

Her fear for Mercy began to morph into anger. It was terrible what the Order was doing. This was not a game. A sweet little girl's life was at stake, and they were *toying with her*. If Salem made it out of here, she would solve this train and feed it to them.

If she made it out of here.

Her leg was growing numb. On one level, the pain cessation was a relief, but it meant there was more blood loss than she thought. A muffled, off-kilter feeling crept up her spine. She must not lose consciousness. She needed to reach the top. If she perished down here, this clue was lost forever.

And Mercy would die.

Salem jammed her foot in a toehold. She reached for a new handhold. She'd climb out of the sea cave one inch at a time. It didn't matter how long it took.

Her concentration was so absolute that a *whisking* sound overhead startled her.

A rope had dropped down.

Her heart hammered at her chest. If she weren't clinging to a wall, she'd have jumped away from the rope like it was a snake. She studied it, wary. She reached out and tugged. It held. She glanced up at an unbroken sliver of sky. Bode had shown her how to string her harness. She could do it, but she didn't know who had thrown the rope down, if they were friend or enemy.

She'd have to confront the person sooner or later. Might as well conserve her remaining strength and reach the top the easiest way. She threaded the rope through her harness. She felt around until she found a sharp wedge of stone she could palm.

And then she hoisted herself toward the opening, not knowing who or what awaited.

CHAPTER 40

The Tea Room, London

Clancy had waited in the Dublin Airport for three more hours but never spotted anyone else he recognized. Not Lucan Stone, not Jason, not Salem or her British friend, no one wearing a cap with I'M THE GRIMALKIN emblazoned across it.

His curiosity had its limits. He'd caught a flight back to London. Did it have something to do with the Order sending him the coordinates to the Tea Room, the mythical meeting spot whose location always moved, famous for its succinct invitation—just the words *Tea Room* plus coordinates—and the sensitive nature of transactions it hosted?

Damn skippy.

Matter of fact, he'd carried his balls in his throat since he'd received the invitation. The Tea Room's dealings routinely included murder. But if the Order was going to kill him, he'd prefer they be quick about it, and so he'd rented a car at Heathrow and driven to the location. Smartphones made life so much easier.

His navigation software brought him to a nondescript office in London's Camden neighborhood.

The building's front door was unguarded, the foyer necessarily spare. The Tea Room's location moved daily, sometimes hourly, so the intelligence community could not trace it. That left little time for decorating.

"Back here."

The accent was unmistakably Russian. Clancy was surprised by the serenity that suffused him as he walked toward the single open door off the foyer. He hadn't necessarily lived a good life, but it had had its moments. He'd made peace with the reality that in this life, there are no second chances, no opportunities to make amends, not really. You couldn't erase what you'd done, only beg clemency, and that had never been Clancy's style. It was ungracious to ask someone else to bear the burden of your mistakes, which was what forgiveness seemed to be to him.

"Thank you for coming."

Clancy's eyebrows twitched, but he contained his surprise beyond that. He recognized Mikhail Lutsenko sitting behind the desk. Most would. The man had a face like a wolverine above shoulders as broad and solid as a railroad tie. He wore his bespoke suit well, but he'd worked for his wealth, clawing his way from beggar to steel magnate, today one of the richest and most feared men in the world. And here he was, alone in a gray room featuring only a desk and two chairs, not a weapon in sight.

"Thank you for having me." Clancy took the chair opposite the desk.

Lutsenko wasted no time. "Did Linder request you retire both the president and vice president?"

Before Carl Barnaby had gone to jail, he'd been the one to give Clancy all his assignments. Since Barnaby had been sent upstream, Clancy wasn't sure who held the power at the Order. For all he knew, it might be Linder, and this was a test to see if Clancy was loyal. "If Linder issued me any command, it would have come during a private meeting."

"Linder is an idiot. If you want to live, you will tell me whether he asked you to retire both or one."

Well, that mystery was solved. "He told me to remove both of 'em."

Lutsenko was holding back either a laugh or an appendix attack. Clancy didn't know him well enough to say. Neither fully manifested. "You will dismiss only one tomorrow," Lutsenko said after he'd composed itself. "I don't care which. The schedule hasn't changed. It must occur between twelve hundred and thirteen hundred."

Clancy kept his face still, but his brain was slipping like a drunk on ice. Linder had gone rogue. He wanted the president and vice president dead—of course he did; then he automatically became president—but the Order wanted only one assassinated now, just enough to destabilize, not destroy, the United States. Linder likely had planned to set up Clancy to take the fall, and why not? He'd already bungled one assassination.

Clancy discovered a short-lived respect for Linder, quickly squashed under the awareness that the Order had predicted exactly what Linder would do with the power they'd given him.

And damn if Lutsenko wasn't reading him like a book right now with those shrewd Russian eyes, squinty and probing.

Lutsenko rested an elbow on the desk separating them. "Have you met the man?"

Clancy adjusted to the conversational tangent. "I read his file when I was with the FBI. Never met him in person. I've only talked to him on the phone."

"You are not stupid."

Smart enough to know I'm in the middle of an operation going south, anyhow. Only explanation for giving any power to Linder, now that he's proved himself a traitor.

Lutsenko continued, reading Clancy so skillfully for the second time that Clancy wondered if he'd been hypnotized into speaking his thoughts out loud. "You suspect Linder is an idiot, and now you know he's a useful idiot. Eagerness is not the worst sin. Understand?"

"Perfectly," Clancy said, relieved. Linder thought he was in charge, but he was their puppet. They'd give him enough rope to hang himself.

"I still see worry on your face. You must know we have the best men for the job. Any job."

Clancy nodded. It didn't matter much to him. He stood, sensing the meeting was over. "Anything else?"

Lutsenko cleared his throat. "Don't fuck this one up."

Clancy may have walked out if not for that last comment, but it poked his stubborn streak, and Clancy found that he had a thread of integrity still running through him, though it'd grown rusty from disuse. "You have the little girl? Mercy?"

Lutsenko evaluated Clancy. Clancy would never know what Lutsenko saw, or why he decided to tell the truth.

"Not here."

Kidnappers of children. Well, Clancy guessed he already knew that, so he didn't know why he'd even asked. It was too late for him to make changes or amends.

He walked toward the door, his spine prickling, bracing for the cold punch of a slug right up until he found himself standing on the sidewalk, out of Lutsenko's range. He was surprised by his palpable relief. Guess he wanted to live more than he'd thought. He was so happy, he wasn't bothered by all the new-age hippies on the street, gathering in front of the bright buildings and under dirty awnings in this counterculture neighborhood. He found he liked it, in fact. They reminded him of his own teens.

Once he was behind the wheel of his rental, he even let himself think about Vietnam, and the day he'd been called in for his medical exam, all of eighteen years old and as green as a spring apple. They only needed to send over ten soldiers that day. Clancy was the eleventh. The recruit ahead of him, the last man who was supposed to go to war, claimed he had vertigo, which meant Clancy had to go Vietnam after all.

Life could hang on a dime like that.

CHAPTER 41

Orkney Islands, Scotland

The Gloup

The warmth of the sun on her shoulders was at odds with the cave darkness that still enveloped her lower body and the bone-shivering that had overtaken her since she'd threaded the rope through the harness. She hoisted herself over the lip with her last bit of energy, crawling up the grassy incline leading to the prairie and the trail.

Two bodies lay on the ground.

Charlie was slumped over the anchoring rope, Bode on the trail halfway between the car and the sea cave entrance. Salem dropped her rock shard and ran-limped toward Charlie, flipping him over. He'd been struck hard, his cheek split like a ripe plum. The front of his shirt was tacky with blood. His chest wasn't moving.

She reached for his wrist to take his pulse.

The middle finger of his left hand was missing.

Salem recoiled. "Charlie!"

He still didn't stir. She pushed through her squeamishness and grabbed his wrist. She felt a pulse, weak but present. She twisted and scoured the landscape. Unless the attacker was hiding behind a hillock, he was long gone. The bleeding from Charlie's finger stump was steady but slow. He was stable. She needed to get to Bode.

Her leg gave way when she stood. She fell hard to the ground, jostling Charlie.

"Salem?" He blinked. One eye was swollen shut, but the other tracked and found her. "You made it." He tried to sit up and collapsed backward.

"What happened?"

"We were ambushed."

"Bode?"

"Dead."

Salem jerked toward the guide's slumped form, her eyes hot. She'd known from the way he was bundled, like a bag of clothes thrown out a window, that he wasn't alive, but she'd locked that away in a compartment to deal with Charlie.

"Who was it?"

Charlie succeeded in sitting up this time, his hand clutched close to his chest. "Two men. One was the gray-haired guy who was behind the breakfast counter at the inn. The one with the tufts of hair over his ears, talking to the innkeeper? I didn't recognize the other one."

"We need to get out of here," Salem said. "And get to a hospital. Can you walk?"

"Can you?" Charlie pointed at her leg, the blood so thick it had grown black.

Salem nodded and stood so she could free herself from the harness. "I have to."

Charlie watched her, his usually pale face an odd gray shade with shock.

"I found it," she said quietly.

Charlie stiffened. "The end of the Stonehenge train?"

"I don't know. It's a box."

She helped Charlie to his feet. Once he gained his equilibrium, some of his strength appeared to return.

"Lean on me," he said. "My legs are fine."

She did. They shuffled like zombies toward Bode, who lay face down. Salem felt part of herself detaching. "The Order was down there before me. Recently. They hid a drawing from Mercy in the same alcove where I found the box."

Charlie drew a sharp breath. "Dammit. Is the box encoded?"

"I don't think so," Salem said. "I haven't examined it yet."

They reached Bode.

"They sliced his throat," Charlie said. "You don't want to turn him over."

"We can't leave him here."

"I'm sorry, Salem."

A black rage flooded her. "We are *not* leaving him here."

Charlie sighed. "I'm sorry, love. Neither of us is in any shape to move him, and if we call the local constable, we'll get tied up in paperwork for hours, if not days. We might lose your girl. I can bring the car over here to spare you the walk, but then we have to leave."

Salem dropped to the ground next to Bode. His position reminded her of a sleeping boy, butt in the air, blankie tucked underneath him. From this angle, she could see the dark gash to his throat, the puddle of blood his face rested in. She reached out and slid her hand inside his.

"I'm so sorry," she whispered.

The black rage returned, shoving aside the sadness. The burning anger made her feel powerful, huge, a vengeful Shiva. She was going to find the men who did this, the same ones who kidnapped Mercy, and she was going to make them pay. She would take their money, and their power, and she would show the world she'd beaten them. She would string them up by their testicle hair and sell piñata sticks to everyone they'd hurt.

And when they finally dropped to the ground, *she'd kill the motherfuckers.*

The labored breathing of an animal pulled her back into the present.

It was her.

She yanked her hand free from Bode's. Her wits had scattered. She called them back.

A car rumbled to life. Charlie would soon be here.

She retrieved the jewel-encrusted box from her bandolier. It glittered in the sunlight, carpeted in diamonds the size of marbles, deep red rubies, emeralds a green so rich they reminded her of the rolling Irish hills. A simple clasp held it closed.

She popped it with her thumb and lifted the lid.

CHAPTER 42

Orkney Islands, Scotland

The Gloup

"We need to fly back to Ireland."

Charlie had left the car running and walked over to help Salem get inside. "What?"

She held the box toward him. Inside lay a silver pendant, its center the size of a quarter. Four arms radiated off the midpoint, each with a silver tie at the end. The metal was worked to resemble reed.

He whistled. "St. Brigid's cross. It's to Kildare for us?"

"That's my best bet." Salem flipped it. "But there's more. A mix of letters and numbers. The print is tiny, but it looks like 8CH3COOH."

"A transposition cipher?"

Salem grimaced. Transposition ciphers were some of the simplest, so it made sense that someone not deep into the code world, like Charlie, would go there first. Any high school algebra student recognized transposition in a formula like $y = f(x)$. A transposition cipher was created similarly using a bijective function, meaning each letter or number of the unencrypted information was matched with another letter or number and *only* that letter or number. Transposition codes were solved inversely, or by walking the original encryption backward.

"Maybe, but the mix of numbers and letters makes it unlikely, or at least nearly impossible to crack without knowing what key was used to create it."

Salem had been eight when Daniel taught her how to crack the Affine Cipher.

It was the first day of spring. In Minnesota, that meant a snowstorm so dense it changed the properties of sound and sight. The whole world was muffled, like Mother Nature had knit fluffy white earmuffs for everyone, and every outdoor surface glittered with prismatic flakes.

Twelve inches of snow had fallen, but public transportation was still running, and Vida insisted on maintaining her office hours even though the college had canceled classes. Daniel had no such work ethic, or at least not one that trumped what he called "Salem Time." He'd asked her about the Affine Cipher on their way back from the sledding hill. Salem's legs had felt like they'd been filled with cement, she'd walked back up that sledding hill so many times, but when Daniel had offered to pull her home on the sled, she'd chosen instead to walk alongside him.

"A fine cipher?"

He'd laughed and stopped to spell it in the snow, his mittened finger gliding through the powder like a skier, leaving behind his looping cursive. "Close. It's spelled like this—a-f-f-i-n-e. You remember what a Caesar cipher is?"

Her dad had been doing some form of puzzle with her since before she could walk, starting with a wooden alphabet puzzle with dowels sticking out of each letter. Salem could put the correct letter in the correct spot before age one, graduated to jigsaw puzzles, and moved on to Japanese puzzle boxes and Rubik's cubes before hitting mathematical ciphers. The Caesar shift was one of the most basic. Julius Caesar used it in his correspondence, settling on a single number and then substituting every letter in the alphabet for the letter that number of shifts from the original. So if he selected the number three, *A* would become *D*, *B* would become *E*, and so on down the line.

"Sure," Salem had said, holding out a tongue to catch a snowflake. Her dad had promised hot chocolate when they returned to the house.

"The Affine is a substitution cipher, just like the Caesar, but more complex. Here's the formula it uses." He scooted to a clean patch of snow and carved these letters:

$$E(x) = (ax + b) \bmod m$$

Salem's third-grade class had not yet covered algebra, but her private tutor had. "What does 'mod m' stand for?"

Daniel had grinned. Salem loved that smile, the one that said he was proud of her. "The number of letters in the alphabet. So if we are using the English alphabet, the m is . . ."

"Twenty-six!"

"You betcha. The x represents the normal position of the letter in the alphabet. If we're still using English, that means a is a one, b is a two, c is a three, and so on. Make sense?"

Salem had nodded. The math formula glistening in the pristine snow, her dad at her side—everything was right in the world. "Can I crack one?"

Her dad had laughed out loud. He erased the formula—he knew she'd already stored it in her head—and replaced it:

$$dbinl\ arhfd$$

It took Salem three minutes to realize she'd need a slightly different formula to decrypt, another minute to create it, and two more to crack the code. "It says 'Salem rocks'!"

Daniel had whooped, drawing the stares of families still on the sledding hill. "She sure does. And I think she's earned a helping of whipped cream on her hot chocolate. What do you think?"

"A double helping," Salem had said, a smile on her face.

Daniel beamed at her, then glanced back at the snow writing. A worried expression flashed across his face. He glanced up and then to each side, as if someone would care that a father and daughter were writing in the snow.

"What's wrong, Daddy?" Salem asked as he erased his writing.

"Nothing." His smile was planted back on his face when he stood up, but Salem wasn't buying it.

"You look scared," she said.

He tapped his chin, his smile becoming more natural, almost mischievous. "I see you're not only good at math. You're also a wizard at reading people." He crouched so they were eye to eye. His cheeks and nose were rosy from the cold. "You know how sometimes girls don't get as much talking time as boys?"

Salem puffed up her cheeks. She sure did. The conversation had started last year, when only boys were elected to the second-grade student council despite Salem and another girl running. Then Salem had noticed there were not very many pictures of girls in any of her schoolbooks, particularly her history textbook.

It had come to a head when they reached the civics unit in their workbook and Salem and her classmates discovered there were only sixty-seven women between both houses of Congress, while there were 468 men. And only a handful of those women had brown skin, like Salem's own mother. Salem had never been a fighter, not like Bel, but fair was fair.

"Yeah?" she said.

"Well, it's not right, but it does have benefits." He leaned over to whisper. "If you spend your whole life living on the outside, you learn to study those inside the circle, the powerful, the men who make the decisions. Learn to read them, Salem, and to trust your own instincts. If the world isn't smart enough to see you, use that to your advantage."

His words had tickled. She'd nodded, not because she understood but because she wanted hot chocolate. She'd grabbed his hand and they'd walked home together, silent.

He'd taught her to read much more complex ciphers after that, but none of what she'd learned seemed to apply to the code carved into the back of the St. Brigid's cross.

"It could be an address," Charlie offered.

Salem was committing the code to memory, her brain working angles and algorithms. "Possibly. Or a date. I need to get at the B&C."

Charlie held out his good hand, pulled it back, and then offered it again. "May I?"

Salem nodded, and he took the box from her. He squinted as he studied it. "We've traveled forward a bit in time, eh? Cut jewels inlaid in silver is a far cry from two-ton rocks transported and scratched on."

"Yeah," Salem agreed. "We're no longer dealing with Neolithic cryptographers, for sure." She stood, favoring her injured leg. "Whoever originally built Stonehenge meant it as a clue directing the seeker to the Standing Stones of Stenness. The flowers around the Standing Stones would have then sent a person in the know to the Flower Rock. Bode said the Flower Rock was originally a slab covering some sort of container. My guess is that whatever was originally at the end of the Stonehenge train was hidden inside."

"A bit far-fetched."

"Not back then," Salem said. "There were few monuments at the time. Stones and flowers would have been excellent markers—permanent ones—to a people who had not yet learned to write. A treasure buried three clues deep, whispered only among a select group, would be safe through the ages."

"Until the Order, or the Underground, began sniffing around."

Salem squared her shoulders. "I think the Underground originally built Stonehenge."

Charlie scowled, or at least appeared to. When he began laughing, she realized his wounds had disguised his laughter as the opposite. "Now you're cooking with gas!"

"You agree?"

"Of course I do. I told you that my mother was a spy for the Underground. I guess I've always been an honorary member, and now I'm actively serving. On accident."

The sun ducked behind a gray cumulus cloud, dousing them in shadow.

Charlie continued. "And so, the Underground, five thousand years ago, hid a treasure three clues deep, with Stonehenge being the first. Then what?"

Salem had been wondering the same thing. "Something spooked them. Maybe the Order found out, or some random archaeologist was close to stumbling across whatever is at the end of the train. The Underground sent a member to move the treasure further out, creating more clues between the beginning and the end of the train. The same thing happened with the Beale train. The Underground thought someone was getting close and had Emily Dickinson move it deeper. If that's what happened here, we can expect the clues to get much more complex moving forward, more modern. The Order must not have been able to crack them. That's why they brought me in."

A thought struck Salem that punctured her hypothesis. "But then why would they have attacked us here? Cut the rope with me at the end?"

"The Grimalkin."

Salem shook her head. She wasn't familiar with the term.

Charlie winced. Salem couldn't tell if it was the words or the pain of speaking. "He's an assassin with the Order. Nobody knew what he looked like, before today. He's famous for three things: his anonymity, his cleverness, and his penchant for toying with those he eventually kills."

"The Grimalkin *plays* with his victims?"

"Yeah. Gets his rocks off on it. Based on what I've heard—and mind you it's thirdhand rumors—he'd get a real giggle at making this endeavor more difficult for you. He still wants you to reach the end, but it's entertaining to him if you know he holds the strings."

Charlie closed his eyes and flexed his hand, his voice growing distant. "The car pulled up a half an hour after you dropped into the cave. Bode said he'd check it out. Figured it was tourists, and he could send them on their way by flashing his geological access pass, tell 'em something about the area being closed due to unstable conditions. Only the driver got out. He looked like a regular Scot. I half watched them, half kept an eye on the hole, ready to call you back up.

"I heard you yell something, so I tried to get closer to the edge. When I looked over my shoulder, Bode was on the ground. I stood at the same time the bloke from the inn exited the passenger side of the car. He was smiling. He hit me with something." Charlie lifted his chin, revealing a bull's-eye pattern, the center of it a black hole the size of a pen tip. "I dropped like a deer. Feels like they smashed my face pretty well, and I'm missing a finger."

Charlie tried a laugh, but the sound grew dark at the end. "Hopefully that's all they did to me, eh? I grabbed a moment of consciousness, just enough to kick the backup rope to you, and then I went back to la-la land."

"I saw him, the man you were talking about, at the inn. He was watching us leave. He reminded me of a . . . cat." Salem's throat grew dry. "You think he was the Grimalkin, and that he put the drawing down there?"

Charlie nodded somberly. "Which means he's solved the train, at least this far."

Salem swallowed. "Jesus. He's insane." A salt-laced wind blew across the prairie, trembling the yellow flowers clustered near the sea cave's entrance. "Why'd they kill Bode?"

Charlie glanced over at the body. "Because they could. My guess is I'm only alive because you need me, and you're only alive because they need *you*. Once we arrive at the end of the Stonehenge train, the Grimalkin will kill us both. He obviously knows about the cross that was in the box. He'll be waiting at St. Brigid's Cathedral, sure as the sun rises."

Salem had already reached that conclusion. "We have to figure out a way to get ahead of him. If not in location, at least in logic. It would be helpful if we knew which member of the Underground was tasked with adding on to the Stonehenge train, like Emily Dickinson did for the Beale train."

"Have you dug around in the box?"

Salem had not. The inside contained fragments of red silk at the edges where someone had removed the lining. She ran her fingers along the smooth silver interior. When that produced nothing, she pulled a penknife from her bandolier to feel along the cracks.

"Just smooth silver."

Charlie was watching her with total concentration verging on desperation. "What if there were two clues, and without the second, we go to the wrong spot? I don't want to have lost my finger for nothing."

Salem's brow furrowed. "I can't find anything more."

"Can I see it again?"

She handed the box back to him. He examined every jewel, crack, and corner. He smelled it. He looked ready to lick it. "I agree. The cross must be all there is."

Salem nodded and reached for the open box as the sun escaped the clouds.

A flash of light dotted the bloody front of Charlie's shirt. Salem's heart squeezed.

She moved the lid of the box. The flash of light appeared again. It was not a reflection off a jewel.

"What do you see?" Charlie asked.

Salem closed the lid and brought it to her face. She'd been rolled flat and pumped back up. She peered into an inset diamond, not wanting to utter her theory out loud until she was sure.

"Holy. Shit." Her hands were shaking.

Charlie crawled closer. "You found something."

She pulled the box away from her eye, blinked to reset her focus, and peered in the diamond again, only it had turned out not to be a diamond after all. It was a lens. Her voice quavered. "Do you know what a Stanhope is?"

"Never heard of it."

Salem wasn't surprised. If she hadn't been raised by Daniel Wiley, master of all things hidden, she likely never would have heard of them, either. He'd given her a Stanhope ring for her tenth birthday. It had a thick pewter band, a diamond-shaped head the size of a pencil eraser and also made of pewter, and a hole punched into the side of the head. He'd told her to peek into the hole. Salem had been delighted to see the image of her mother and father inside her Stanhope ring. She hadn't thought of it in years. Last she'd checked, it was nestled in her childhood jewelry box back home.

"The name comes from the third Earl Stanhope, who invented a small, one-piece microscope in the 1800s. A different guy developed the microphotograph a little while after that. In 1857, a French inventor named Dagron combined the two, mounting a microscopic image on the end of a convex magnifying lens, the whole unit the size and shape of a Lite-Brite peg. The result is basically a stand-alone peephole; you hold it up to the light, peek in, and can see a single photograph. It was the original viewfinder."

Charlie appeared hypnotized by her words.

Salem's voice was shaking as she finished her explanation. "Dagron was a spectacular salesman and designed hundreds of novelty items with nearly invisible Stanhopes built into them: rings with pictures of naked ladies, crosses with the Lord's prayer, pens with a photo of the Eiffel Tower, all of it hidden unless you knew to look through the tiny hole."

She held the box out to him and pointed at what she had thought was a recessed diamond.

He held it up to his face.

When she blinked, she could still see the image on the inside of her eyelids. It was a negative of a muddy black X drawn in a staccato hand, a white circle marking where the two lines of the X crossed. The gray background broke in a diamond shape around the X, its blurriness suggesting movement, a gyroscope forever spinning as the world stood still.

When Charlie lowered the box, it was clear he'd also recognized the image inside the Stanhope.

It was a copy of Rosalind Franklin's famous Photo 51, the X-ray that proved DNA's double helix structure.

CHAPTER 43

Orkney Islands, Scotland

They huddled in the car outside the apothecary. Charlie had volunteered to go in. If his parka was zipped to his throat, most of the blood soaking his shirt was hidden. There was no way to hide the damage to his face, which was taking the color and shape of overcooked pot roast, but at least he could walk without dragging a limb.

Salem stuffed money into his unmangled hand. The other would remain in his pocket. He would buy clean shirts, pants if they carried them, antiseptic, bandages, and painkillers. Wounds licked and clothes swapped out, they'd do their best to get on the next plane to Dublin.

Bode's body was back at the Gloup, a blanket tossed over him.

It had broken Salem's heart to leave him there, but she'd agreed it was the only option. They could not involve local police. She'd wanted to contact Agent Bench, or have Charlie pull strings at MI5, so at least Bode could get a proper burial.

"There's good points to that," Charlie had said, driving one-handed. "And it's possible that the only reason the Grimalkin has been so effective at following us is he knew all along where we'd be going, at least up until the next step, St. Brigid's Cathedral. But what if there's more to it? What if my boss, or yours, is filling the Order in on our activities? Wouldn't be the first time."

No, Salem thought, *it certainly wouldn't.*

Still, when Charlie walked into the apothecary, she'd held her phone. It itched in her palm. She wanted to tell Lucan Stone what they had learned and where they were going next. But what if he was the one who'd been feeding the Grimalkin the information she'd sent to him?

She tucked her phone back into her pocket, watching locals walk down the street. Kirkwall appeared to be a lovely town. She imagined it was full of salt-of-the-earth people. They deserved better than conspiracy and murder. She and Charlie needed to get out of here before they brought more bad. He was right that it would be best to call in an anonymous tip on Bode once they were safely in Dublin. It didn't feel good, but she couldn't risk being detained here.

The driver's door opened. Charlie slid in. "The pharmacist asked if I'd been in a good fight. Told him he had no idea." He held a large bag toward Salem. "Got everything we need, though. You take care of yourself while I drive, and I'll wash up at the airport parking lot, yeah?"

Salem nodded. She dug around in the bag and pulled out a pair of gray sweatpants. They were so clean, so normal, that they made her want to weep. Underneath them was a roomy navy-blue T-shirt with ORKNEY ISLANDS written across the front in plaid.

"Limited selection," Charlie said apologetically.

Salem returned to the bag, searching until she hit on the bottle of antiseptic, a roll of gauze, butterfly closures, and a scissors. She set the rest of the bag in the back seat and took the scissors to her jeans. Her leg was too swollen to take them off naturally, so she'd need to slice them, all her modesty gone out of necessity. The waistband was difficult to cut through. Once she'd breached that, she could rip the rest of the way down, working toward her ankles.

She was grateful to see that her underpants, at least, were still clean. The first bruise showed up halfway down her left thigh, a matching, cantaloupe-size blotch of yellow and green near her right knee. She needed the scissors again to cut through the slipshod bandage she'd fashioned around her shin wound.

A lightheadedness washed over her when she grabbed them. This was where it would get tough.

She'd have to look at the gash in her leg straight on, in the cold light of day.

Her blood had made her pants leg stiff as a cast. The cloth remained rigid as she cut through it, revealing the wound beneath. The laceration had gone swollen and puffy around the edges, the alarming white of bone visible in the center. She would need to sanitize the wound or risk losing her leg to gangrene, but the pain of pouring antiseptic into the wound was unimaginable.

"Let me help you with that," Charlie said quietly.

Salem looked over at him. She could feel the early stages of shock murmuring in her ears, a numbness creeping over her. It was the perfect time. She grabbed the bottle of antiseptic, twisted off the top, and poured it into the gash.

The pain was exquisite, searing, so loud she had to fight to stay above it.

And then it passed, leaving nausea and a sick heartbeat. "Holy hell," Charlie said. "I've never seen anyone do that."

Salem couldn't answer. If she opened her mouth, she'd throw up. Using a clean edge of her shredded pants, she wiped at the perimeter of her wound, cleaning it as best she could. After she'd removed the blood and dirt she could bear to touch, she ripped open the package of butterfly strips. After testing to make sure she could remove their adhesive covers with one hand, she called up a mental image of Mercy and Bel, arms around each other, safe, smiling encouragingly at her.

She could do this. She *would* do this.

She drew in a deep breath and then squeezed her wound closed, tearing the healing flesh and producing deep-red blood. Once the sides of the wound were touching, she held them together with one hand. With the other, she began applying the butterfly closures.

When she was done, her patch job wasn't pretty, but it would suffice. She slathered the area with bacitracin and wrapped the gauze tightly around the butterflied wound, both to keep the flesh in place and to repel bacteria. Removing the last of her pants, she discovered no more serious wounds. The fleece sweatpants felt so good against her skin that she couldn't keep in the moan when she pulled them on. As an afterthought, she cut Mrs. Molony's sachet from her wrecked jeans and fastened it to the sweatpants' drawstring.

She traded out her ripped and bloody blouse for the Orkney T-shirt, yanked a zip-up wind parka over that, brushed her hair and tied it in a bun, used some wet wipes she found in the glove box to clean her hands and face, chewed a handful of aspirin plus two Ativan from her bag, and felt almost normal.

"Your turn," she said to Charlie.

"Just in time." He pointed ahead. "I'll park at the far side of the lot, close enough to those cars so as not to draw suspicion but far enough from the door so we have privacy."

Salem was prepping to treat his wounds. "Do you have any cuts besides the one on your face and your—where your—"

She couldn't finish. Someone had cut off Charlie's finger. Not out of self-defense. Not to get any information out of him. *Just because they could.*

"Ah, love, it's not that bad," he said, smiling weakly. "It'll make it harder to get pissed off at people while driving, is all."

It took her a moment, but when he held up his mutilated hand, she understood. They'd taken his middle finger.

"I bet they have prosthetic ones."

Charlie chuckled as he parked the car. "Like what fans hold at football games, maybe? A big foam finger? I like the sound of that."

His laughter warmed her. Their eyes connected, and she returned his smile, amazed at how bright-eyed he looked, how rosy his cheeks. For the first time, she thought they might get through this. "We should wash off your hand and your face before you change. That way, you won't get any blood on the new clothes."

Charlie nodded, holding out his injured hand. Salem wadded her jeans underneath it to catch any liquids that would wash down when she cleaned the wound. She steeled herself to examine the stump. Her jaw clenched. It had been cleanly sliced between the base and first knuckle, leaving a half-inch stub. The steady blood flow had slowed to a seeping. The white of the bone was centered in the flesh, no splinters, the whole of it reminding Salem of a cartoon rendering of a pork chop.

"I think they cut your finger with the same knife they sliced my rope with."

"Makes sense," Charlie said through gritted teeth. "Ready?"

He jerked his head by way of a nod and started to speak, but Salem was already pouring the antiseptic. He yanked his hand away, but she was done. All that was left to do was clean it off.

"Jesus, Mary, and Joseph does that sting," he said. "Give me some cloth."

She found a clean spot on her blouse and handed it over. He scrubbed around his wound. When his hand was spotless, she slathered it in the salve and gently wrapped a bandage over the stump and around the base of his thumb, making several rounds to protect it. Next, she cleaned up his face, closing the cut on his cheek with another butterfly closure. She left him to clean off his face in the rearview mirror, which he angled down.

"Bloody hell. It's a good thing you didn't let me look at myself before going into the apothecary. I might have chickened out."

"Here's a new shirt." Salem folded it onto the dashboard and shoved their soiled clothing and bandages into the bag, which she intended to leave on the floor.

Their overnight bags plus the B&C rested on the seat. They could walk away from this. Once they'd solved the Stonehenge train and Mercy was safely at home, she'd track down Bode's family and let them know what a hero their son had been.

"Down!" Charlie yelled, reaching for his gun and shoving Salem's head toward the floor of the car.

But not before she caught a glimpse of Alafair peering through her window.

CHAPTER 44

Orkney Islands, Scotland

Kirkwall Airport

"Put your weapon down!" Salem ordered Charlie. She hadn't seen Alafair since London, hadn't thought of her since she'd programmed GAEA to see who she worked for or with. It made no sense that she was in the Orkneys, but things had stopped making sense a while ago. "I know her."

Charlie kept his gun trained on Alafair. Alafair glared at Charlie through the window.

"Charlie," Salem said. "Please."

"If you tell me who she is," Charlie said. His voice was a snarl.

"A freelance computer hacker."

"Why's she here?"

"I don't know. Put your gun down and we can ask her."

Charlie grumbled but complied, shoving his weapon into its holster. Alafair rolled her eyes and signaled for them to exit the car. They obliged, Salem keeping as much weight as she could off her wounded leg, Charlie scanning the perimeter.

"You're far from home," Salem said.

Alafair cocked an eyebrow. Her dark hair was loose, flowing down her back. She wore a leather jacket that fit her upper body like a brace, black jeans, and scuffed leather boots that zipped up her calves. "Not as far as you," she observed. She studied Salem, pausing at each of her bruises, even the ones covered by cloth. "He found you," she said, matter-of-factly.

"What do you want?" Salem asked. For all she knew, Alafair was an assassin working for the Order, though they probably didn't hire women for that sort of work. Salem bit down on the laugh before it escaped.

"I want to give you a ride. To Dublin, and then Kildare." Alafair pointed behind her, toward the terminal and the tarmac. More than a dozen people sat inside the building. Two small airplanes were parked. The flatlands of Scotland rolled for miles beyond that.

"The nearest plane is mine, and my pilot is waiting. I've also got a driver on the ground in Dublin. We can be standing at the foot of St. Brigid's Cathedral inside of three hours."

Salem and Charlie exchanged grim looks. "How do you know where we're going?" Charlie asked.

"I can explain that in the plane, or we can talk about it here." Alafair tipped her head toward Kirkwall. "You can just see the constable making his way over. Seems a gentleman recently entered the apothecary looking a little too tough for a regular fight, even for a Brit."

Still, Salem and Charlie hesitated.

"A scientist has gone missing as well. An American student hired out to help two FBI agents. Too soon to file a missing person's report, but there is interest," she said, tapping the trunk of the car. "I'm sure the police would like to ask you about that."

"Not much of a choice, then," Charlie said, reaching into the car for the clean shirt. "If one of you can help me change, we can be on our way."

Salem walked around the car to assist him. She tucked the old shirt under the seat and reached for their bags before casting a final look toward town. The Orkney police car's bright yellow and blue decals were now visible.

"It's quicker to walk across the tarmac," Alafair said, "but we'd be in plain sight. Better to enter through the terminal and exit out the back." She unzipped the front of her jacket and tugged out a phone. She spoke as she walked, taking one of the bags from Charlie to lighten his load. "We're on our way. Three passengers total. Be ready for immediate takeoff."

An airplane engine rumbled to life on the opposite side of the tarmac. Alafair tucked her phone away and addressed Salem. "Try not to limp if you can."

Salem grimaced. She walked as naturally as she could, the butterfly strips tugging at her flesh but holding. Charlie threw back his head and laughed. The gesture startled Salem, but Alafair understood immediately, mimicking Charlie's laughter. Three regular people, sharing a joke.

The police car was close enough that Salem could see it contained two officers. They didn't appear to be speeding. She didn't want to give them a reason to. At its current pace, the police vehicle would reach the parking lot in three minutes, which was how long it would take them to reach the terminal.

Alafair and Charlie carried on their fake conversation. Salem dragged herself behind. They entered the terminal. An elderly couple spotted them first, polite smiles dropping off their faces as they took in Salem's and Charlie's visible injuries. One look at their expressions and Salem realized they never would have been allowed to board a regular flight.

A child pointed, and a mother shushed them. A low hum traveled along the small terminal as more people whispered about the threesome. Once they were away from the glass windows, Alafair uttered a one-word command.

"Run."

Salem did her best, tears of pain welling in her eyes. Their feet pounded on the floor. Alafair led them toward the rear of the building. Salem kept up despite the agony, ignoring the dot of red that had appeared on her sweatpants. They left through an emergency exit, its wire cut. No alarm.

"Just ahead."

Salem risked a glance back as they neared the plane. The police had parked in front of the terminal, two officers stepping out and stretching.

An oval-shaped door on the side of the plane opened and unfolded into steps. Alafair ushered Salem and then Charlie up them, taking up the rear. She began pulling the door closed, barking orders at the woman who had let them in. "We better be in the air before my ass hits that seat."

The woman hurried to the cockpit. Alafair sealed the door, slamming it into place. Salem fell into the nearest seat, one of six, three to a side. The upholstery was out of date, the interior of the plane carrying a distinct 1970s aesthetic, but it was clean, and it was getting them out of here. Charlie took the chair in front of her, and Alafair sat across from Salem.

The engine surged, the sound of the propeller roaring to life reaching the inside of the plane.

Alafair pointed to a silver rectangle on the side of her chair. "They swivel."

She pushed hers and used her feet to turn toward Salem.

Salem did the same, and then Charlie, so they were all facing each other.

"It's time to talk," Alafair said, her eyes glittering.

Salem fell stubbornly silent. Charlie, not so much. "Are you with the Order or the Underground?"

"Neither. Freelance." Alafair leaned forward and Charlie pulled back. "Let me see your hand."

He scowled.

She arched an eyebrow, smirking. "If it makes you feel better, I'll let you hold your gun while I do it."

Charlie offered his hand, still sullen. Alafair reached for it, feeling gently around the wrist, pushing up his sleeve to examine his forearm, levitating her hand just over the stump. She didn't touch it, but the suggestion that she could made Charlie twitch.

Alafair held firm. "This is already infected. Feel for yourself. It's giving off heat like a stove. What was used to cut off your finger?"

"I don't know. I was unconscious."

Alafair relaxed, a look like pity flitting across her face. "I'm sorry to hear that. It's a particular horror to have things done to you when you're asleep, yes?" She turned her attention to Salem. "Your leg is all right for now. Its blood is clean, and your cheeks aren't flushed like your friend's."

Salem's stubbornness melted. "Do you have anything to help him?"

"Not on the plane. We can pick up supplies when we land." The unspoken fact that they would not visit a hospital lay solid between them.

"You lied about wanting me to help you find Rosalind Franklin's research," Salem accused.

Alafair watched her, mirth dancing in her eyes. She was waiting for Salem to put the pieces together.

It took Salem only seconds, the puzzle falling into place as the plane shuddered off the ground. It shouldn't have taken her that long. *Photo 51.* She'd thought it was part of the 8CH3COOH code, but it wasn't. It was the signature of the woman who'd left the code. "Franklin is the one who added on to the Stonehenge train."

Alafair's eyes sparkled. "I've never been able to prove it, but I believe so."

"Her DNA research is at the end of the train?" Salem asked.

"That's our best bet. And not just Franklin's research. A treasure of women's wisdom, if the rumors are true. Scientific discoveries, medical breakthroughs, poems and plays—all of it either hidden or incorrectly attributed to men all these years."

"That would be something," Charlie said, but his words slurred. He started to slump but then sat up straight. "You're Indigo."

His words puzzled Salem, until she remembered the super-wealthy, clandestine, and independent cryptanalysis group GAEA had uncovered. Her eyes flew to Alafair, who was watching Charlie with a peculiar focus.

"That would be quite a thing if I were," Alafair said by way of a response. She stood and walked over to a cabinet. She opened a pill bottle and grabbed water, bringing both back to Charlie. "I can't imagine it will touch the bone pain, but it'll keep your fever at bay until we have something stronger."

Charlie took both without argument. His hands were shaking so much that he dropped the pills. Salem handed them back to him, horrified at how quickly the infection had set in. What she had thought was good cheer as she'd cleaned his wound was the pre-glow of blood poisoning. Charlie popped three pills into his mouth, followed by a glug from the water bottle.

"Finish it," Alafair commanded, pointing at the water. "Take as much fluid as you can keep down. You too, Salem. You're the color of snow. Not a pretty shade for a half Persian."

Salem sipped the water she was offered. Her stomach clutched, pushing back, and then once it realized what it was, begged greedily for more. Salem downed the bottle. "May I have another?"

"Wait to see how long that one stays down," Alafair cautioned. "They don't make this carpeting anymore."

"You knew we'd be at the Gloup?" Salem asked.

"I hate to hurt your spy feelings," Alafair said, directing her derision in Charlie's direction, "but you are not the first to track it this far. I've no idea who first discovered that Stonehenge was a code, or when, but the rumor has been alive longer than my great-great-great-grandmother. The reports of treasure at the end—jewels and gold, originally—created a great interest in Stonehenge." She cocked her head. "I know of two groups that cracked the Underground's original code—the Order and the Roma. My people followed the Stonehenge clue to Stenness, then the Ness of Brodgar, which got us to the Gloup, and the jeweled box. What took us centuries, you solved in a day."

Her tone made it more annoyance than compliment.

"I have seen St. Brigid's cross inside that box, ran my fingers across the $8CH3COOH$ carved into the back, as have many of my ancestors. They were after jewels. Me? I was there in the hopes that the rumors that Rosalind Franklin had been sent by the Underground to move the treasure were true. Because if they were, that meant that her discovery of a way to reverse paralysis could also be true."

"But if you've seen the cross, then it's already sent you to St. Brigid's," Salem argued.

"Aye. My people've probably written a bloody folk song about it, that clue's been around so long. But I've never been able to definitively connect the jeweled box to Rosalind Franklin, and no one among us, not the Roma or the Order, have ever solved it beyond St. Brigid's. It was a gentleman's agreement, I suppose, that we both left the jeweled box at the Gloup. Our only chance at getting to the riches of the ages was for someone to crack its secret, to discover the meaning of the code on the back of the cross."

"How long will it take us to get to Ireland?"

"Two hours."

"And then to Kildare?"

"Another hour." Alafair pursed her lips. "I don't know if the devil's on your side, but today is Kildare's fall festival, celebrating the equinox. It will be easy to blend in, for you as well as those hunting you."

Charlie snuffled. He had drifted into a troubled sleep.

"Best thing for him," she said, her tone gone acid. "That's the Grimalkin's work, amputating a finger after he has knocked you out. You spend the rest of your life wondering what else he took from you."

"Are you going to protect us?"

Alafair raised an eyebrow. "The Roma as well as the Indigo are neutral in all matters historical and political. Our interests have crossed over in this, yours and mine. I will help you if it will help my brother, but I speak only for myself." She lifted her nose in Charlie's direction. "How well do you know him?"

"He saved my life. If he hadn't gotten the rope down to me, I never would have made it out of the Gloup."

Alafair nodded thoughtfully. "He is familiar to me, but I don't know how. And I don't trust him."

Salem didn't tell her that Charlie worked for MI5. She knew him better than she knew Alafair and intended to protect him as he had protected her. "If we crack the Stonehenge code and Rosalind Franklin's research is found, how long until her cure would be a reality?"

"We have scientists who have the equipment. We just need the data. Depending on how advanced it is, months. Maybe even weeks if she tested it herself."

That made up Salem's mind. She reached for her overnight bag, into which she'd transferred the jeweled box. "I have something to show you."

CHAPTER 45

Kildare, Ireland

St. Brigid's Cathedral

A car was waiting for them at the Dublin Airport, as promised.

Charlie rested in the back seat, some of his color returning. Alafair drove. Salem took the passenger seat, firing up GAEA so she could add an additional command to the algorithms she was currently running, this one with a code-breaking bend.

GAEA must break 8CH3COOH before they reached Kildare. Salem fed her the string of code and then checked her nets. She hadn't caught anything immediately noteworthy, only unrelated and isolated information about Franklin possibly dating Jacques Mering, the married director of the Paris lab she began her career at; some late-chiming groups taking credit for the bombing but having their facts wrong; and thousands of social media posts threatening to kill Hayes, but all of them so redundant in wording that, after collating all background information on each poster to verify they were impotent, GAEA presented it as a one-sentence report: "Dismissed 74,036 online threats against Hayes."

Salem lifted her head. Alafair was taking back roads as a precaution. It was a long shot that the Kirkwall police had discovered Bode's corpse at the Gloup and connected it to the private airplane that took off, but they could not risk being detained. The country roads would add only minutes to the travel time, Alafair had promised.

Salem didn't mind. The close sky of Ireland healed something inside her each time she returned here. She wondered if her dad's people still lived here. She could ask around, once they solved this. Yes, she liked imagining a future, one with Mercy in it.

Whitewashed cottages protected by waist-high rock walls sped past her window, broken by great swaths of verdant green interspersed with raspberry brambles as large as a house and bursts of dusty purple and orange flowers. "What are those?"

Alafair flicked her eyes. "The flowers? The tall fire bursts are montbretia. The violet ones are heather. My mother used to feed us heather tea when we were ill. It cleaned you out, that's for sure. I think it would have tasted even more bitter, but she went heavy on the honey."

"Hmmm." Salem rubbed her face. Electric poles were the only modern touch on this stretch of road. Treetops met one another above the road, their hanging branches trimmed by tall trucks into a perfect truck-shaped hole. She pulled her attention back to the laptop. GAEA's Moscow/London server collator had flagged another business email sent between the two. Like the previous email she'd caught, this one didn't make clear what the businesses were.

Our onetime offer is only on the table briefly—23 September, 12:00–12:30. Whereas the first email had originated in Moscow and gone to London, this one had traveled in reverse. As with the previous email, this one had been snagged because of the date. Salem didn't hesitate in sending it on to Stone. She wouldn't fill him in on the Stonehenge train any longer, but it would be irresponsible to withhold information related to the bombing or, potentially, to the president's visit.

That's all there was in GAEA's nets. Salem paused to think about Rosalind Franklin. Alafair had been excited—no, more like vindicated— to see Franklin's Photo 51 inside the jeweled box. It was incontrovertible evidence that Franklin had been the one who'd picked up the Stonehenge train at the Gloup and moved it out.

Alafair had also infected Salem with her confidence that Franklin had discovered a way to reverse paralysis. Salem had seen enough proof in Franklin's genius and her work with DNA to believe there was hope for Bel to walk again at the end of the Stonehenge train. The pressure to protect the president, save Mercy, and find a treatment for Bel was immense. Salem had to shove all that to the corner of her mind and focus on the next step, which was to find out everything she could about St. Brigid. She programmed GAEA to scour the internet for anomalies in the background while Salem completed a surface search.

She discovered that the Catholic Church had claimed Saint Brigid of Kildare for one of Ireland's patron saints, but they'd almost certainly co-opted her from the stories of a fourth-century priestess to Brigid, the Celtic mother goddess. The Christian festival in celebration of St. Brigid was scheduled to replace Imbolc, the pagan celebration of spring. On that day, the first of February, celebrants wove St. Brigid's unique rush crosses and hung them over their doors to protect their homes.

According to sixth-century texts, the pagan priestess first plaited the cross at her dying father's bedside. She was a healer, skilled with metalwork, and exceedingly generous. When she converted to Christianity, she built an abbey on what was then a Celtic shrine in honor of the goddess Brigid.

The woman, who had also started calling herself Brigid, created a school devoted to piousness and the arts. Her nuns attended the eternal flame in the Fire Temple. Brigid died in 525, and a shrine was built soon after near the temple. This was destroyed and rebuilt many times during subsequent centuries, most notably in 1223 and 1686. An almost entirely new building was erected on the same location in the late nineteenth century.

Also within a stone's throw of the Fire Temple's foundation, a tower—its design unique to Ireland—was erected in the twelfth century. It was still standing, one of only two such towers in Ireland that allowed access. Salem, Charlie, and Alafair were on their way to the nineteenth-century cathedral and twelfth-century tower right now, but none of Salem's research revealed a connection to 8CH3COOH, which itself might be a keytext rather than a clue.

GAEA pinged with preliminary research on what the numbers could potentially represent if they were isolated from the letters and then combined or taken alone. Numerology suggested that thirty-eight represented creative relationships; eighty-three, business collaborations. The number thirty-eight referred to a revolver, was the atomic number of strontium, a factorial prime, how many Bach flower tinctures were created in the 1930s, and the number of slots there are on a roulette wheel.

The number eighty-three was used by white supremacist groups as a greeting, appeared once in the Bible, was bismuth's atomic number, the age at which a practicing Jew can celebrate their second bar mitzvah, and a Sophie Germain prime—a computationally secure prime named after the famous eighteenth-century mathematician. The third letter of the alphabet was C, and the eighth H, two of the three letters used in the code carved into the back of the St. Brigid's cross.

The number three was the second Sophie Germain prime, a rough approximation of pi, representative of the Holy Trinity, and a Fibonacci number; meant "end of text" in binary code and represented St. Peter (who three times denied and three times accepted Jesus) in Christianity; and was the accepted number of times bad luck appeared.

The number eight was the infinity symbol, could represent the equinox, was also a Fibonacci number, and was the second magic number according to nuclear physics. In Greek numerals, where Greek letters were still used to symbolize numbers, eight was written as the letter *eta* with an acute accent, roughly translating to H.

"Here we go."

The slowing of the car dragged Salem out of her number research and into the present. That, and the smell of burgers grilling and the sight of packed crowds making the road ahead nearly impassable. "Wow."

"Yeah," Alafair said. "The festival will make it hard to park. I think we should leave your guy in the car."

"That sounds about as fun as a pet fish," Charlie said from the back seat.

Salem turned. His eyes were closed, and he was lying down. "You should rest."

He dragged himself to a sitting position. His color dropped and then returned. "I'm going with."

Alafair sniffed but didn't argue. "I'll drop you both off at the cathedral and then meet up with you after I park."

"Thanks." Salem didn't want to lug the B&C through the crowds, but she couldn't leave it behind. She set GAEA to chime if she found anything remarkable, put the computer in its case, zipped it, and slid the strap over her shoulder in anticipation of exiting the car. People were ten deep on each side, smiling, talking, wearing bright scarves and caps. They moved to let the car past and then closed the space behind it. "This festival is a pretty big deal?"

"To the Irish, every festival is a big deal. This is one of the originals, though. It's a harvest festival, a time to celebrate the fruits of the year and connect with your neighbors before battening down the hatches for winter. While its roots come from an agricultural community, most of the celebration happens in town. As you can see, the cathedral gets its share of spillover."

Alafair pointed forward, to where a grand church on a hill was emerging into view. The majestic gray stones made Salem gasp. The building was compact yet grand, Celtic stone high crosses peppering the ground between the entrance and the cathedral in the typical Irish graveyard.

Alafair put the vehicle into park. "Can't take you any farther."

Salem opened her door as far as she could in the crowd and slid out, closing it before going back to help Charlie. Her leg protested with a sharp ache, but it wasn't bleeding. Charlie was not emanating as much heat, either. The aspirin must have cut his fever. "Meet you inside the grounds," Salem said to Alafair.

"I got this," Charlie said, smiling his lopsided smile as Salem tried to support him on her shoulder.

Salem was going to argue but decided against it. "I don't yet know what we're looking for," she said, pitching her voice so it traveled below the hum of the crowd.

"Hasn't stopped us yet," Charlie said.

A grateful warmth suffused Salem. "It makes the most sense to start in the main cathedral. It was built hundreds of years after Brigid died, but this part of the train was put in place recently, before Rosalind Franklin died."

"When was that?"

"1958. All the structures here were well in place by then. We're looking for a spot that would make sense to a scientist, or a Brit."

"Or a woman."

Salem's mouth twitched. "Yeah, or a woman. Plus, a connection to the numbers eight or three, any combination thereof, and the letters *C, O,* or *H.*"

They breached the open gate. The crowds were lighter inside, soberer.

"I'll walk the grounds," Charlie offered. "Count headstones, look for other structures there might be three, eight, or eleven of. You go inside, and we text each other if we find something, deal?"

"Works for me." Salem felt bad leaving Charlie. His fever was down, but he'd lost something since the attack, something less obvious than a finger. She clapped her hands together once, sharply, to startle herself out of her thoughts. There wasn't time for pity. She had a code to crack. Maybe they'd even locate the end of the Stonehenge train today. If the Underground was in charge, it'd make sense they'd move it to a church founded by a woman.

The cathedral's main entrance was propped open, a disconcertingly small door opening into the short end of the building that was shaped like a Christian cross from above. There was a line to enter, but it was fast-moving.

"Buy a cross?"

Salem smiled at the middle-aged man holding a St. Brigid's cross toward her. His Irish brogue was thick. His belly stretched the fabric of the Def Leppard concert T-shirt he wore. The cross was made of straw. It was simple but lovely.

"It's beautiful," she said.

He winked. "Long winters here. We either become artists or alcoholics." He pointed upward. "He prefers the former. Can I interest you in one?"

"Sure." Salem unzipped her parka to reach for money.

"Thank you. All the money raised goes to support the cathedral." She became flustered when she realized she carried no cash. All the clothes she wore were from the apothecary. Charlie had handled the money. "I'm so sorry. I don't have my wallet."

He cocked his head. "It's all right, love. We share the harvest." He handed her a cross.

"I can't take this."

"You can and you will." He pressed it in her hand, tipping his head toward her waist. "And tell the mothers that we were good to you here in Kildare, will you?"

Her eyes darted downward. Mrs. Molony's red-flowered sachet was still looped through the drawstring of her sweatpants. Her pulse ratcheted. She wanted to ask the man what he meant, but he was already chatting with the family behind her. Mrs. Molony had told her the sachet would protect her. She'd assumed it was an old wives' tale tied to the herbs inside, but it had meant more to Alafair, and to this man. She touched it, rubbed the cloth between her fingers, following the crowd as they entered the cathedral and then began walking its perimeter, oohing and aahing at the treasures it contained.

She understood their awe. Stained glass windows let in colored light, which washed over stones and structures hundreds of years old.

The foyer held glass dioramas depicting twelfth-century society in Kildare. Salem glanced at them only briefly, walking ahead toward rows of pews beneath lancet windows.

The gray and white stone walls on each side of the pews held a cacophony of relics, including the sixteenth-century tomb of Walter Wellesley, a stone baptismal fount so eroded by age that it appeared to be built of foam, carved bits of rock, fifteen mismatched tiles framed like a larger-than-life sliding block puzzle, microwave-size stone casts of nautilus shells, religious seals, and St. Brigid's woven crosses tucked into alcoves built into the walls. Nothing was behind a rope or under glass, all of it accessible to the masses, all of it embalmed in the acrid odor of age.

Taken together, the cathedral's interior was grand and overwhelming.

Salem did not know where to begin.

She chose as a random starting point a straw St. Brigid's cross nailed below the window nearest her. She would examine every nook and cranny before moving on. A pop of color behind a stone caught her attention. She leaned forward, peeking behind the shield-shaped rock propped against the wall.

It hid a red ball of yarn.

Her flesh crawled. It was a cat's toy. She spun, looking for the Grimalkin, though she had no clues about the assassin's appearance. No one was paying any attention to her. That didn't help. She was so wound up that she jumped when her phone buzzed. It was a text from Charlie.

Meet me in St. Brigid's kitchen. Burial vault to the right of path we came in on.

Salem's skin tingled. She wove her way through the crowd, leaving via the door she'd entered through. She was in such a hurry to reach Charlie that she bumped into a man. "Sorry!"

"No worries," the gentleman said, tipping his tweed cap and smiling as he disappeared into the crowd.

"Over here!"

Salem spotted Charlie's waving hand and walked toward it as fast as her leg would allow. "What'd you uncover?"

"Maybe nothing." He glanced at her leg. "Can you manage the stairs?"

"Yep."

"Then follow me." He pushed gently through the crowd waiting to descend the narrow steps into the earth, pointing at the stone plaque mounted over the stairs. "It was built in the fourteenth century. While almost certainly used as a burial vault, it may have also been the entrance to an underground escape tunnel."

They reached the base of the stairs. Both Salem and Charlie had to crouch to enter the crowded room. Its ceilings were coved. What Salem could see of the space reminded her of the inside of a brick oven. It gave her the shivers. She scanned the walls to pinpoint what Charlie had seen.

"Look up," he said.

She did. Channels like desperate scrapings ran across the ceiling. She lifted her hand and traced her fingers through it, shuddering. It looked like the handiwork of someone buried alive, trying to claw his way out.

"There's thirty-eight of them in this section." A crack separated one chunk from the rest of the ceiling. "Does it mean something?"

Salem pulled out her phone and clicked on its flashlight. The artificial illumination curried some annoyed stares from those presumably trying for an authentic experience, but she didn't care. She retrieved her penknife, too, and dug around the crack and further explored the scrapings. Charlie kept most of the crowd away from her.

"I'm afraid I don't see anything," she said.

He frowned. "Me neither. But I had to be sure."

They swam through the crowd to the surface. After being underground, Salem felt grateful for the cool, fresh air washing over her. She was not yet ready to return to all the potential hiding spots inside the cathedral. "Have you walked through the graveyard?"

Charlie seemed to read her mood. "Not yet. I'll take this side, you take that, and we'll meet in the middle? We can work the interior of the cathedral after that, if we don't find anything."

She wanted to hug him she was so grateful. She walked toward the stone wall that ringed the cathedral grounds. The earth grew springy closer to the wall. The grass wasn't mowed back here, stocky yellow flowers mixed among the clover and brome. A rise in the earth reminded her of the barrows circling Stonehenge.

Neither the wall nor the ground gave up any clues, so she made her way toward the graveyard. A short metal fence surrounded one of the graves. She neared it, poking at a pile of sticks bundled on the ground. They squirmed. She jumped back, causing a streak of pain in her wounded leg.

She'd nudged a mound of slugs, not sticks.

Salem drew a deliberate breath and ignored the writhing pile. She couldn't afford to be squeamish.

The gravestone was eroded beyond legibility, its front speckled with yellow and black lichen. She was surrounded by festivalgoers speaking Irish laced with bits of English. The rich swell of Irish folk music reached her from the village, wafting with it the scent of fresh-baked bread and something malty.

Her eyes grew hot. She blinked to clear a spot blurring her vision. It had appeared as a light on the ground in front of her. Rubbing her eye sockets did not make it disappear. The circle of white-yellow was as big as the bottom of a soda can. It reminded her of a larger version of the Stanhope's reflection onto Charlie.

She shaded her face and stared up toward the tower.

It was constructed of the same lichen-dappled gray stones as the cathedral, its workmanship smooth. Two-story metal stairs led to a single door on its face. Another window was built into the side two-thirds of the way up, the only aperture until the rung of archer's windows at the very peak, beneath the tower's castellated ridge.

The light seemed to have come from the midway window, but it had disappeared. A reflection from someone's watch face?

"You should see inside that window at the equinox. It's tonight, you know. Reason for the festival." It was the same man Salem had bumped into leaving the cathedral. He was tall and bear-shaped with a nose that hooked as if it had been broken several times. "The equinox is the only time all year the sun shines directly inside, and just for a minute."

His words flipped on the klieg lights of Salem's consciousness. The equinox was represented by the number eight.

Eight was the first number of the code on the St. Brigid's cross. The whiteboard of her mind began madly scribbling hypotheses, erasing them, redrawing new ones. The light through that window for only one minute of every year, shining in on a clue that would otherwise be invisible. That would explain why no one had solved the Stonehenge train beyond the Gloup. A time-based clue would be appealing to a scientist like Rosalind Franklin.

While Salem's brain worked out all the possible angles, her mouth addressed the immediate one. "Do I know you?"

The Irishman tapped the side of his nose before pulling back one side of his parka to reveal a flowered belt in the same pattern as Salem's sachet. "I don't believe so. As I was saying, the light shines in there once a year. People like to go inside for that, so it can be quite a scramble to reach the location. Seen it before myself. Can't say it was too impressive, but of course I live here." He winked again. "Do you know there's six floors inside? The ladders connecting them are near vertical, a hundred thirty steps total. It used to be a bell tower, back in its prime. A place to hide riches, too, though I suspect it's been combed clean."

"What time is it?"

He glanced at his watch. "It's quarter to nine." He shoved his hands deep in the pockets of his corduroy pants and returned his attention to the tower, as if they were two old friends discussing the weather. "This year, the equinox occurs at 9:02, is over by 9:03. Such a short moment."

Salem's heart somersaulted. She began to calculate the distance between her and the tower but realized it didn't matter: she had to get there. She limped forward, skimming the crowd for Charlie. She needed him. He knew masonry. He could navigate a crowd. If he pulled out his MI5 ID badge, people would have to move aside for them.

There wasn't time for her to do it alone. It wasn't possible.

She almost wept with relief when she spotted him slouching against the far wall, behind and to the left of the tower. He was staring at his phone, likely texting her just as she was searching for him. Salem opened her mouth to shout for him.

His name left her lips at the same moment another man walked through the opening and turned to Charlie. Something in the way he carried himself chilled Salem to her core. When he looked her direction, she understood why.

It was Jason, the man who had tortured her mother, the snake who could change all his appearance except for his eyes. He was after Charlie.

CHAPTER 46

Kildare, Ireland

St. Brigid's Cathedral

Jason had swallowed his displeasure when the Grimalkin commanded him to hide the ball of yarn, but he could not contain himself when the Grimalkin ordered him not to retire Salem Wiley's associate. It would have been so easy to stick with the plan, for the Grimalkin to shadow Salem and for Jason to terminate her colleague so Salem would no longer be distracted and could not escape. It's what they'd agreed on during the drive from the airport.

But the Grimalkin would not, could not, follow a plan straight. The assassin had pulled Jason away from what he was doing, ordered him to pivot.

"I've got an update," the Grimalkin said. "A new plan."

Jason scowled, waiting. He estimated over two thousand people crowded the streets of Kildare. The bustle disguised their argument, but it also irritated Jason.

"Do you want to know what it is?"

Jason still refused to answer. He would not be the Grimalkin's toy, a distraction from the frustrating efficiency with which Salem was solving everything thrown her way. Jason had watched her inside the cathedral, nervous, limping even though she'd gone to great efforts to hide that weakness, deep bags under her eyes. She was stumbling around like a wounded bird yet was seemingly able to spot clues that the rest of the world was blind to. It must chafe the Grimalkin greatly to have someone so outwardly weak be so much better at code breaking.

"Aw, come on now," the Grimalkin said, wheedling. "Lean in and let me tell you the new plan, the one that involves *me* killing the colleague in the next five minutes and *you* getting the glory of shadowing Wiley when she breaks the uncrackable next level of the Stonehenge train like the idiot savant that she is."

Despite himself, Jason bent toward the Grimalkin ever so slightly.

The Grimalkin had grinned. "There it is, such a good teammate you are."

Jason saw it coming but could not move fast enough. The Grimalkin's legendary speed was not a myth. Jason was outdrawn.

He saw only the blur of a hand, felt only a prick at his throat.

Even as he fell to the ground, he did not know whether the weapon had been a needle or a knife.

CHAPTER 47

Kildare, Ireland

St. Brigid's Cathedral

"Salem!"

She turned to see Alafair walking around the side of the cathedral.

When her head whipped back to the spot Charlie had been, both he and the assassin had vanished.

Salem stared wildly at the tower, then at the spot where Charlie had disappeared.

The sun was dropping.

She could save her partner, or she could crack the next clue of the Stonehenge train.

"I saw the fellow in the long coat watching your man. Did he reach him?" Alafair asked.

Salem nodded, Alafair trailing her as she limped toward the spot where Charlie had been texting, her mind made up. Enough people had died. She would discover another way to crack the code. "I think so. We've gotta help him. If they haven't taken him too far, I can maybe get back in the tower before the equinox is over."

Alafair stopped her. "What's this?"

Salem pointed toward the tower's window. "I think that the St. Brigid's cross is sending us to the tower, that the only reason no one has unlocked its secret is because it's only visible once a year, at the exact moment of the equinox, when the sun shines through that single window."

Alafair steered Salem toward the tower. "Go."

"I can't." Salem pulled free. "I have to rescue Charlie."

Alafair laughed unpleasantly. "You and your bum leg against a man trained for battle? I will save your friend, if there's anything left of him. You crack the code."

Salem drew in a breath to fight, to argue that she couldn't trust a near stranger with Charlie's life, but she heard the sense in Alafair's words. It pained her to leave her friend, but she had to do it. "Thank you."

She felt someone's gaze on her as she hurried toward the tower, maybe the Grimalkin's, wanting her to solve the puzzle so he could swoop down and snatch it from her before murdering her. The thought stoked that same black rage that had consumed her back at the Gloup. She picked up her pace, her leg openly bleeding.

She flung out her elbows, but there was no need to jostle. The crowd parted for her, stepping aside to let her charge up the metal stairs. The design above the door featured the same V shapes as on the Flower Rock and the Gloup—more refined, yet the same flower symbols nonetheless. She wanted to yell her exultation. She was in the right place.

At the first landing, the tower was no wider than six feet across, bisected by a wooden ladder that pierced the ceiling above. It was agony to bend her leg at each of the steps, but she pushed through to the second landing.

This level was packed with people, but they hugged the walls when she neared. When a rare person turned to chide her for shoving, a nearby friend silenced them.

I must look the ghoul, she thought, bleeding and wild-eyed, bent on climbing upward.

The tower narrowed slightly at the third level, the crowds here treating her with the same cautious deference. Sweat dripped down her back.

Her jacket was too hot for this physical exertion. She dropped it halfway up to the fourth level.

The level with the window.

The light was different even before she breached the floor separating the third floor from the fourth. This room was so packed with people that it was impossible to stand in it, but as if urged by some whisper network, people moved up the ladder to make room.

Salem got her bearings. The circumference of this space was also about six feet. The window was to her left, deeply recessed, revealing the walls to be at least four feet thick. The window was more of an archer's opening than a true aperture, and bright green clumps of flowers grew in the chinks of stone near its outer rim.

The sun was tickling the window's edges.

"What time is it?" Salem demanded of a woman standing near her, one of the few who'd remained.

"Nine p.m. pure, ma'am," she said, her Irish accent thick.

"You're sure?"

"Yes."

Salem nodded. She stepped away from the path of light, eyes trained on the spot she guessed the equinox sunset would illuminate.

She didn't remember inhaling or exhaling. Only waiting. The light came.

Its shape, through a trick of the stonework, appeared as a St. Brigid's cross.

Those remaining on the fourth floor gasped.

Salem leaped forward, slapping her hand in the center of the cross. The warmth of the sun heated it. She reached for her phone and snapped a one-handed photo. Then she peered at the shape, eyes and mind racing to find what CH_3COOH—the original code minus the eight that had brought her here—would have meant to Rosalind Franklin in this context.

She had less than a minute.

"Here you go."

The woman who'd told Salem the time was holding a tube of lipstick, its red tip poking out. Salem didn't understand.

The woman stepped forward tentatively, as if offering a treat to a mad dog. "It's for the shape, now. Trace it with the lipstick before it disappears."

Salem accepted it gratefully, completing the four-armed outline just before the sun moved its trajectory and the light cross disappeared. She handed the tube back. "I'm afraid it's ruined."

The woman smiled. "The color never suited me."

Salem studied the outline. The rock in the center of it was the same unbroken limestone as the rock beyond it. There were no holes, no imperfections. She could scrape at it, pound it, but she wouldn't get far before the police dragged her away. She was surprised the locals had not already thrown her out of the tower, if she paused to think about it. They were surely texting for help, afraid to disrupt the crazy woman. She didn't have much time.

CH3COOH.

If she removed the remaining number, it spelled *CHOOCH*. Like the noise a train made? Except that didn't help. She dropped to the floor, keeping her wounded leg as straight as possible, and removed GAEA from her case. She flipped her open, the lipstick outline garish, almost swastika-shaped, above her.

She inputted the letters. And waited.

And waited.

GAEA was testing billions of hypotheses. Salem had to help her, must narrow it down. She felt the eyes of the people lining the walls, crowding the stairs, but she had to pretend as if they weren't there.

How could she narrow it?

"Science!"

When a young man on the ladder jumped, she realized she'd yelled that out loud. Rosalind Franklin had been a scientist. She would have chosen a code in her own milieu, a formula.

Salem's fingers flew like birds across the keys.

GAEA provided the result in less than thirty seconds. CH_3COOH was the chemical formula for acetic acid.

Salem whooped. She tweaked GAEA's data input to discover that acetic acid was a simple carboxylic acid produced by certain bacteria, naturally present in the vaginal lubrication of primates and synthetically produced for use as an antifungal and antibacterial in ear drops as well as to create vinegar, wood glue, and photographic film. The last use was almost certainly how Rosalind Franklin had come into contact with it. And she would have known of its singularly unusual property: it melted limestone.

Salem shot back to her feet. "Who has ear drops?"

The woman who had given her the lipstick shrugged. "Not me."

"Vinegar?" Salem asked, without much hope.

"Well, you heard her," the woman said to the person standing at the top of the ladder. "Spread it up and down. We need ear drops or vinegar."

Those who had been watching Salem began buzzing, the sound traveling along the tower. They might think she was off her rocker, but they wanted to help.

"I can't believe you aren't having me arrested," Salem said to the woman.

She winked. "You're in Ireland, love. We take the person whole. And in any case, we Kildaren know about the cross lighting up for the same minute every year. Wouldn't mind knowing what's behind it. Here we go now." A bottle of ear drops was handed down. Five condiment packets of malt vinegar appeared from below.

"Is that it?" the woman asked. The humming traveled up and down and back again. When it returned empty, she shrugged. "This'll have to do," she told Salem.

The bottle of ear drops was half-full at best. The packets combined would provide no more than three tablespoons of vinegar by Salem's guess. She wasn't hopeful, but she had no choice. She approached the wall.

"Can you shine a light on it?"

The remaining people crowded in the room with her turned on their phones, lighting up the wall like a film shoot.

Salem drew a deep breath. She removed the cap from the ear drops. She aimed toward the center of the cross and sprayed, pointing the nozzle so all the drops landed within the lipstick boundary.

The bubbling was immediate. Those on the landing cheered.

Salem squirted some more above that spot. The foaming grew more aggressive. She emptied the whole bottle and moved on to a packet of vinegar, squirting it at the top of the cross so any overflow rolled down. The acrid smell curled the flesh inside her nose.

She poured the other four packets within the cross.

Careful not to disturb the work of the acetic acid, she explored with the tip of her penknife. It was difficult to see what was happening under the bubbling brown-yellow, but it seemed as if the knife went in deeper than it would have before she'd doused the wall.

She pushed and twisted.

A pitted block of limestone fell near her feet. It revealed a square of metal underneath. "She's found something!"

This cheer traveled all the way to the top of the tower.

Salem put her shoulder into it, chipping away the now-loosened limestone to reveal more metal. Once it was fully exposed, she saw it had the same trip mechanism as the drawer in the Gloup.

She pushed the switch. A drawer slid open, drawing gasps.

Salem reached inside. She removed a glass test tube holding a scroll of paper.

"We've got to see what's on that," the lipstick woman said.

Salem popped the stopper off the tube.

She drew out the paper.

Unrolled it.

It was blank.

The room was quiet, charged.

"Well, that's a bucket of shite," the woman finally said.

Salem let the scroll snap closed. Rosalind Franklin had been a brilliant woman, a hunted woman. She would not have gone through all this trouble to conceal a blank sheet of paper. Either the Grimalkin had come ahead and was playing with her yet again—unlikely, given the timing and the state of the wall before she'd doused it with acid—or Franklin had used invisible ink to throw off anyone who accidentally stumbled across the clue.

Regardless, Salem had to get out of there.

"Thank you for your trouble," she said to the woman, and then directed it at everyone she could see. "Sorry to all of you for damaging the inside of your tower."

"Best time we had in a while," the woman said. "And we can see you'd like to go. Can't say as I blame you. We'll clean up here. Be off with you."

The adrenaline drained away, leaving Salem soggy-brained, like she was part of a massive prank being filmed, maybe playing across screens right now. Her leg was hot and tight, and fresh blood had begun to soak her sweatpants. She didn't need to make sense of this; she needed to leave.

She tucked the paper inside the glass. She closed the B&C and hoisted its strap over her shoulder. "Thank you."

People made way for her. She limped down the steep stairs. Someone handed her parka back to her and kept moving. Once outside, she sucked in the fresh air, clearing her head. The grounds of St. Brigid were still crowded, all but the people at the entrance oblivious to the drama that had gone on inside.

Salem melted gratefully into the crowd, walking as naturally as a woman in bloody sweatpants could, toward the hole in the wall where Charlie had disappeared. Traveling musicians played a jig down the road to her left. The smell of burgers had been replaced by the scent of frying fish. A performer must be preparing to her right because a clot of people seemed to be forming a circle around something.

She intended to circumvent the throng, but she caught a glimpse of someone lying on the ground in their center. Her heart slid sideways. Was it Charlie? Had she sacrificed him to find the clue?

She walked slowly toward the body, getting jostled and pushed. She didn't want to see who it was, but she had to. The way the crowd was responding—no urgency, no action—the person on the ground must be beyond help.

Her hand was up to push aside the only person left standing in her way when someone grabbed her and pulled her back. Salem struck out to defend herself, but her B&C twisted in front of her, throwing her off balance.

"It's me," Alafair said. "You don't want to see the body."

Salem's heartbeat thundered at her neck. "Who is it?"

"Some guy's been knifed."

"Charlie?"

"Ach. No. He's at the car, waiting for us, though he's not looking good. I went to round up a remedy for him and you both, and then to find you. Did you break the code?"

The far-off wail of an ambulance cut through the jangly notes of the folk music and the somber murmurings of the people gathered around the body. Salem wanted to run, to follow Alafair away from the crowds and the noise, but something in the Romani woman's demeanor was unsettling. "You made Charlie walk all the way to the car?"

Alafair's eyes grew veiled. "It's not that far. Come on." She grabbed Salem's arm, pulling her away from the body.

Salem strained to see who was on the ground. She could not. The crowd closed behind her.

The ambulance was growing closer, its siren piercing. Whoever was hurt would be cared for, if they were alive.

"You didn't answer me," Alafair said. "Did you find the next clue?"

"Yes." Salem touched the glass vial through her parka. "But how do you know it's not the last clue?"

Alafair tossed a disturbed glance back at Salem, not losing speed as she cut a swath through the inebriated and celebratory. "I don't. Car's up here."

Salem nodded. Her feet were heavy, her arms were cement, her eyes were sandpaper. Everything felt feverish and swollen. She'd slept four hours in as many days. She was cut and bruised and traumatized, and she'd just about had enough.

The car peeked through the crowd. Charlie sat in the front seat, his head dangling to the side. Her relief was solid. She'd been sure he was the one back in the square, dead, killed by Jason.

Or Alafair.

Paranoia itched at her. She ignored the look Alafair tossed her, her hungry expression as Salem slid into the car's back seat. If she could simply be still for a moment, she could center herself.

She would decide what the next move was. Everything would become clear.

Her last thought was of the saffron outline of the sunlight in the shape of St. Brigid's Cross.

SATURDAY

September 23

CHAPTER 48

Heathrow Airport, London

The seismic shift of going from air to ground lurched Salem awake. She sat up, the movement triggering a searing headache. She blinked back the pain, her eyes watering.

"Here's some water."

She pushed away the pressure at her mouth, swiping at her face. "Charlie?"

"Yeah."

His blurry image came into focus. They were on Alafair's plane. Alafair was sitting across from Salem, her face sharp. Charlie was kneeling in front of Salem. He appeared peaked, but better.

"I thought you were dead," Salem said.

Charlie smiled his crooked grin. "I *felt* dead. And you were on your way to joining me. I don't know what was in those remedies Alafair gave us, but it brought us back from the brink."

Salem was wearing different clothes. Her windpipe squeezed. "My parka."

Alafair tossed her chin toward the pull-down table. "All your clothes are over there. I've not removed anything from your pockets."

Salem glanced from Charlie to Alafair. "How long have I been out?"

"It took us three hours to receive clearance to fly out of Dublin. We were in the air a little shy of two hours."

"I came to about an hour ago," Charlie offered. "We'd both been put in new clothes."

"You'd pissed yourself," Alafair told Charlie. "Your fever had returned. I cleaned and dressed both your wounds and put you in new clothes. I also injected you both with antibiotics my pilot obtained while we were in Kildare."

Salem stretched her leg in front of her. It was stiff but no longer felt hot. She rubbed her hand along the front of the soft pants Alafair had dressed her in. The wound was well bandaged, tender but contained. She drew in several deep breaths, her headache receding. "Thank you."

"She wouldn't let me look at the clue," Charlie complained, but it sounded good-natured. "Said we had to wait until you woke up."

Salem shoved open the window covering. Except for the landing lights, it was dark outside. "Where are we? What time is it?"

"Heathrow, this side of four a.m.," Alafair said. "A body was discovered at the Gloup in Kirkwall. The ID was for Bode Janus, an American. It's only a matter of time until they connect you to him and then track our plane to Dublin. We needed to get out, and London was the closest. The question is, Where to next?"

Salem waited until the plane came to a full stop before testing her leg. It was weak but held her. She walked to the table, riffled through her parka pockets, and tugged out the stoppered glass test tube. "Charlie," she said, the time at Kildare coming back to her in fits and bursts. "I saw you get taken by a guy in a long coat. You were leaning against the church wall, and then you weren't."

He grew pale. "Yeah. I think it was the Order's number-two assassin. A man who can supposedly change the shape of his face. I don't know what he intended to do with me. But then the Grimalkin jumped him, same guy as from the Gloup. Slid a knife right into his throat. I fell back, did my best to blend into the crowd. That's when Alafair found me and shooed me back to the car."

Alafair's eyes glittered like sharp ice. "I needed to get us away from the body on the ground." She turned her attention to Salem. "And I found you shortly after."

Salem nodded. Something was nagging at her. She needed to be alone with her thoughts to sort it out. She returned to her seat, removing the stopper and the scroll of paper. She palmed it flat against her tray table, noting that neither Alafair nor Charlie seemed surprised by its blankness. "I need the B&C. And—"

"Research on sympathetic ink?" Alafair asked. Salem frowned.

Alafair shrugged. "You're not the only one who knows her way around codes. It's a blank sheet of paper, isn't it? Must be an invisible ink, and not an organic fluid, like lemon juice or artichoke dye. Wouldn't stand the test of time. That leaves sympathetic inks, which would make more sense anyways, given Franklin's scientific background."

"Your pilot picked up iodine with the first-aid supplies?"

"I think so." Alafair reached for a bag and dug around, producing a plastic bottle of brown-purple skin disinfectant. Her expression said she was curious but was going to watch and learn rather than interrupt with questions.

Not so Charlie. "Don't you have to know what sort of ink was used to decide what will reveal it?"

Salem shook her head. "In World War I, both the Germans and the Americans used invisible ink. Because most organic inks could be revealed by exposing them to heat, they weren't considered reliable. Sympathetic inks made from copper sulfate, iron sulfate, and cobalt salts were harder to decrypt. The Allies discovered that exposing paper to iodine vapor will turn any of the paper's altered fibers brown. So anything that was wet will change color."

Alafair strode to a cupboard. "You'll need to heat the iodine." She dug around and came up with a one-cup electric teapot. "This should do the trick."

Salem plugged the pot in before filling it with iodine. "Cover your nose and mouth," she said. "You're not going to want to breathe this in."

Her eyes started watering immediately. When the purply surface rippled, the hot, inky smell scalded her mucous membranes even through her sleeve. "You two don't have to stay so close."

"You couldn't pay me to leave," Charlie said, the collar of his T-shirt hooked over his nose and ears.

Alafair didn't even bother to respond.

A bubble burped through the surface, followed by another. Soon, the iodine was at a rolling boil, its violet vapors floating up, turning the teapot into a witch's cauldron. Salem held the unrolled scroll above, close enough to feel the heat on her knuckles. The paper sucked up the vapor. She allowed some doubt to seep in. This might not work. The scroll may be truly blank. Or, if someone had discovered it before Salem and already heated the ink, the clue would not be recoverable.

A new thought struck her: some inks revealed their code only briefly, and then it was gone forever.

"Charlie, take out your phone. I need you to snap a photo of anything that appears."

He dug in his pocket with his good hand.

A kiss of color appeared on the corner of the paper. The softest moan of pleasure escaped Alafair.

The spot of brown expanded as if a ghost were writing in front of them. The shapes appeared slowly, then faster, a furious staccato of brown flowing from the left to the right as the iodine vapor breathed life into the paper.

And then it was done. The clue revealed.

"Another code," Charlie said, snapping a photo, his disappointment heavy in his voice.

Alafair's stare drew Salem's like a magnet. They both understood. It wasn't a code; it was the *original* code: written language, breakable only by those who knew the alphabet.

Or in this case, the aleph-bet.

"It's Hebrew," Alafair declared. "Rosalind Franklin's second language."

Salem unplugged the pot of iodine and put the lid over the top to make room for the B&C Alafair was handing her. "Send me that photo," she ordered Charlie.

It arrived in her email simultaneous to her getting online.

GAEA scooped up the image Charlie sent and immediately translated it into English.

No justice without mercy.

Salem swallowed past the poisonous tang in her throat. Justice. Mercy.

She knew exactly where Rosalind Franklin wanted them to go.

CHAPTER 49

Heathrow Airport, London

Private planes at Heathrow taxied to and parked at a dedicated section of the airport. Still, their passengers needed to pass through Customs before being allowed to leave the airport. Alafair had assured them that the plane was registered under her family business, a legal corporation. If the law had questions about who was transported from Kirkwall to Dublin and then to Heathrow, they would first question the pilot, who had been instructed to say she'd transported only Alafair.

By the time they were done questioning the pilot, if they even did, Charlie and Salem would already be through security.

Salem told herself all this, but it didn't stop her pulse from fluttering as the uniformed agent glanced from her to her passport and back to her, his lined face impassive. "Your business in London?"

Salem considered lying and discarded the idea almost immediately. She was in the system. "I'm here on a work visa."

"Where were you traveling from?"

"Dublin."

"I see you were just there. A return visit?"

Was he asking more questions than usual? Detaining her until the Order arrived to take her clue, kill her? "Yes."

The agent held her gaze, his eyes inscrutable. The line behind Salem shifted. Two lanes over, Charlie passed through quickly. Alafair had cleared security moments earlier.

"Lovely country, Ireland."

"Yes." Salem's voice cracked on the one-syllable word. "I'd like to go back. Someday."

The Customs agent nodded, snapped her passport shut, and handed it back to her. "Welcome back to London, then." He looked toward the head of the line. "Next."

Salem carried the B&C and her overnight bag. She stuffed the passport back into the duffel, feeling all kinds of conspicuous. She walked, head down, toward Terminal 2's WHSmith shop. The plan was to meet up with Alafair and Charlie. They would share a cab to Parliament, the home of justice, and figure out some way to access the Robing Room.

There, Salem would examine William Dyce's mercy painting. If her hunch was correct, inside the painting they would find the final code, the one that would direct them to the treasure at the end of the Stonehenge train.

Rosalind Franklin's DNA work, a secret history, incalculable wealth.

No justice without mercy.

Except Salem was uneasy. Something had happened back at St. Brigid's, something between Charlie and Alafair. One had a reason to be suspicious of the other, Salem could sense it in how they paced each other, waiting for a misstep so they could pounce. Their stories also didn't add up, both featuring an ambiguity that Salem could not puncture.

She'd seen the assailant grab Charlie and recognized him as Jason, the assassin who had kidnapped her mother. Alafair had located her soon after, offering to rescue Charlie. Salem had then gone to the tower, spending fewer than twenty minutes there. Alafair had almost been waiting for her when she exited, deliberately leading Salem around a body, one dressed in the same color and style of clothes she remembered

Jason wearing. Charlie had been in the car when they reached it, just as Alafair had said he would be.

The timeline matched up, but there was something not right in the details.

Salem spotted them both ahead, Charlie leaning against the cobalt-blue wall of the WHSmith, glancing at his phone, Alafair pretending to look at a rack of crisps. They appeared to be together, but not together, the same road weariness to their shoulders, wariness to how they moved. The airport crowds murmured past, pulling roller bags, hoisting purses, unfolding maps, but Alafair and Charlie seemed to move separate from that sea.

They hadn't spotted her yet.

Instincts convinced Salem to take a sharp left into the women's bathroom, beelining to an open stall. The mirrors were crowded with teenagers all wearing the same blue jacket emblazoned with the name of a South American soccer team. Salem locked the door behind her and hung her B&C and then her duffel over the hook. She fished her phone out of her bag.

Bel's folder was pulsing. Salem imagined it was packed with rage. Salem's texts to Agent Lucan Stone had gone unanswered.

He may not even be receiving them. If he was, he could be choosing not to respond for security reasons or something else entirely. Maybe it had been stupid of her to reach out to him, to send him these messages in a bottle and hope that he was getting them, using them, building a case on his end.

But she had to communicate with someone, now more than ever. She wrote him the last message she'd send on this mission. **The final clue is in the Robing Room at Parliament. Going there now. Will need access.**

She was returning her phone to the duffel when it buzzed. Her mouth grew dry.

She flipped over the phone.

It was a response from Stone. You've been compromised. The Grimalkin is with you. Come alone.

Her veins filled with ice. She tucked the phone away, hoisted both bags over her shoulders, and slid into the exiting herd of soccer players, walking away from the WHSmith, her eyes on the ground.

CHAPTER 50

Kensington Palace Gardens

London Offices of the Order

Lutsenko's special phone lit up, causing a not-unpleasant tightening in his groin. The Grimalkin had never called him before. The assassin's reputation was a thing of terrible beauty. While the Order considered the Grimalkin their employee, the truth was that the assassin was a freelancer, capable of executing Lutsenko—anyone—and then disappearing forever.

Killing without consequence.

It engendered a certain excitement, dealing with someone so lethal.

"Hello?"

"She's on her way to Parliament."

Lutsenko had not gotten to the board of the Order by being stupid. "The final clue?"

"I believe so."

"You're with her?"

A pause. "I can see her." The background noise sounded like an airport or a subway, a location where crowds gathered in transit. "We need to remind her what's at stake."

"The girl." It wasn't a question. Standard procedure, really.

"Yes. When you send the reminder, tell her she has four hours. I'll need current coordinates to the Tea Room plus exclusive use of it. I'll take it from there."

The command chafed, but only momentarily. Lutsenko had no ego in this. He wanted what was at the end of the Stonehenge train. Any man would. They were stupid, ignorant, or lying if they thought otherwise. "Fine. Is that it?"

The Grimalkin had already hung up.

CHAPTER 51

Journey to Parliament, London

A Piccadilly train had been waiting at the terminal. Salem leaped on as the doors closed behind her. She thought she caught a glimpse of Charlie, but the crowd had surged when the doors whisked closed. She pushed toward the front of the train, feeling exposed.

Stone had not texted again. Salem pulled up a transportation app and inputted her final destination. The instructions were immediate. She'd alight at Hammersmith and walk across the platform to the District Line, which would take her to Westminster. From there, she'd limp to Parliament, hoping the guards would let her in, praying Charlie or Alafair didn't get there first.

If the trains ran on time, and she had spit and luck, she'd reach Parliament in under forty minutes. Her heartbeat thudding in her ears sounded like footsteps. She kept glancing around at her fellow travelers, seeing who was watching her, coming for her. The man with his back to her, was it Charlie? No.

Breathe. Breathe.

The B&C weighed down her shoulder. She was loath to pull it out. It would make her too vulnerable, too distracted. But she needed to research. The painting would not give up its secrets easily. She needed to find a corner of the train car that she could lean against and then run old-fashioned phone research.

A seat opened up. She slid into it, almost weeping with relief at alleviating the pressure from her leg. Her phone's battery was low. She dug in her bag for her remote charger and hooked it up. The phone greedily soaked up the juice.

Salem's first search was for the history of the Robing Room's art. Her first hit surprised and worried her. Dyce's paintings were frescoes, which meant they'd been painted on wet plaster rather than canvas. It would have been difficult for Rosalind Franklin to alter a painting that was part of the wall.

She pulled up the history of Dyce's mercy painting, the one Hayes had pointed out to Salem. It depicted Sir Gawaine kneeling at the feet of his queen. According to legend, Sir Gawaine had intended to slay a knight who'd killed Gawaine's hunting dog, but a woman rushed to defend the knight. Gawaine slew her by accident. He rode to his queen at Camelot, begging forgiveness, and was tasked with protecting women forevermore. Thus the description beneath the painting: Sir Gawaine swearing to be merciful and "never be against Ladies."

That was all she could discover on that specific painting. Her next search was "Rosalind Franklin processes." She'd read the basics on Franklin's life and career, but nothing had stood out indicating how Franklin would hide a clue originally painted onto wet plaster a hundred years earlier.

Salem knew Franklin was famous for her work with X-rays. She did not know that Franklin had primarily used two methods: two-dimensional fiber diffraction to discover the shape of DNA and three-dimensional crystallography to study the molecular structure of any substance that could form a crystal, including salt, water, minerals, and fatty acids.

None of that information actually helped Salem, unless Franklin had created a dye at the molecular level that blended perfectly with Dyce's paint and used it to create some sort of map over the top of the mercy fresco. Salem snorted at the thought, but it inspired another: if Franklin had hidden a clue in the Robing Room, she would have needed access, possibly while wearing a disguise. GAEA could run a history of work orders and private events recorded in the Parliament building during Franklin's adult life, approximately 1938 through 1958. It would be impossible on her phone.

The train shivered to a stop. Salem's attention clicked back to real time. *Hammersmith.* She raced out, pushing through the crowds, not risking a glance behind. She was thankful for the crush of tourists and Londoners, but surprised to see Saturday crowds this early in the day, before she remembered that today was the headlining day of the International Climate Change Summit. The city would be pulsing with people. A good cover, but it also meant security would be extra tight around Parliament.

She wondered where in the city her mother was. Vida was surely remaining in London until they located Mercy. The District Line pulled up to the platform. Salem boarded and made her way to the rear of the nearest car, planting her back to the wall. The train filled and took off. A variety of languages jammed the interior of the car, people from all over the world gathering, moving as a single animal, swaying forward then back as the train groaned around corners.

The stops sped by. Salem had no plan. She held her phone, suddenly desperate to call Bel. So what if Bel hated her for letting Mercy get kidnapped? She'd still want to help Salem find her. Except that would be selfish because there was nothing Bel could do. Salem would only be calling her to get her sympathy, her love, to fill up that hollow spot that was Salem's heart.

"Westminster stop."

The train jostled to a halt. Salem followed the stream out and up the Bridge Street exit stairs. The fresh air slapped her face when she hit topside. She squeezed her jacket tighter around her neck, self-conscious about her rough appearance. She needn't have bothered. Most of the people were staring up at the Elizabeth Tower housing Big Ben, snapping photos, taking selfies. An animal-rights group was holding a protest blocking the sidewalk, so she stepped into the road, where she was whistled back by an irate police officer.

"The light has to change!"

She apologized, walking toward the Parliament entrance Charlie had driven them through the first time she'd entered. The gate was open, armed guards standing in front. She craned her neck to see the tourist entrance. It appeared to be closed.

She'd have to try the guards. She still had her FBI identification. It might be enough.

The throng pushed her toward the guarded gate and then veered right, toward Westminster Abbey, the abrupt change in movement making her stumble. She grabbed a nearby bench to keep from falling. She'd almost righted herself when a force struck her in the center of her back. She hit the ground, unable to draw a full breath. She rolled to her back, hands up to block another hit.

But no one was there.

No one was even looking her way. What had hit her?

She pulled herself onto the bench, stretching her hand behind her to feel the spot where she'd been assaulted. The weight of something in her pocket brushed against her thigh. It wasn't her phone, which she still clutched.

It was a gift box, pink, wrapped in a ribbon.

Her eyes darted around, panicked, looking for who had slid it into her pocket.

No one was paying her any mind. A climate-change protest group had begun a chant. *Fossil fuel is too cruel. Fossil fuel is too cruel.* A nearby food cart was hawking gyros, the Mediterranean spices redolent in the cool air. Another vendor sold stovepipe Union Jack hats.

The world spun in carnival colors, too busy for her.

Salem tugged the ribbon. It fell to the ground. She lifted the lid. A single note lay inside, its message written in pencil.

Once you have it, come to the Tea Room alone. 51.534761, -0.057631 until 1200 23.09 and then gone to you forever.

She lifted the note. Underneath, in a bed of cloudy cotton stained with drops of red, lay a severed ear, a pink rosebud earring resting in its lobe.

Mercy's ear.

Salem's hands shook. She slammed the lid back on the box before it could fall from her hands. She shoved it in her pocket, as much as it horrified her to have the child's flesh in her jacket.

She stood, her knees wobbling.

Get yourself together.

She did not have the luxury of hysteria. With concentration, she moved one leg, and then the next, toward Parliament. She'd gone forward ten whole feet when the crowd parted, revealing Agent Lucan Stone ten feet in front of her.

Watching her.

She reached in her pocket for the box.

His eyes widened. He yelled something, his words swallowed by the firework clap of a gunshot. The left side of his upper body flew back, punched by an invisible giant. The red began to flower on his shirt before he hit the ground.

Someone screamed.

Salem ran to him, fell beside him, ignoring the rip of pain in her leg. She placed her hands over the bleeding, pushing down, feeling the hot liquid pulse of his life leaving him. The screaming grew louder.

She searched the crowd for help. *Call an ambulance!*

No one seemed to be responding. Salem felt the world collapsing onto her, moving so slowly, burying her. Lucan Stone could not die right now. Why was no one helping?

The crowd parted. Charlie appeared, and with him, her supervisor, Robert Bench. Salem sobbed with relief. "It's Lucan! He's been shot!"

The men took immediate action. Charlie yelled into a walkie-talkie. Bench knelt across from Salem. He put his hand over hers, gently pulling hers out from under. "I'll stay with him until the ambulance arrives. You need to get inside Parliament."

The ambient noise was loud—yelling, questions, someone weeping—but somehow Bench's words reached her ears clearly, as if they were alone in a room. She was slipping into shock. She searched for an anchor point, something to ground her. She spotted Agent Len Curson nearby, something off-balance in his face as he glanced at Salem before taking charge of crowd control, creating a perimeter around the fallen agent.

Salem was frozen.

Bench's voice was quiet but commanding. "*Now*, Agent Wiley."

Salem sat back on her heels. Her hands were cold apart from Agent Stone's body. She could only sip at the air. "What . . . ?"

"Agent Stone is the Grimalkin," Bench said. "We've finally caught him. Now get inside and save the girl. They're expecting you."

CHAPTER 52

Parliament, London

Salem was shuffled through hallways, someone appearing with a towel to wipe her hands free of blood, men murmuring, exchanging glances, ferrying her toward the Robing Room as quickly as they could.

Snippets of conversation swirled around her. *The president and vice president will be arriving in different vehicles, same time—twenty minutes out. Water leak near Jubilee Café. The prime minister is in the building. Russian security wants a word. Can you believe the size of the crowds?*

Salem let herself be led. Agent Lucan Stone was the Grimalkin. She had fed him clues the whole way, told him everything he needed to know to kill Bode, slice off Charlie's finger, and be waiting for her at St. Brigid's and then outside Parliament.

Her mother was right about her.

She was worse than useless. She was dangerous.

They reached the Robing Room's gilded door. Waiters and guards, butlers and secretaries pushed past. The summit was reaching a fever-ish pitch, separate from Salem, who was moving inside a bubble. The Robing Room door was opened for her.

She was pushed inside.

Alone.

The silence was heavy.

The door across the long room clicked open. Charlie stepped inside. Salem instinctively backed toward the door behind her.

He held up his hands, all nine fingers. "Wait! I'm sorry." She was numb.

He walked toward her. "It's terrible it went down like that, love. We'd had an idea for a while but weren't sure until he planted that box on you. He's given you a piece of the girl, hasn't he? Right in line with his pattern."

Salem's mouth creaked open. Words didn't come. She reached in her pocket for the box instead and held it out to him.

He walked toward her, keeping his hands where she could see them, eyes and mouth soft, as if approaching a skittish forest creature. "Just let me put some gloves on, and then I'll take that from you." His wounded hand disappeared into his pocket and came out with a rubber glove, which he slid on his free hand. He plucked the box from her palm and set it on top of a nearby table. He removed the lid.

"Damn it all to hell," he whispered. "There isn't much time. You know of the Tea Room?"

She shook her head.

"It's shorthand for a drop site. Terrorists, kidnappers, anyone looking for an exchange of money or information meets at the Tea Room. It's not a set place but a movable location, and after it serves its purpose, it's gone."

A balloon was building in her stomach, expanding, rising to remove her head with it. "I'm sorry."

He glanced at her. "For ditching me back at the airport?" He attempted a smile, but the situation was too dire. "You needn't be. In fact, it was a smart move, knowing what you knew. But we're here now. We've got to crack this code. Have you got anything?"

He stepped aside so she had a clear view of the painting. He was right, she knew that, understood she needed to get it together, but how was such a thing possible? She pressed her hand to her mouth, biting back the scream that threatened to consume her. She swallowed her disbelief, terror, and shame, shoved them all into a chest, and locked them up tight.

There was no room for feeling anymore. Only math. Computation. Order.

She unzipped the B&C as she approached the painting. She placed it on a table immediately below Dyce's mercy fresco, waking GAEA and asking her to pull any unusual history on the room. While GAEA worked, Salem stood, glancing behind the wood. "I need a chair," she said.

Charlie obliged.

She stood on it and was able to feel farther up the wood. No aberrations jumped out at her. Leaning forward, she peeked behind the frame but couldn't move it. It had been mounted around the plaster rather than hung on the wall like a standard canvas painting.

"I think I'll need a ladder and a flashlight," Salem said. GAEA pinged.

Salem eased herself off the chair and peered at the screen. What she saw exploded a ball of heat square in her chest. "And a roll of butcher paper, plus a box of crayons or a charcoal stick."

CHAPTER 53

Tower Bridge, London

Penthouse

The people below swarmed like ants.

It was a cliché, but for Clancy, there was a reason certain sayings settled into the language and claimed their spot. They fit exactly the situation they meant to describe.

The Order's Tower Bridge penthouse was overkill—pun intended—for the job he was meant to do, but he could treat the lavish furniture and priceless paintings as the props they were. The only thing he cared about was the single square window no larger than a bread box, a reference he didn't think kids these days would get.

The window slid upward. Unless something was sticking out of it—which his bionic sniper rifle would soon be—there was no reason to glance up here, and even then, you'd have to have eagle eyes or, better yet, a pair of binoculars trained on the window to catch the movement.

He was peering through his own set of binoculars as Agent Stone was shot and dropped. Clancy'd worried that it would screw up his plans, but his contact inside Parliament assured him that the proceedings were on schedule. President Gina Hayes and Vice President Richard Cambridge would be arriving in seven minutes and counting. He could see their motorcades coming from different directions.

Worked for Clancy.

He found himself grateful for the opportunity to rectify his past mistake. It wasn't personal. It was pride. A twinge he recognized as self-pity tickled his nose. He was thinking of his wife and kids. They were nice enough folks. Sometimes he missed them. But nuts to that. There are no amends in this life. You do what you do and you take the hits.

Still, he wouldn't hate seeing his kids one more time.

He set down his binoculars to give his sniper rifle a final check. It looked good. He slid it along the window ledge and lined up his shot, the wind biting his cheeks.

The president and vice president exited their vehicles on schedule, walking toward each other, hands outstretched. Grins flashed and cameras snapped.

Clancy set his sight. He pulled the trigger.

The bullet sank in, traveled through, and exited the other side. There was no surviving that, but Clancy was a professional. He took one more shot.

CHAPTER 54

Thundering footsteps pounded outside the door, but Salem's focus was absolute. She was taping butcher paper, taken from the cafeteria, to the edges of the painting. Once she had it in place, Charlie handed her the black crayon he'd found in a box left in the lost and found.

GAEA had come though.

No private events had been scheduled in the Robing Room during the twenty years of Rosalind Franklin's adult life. It was either open to the public or closed for the single day a year the queen required it. In addition, the Robing Room frescoes had remained untouched since their creation, the only exception being in 1956, when the room was closed off so the frescoes could be sprayed with a clear sealant to protect them from the vagaries of time.

If there was a clue to be discovered, it was on the surface, sprayed over the top of the painting by a skilled chemist and X-ray crystallographer, one familiar with the two-dimensional patterns expanded through the science of fiber diffraction.

Salem stripped the paper from the black crayon, the waxy smell taking her back to kindergarten. She laid it across the upper left corner the long way and rubbed. The method was commonly used on gravestones to lift images. Charcoal or a disc of rubbing wax would be the standard media, but she worked with what she had.

The image began appearing almost immediately.

Charlie hollered triumphantly. "Salem Wiley, you are a genius."

She applied enough force to pick up the delicate fiber pattern.

Franklin had sprayed over the top but not so much that she would damage it. The upper left quadrant of the paper revealed a rudimentary drawing of a woman, her right hand raised in supplication, and then her face, emerging like ancient ghosts from a mist. The upper right quadrant revealed a mirror image of that woman, her left hand raised. The women's identical heads were framed by a blunt headdress and kohl eyes reminiscent of Egyptian tomb art.

The crayon was growing hot from the rubbing. "Can I have another, please?"

Charlie stripped the paper off a royal-blue crayon and handed it to her.

She stretched her fingers, working out a cramp from holding the black one so tight. She started rubbing the lower left quadrant from the bottom edge, working her way upward. The woman's foot appeared first, flat and pointed to the left. The right foot was the same, but a shape was curling behind it.

Salem brought the crayon upward, rubbing, the smell of warm wax comforting. The woman wore a simple shift, the shape near her feet curling behind her form. Her left hand was outstretched toward something. Salem stayed on the image, expanding it from the center and out.

"It's a dragon," Charlie said, his voice tight. "The women are holding hands through the middle of a dragon's head."

Salem kept rubbing, though she knew he was right. Mostly. The Egyptian aesthetic had thrown her off, but otherwise, the image was as she'd expected, a Neolithic message sent through time from a people who had no written language.

It was a pictographic map.

Charlie understandably thought the giant, snaking creature between the two women was a dragon, their hands piercing its eyes and meeting at the orb of its brain, its mouth drawn down in pain.

But it was no dragon.

The vulnerable tightness of hope squeezed Salem's throat and chest. Rosalind Franklin had known all along where women's ideas and inventions had been hidden. The Order or archaeologists had sniffed too near this final map, originally hidden under the Flower Rock, so she'd moved it—or this fresco-sprayed replica of it—three stops out, from Brodgar to the Gloup, the Gloup to St. Brigid's, and St. Brigid's to here.

The map didn't show a dragon, a mythical beast that would have been unfamiliar to the Neolithic people. It showed an eel.

Salem knew where the treasure was hidden.

"I have to get this to the Order." She peeled off the tape and began rolling up the map.

"What?" Charlie's voice was sharp. "Get *what* to them?"

She would not tell him. If she did, he might try to talk her out of it, or report the location to their superiors, whose actions may cost Mercy her life. Salem stepped gingerly down from the chair. "I need to go to the Tea Room. Alone."

He looked ready to argue but swallowed it. "You have the coordinates?"

Salem glanced at the box on the table. She didn't want to open it again.

"I'll send you a photo." He walked briskly to the box and clicked a picture of the paper on top. Her phone buzzed three seconds later. "For the record, I don't like sending you alone, but I understand why it needs to be that way."

Her eyes filled. They'd been through a lot. Once she returned to Minnesota, she could process it all, come up with the correct response. She had nothing now. She tucked her chin and walked toward the door.

"Not that one," Charlie said, laying his hand on her shoulder and steering her toward the rear exit. "By the sounds of it, there's something unpleasant happening out front. We need to get you out the back. And fast. You have money?"

"God, no."

He yanked his wallet out of his back pocket, opening the door at the same time. The hall was relatively clear, only a thin stream of workers using the back area. Charlie handed her a wad of bills. "Follow me."

Heads down, they walked against the flow. It was mostly caterers and maintenance staff in the back hallway, but the snatches of conversation Salem caught proved Charlie right. Something had happened in Parliament. Someone was hurt.

Dead.

It couldn't be Agent Stone, could it?

Charlie kept them both moving, no time for questions. He flashed his identification at the guards watching the west rear Parliament exit, and they opened the door briskly. A cab was waiting outside.

"I needn't tell you how to turn coordinates into an address," Charlie said, cupping her open window with his good hand after he closed the door behind her. His boyish face churned with barely contained emotion. He leaned forward. Salem thought he was going to hug her, but he stopped himself.

"Take care of her," he ordered the cabbie before stepping back.

"Salem!" It was a scream from the crowd being herded away from the rear of Parliament.

Salem craned her head out to see who was shouting for her.

Her heart jumped into her mouth. It was Bel, steering her wheelchair toward the cab, held back by guards. Salem reached for the door handle. It was instinct. Her higher brain shocked her awake before she pulled the door open, though. She didn't have time to talk to Bel. She had to save Mercy.

Salem fell back into her seat as the black cab pulled away.

CHAPTER 55

Washington, DC

Speaker of the House Vit Linder reclined in his squeaky leather chair in his too-small office in the Longworth House Office Building. He hadn't been offered an upgrade when he'd been elected Speaker. Subsequently, the office did not reflect his importance.

That would soon be rectified.

Can't beat the Oval Office for lighting.

In the meanwhile, his current headquarters were the perfect place to receive the news of the death of the president or vice president. He guessed Clancy would only kill one, but he wasn't sure. In the end, it wouldn't matter. Either Clancy followed orders and made Vit president, or he told on Vit and the Order marked him as stupid. Either scenario worked for Vit.

People always underestimated him.

Always.

Not for much longer, not once he was president of the United States of America.

If Hayes went down, Cambridge would be sworn in. Cambridge and Vit were different parties, opposite worldviews. Cambridge would never name him Veep; he would nominate someone else, and that someone else would need to be approved by a Senate and House both led by the opposition party, both in Vit's control. They would stall, as commanded. The same would happen, more or less, if Cambridge was the one killed.

With the sand loosened beneath democracy, it'd be easy to convince the Order to kill off the survivor of today's assassination, allowing Linder to walk into office, hands clean.

He'd be the president within a year. His life would finally have meaning.

He heard footsteps padding down the hall toward him, their beat urgent. He'd purposely not watched the news. He wore the exact correct face. He'd played it perfectly, strategized, gotten his pawns into place.

Just like a game of checkers, he congratulated himself.

CHAPTER 56

Tower Bridge, London

"This is it."

Salem looked at the museum of oddities the driver indicated. "That?"

He tapped his GPS, into which he'd typed the coordinates rather than have her search a street address. "I don't think so. I think it's that door between the museum and the Indian restaurant."

"Thanks." She paid and tipped him and stepped out, clutching her phone, the roll of butcher paper tucked under her arm. The streets were busy, but nothing compared to the chaos surrounding Parliament. Her heart hitched up her chest. She must live long enough to rescue Mercy. The awareness was out-of-body. She felt like she was watching from above, directing a Salem puppet.

She walked toward the door.

Mercy might be inside. Salem hoped she could hold her, nuzzle her sweet-soft hair, tell her everything was going to be okay even though it was a lie. Her only bargaining chip was the thin hope that the Order would not recognize the significance of the image of two women and the eel. With their main code breaker, the Grimalkin, down, they might need her to lead them to the final treasure. She'd figure out how to free Mercy in that time, even if she had to push the child out of a moving vehicle to save her.

The door creaked open as she raised her hand to knock.

She stepped into a dark hallway. A single table broke the flow, a vase of plastic roses set on top of it. She walked past, engaging the flashlight on her phone to light her steps. Dishes clanked in the restaurant next door. The air smelled like curry and dust. Two closed doors branched off the end of the hallway, one going each direction.

They were identical, both with old brass knobs and peeling yellow paint. She didn't know which one to take and so chose right. Her hand gripped the cool knob.

"Don't!"

She turned. It was Charlie, coming through the door she'd entered.

"What are you doing here?"

He walked toward her, his face wrecked with worry. "I can't let you do this, Salem. It's a trap. The Order has no reason to give you the girl. Not right now. MI5 thinks you're expendable if it gets them something concrete on the Order. I don't."

A vise squeezed Salem's head. "You can't do this. It's not up to you. I have to save Mercy."

His face dissolved into tears, unsettling her. But she had too much forward momentum. She pulled open the door. A brick wall was on the other side. She pushed on it, the solid rough surface scraping her palms.

She turned to the other door and opened it. Another brick wall.

Now Charlie was weeping. Salem stepped toward him, almost reached him, when she realized it wasn't tears but laughter, a breathy pinch of horrible dry, wicked humor. Charlie darted to the side, grabbed a plastic rose, and held it toward Salem.

"Smell it."

She recoiled.

"You can't," he said. "It's fake. My idea. Nice touch, yeah? Bet you wish you'd trusted the flowers, like Mrs. Molony told you."

All Salem could hear was the single knock of her heartbeat.

Thump.

Charlie bent forward as if to tie his shoes, but began licking his arm instead. Like a cat.

Thump.

With the back of his hand, he rubbed over his ears, tufting out his hair. He smiled up at her and meowed, bringing his cat and mouse game full circle.

Thump.

She realized what had been nagging her on the plane ride from Dublin to Heathrow. Back at St. Brigid's, Charlie hadn't seemed surprised or worried to see Jason, only irritated. It wasn't Alafair who'd made her uneasy. Alafair, who hadn't trusted Charlie from the moment she'd laid eyes on him.

It was Charlie.

Thump.

He stood between her and the door.

The Grimalkin stood between her and the door. "You shot Lucan, you bastard."

He darted forward and grabbed the phone out of her hand. "Killed him, too, with any luck. My car is out front. I presume you won't tell me what the map means until you see the girl, so off we go."

Bile burned the back of Salem's throat. "You have the FBI on your side?"

"Only a few. Only when I need them." He pushed her outdoors, his too-hot hand holding the back of her neck to steer her.

"Jesus, you cut off your own finger."

"I like to embody my roles."

She was struck by a final, shameful understanding, something she should have put together earlier. Back at the Gloup, Charlie had said Bode's throat had been slit when Charlie looked back toward the hole, but that Bode had been face down when Charlie came to. He couldn't have known how Bode had died unless he'd witnessed it.

Or done it.

Agent Len Curson held the door open. Salem glared at the turn-coat. He held her stare, coolly, leading her toward a car. A suit Salem didn't recognize sat behind the wheel. The Grimalkin tossed Salem's phone into a trash bin and then forced her into the car. He and then Curson followed, one sitting on each side of her in the back seat.

"Probably no small talk, right?" Charlie said. "It's been exhausting listening to your every little thought the past four days, by the way, ful-filling your fix-it fantasies by telling you about my parents, hearing you whine about Bel. *Blah blah blah.* Bloody hell, you should have called her. She would have told you it wasn't your fault Mercy was taken. She would have helped you crack the code."

Salem couldn't stay on top of the quicksand that had become her life. Her brain was flying, but it wasn't moving fast enough. She was going under.

Mercy.

"Where is she?"

Charlie ducked his head and pointed. "Up there."

She followed his finger. Tower Bridge—close, far too close. Salem's panic began a high keen. She dulled it, swallowed it, buried it. "You were working with someone else."

"Jason. Useless, except when it comes to disguise. You know him. Or your mother does. And can we talk about your mother? What a piece of work. She'd fuck up a saint, that one."

The Heel Stone. The Eel Stone. The Heel Stone. The Eel Stone. Salem sang the words inside her head, biting down on them when they grew too slippery.

"Is your name really Charlie?"

He nodded, his smile even. "Charles Arthur Thackeray. My mother was a spy for the Underground. Father, too, though I may have failed to mention that. Cost them both their lives, and for what? Shite."

They pulled up to a Tower Bridge side door. Agent Curson exited first, running around to open Charlie's door, then escorting Salem inside the Tower Bridge, gripping her arm. He should have known she wouldn't run, not with Mercy inside.

Charlie led them to an elevator. Curson entered first with Salem. Charlie followed. As the elevator shot up, Salem's stomach dropped. "That's right," he said. "You're a bit of an agoraphobe, though you seemed to do just fine on our little road trip. You're not going to like what you see up here. The whole world, no protection, spread out as far as your eyes can see."

Salem's tiny world grew smaller. "What *is* Mercy?"

Charlie's eyes stopped their frantic spin and focused. "She's the one-pad cipher. As was her mother before her, and her mother before that, so on down the line to the inception of the Underground. It's nothing to do with her blood, at least not in a way measurable by current technology."

DNA. Genetic instructions as code.

"I see your brain working. If you could solve that one, the Order would certainly love you, yes they would. But no one can break it, not with the knowledge we have now. If we crack a few more trains, however, it should be easy peasy. All glory to the Grimalkin." He giggled.

The elevator door slid open to an opulent room the size of a hotel lobby.

Mercy sat in the center, huddled on a blue velvet couch. A familiar-looking man sat near her. She wore corduroys and a Disney princess T-shirt. Her head was bandaged over her left ear. She seemed smaller than she had days ago, her expression haunted, her focus on some spot on the floor even though a coloring book and crayons rested next to her.

Salem cried out.

The child glanced up. A heartbreak of emotions played across her face—hope, suspicion, terror, love. She leaped off the sofa and into Salem's arms, shivering, her frame slight, clinging so tightly to Salem that she stole her breath.

Salem held her like her life depended on it, weeping with grief and joy. The connection she felt embracing the child overwhelmed her. She'd never felt such pure love, or horror. Mercy was a part of her, she knew that now, but there was something shriveled and stunned about the child, a vital part of her spirit broken. The men had stolen something from her, something precious. Salem didn't know if they could get it back, and that realization crushed her.

"I'm sorry I'm sorry I'm sorry," she murmured repeatedly, choking on the words.

The familiar man rose from the couch. Salem realized where she knew him from. He'd been Stone's partner last year, following her and Bel as they'd tried to save Hayes. He'd had a different nose then, but he was the same man, a dead ringer for Ed Harris.

"It's done," he said.

Charlie walked to the window and looked down. "You've caused quite a stir, haven't you, Clancy?"

The sky beyond the high wall of windows was unbroken blue. They must be in a penthouse suite attached to the top of one of the bridge's supports. Salem shifted her weight, causing Mercy to whimper and snuggle deeper. The shivering warmth of the frail child woke something deep in Salem, a primal maternal rage. She wanted to scream, fight, and tear at the monsters who'd stolen the girl, yet her fury was tempered with a sharp terror that two of them might not make it. They were outnumbered, their adversaries too potent, too cunning.

No, she would not let the child die here. How could she offer her life to save Mercy's?

Charlie spun and strode toward Salem, cutting off her train of thought. "I'll take the rubbing from you, then, and you can explain exactly what it represents."

If she did, he would kill her immediately. They might let Mercy live, or they might not. Her mind raced, searching for an out. The elevator was the only entrance she could see. No way to get that door open and safely closed without alerting the men. She knew where Curson carried his gun; the outline of it was clear at his hip as he leaned near the elevator buttons. That's also where Charlie carried his piece.

Probably Clancy, the Ed Harris look-alike, carried a gun in the same spot. She would snatch one of their weapons, and she'd shoot all three dead center in their foreheads. She'd have to. There was nothing to lose. It was now or never. She gave Mercy one last squeeze and tried to separate from her. The child clung to her like a baby monkey.

"She's been through a time," Clancy said.

Salem glared at him. Was he really trying to empathize with the child he'd helped kidnap?

Then her pocket buzzed, a loud but unmistakable hum against her flesh and Mercy's. Salem held her breath, and for a moment, Mercy's trembling stopped. It was almost as if time stood still, the spell broken as Clancy lunged toward her, moving startlingly fast.

"Jesus Christ, you didn't search her?"

"I confiscated her phone," Charlie said, his voice high and reedy.

Clancy wrenched Mercy out of Salem's arms, the child clawing and screaming. Salem fought him like a wildcat, bereft without Mercy's weight, but he was able to dip the phone out of her pocket and step away before she could get at his gun.

He clicked its power button, lighting up the screen and reading the information it revealed. "But you didn't confiscate Stone's phone."

Charlie blanched.

Salem didn't know why she'd snatched it from Stone's pocket when he slumped, bleeding, in front of Parliament. She'd felt it under her hand, and she'd wondered about him, about who would survive him, who would tell his story. She'd slipped his phone into her pocket without thinking too hard about it.

The elevator light pinged. Someone was riding it up.

CHAPTER 57

Tower Bridge, London

Charlie, Clancy, and Curson were the only Order employees in the penthouse. Salem could tell by the startled glances they exchanged that they hadn't expected anyone else. All three of them moved toward the door, their attention momentarily distracted from Salem and Mercy.

Salem backed up, shielding the child, a mix of hope and desperation buoying her. She still didn't see another way out besides the elevator, but there had to be one. She gave Mercy what she prayed was a reassuring glance, holding her finger over her mouth as a signal to be silent. The dull look in Mercy's eyes cut straight to Salem's heart. The little girl had been terrorized, that much was clear.

Salem's fury returned.

She would find a way out, even if it meant exiting through one of the windows. She studied all the panes of glass, moving her head as little as possible so as not to attract attention. Her hope surged when she realized the floor-to-ceiling window fifteen feet behind them was actually a sliding glass door leading to the smallest of balconies. Beyond the balcony's railing was the blue roof of the pedestrian walkway twenty stories above the frigid waters of the Thames.

The elevator's light changed, indicating it had reached their floor. Clancy and Curson pulled their weapons. Charlie kept his holstered.

The door slid open.

Alafair stood inside, smiling broadly, confidently, every inch of her body declaring that she belonged here. She wore her standard gear: leather jacket, formfitting jeans, zip-up boots. Her hands hung loosely at her sides.

Salem felt a sear of betrayal—it appeared that Alafair had been working with the Grimalkin all along, using Salem to solve the train—but she didn't give it oxygen. It didn't matter why Alafair was here as long as it was causing a distraction. She leaned over to Mercy, holding her pointy chin with her thumb and forefinger. "You need to get out of here, sweetheart, any way you can."

Mercy clutched Salem's hand, shaking her head violently. When they'd first met, Mercy had been resourceful. She'd survived on the road with her older brother for most of her life. But the Order had profoundly wounded her. Salem could see it in the tightness of the child's eyes, the hollowness caving her cheeks.

"Honey, you have to get out of here." She tried to peel Mercy's sweaty, tiny hands off hers, biting back the tears. "Please. It's the only way."

Alafair's voice poured like chocolate over Salem's. She spoke directly to Charlie. "I have something to offer you."

Salem glanced over, she couldn't help it. Alafair stepped into the room, her hands held in front of her, palms out. Salem knew how fast those same hands could produce a knife, but she also wasn't sure whom to trust. Charlie seemed to be experiencing the same struggle.

"I don't need you," he said. He reached around for his weapon.

Something about his movement rocked Mercy, crashing through her trauma. "Noooooo!" she screamed. Her voice was dry and cracked but piercing. She dropped Salem's hand. At first, it looked like she would run toward Alafair and the elevator, but instead, she charged toward the sliding glass door. She yanked it open. An unforgiving wind blustered into the room. Mercy didn't hesitate, running to the edge of the balcony, then hoisting herself over it.

Charlie raced toward Mercy.

They do need her; somehow, they know what she's the one-pad cipher for.

But those thoughts didn't move as fast as her feet, which flew toward Mercy.

Charlie reached the balcony first, but Mercy was already over it, balanced on the roof of the tourist walkway that connected one bridge support to the other. A gust of wind momentarily lifted her off her feet.

Salem screamed.

The airstream disappeared as quickly as it had arrived, dropping the child. Mercy tumbled to her knees and grabbed for purchase. She clung to the narrow lip of the roof.

"Salem!" she cried, her voice reedy. "Help me!"

Charlie was crawling over the balcony's railing. Salem grabbed at him, pulling him back, oblivious to the actions of the other three inside the penthouse. Charlie swung, his hand connecting with her cheek with a sharp crack. She reeled back but not before she caught a glimpse of the Thames two hundred feet below, a blue-silver thread that would pop her like a water balloon if she landed on it from this height. Every cell in Salem's body snapped in terror, paralyzing her. She tasted the harsh metal tang of panic.

Charlie was nearly over the railing. Once his boots hit the roof, he'd only have to crawl five feet, and he'd have Mercy.

Fight for her! Bring her back inside!

It was Salem's voice in her head, but they were her dad's words, and Bel's. They'd always believed in her, had been sure she could do anything she set her mind to. It was enough to pierce her paralysis.

Mouth dry, Salem forced her eyes straight ahead and stepped onto the balcony. The wind was powerful, an icy shoulder propelling her back. She leaned into it, dropping one leg over the railing, followed by the other. Because her body was facing the penthouse, she saw the knife fly from Alafair's hands and into Curson's throat. He dropped to the floor near the couch.

Clancy was drawing on her, lining up his sight, a clear twenty feet separating the two of them.

The elevator door had closed behind Alafair, so she had no shelter. Salem wanted to help Alafair, but a cry from Mercy caused her to twist around. Charlie was nearly to her. Salem released one hand and whipped it around to grab the railing behind her, then twisted so she was facing the roof. She wanted to close her eyes, but knew she'd give up and fall if she didn't have a visual anchor. She toppled onto the roof of the walkway, its metal cold beneath her. "Hang on, Mercy! I'm coming!"

Charlie was reaching for the girl with his good hand and for his gun with his wounded one. "Come to me," he commanded her, the wind whipping his voice toward Salem. "I won't hurt you."

"No!" Salem said. She launched herself forward. "Don't do it!"

Charlie swiveled his gun, holding it inches from Salem's head. "Looks like I get to see those beautiful brains up close."

A shot rang out.

CHAPTER 58

Tower Bridge, London

How about them goddamned apples, Clancy thought, a knife hilt-deep in his neck. *It turns out you can make amends.*

He'd started the ball rolling by killing the vice president rather than the president. Nobody'd miss the guy. Gina Hayes, though? That'd be a real gutshot to progress, and it turned out Clancy had developed some strong feelings about that—or at least a healthy dose of curiosity as to what a women-run world might look like. They couldn't fuck it up any worse than the gents, and who knew? It might be an improvement.

He could have stopped there, but then he'd gone and shot the Grimalkin right through the eyes.

Bet that cat doesn't land on his feet.

His wheezing laugh sprayed blood.

He wasn't sure he'd have had the cojones to shoot the legendary assassin if that pretty woman's knife hadn't lodged itself clean against his carotid artery, its tip scratching his spine. The blade was the only thing keeping him from bleeding out. He wouldn't last until the EMTs arrived.

As a dead man shooting, he'd chosen the Grimalkin over the woman, and he felt tickled goddamned pink about that decision.

Pow.

Pulling the trigger had sapped the last of his energy. He fell backward, just missing the sofa. His field of vision was shrinking, like he was looking through a pair of binoculars. He reached toward the knife, planning to pull it out. No use in waiting.

That's when the elevator dinged again. Who was riding it up this time? Captain America? The Dallas Cowboy cheerleaders? Now that was a final surprise he wouldn't mind, but when the door whisked open, he saw something even better.

His old partner, Agent Lucan Stone, his arm in a sling.

Was Stone about to learn that Clancy had done something right, here at the end? *Well, I'll be double-hot-damned. There really is justice in this world.*

The knife came out with a squirt.

Clancy's lifeblood flowed out of him, along with a final thought: Lutsenko and his cronies were going to lose this war.

They may have the best men, but they did not have the best minds.

Hell, it turned out they didn't even have the best fighters.

CHAPTER 59

London Bridge, London

Jason was leaning against a London Bridge railing when the body plummeted off the Tower Bridge's elevated walkway roof. Someone near him screamed, and then everyone began pointing upward or snapping photos, some of them managing both simultaneously.

The body could belong to Wiley or the kid or even a random jumper, but there was the slimmest chance it was the Grimalkin plummeting into the Thames.

Jason smiled.

This wasn't a business for men who played games. Rules were necessary, but not the ones the Grimalkin demanded: *Think of me only as Charlie Arthur Thackeray when I am with Salem, the Grimalkin when I am with you. Never look at me as if you recognize me. Never question my commands.*

The woman standing next to Jason on the bridge, who had been turning to say something about the falling man, stopped when her gaze met Jason's. Her face went soft, her mouth slack. She looked as if she'd entered the Rapture.

Jason felt as beautiful as he appeared.

The Grimalkin had attacked him at St. Brigid's. He'd slid a knife into Jason's neck. Blood had spurted. Jason had fallen to the ground.

And then a miraculous thing had happened. His neck skin had closed over the wound.

He hadn't known he'd possessed that power. He'd lain on the ground until the Grimalkin was gone, and then he'd stood, shoved his way through the gaping crowd, and made his way back to London with the realization that he'd been born again.

He had known the finale would take place at the Order's Tower Bridge penthouse and came by to watch as a tourist. He hadn't dreamed it would go so . . . generously. He shoved his hands in his pockets, his angelic mien still in place.

The Order wasn't going to like this.

Not at all.

Jason smiled.

MONDAY

September 25

CHAPTER 60

Stonehenge

The murmur of a breeze played across the red poppies, teasing them. The sun, the rarest of sights in England, shone fierce and proud overhead. Stonehenge proper had stayed open, with a perimeter around the Heel Stone roped off. The curious and those with good instincts lined up along the rope, snapping photos with their phones, speculating on what the motley crew surrounding the fifteen-foot Heel Stone was up to.

It had always been an odd rock, separate from Stonehenge yet a part of it, its misshapen stone resembling for all the world an eel rising from the ground.

The crew inside the rope totaled ten: a woman in a wheelchair, a man wearing a sling over his muscled shoulder, an older woman wearing a scowl, a curly-haired woman who stood near the wheelchair, a dark-haired woman who carried herself like a dancer, a girl with a bandaged head, two professor types, and two workers setting up a portable scissor lift on each side of the eel head–shaped stone.

The curly-haired woman appeared to be reluctantly in charge.

"Closer, please," Salem told the worker moving the scissor lift near the stone. The wound on her leg burned as she stepped onto the lift, preparing to be hoisted toward the eel's eye. According to the doctor, it could take months for her leg to feel like normal again.

"That'd make it the only part of my body that does," she'd told him.

Alafair had helped Salem and Mercy off the roof of the Tower Bridge walkway. The EMTs who rode the elevator up after Stone had cleared the room rode it right back down, rushing Mercy and Salem to the nearest hospital, where the child grew hysterical at any attempt to separate her from Salem. The doctors had settled on treating them side by side and then assigning them the same hospital room.

Salem had slept for eighteen hours with Mercy curled up next to her. They might have suffered nightmares, but when they woke, Mercy flashed Salem the most beatific smile.

"You're really here," she'd said.

Salem pulled her tight. The little girl had taken the words out of her mouth.

Bel was in the hospital room when they woke. She said it had been all she could do to let them both sleep that long. She hugged them tightly, Mercy's complaint that Bel was smothering her drawing tremulous laughter. When Bel could finally bear to let them go, she called in a doctor, who declared that Mercy's ear and Salem's leg were healing, even though it was too late for stitches and they would each forever carry a deep-purple scar.

Only when the doctor left did Bel lay into Salem. "You didn't return my calls or texts."

"I—"

"I know," Bel said, interrupting her.

The hollows under her eyes and in her cheeks mirrored Mercy's, but she wore her signature smile despite the sleep she'd obviously lost to worry. "You thought I'd be mad at you for allowing Mercy to be captured on your watch. You internalized blame for every problem in your orbit and decided you were the only one who could fix them. Oh, and also that no one really loved you. Am I right?"

Salem grimaced, opening her mouth to confess that all that was true, but a sob slipped out instead. Bel hoisted herself into bed next to Salem and held her friend while she wept. Mercy snuggled between them. When the tears subsided, Bel informed Salem that the bullet that had hit Agent Stone had gone clean through his shoulder, throwing him off his feet. He'd struck the back of his head when he landed, knocking him out.

A bystander called an ambulance before Assistant Director Bench—now in custody—could take charge of the scene. When he came to, Stone realized his phone was gone and put an immediate trace on it.

"That was smart, Salem," Bel said.

Salem wiped her eyes. "It didn't feel smart. It felt like stealing."

"Sometimes you can only judge whether something is right by the results," Bel said. Then her face mellowed. "Alafair followed you from Heathrow. Apparently, when you were passed out on her plane, she snuck a tracker into that bundle of herbs you got in Ireland."

Salem craned her neck to see where Bel was pointing. Mrs. Molony's sachet rested on the bedside table next to a glass of water with a bendy straw poking out of it. Salem laughed. She couldn't help it.

Look for the help that's out there, and remember the water, the flowers, and the power of women.

"I'll explain later," Salem said in response to Bel's quizzical expression.

Bel shrugged and continued. "Alafair witnessed you get off the Tube at Westminster, Stone get shot, you get herded into and then out of Parliament—the whole thing until you hopped into the cab. She relied on the tracker after that. It led her to Tower Bridge just in time to see you forced into an elevator. She watched it go all the way to the penthouse. Then she rode it herself, not knowing what it would bring her to."

Salem pulled back so she could look at Bel. "I can see by your dreamy expression that you've met her."

"Damn," Bel said, her voice growing husky. "I *have*. That woman has—what's the female equivalent of balls?"

"Ovaries. She's got ovaries."

"Those too," Bel said, laughing. "She saved you. Agent Stone and his men were on her heels, but if she hadn't gotten there when she did, things would have ended very differently."

Salem uttered the name that had been haunting her. "Charlie?"

Bel's eyebrows furrowed. "You couldn't have known. He fooled everyone."

"Not Alafair. She told me that the first time she met him, she didn't trust him."

Bel shrugged. "She wasn't told by her FBI supervisor that he was MI5 and assigned to work with her. You were screwed from the word go, Salem, but you survived. Not only that, you saved Mercy. And you solved the mystery of Stonehenge."

Not yet she hadn't, but it hadn't taken long to assemble the necessary team, and here they were, gathered at the Heel Stone, ready to plumb its secrets. Salem really hoped there were some. It would be embarrassing as hell to have come this far for nothing. She tossed the worker a thumbs-up, and he pushed the button that would raise the scissor lift. It groaned to life, elevating her toward the Heel Stone's eye.

One of the two archaeologists inside the perimeter, a woman, climbed aboard the opposite scissor lift. They'd ascertained that the eel's eyes wouldn't be large enough to accommodate a man's hands. Neither archaeologist had a guess as to what they'd find inside, and Salem felt a chill of fear as her scissor lift ground to a halt next to the Heel Stone opening. What if the gaping recess held some sort of trap that smashed her hand?

Bel waited near the base of the lift, her smile reassuring. Vida was also there, at President Hayes's behest. Salem avoided looking at her mother, instead searching the crowd for Mrs. Molony's beautiful lined face. Salem didn't know how the woman had learned about her cracking the final code, but she assumed it had something to do with the Irish arm of the Underground that Mrs. Molony led, their calling card the colorful sachet she'd given Salem.

Mrs. Molony's face was serene. Salem smiled at her before she eased her hand into the hole. The interior of the stone eye socket felt cool, a mini-cave. Salem had told the archaeologist about the drawer releases she'd discovered in the stone of the Gloup as well as St. Brigid's Tower.

The same stonemason who'd constructed those hiding spots had surely been in charge of concealing whatever was hidden in the Heel Stone.

The early afternoon was cool, but Salem was sweating with the effort of searching every surface inside the tunnel, which was nearly as long as and not much wider than her arm stretched to its extreme. Seconds ticked away.

"Are you finding anything?" the archaeologist on the opposite side of the Heel Stone hollered.

"Nothing!" Salem yelled back. "You?"

"Nope."

Salem's heart dipped. Maybe she'd read the Robing Room image wrong. Or someone had already been here and removed the treasure. But she'd come too far to give up. She had to persevere. She closed her eyes, envisioning Bode. He'd told her to use all the senses and to trust the rock. She tucked her ear toward the opening, listening for a change in tenor as she traced her fingertips over the surface.

She finally heard it three-quarters of the way in, a break in noise as her fingers crossed over a dip. She returned to it, pushing her pinkie finger into the hollow. A scraping sound indicated something inside the tunnel had shifted. "I found it!"

"Yeah!" Bel cheered.

Salem yelled instructions over to the archaeologist, who located her own depression at the same distance inside her tunnel as Salem's. "Push it on the count of three," Salem commanded. "One, two, three!"

"Do you feel that?" the archaeologist yelled.

"Yeah," Salem said, heartbeat fluttering. "It feels like it's moving to the right."

"It's moving left for me," the archaeologist said. "I think it's a globe vault. Pull your finger out of the depression and turn the stone at the end of your tunnel, gently."

Salem obliged. The stone moved surprisingly smoothly once they both applied force, twirling to Salem's right like a mounted sphere. It traveled several inches, and then her hand fell into an opening. "I'm in!" She felt paper, coins, containers.

"I'll hold it in place."

Salem drew out what she could, one handful at a time, handing it down to the other archaeologist, who gathered it reverentially in a bin.

"What is it?" Bel asked impatiently.

Vida stood near the base of the scissor lift, her voice quivering with emotion. "Jewels. Gold coins. Scrolls that will surely tell the story of matriarchal cultures, including the female engineers who built Stonehenge to celebrate their queens. Details of women's freemasonry, poems, scientific discoveries. Land deeds returning whole townships to their female owners. It is proof that justice always gets the last word."

Until those words, Vida had been icily quiet since Salem had returned with Mercy. Salem realized her mother had her own demons to work through; she would no longer take them on as her own. She glanced down at one of the loose papers she'd retrieved. It was drawn in the same hand and featured the same code as the single page she'd uncovered in the Beale Cipher.

"Take a picture of that for me," she ordered.

Vida appeared ready to argue but held her tongue.

When Salem had the vault emptied, she stepped down. The archaeologists would return to fully examine the Heel Stone. For now, what they had recovered would be kept safe by the English Heritage, though Salem was not leaving until she had photographed everything.

Alafair stepped forward, pointing toward a scroll of paper whiter than the rest. "May I?"

The archaeologist shrugged. The rules were not clear.

"Yes," Agent Stone said, his gravelly voice the perfect antidote to the surreal situation. "Of course you may. We're in your debt."

Alafair plucked the scroll and unrolled it. She held it up toward the sun, inhaling sharply. "It's real."

Salem stepped next to her. She recognized Rosalind Franklin's handwriting. "Oh my god."

She hadn't told Bel of this possibility. There was so much to catch her up on.

A dot of pink caught her eye. It was Mercy, charging away. She must have grown bored with the paper and the stone. She darted under the rope, through the crowd, and toward Stonehenge. "Mercy!" Salem yelled, suddenly gripped by anxiety. This was the farthest the girl had been from her since they'd been reunited in the Tower Bridge penthouse.

Salem found it difficult to breathe. She lunged toward the rope, but a warm hand slowed her. She turned to see Lucan Stone, powerful, solid, beautiful. Her heart squeezed. She could smell his crisp cologne, imagine his strong arms holding her.

He'd visited her in the hospital after her eighteen-hour nap with an offer. He wanted her and Bel to be his partners in a new endeavor, a three-person team answering only to the president. Their mission would be to discover and crack the Underground's codes. Salem had told him that she needed more rest, but that she'd talk to Bel and they would consider it. She couldn't believe that those words had come out of her mouth, and she was even more surprised to discover that she meant them. Her and Bel working together again, but this time chasing rather than running from the bad guys? That could work. That could work really well.

"She'll be all right," he said, nodding toward Mercy.

Salem wanted to believe him. She glanced back toward the girl. She was darting through the field of red poppies toward the monument, past the guards, and into the center of the stone ring. The child touched the ground near the Altar Stone and charged back toward the Heel Stone like she was playing a game of Red Rover by herself.

She was giggling and breathless when she returned, leaping into Salem's arms. Salem squeezed Mercy, burying her face in the child's sunshine-scented hair. She wanted Mercy to promise she'd never leave her side again, but Stone was still next to her, and his nearness made her feel stronger than she did standing alone. Still, she had to say something. "What were you doing?"

Mercy didn't answer. She snuggled more deeply into Salem, sighing contentedly.

"I think she was being a kid," Agent Stone said, his voice a gentle rumble. "Girls get to play."

Salem turned to him, searching for judgment. All she saw was an easy smile.

She nodded.

Girls get to play.

Author's Note

The historical events, figures, and organizations in this novel are accurately portrayed, including the history of cryptography, the Birka Viking warrior, Five Eyes, and the Black Chamber. Same with the accounts of Rosalind Franklin and Photo 51, St. Brigid, and the achievements and assassinations of Peruvian activist María Elena Moyano, Russian human rights activist and journalist Anna Politkovskaya, and Benazir Bhutto, the first female prime minister of Pakistan. I fictionalized their intersection with the characters in this story. The Vigenère and Beale Ciphers are also real and a fascinating trip through history, if you have the time.

The locations in the book and their history are also accurately described to the best of my ability: the Mayflower pub, Parliament's Robing Room and the frescoes within, Stonehenge, the Gloup, the Standing Stones of Stenness, the Ness of Brodgar, St. Brigid's Cathedral and Tower, and Tower Bridge. While I have renamed the Ness of Brodgar stone the Flower Stone, the art on the stone is accurately described, as are the similar designs found in St. Brigid's Tower.

All the remaining characters in this book are works of fiction.

ABOUT THE AUTHOR

Photo © 2018 CK Photography

Jess Lourey is the Amazon Charts bestselling author of *The Quarry Girls*, *Litani*, *Bloodline*, *Unspeakable Things*, *The Catalain Book of Secrets*, the Salem's Cipher thrillers, and the Murder by Month mysteries, among many other works, including short stories, young adult fiction, and non-fiction. Winner of the Anthony and Thriller Awards, Jess is also an Edgar, Agatha, and Lefty Award–nominated author; TEDx presenter; *Psychology Today* blogger; and recipient of The Loft's Excellence in Teaching fellowship. Check out her TEDx Talk for the true story behind her debut novel, *May Day*. She lives in Minneapolis with a rotating batch of foster kittens (and occasional foster puppies, but those goobers are a lot of work). For more information, visit www.jessicalourey.com.